Praise for *Raven Black*

'A riveting read. Ann Cleeves probes beneath the surface of a community to reveal the darkness that can fester when everyone thinks they know each other's secrets' Val McDermid

'Cleeves creates a convincing world of hostility against outsiders . . . of small snobberies and major jealousies. *Raven Black* breaks the conventional mould of British crime-writing, while retaining the traditional virtues of strong narrative and careful plotting'
Jane Jakeman, *Independent*

'*Raven Black* shows what a fine writer Cleeves is . . . an accomplished and thoughtful book'
Susanna Yager, *Sunday Telegraph*

'Beautifully constructed . . . Cleeves writes with an easy directness that brings alive the tensions in a place where everyone knows everyone else . . . *Raven Black* is a lively and surprising addition to a genre that once seemed moribund' Natasha Cooper, *Times Literary Supplement*

'Ann's characterisation is worthy of the best writers in the field . . . Rarely has the sense of place been so evocatively conveyed in a crime novel' *Daily Express*

'*Raven Black* is a fine and sinister psychological novel in the Barbara Vine style. Cleeves is part of a new generation of superior British writers who put refreshing new spins and twist on the old forms' *Globe and Mail*

'Ms Cleeves weaves a good tale, as intricate and as satisfying as a Fair Isle sweater' Stuart Pawson

RAVEN BLACK

Ann Cleeves lives in West Yorkshire with her husband and their two daughters. As a member of the 'Murder Squad', Ann works with other northern writers to promote crime fiction.

In addition to *Raven Black*, she has written five stand-alone novels of psychological suspense. Ann is also the author of the Inspector Ramsay novels. Her new novel, *Hidden Depths*, will be published by Macmillan in 2007.

Visit her website at www.anncleeves.com

Also by Ann Cleeves

ANN CLEEVES

RAVEN BLACK

PAN BOOKS

First published 2006 by Macmillan

First published in paperback 2006 by Pan Books
an imprint of Pan Macmillan Ltd
Pan Macmillan, 20 New Wharf Road, London N1 9RR
Basingstoke and Oxford
Associated companies throughout the world
www.panmacmillan.com

ISBN-13: 978-0-330-44114-8
ISBN-10: 0-330-44114-0

1 3 5 7 9 8 6 4 2

A CIP catalogue record for this book is available from
the British Library.

Typeset by IntypeLibra, Ltd
Printed and bound in Great Britain by Mackays of Chatham plc, Chatham, Kent

For Ella. And her grandfather.

Acknowledgements

It was foolhardy to attempt a book set in Shetland while living in West Yorkshire. It would have been impossible without the help and support of Shetlanders. Thanks to Bob Gunn, to everyone at the Shetland Arts Trust, especially Chrissie and Alex, to Morag at Lerwick Library, to Becky and Floortje for an insight into what it is to be young, and to Becky again for her detailed advice on the script. A special mention for Fair Isle, where it all started and for our friends there. Despite this help, there will probably be inaccuracies. They are all mine.

Chapter One

Twenty past one in the morning on New Year's Day. Magnus knew the time because of the fat clock, his mother's clock, which squatted on the shelf over the fire. In the corner the raven in the wicker cage muttered and croaked in its sleep. Magnus waited. The room was prepared for visitors, the fire banked with peat and on the table a bottle of whisky and the ginger cake he'd bought in Safeway's the last time he was in Lerwick. He could feel himself dozing but he didn't want to go to bed in case someone should call at the house. If there was a light at the window someone might come, full of laughter and drams and stories. For eight years nobody had visited to wish him happy new year, but still he waited just in case.

Outside it was completely silent. There was no sound of wind. In Shetland, when there was no wind it was shocking. People strained their ears and wondered what was missing. Earlier in the day there had been a dusting of snow, then with dusk this was covered by a sheen of frost, every crystal flashing and hard as diamond in the last of the light, and even when it got dark, in the beam from the lighthouse. The cold was another reason for Magnus staying where he was. In the bedroom the ice would be thick on the inside of the window and the sheets would feel chill and damp.

He must have slept. If he'd been awake he'd have heard them coming because there was nothing quiet in their approach. They weren't creeping up on him. He'd have heard their laughter and the stumbling, seen the wild swaying of the torch beam through the uncurtained window. He was woken by the banging on the door. He came to with a start, knowing he'd been in the middle of a nightmare, but not sure of the details.

'Come in,' he shouted. 'Come in, come in.' He struggled to his feet, stiff and aching. They must already be in the storm porch. He heard the hiss of their whispers.

The door was pushed open, letting in a blast of freezing air and two young girls, who were as gaudy and brightly coloured as exotic birds. He saw they were drunk. They stood, propping each other up. They weren't dressed for the weather yet their cheeks were flushed and he could feel the health of them like heat. One was fair and one was dark. The fair one was the prettier, round and soft, but Magnus noticed the dark one first; her black hair was streaked with luminescent blue. More than anything, he would have liked to reach out and touch the hair, but he knew better than to do that. It would only scare them away.

'Come in,' he said again although they were already in the room. He thought he must sound like a foolish old man, repeating the same words, making no sense at all. People had always laughed at him. They called him slow and perhaps they were right. He felt a smile crawl across his face and heard his mother's words in

his head. *Will you wipe that stupid grin from your face.
Do you want folk to think you're dafter than you really
are?*

The girls giggled and stepped further into the
room. He shut the doors behind them, the outside door
which had warped with the weather and led into the
porch, and the one into the house. He wanted to keep
out the cold and he was frightened that they might
escape. He couldn't believe that such beautiful crea-
tures had turned up on his doorstep.

'Sit down,' he said. There was only the one easy
chair, but two others, which his uncle had made from
driftwood, stood by the table and he pulled these out.
'You'll take a drink with me to see in the new year.'

They giggled again and fluttered and landed on the
chairs. They wore tinsel in their hair and their clothes
were made of fur and velvet and silk. The fair one had
ankle boots of leather so shiny that it looked like wet
tar, with silver buckles and little chains. The heels
were high and the toes were pointed. Magnus had
never seen footwear like it and for a moment he
couldn't take his eyes off them. The dark girl's shoes
were red. He stood at the head of the table.

'I don't know you, do I?' he said, though looking at
them more closely he knew he'd seen them passing
the house. He took care to speak slowly so they would
understand him. Sometimes he slurred his speech.
The words sounded strange to him, like the raven's
croaking. He'd taught the raven to speak a few words.
Some weeks, he had nobody else to talk to. He
launched into another sentence. 'Where are you from?'

'We've been in Lerwick.' The chairs were low and
the blonde girl had to tip back her head to look up at

3

him. He could see her tongue and her pink throat. Her short silk top had become separated from the waist-band of her skirt and he saw a fold of flesh, as silky as the material of her blouse and her belly button. 'Partying for Hogmanay. We got a lift to the end of the road. We were on our way home when we saw your light.'

'Shall we have a drink, then?' he said eagerly. 'Shall we?' He shot a look at the dark girl, who was staring at the room, moving her eyes slowly, taking it all in, but again it was the fair one who replied.

'We've brought our own,' she said. She pulled a bottle from the woven shoulder bag she'd been clutch-ing on her knee. It had a cork jammed in the top and was three-quarters full. He thought it would be white wine, but he didn't really know. He'd never tasted wine. She pulled the cork from the bottle with sharp, white teeth. The action shocked him. When he real-ized what she intended doing he wanted to shout to her to stop. He imagined the teeth snapped off at the roots. He should have offered to open it for her. That would have been the gentlemanly thing to do. Instead, he only watched, fascinated. The girl drank from the bottle, wiped the lip with her hand, then passed it on to her friend. He reached out for his whisky. His hands were shaking and he spilled a couple of drops on to the oilcloth when he poured himself a glass. He held out his glass and the dark girl clinked the wine bottle against it. Her eyes were narrow. The lids were painted blue and grey and were lined with black.

'I'm Sally,' the blonde girl said. She didn't have the dark one's capacity for silence. She'd be one for noise, he decided. Chatter and music. 'Sally Henry.'

'Henry,' he repeated. The name was familiar, though he couldn't quite place it. He was out of touch. His thoughts had never been sharp, but now thinking took an effort. It was like seeing through a thick sea fog. He could make out shapes and vague ideas but focus was difficult. 'Where do you live?'

'In the house at the end of the voe,' she said. 'Next to the school.'

'Your mother's the schoolteacher.'

Now he could place her. The mother was a little woman. She'd come from one of the north isles. Unst. Yell, maybe. Married a man from Bressay who worked for the council. Magnus had seen him driving around in a big 4x4.

'Aye,' she said and sighed.

'And you?' he said to the dark girl, who interested him more, who interested him so much that his eyes kept flickering back to her. 'What do they call you?'

'I'm Catherine Ross,' she said, speaking for the first time. Her voice was deep for a young lassie, he thought. Deep and smooth. A voice like black treacle. He forgot where he was for a moment, picturing his mother spooning treacle into the mixture for the ginger cakes she'd made, twisting the spoon over the pot to catch the last sticky threads, then handing it to him to lick. He ran his tongue over his lips, became embarrassingly aware of Catherine staring at him. She had a way of not blinking.

'You're not local.' He could tell by the accent. 'English?'

'I've lived here for a year.'

'You're friends?' The idea of friendship was a

ANN CLEEVES

novelty. Had he ever had friends? He took time to think about it. 'You're pals. Is that right?'

'Of course we are,' Sally said. 'Best friends.' And they started laughing again, passing the bottle backwards and forwards, throwing back their heads to drink, so their necks looked white as chalk in the light of the naked bulb hanging over the table.

Chapter Two

Five minutes to midnight. They were all on the streets of Lerwick around the market cross and it was jumping. Everyone was steaming, but not fighting drunk, just mellow and you felt that you belonged, you were a part of the laughing, drinking crowd. Sally thought her father should have been here. He'd have realized then that there was nothing to get uptight about. He might even have enjoyed it. Hogmanay in Shetland. Like, it wasn't New York, was it? Or London. What was going to happen? Most of the people here she recognized.

The thud, thud of a bass came up through her feet and rolled around her head, and she couldn't work out where the music was coming from, but she moved along with it like everyone else. Then came the bells for midnight and 'Auld Lang Syne' and she was hugging the people on either side of her. She found herself snogging a guy and realized in a moment of clarity that he was a maths teacher from Anderson High and he was more pissed than she was.

Later, she wouldn't remember what happened next. Not exactly and not in sequence. She saw Robert Isbister, big as a bear, standing outside The Lounge, a red tin in his hand, looking out at them all. Perhaps

7

she'd been looking out for him. She saw herself sauntering up to him in rhythm to the music, hips swaying, almost dancing. Standing in front of him, not speaking, but flirting all the same. Oh certainly flirting, she was sure of that. She put her hand on his wrist, didn't she? And stroked the fine golden hair on his arm as if he was an animal. She'd never have done that if she'd been sober. She'd never have had the nerve to approach him at all, though she'd been dreaming of this for weeks, imagining every detail. He had his sleeves rolled up to his elbows although it was so cold and he wore a wristwatch with a gold bracelet. She'd remember that. It would stick in her head. Perhaps it wasn't real gold, but with Robert Isbister, who could tell?

Then Catherine was there, saying she'd wangled them a lift home, as far as the Ravenswick turning, at least. Sally was all for staying, but Catherine must have persuaded her because she found herself in the back of a car. It was like her dream too, because suddenly Robert was there too, sitting next to her, so close that she could feel the denim of his jeans against her leg and his bare forearm on the back of her neck. She could smell the beer on his breath. It made her feel sick, but she knew she couldn't allow herself to throw up. Not in front of Robert Isbister.

Another couple was crushed into the back of the car with them. She thought she recognized them both. The lad was from South Mainland somewhere and was away in college in Aberdeen. The girl? She stayed in Lerwick and was a nurse in the Gilbert Bain. They were devouring each other. The girl was underneath, the lad lying on top of her, nibbling at her lips and her neck and her earlobes, then opening his mouth wide as if he intended to swallow her piece by piece. When Sally turned back to Robert, he kissed her, but slowly and gently, not like the wolf from Red Riding Hood. Sally didn't feel that she was being eaten up at all.

Sally couldn't see much of the lad who was driving. She was directly behind the driver's seat and all she could make out was a head and a pair of shoulders clad in a parka. He didn't talk, either to her or to Catherine who was sitting beside him. Perhaps he was pissed off about giving them a lift. Sally was going to chat to him, just to be friendly, but then Robert kissed her again and that took up all her attention. There was no music playing in the car, no noise at all except for the engine which sounded really rough and the slobbering of the couple squashed beside her.

'Stop!' That was Catherine. It wasn't loud, but coming out of the silence it shocked them all. Her English voice jarred on Sally's ears. 'Stop here. This is where Sally and me get out. Unless you want to give us a lift down to the school.'

'No way, man.' The student broke away from the nurse just long enough to comment. 'We're missing the party as it is.'

'Come with us,' Robert said. 'Come on to the party.'

His invitation was seductive and meant for Sally, but Catherine answered. 'No, we can't. Sally's supposed to have been at our house. She wasn't allowed into town. If we're not back soon, her parents will come looking.'

Sally resented Catherine speaking for her, but knew she was right. She mustn't blow it now. If her mother found out where she'd been, she'd go ape. Her father was reasonable left to himself, but her mother was crazy. The spell was broken and it was back to the real world. She untangled herself from Robert, climbed over him and out of the car. The cold took her breath away, made her feel light-headed and euphoric as if she'd had another drink. She and Catherine stood side by side and watched the tail lights of the car disappear.

'Bastards,' Catherine said, with so much venom that Sally wondered if something had gone on between her and the driver. 'They could have given us a lift.' She felt in her pocket, brought out a thin torch and shone it on the path ahead of them. That was Catherine for you. Always prepared.

'Still,' Sally felt a soppy smile spread over her face, 'it was a good night. A fucking good night.' As she slung her bag over her shoulder something heavy banged against her hip. She brought out a bottle of wine, opened, with a cork stuck in the top. Where had that come from? She didn't even have a fuzzy memory. She showed it to Catherine in an attempt to lift her gloom. 'Look. Something to keep us going on the way home.'

They giggled and stumbled down the icy road.

The square of light seemed to come from nowhere and surprised them. 'Where the shit are we? We can't be back yet.' For the first time Catherine seemed anxious, less sure of herself, disorientated.

'It's Hillhead. The house at the top of the bank.'

'Does anyone live there? I thought it was empty.'

'It belongs to an old man,' Sally said. 'Magnus Tait. He's daft in the head, so they say. A recluse. We were always taught to stay away from him.'

Catherine wasn't frightened now. Or perhaps it

10

was just bravado. 'But he's there, all alone. We should go in and wish him happy new year.'

'I've told you. He's soft in the head.'

'You're scared,' Catherine said, almost a whisper.

I am, shit-scared, and I don't know why. 'Don't be dumb.'

'I dare you!' Catherine reached into Sally's bag for the bottle. She took a swig, replaced the cork and handed it back.

Sally stamped her feet to show how ridiculous this was, standing out in the cold. 'We should get back. Like you said, my folks will be waiting.'

'We can just say we've been first-footing the neighbours. Go on. I dare you.'

'Not on my own.'

'All right. We'll both go.' Sally couldn't tell if this was what Catherine had intended from the beginning, or if she'd boxed herself into a position she couldn't escape from with her pride intact.

The house was set back from the road. There was no real path. As they approached Catherine shone her torch towards it and the beam hit the grey slate roof, then the pile of peats to one side of the porch. They could smell the smoke coming out of the chimney. The green paint on the porch door rose in scabs over bare wood.

'Go on then,' Catherine said. 'Knock.'

Sally knocked tentatively. 'Perhaps he's in bed, just left the light on.'

'He's not. I can see him in there.' Catherine went into the porch and thumped with her fist on the inner door. *She's wild,* Sally thought. *She doesn't know what she's messing with. This whole thing's crazy. She* wanted to run away, back to her boring and sensible parents, but before she could move there was a sound from inside and Catherine had the door open and they stumbled together into the room, blinking and blind in the sudden light.

The old man was coming towards them and Sally stared at him. She knew she was doing it but couldn't stop herself. She'd only seen him before at a distance. Her mother, usually so charitable in her dealings with the elderly neighbours, usually so Christian in her offers to go shopping, to provide broth and baking, had avoided any contact with Magnus Tait. Sally had been hurried past the house when he was outside. 'You must never go there,' her mother had said when she was a child. 'He's a nasty man. It's not a safe place for little girls.' So the croft had held a fascination for her. She had looked across at it on her way to and from the town. She had glimpsed his back bent over the sheep he was clipping, seen his silhouette against the sun as he stood outside the house looking down to the road. Now, this close, it was like coming face to face with a character from a fairy tale.

He stared back at her and she thought he really was like something from a picture book. A troll, she thought suddenly. That's what he looked like, with his stumpy legs and his short, thick body, slightly hunch-backed, his slot-shaped mouth with the teeth jumbled and yellow inside. She'd never liked the story of the Billy Goats Gruff. When she was very small she'd been terrified to cross the bridge across the burn to get to her house. She'd imagined the troll living underneath, his eyes fiery red, his back bent as he prepared to charge her. Now she wondered if Catherine still had her camera with her. The old man would make some picture.

Magnus looked at the girls with rheumy eyes which seemed not quite to focus. 'Come in,' he said. 'Come in.' And he pulled his lips away from his teeth to smile.

Sally found herself chattering. That was what happened when she was nervous. The words spilled out of her mouth and she didn't have an idea what she was saying. Magnus shut the door behind them, then stood in front of it, blocking the only way out. He offered them whisky but she knew better than to accept that. What might he have put into it? She pulled the bottle of wine from her bag, smiled to appease him and carried on talking.

She made a move to stand up, but the man had a knife, long and pointed with a black handle. He was using it to cut a cake which had been standing on the table.

'We should go,' she said. 'Really, my parents will be wondering.'

But they seemed not to hear her and she watched in horror as Catherine reached out and took a piece of cake and slipped it into her mouth. Sally could see the crumbs on her friend's lips and between her teeth. The old man stood above them with the knife in his hand.

Sally saw the bird in the cage when she was looking round for a way out.

'What's that?' she asked abruptly. The words came out of her mouth before she could stop them.

'It's a raven.' He stood quite still, watching her, then he set the knife carefully on the table.

'Isn't it cruel, keeping it locked up like that?'

'It had a broken wing. It wouldn't fly even if I let it go.'

But Sally didn't listen to the old man's explanations. She thought he meant to keep them in the house, to lock them in like the black bird with its cruel beak and its injured wing.

And then Catherine was on her feet, dusting the cake crumbs from her hands. Sally followed her. Catherine walked up to the old man so she was close enough to touch him. She was taller than him and looked down on him. For an awful moment Sally was afraid that she intended to kiss his cheek. If Catherine did that she would be obliged to do it too. Because this was all part of the same dare, wasn't it? At least that was how it seemed to Sally. Since they had come to the house, everything had been a challenge. Magnus hadn't shaved properly. Hard, grey spines grew in the creases in his cheeks. His teeth were yellow and covered in saliva. Sally thought she would rather die than touch him.

But the moment passed and they were outside, laughing so loud that Sally thought she would piss herself, or that they would collapse together into a heap of snow. When their eyes got used to the dark again they didn't need the torch to show them down the road. There was a near-full moon now and they knew the way home.

Catherine's house was quiet. Her father didn't believe in new year celebrations and had gone to bed early.

'Will you come in?' Catherine asked.

'Best not.' Sally knew that was the answer she was supposed to give. Sometimes she could never tell what

Catherine was thinking. Sometimes she knew exactly. Now she knew Catherine didn't want her going in.

'I'd better take that bottle from you. Hide the evidence.'

'Aye.'

'I'll stand here, watch you to your house,' Catherine said.

'No need.'

But she stood, leaning against the garden wall and watched. When Sally turned back she was still there.

Chapter Three

If he'd had the chance, Magnus would have liked to explain to the girls about ravens. There were ravens on his land, always had been, since he was a peerie boy, and he'd watched them. Sometimes it was as if they were playing. You could see them in the sky wheeling and turning, like children chasing each other in a game, then they'd fold up their wings and fall out of the sky. Magnus could feel how exciting that must be, the wind rushing past, the speed of the dive. Then they'd fly out of the fall and their calls sounded like laughter. Once he'd seen the ravens in the snow sliding down the bank to the road on their backs, one after another, just as the boys from the post office did on their toboggans until their mother shouted them away from his house.

But other times ravens were the cruellest birds. He'd seen them peck the eyes from a new sickly lamb. The ewe, shrieking with pain and anger, hadn't scared them away. Magnus hadn't scared the birds off either. He'd made no attempt. He hadn't been able to take his eyes off them, as they prodded and ripped, paddling their talons in the blood.

In the week after new year he thought about Sally and Catherine all the time. He saw them in his head when he woke up in the morning, and dozing in his chair by the fire late at night he dreamed of them. He wondered when they would come back. He couldn't believe that they would ever return but he couldn't bear the idea that he would never talk to them again. And all that week the islands remained frozen and covered in snow. There were blizzards so fierce that he couldn't see the track from his window. The snowflakes were very fine and when the wind caught them they twisted and spiralled like smoke. Then the wind would drop to nothing and the sun would come out and the reflected light burnt his eyes, so he had to squint to see the world outside his house. He saw the blue ice on the voe, the snowplough cutting a way down from the main road, the post van, but he didn't see the beautiful young women.

Once he did catch a glimpse of Mrs Henry, Sally's mother, the schoolteacher. He saw her come out of the schoolhouse door. She had fat fur-lined boots on her feet. A pink jacket on, with the hood pulled up. She was a lot younger than Magnus, but she dressed like an old woman, he thought. Like a woman who didn't care what she looked like, at least. She was very small and moved in a busy way, scuttling as if time was important to her. Watching her, he was suddenly scared that she intended to come to him. He thought she had found out that Sally had been in the house at new year. He imagined her making a scene, shouting, her face thrust so close to his that he'd smell her breath, feel the spit as she screamed at him. *Don't you dare go near my daughter.* For a moment he was confused. Was that scene imagination or memory? But she didn't come up the hill towards his house. She walked away.

On the third day he had run out of bread and milk, oatcakes and the chocolate biscuits he liked with his tea. He took the bus into Lerwick. He didn't like leaving the house. The girls might come when he was out. He imagined them climbing the bank, laughing and slipping, knocking at the door and finding no one at home. The worst thing was that he would never know that they had been. The snow was packed so hard there that they would leave no footprints.

He recognized many of the other passengers on the bus. Some of them he had been to school with. There was Florence who had cooked in the Skillig Hotel before she retired. They had been pals of a kind when they were young. She had been a pretty girl and a fine dancer. There'd been one dance in the hall at Sandwick. The Eunson boys had been playing and there'd been a reel when the music had gone faster and faster and Florence had stumbled. Magnus had caught her in his arms, held on to her for a moment until she'd run off laughing to the other girls. Further down the bus was Georgie Sanderson, who'd hurt his leg in an accident and had had to give up the fishing.

But Magnus chose a seat on his own and none of them spoke to him or even acknowledged his presence. That was how it always was. Habit. They probably didn't even see him. The driver had turned the heat full on. Hot air blew from under the seats and melted the snow on everyone's boots until water trickled down the central aisle, backwards and forwards depending on whether the bus was going up or downhill. The windows were covered in condensation, so he only knew it was time to get out because everyone else did.

Lerwick was a noisy place now. When he was growing up he'd known everyone he met in the street. Recently even in the winter it was full of strangers and cars. In the summer it was worse. Then there were tourists. They came off the overnight ferry from Aberdeen, blinking and staring, as if they'd arrived at a zoo or a different planet, maybe, turning their heads from one direction to another looking all around them. Sometimes huge cruise ships slid into the harbour and sat there, towering over the buildings. For an hour their passengers would take over the town. It was an invasion. They had eager faces and braying voices, but Magnus sensed they were disappointed by what they found there, as if the place had failed to live up to their expectations. They had paid a lot of money for their cruise and felt cheated. Perhaps Lerwick wasn't so different after all from the places they had come from.

This morning he avoided the centre and got off the bus at the supermarket on the edge of the town. Clickimin Loch was frozen and two whooper swans circled it searching for a patch of open water to land. A jogger ran along the path towards the sports centre. Usually Magnus enjoyed the supermarket. He liked the bright lights and the coloured notices. He marvelled at the wide aisles and the full shelves. Nobody bothered him there, nobody knew him. Occasionally the woman on the checkout was friendly, commenting on his purchases. And he'd smile back and remember what it was like when everyone greeted him in a friendly way. After completing his shopping he would go to the café and treat himself to a mug of milky coffee and something sweet – a pastry with apricots and vanilla or a slice of chocolate cake, so sticky that he had to eat it with a spoon.

Today he was in a hurry. There was no time for coffee. He wanted to get the first bus home. He stood at the stop with two carrier bags at his feet. Although the sun was shining there was a flurry of snow, fine like icing sugar. It settled on his jacket and on his hair. This time he had the bus to himself. He took a seat near the back.

Catherine got on twenty minutes later when they were halfway to his home. At first he didn't see her. He'd rubbed a clear circle in the mist on the window and was looking out. He was aware of the bus stopping but was lost in his dreams. Then something made him turn round. Perhaps it was her voice when she asked for her ticket, though he hadn't consciously heard it. He thought it was her perfume, the smell she'd brought with her into his house on New Year's Day, but it couldn't be, could it? He wouldn't smell her from the front of the bus. He lifted his nose into the air but all that reached him then was diesel and wet wool.

He didn't expect her to acknowledge him. There was enough excitement in seeing her. He had liked both the girls, but Catherine had been the one who fascinated him more. She had the same blue streaks in her hair, but was wearing a long coat, a big grey coat which reached almost to her ankles and which was wet and slightly muddy at the hem. Her scarf was hand knitted, bright red, red as new blood. She looked tired and he wondered who she could have been visiting. She slumped on the front seat without noticing him, too exhausted, it seemed, to walk further up the bus.

He couldn't quite see from where he was sitting, but he thought she had her eyes closed.

She got out at his stop. He stood back to let her out first and still, it seemed, she wouldn't recognize him. How could he blame her? All old men would look alike to her, just as all tourists did to him. But she stood at the bottom of the steps and turned and saw him. She smiled slowly and held out her hand to help him down. She was wearing woollen gloves so he couldn't feel her skin against his but the contact gave him a thrill all the same. He was surprised by his body's response to her, hoped she didn't sense his excitement.

'Hello,' she said, in her black treacle voice. 'I'm sorry about the other night. I hope we didn't disturb you.'

'Not at all.' His voice was breathless with nervousness. 'I was glad that you came by.'

She grinned at him as if he'd said something to amuse her.

They walked on for a few steps in silence. He wished he knew what to say to her. He could hear the blood rushing in his ears as it did when he'd worked too long singling turnips, bent over the hoe in the field in the sun, when the breath came in pants.

'We're back at school tomorrow,' she said suddenly. 'It's the end of the holidays.'

'Do you like school?' he asked.

'Not really. It's a bore.'

He didn't know how to answer that. 'I didn't like school either,' he said after a while, then he added for something to say, 'Where have you been this morning?'

'Not this morning. Last night. I stayed with a friend. There was a party. I got a lift to the bus stop.'

'Sally didn't come with you?'

'No, she wasn't allowed. Her parents are very strict.'

'Was it a good party?' he asked, genuinely interested. He'd never gone much to parties.

'Oh,' she said. 'You know . . .'

He thought she might have had more to say. He even had the sense that she might tell him something secret. They had reached the place where he would have to turn to climb the bank to his house and they stopped walking. He waited for her to continue speaking, but she just stood. There was no colour on her eyes this morning, though they were still lined with black, which looked smudged and dirty as if it had been there all night. At last he was forced to break the silence.

'Won't you come in?' he asked. 'Take a dram with me to keep out the cold. Or some tea?'

He didn't for a minute think she would agree. She was a well brought-up child. That was obvious. She would have been taught not to go alone into the house of a stranger. She looked at him, weighing up the idea.

'It's a bit early for a dram,' she said.

'Tea then?' He felt his mouth spread into that daft grin which had always annoyed his mother. 'We'll have some tea and chocolate biscuits.'

He started up the path to the house, quite confident, knowing she would follow.

He never locked his door, but he opened it for her and stood aside to let her in first. As he waited for her to stamp her boots on the mat he looked around him. Everything was quiet outside. No one was around to see. No one knew he had this beautiful creature to visit him. She was his treasure, the raven in his cage.

Chapter Four

Fran Hunter had a car but she didn't like using it for short trips. She cared about global warming and wanted to do her bit. She had a bike with a seat on the back for Cassie, had brought it with her on the Northlink ferry when she moved. She prided herself on travelling light and it had been the only bulky item in her luggage. In this weather though a bike was no good. Today she wrapped Cassie up in her dungarees and coat and the wellingtons with the green frogs on the front and pulled her to school on a sledge. It was January 5th, the first day of the new school term. When they set off it was hardly light. Fran knew Mrs Henry already disapproved of her and didn't want to be late. She didn't need more knowing looks and raised eyebrows, the other mothers talking about her behind her back. It was hard enough for Cassie to fit in.

Fran rented a small house just off the road into Lerwick. It stood next to a stern brick chapel, and was low and unassuming in comparison. There were three rooms, with a basic bathroom built more recently on the back. They lived in the kitchen, which was much as it had been since the house had been built. It had a range where they burned the coal brought every month in a lorry from the town. There was an electric cooker too, but Fran liked the idea of the range. She was a romantic. The house had no land now, though once it must have been attached to a croft. In the season it became a holiday let and by Easter Fran would have to make a decision about her and Cassie's future. The landlord had hinted that he might be prepared to sell. She was already coming to think of it as home and a place to work. Her bedroom had two big skylights and a view to Raven Head. It would do as a studio.

In the grey dawn Cassie chattered and Fran responded automatically, but her thoughts were elsewhere.

As they rounded the bank near Hillhead, the sun was rising, throwing long shadows across the snow, and Fran stopped to look at the view. She could see across the water to the headland beyond. It had been right to come back, she thought. This was the best place to bring up a child. Until that moment she hadn't realized how unsure she had been about the decision. She was so good at playing the part of aggressive single mother that she'd almost come to believe it.

Cassie was five and as assertive as her mother. Fran had taught her to read before she started school – and Mrs Henry had disapproved of that too. The child could be loud and opinionated and there were times when even Fran wondered, despising herself for the dreadful suspicion, if she had created a precocious monster.

'It would be nice,' Mrs Henry said frostily at the first parents' evening, 'if occasionally Cassie did as she was told first time. Without needing a detailed explanation of why I'd asked her to do it.'

Fran, expecting to be told that her daughter was a

genius, a delight to teach, had been mortified. She had hidden her disappointment with a spirited defence of her philosophy of child rearing. Children should have the confidence to make their own choices, to challenge authority, she'd said. The last thing she wanted was a child who was a meek conformer.

Mrs Henry had listened.

'It must be hard,' she had said when Fran ran out of steam, 'to bring up a child on your own.'

Now Cassie, perched on the sledge like a Russian princess, was beginning to get restive.

'What is it?' she demanded. 'Why have you stopped?'

Fran's attention had been caught by contrasting colours, the possibility for a painting, but she pulled the rope and continued. She, like the teacher, was at the whim of Cassie's imperious demands. At the top of the bank she stopped and climbed on to the back of the sledge. She wrapped her legs around her daughter's body and held a loop of rope firmly in each hand. Then she dug her heels into the snow and launched the sledge down the hill. Cassie shrieked with fear and excitement. They bounced over the icy ruts and picked up speed as they reached the bottom. The cold and the sunlight burned Fran's face. She tugged on the left-hand rope to guide them into a soft snowdrift piled against the playground wall. Nothing, she thought, will compare with this. This is about as good as it gets.

For once they were early. Fran had remembered Cassie's library book, her packed lunch and a change of shoes. Fran took Cassie into the cloakroom, sat her on the bench and pulled off the wellingtons. Mrs Henry was in the classroom, sticking a series of numbers on to the wall. She was perched on her desk but still found it hard to reach. She was wearing trousers of some man-made fibre, slightly shiny, puckered at the knees, and a cardigan, machine knitted, with a vaguely Norwegian pattern. Fran noticed clothes. She had worked as assistant fashion editor on a woman's magazine after leaving university. Mrs Henry was ripe for a makeover.

'Could I help you?' She felt ridiculously afraid of being rejected. She'd managed photographers who could make grown men cry, but Mrs Henry made her feel like a nervy six-year-old. Usually she arrived at school just before the bell. Mrs Henry was already surrounded by parents and seemed to be on personal terms with them all.

Mrs Henry turned round, seemed surprised to see her. 'Would you? That would be kind. Cassie, come and sit on the mat, find a book to look at and wait for the others.'

Cassie, inexplicably, did just as she was told.

On the way back up the hill dragging the sledge behind her, Fran told herself it was pathetic to be so pleased. Was it such a big deal? She didn't even believe in learning by rote, for Christ's sake. If they'd stayed south she'd have considered Cassie for a Steiner school. Yet here she was, thrilled to bits because she'd stuck the two-times table on the classroom wall. And Margaret Henry had smiled at her and called her by her first name.

There was no sign of the old man who lived in Hillhead. Sometimes when they were going past he came out to greet them. He didn't often speak. Usually it was just a wave and once he'd thrust a sweetie in

Cassie's hand. Fran didn't like Cassie having sweets – sugar was nothing but wasted calories and think of the tooth decay – but he'd seemed so shy and eager that she'd thanked him. Then Cassie had thrust the slightly dusty striped humbug into her mouth, knowing Fran wouldn't stop her in front of the old man and Fran could hardly ask her to spit it out after he'd gone back inside.

She stopped there to look down at the water again, hoping to recreate the image she'd seen on the way to the school. It was the colours which had caught her attention. Often the colours on the islands were subtle, olive green, mud brown, sea grey and all softened by mist. In the full sunlight of early morning, this picture was stark and vibrant. The harsh white of the snow. Three shapes, silhouetted. Ravens. In her painting they would be angular shapes, cubist almost. Birds roughly carved from hard black wood. And then that splash of colour. Red, reflecting the scarlet ball of the sun.

She left the sledge at the side of the track and crossed the field to see the scene more closely. There was a gate from the road. The snow stopped her pushing it open so she climbed it. A stone wall split the field in two, but in places it had collapsed and there was a gap big enough for a tractor to get through. As she grew nearer the perspective shifted, but that didn't bother her. She had the painting fixed firmly in her mind. She expected the ravens to fly off, had even been hoping to see them in flight. The sight of them aloft, the wedge-shaped tail tilted to hold each steady, would inform her image of them on the ground.

Her concentration was so fierce, and everything seemed unreal here, surrounded by the reflected light which made her head swim, that she walked right up to the sight before realizing exactly what she was seeing. Until then everything was just form and colour. Then the vivid red turned into a scarf. The grey coat and the white flesh merged into the background of the snow which wasn't so clean here. The ravens were pecking at a girl's face. One of the eyes had disappeared.

Fran recognized the young woman, even in this altered, degraded state. The birds had fluttered away briefly as she approached but now, as she stood motionless, watching, they returned. Suddenly she screamed, so loudly that she could feel the strain in the back of her throat and clapped her hands to send the birds circling into the sky. But she couldn't move from the spot.

It was Catherine Ross. There was a red scarf tight round her neck, the fringe spread out like blood on the snow.

Chapter Five

Magnus watched from his window. He had been there since first light, before that even. He hadn't been able to sleep. He saw the woman go past, dragging the little girl on the sledge behind her and felt the stirrings of envy. He had grown up in a different time, he thought. Mothers had not behaved that way with their children when he was a boy. There had been little time for play.

He had noticed the little girl before, had followed the two of them up the road on one occasion to see where they were staying. It had been in October because he'd been thinking of the old days, when they used to go guising for Hallowe'en in masks, carrying neepy lanterns. He thought a lot about the old days. The memories clouded his thoughts and confused him.

The woman and the girl lived in that house where the tourists came in the summer, where the minister and his wife once stayed. He had watched for a while, though they hadn't seen him looking through the window. He had been too clever to get caught and besides, he hadn't wanted to frighten them. That was never his intention. The child had sat at the table drawing on big sheets of coloured paper with fat crayons. The woman had been drawing too, in charcoal with quick fierce strokes, standing next to her daughter, leaning across her to reach the paper. He'd wished he'd been close enough to see the picture. Once she'd pushed her hair away from her face and left a mark like soot on her cheek.

He thought now how pretty the little girl was. She had round cheeks, red from the cold, and golden curls. He wished the mother would dress her differently though. He would like to see her in a skirt, a pink skirt made of satin and lace, little white socks and buckled shoes. He would like to see her dance. But even in trousers and boots, there was no mistaking her for a boy.

He couldn't see down the brow of the hill to where Catherine Ross lay in the snow. He turned away from the window to brew tea, then took his cup back with him and waited. He had nothing to get on with. Nothing urgent. He had been out the night before with hay for the croft sheep. He had few animals on the hill now. On these freezing days when the ground was hard and covered with snow, there was little else for him to do outside.

The devil makes work for idle hands. The memory of his mother saying those words was so sharp that he almost turned round, expecting to see her sitting in the chair by the fire, the belt filled with horsehair round her waist, one needle stuck into it, held firm, while the other flew. She could knit a pair of stockings in an afternoon, a plain jersey in a week. She was known as the best knitter in the south, though she'd never enjoyed doing the fancy Fair Isle patterns. *What point is there in that?* she'd say, putting the stress on the last word so she'd almost spit it out. *Will it keep dee ony warmer?*

He wondered what other work the devil might find for him.

The mother came back from the school, pulling the empty sledge behind her. He watched her from right at the bottom of the hill, leaning forward, trudging like a man. She stopped just below his house and looked back across the voe. He could tell that something had caught her attention. He wondered if he should go out and call her in. If she was cold she might be distracted by the thought of tea. She might be tempted by the fire and the biscuits. He still had some left and there was a slice of ginger cake in the tin. He wondered briefly if she baked for her daughter. Probably not, he decided. That would be another thing to have changed. Why would anyone go to all that trouble now? The beating of sugar and marge in the big bowl, turning the spoon as it came out of the tin of black treacle. Why would you bother with that, when there was Safeway's in Lerwick, selling pastries with apricot and almond and ginger cake every bit as good as the one his mother had baked?

Because he'd been preoccupied with thoughts about baking, he missed the moment when he could have invited the woman into the house. She'd already wandered away from the road. There was nothing he could do now. He could just see her head – she was wearing a hat, a strange knitted bonnet – as she slid down the dip in the field, then she was lost to view altogether. He saw the three ravens, scattering as if they'd been shot at, but he was too far away to hear the woman screaming. Once she'd disappeared from view he forgot about her. She wasn't important enough to feature as a picture in his head.

The teacher's man drove up the road in his Land Rover. Magnus recognized him but had never spoken to him. It was unusual for him to be so late, leaving home. Usually he left the schoolhouse early in the morning and returned after dark. Perhaps the snow had altered his plans. Magnus knew the movements of everyone in the valley. There had been nothing else to take his interest since the death of his mother. From overheard gossip in the post office and the bus, he had learned that Alex Henry worked for the Islands Council. He was something to do with the wildlife. Magnus had heard the men complaining. A local man should know better, they said. Who did Henry think he was, laying down the law to them? They blamed the seals for taking fish and thought they should be allowed to shoot them. They said people like Henry cared more for animals than men's livelihoods. Magnus liked to see the seals – he thought there was something friendly and comical about the way they stuck their heads out of the water – but then he'd never gone to the fishing. The seals made no difference to him.

When the car stopped, Magnus had a repeat of the panic he'd experienced when he'd seen Margaret Henry. Perhaps Sally had talked. Perhaps the father was here to complain about Magnus taking the girls into the house. He thought Henry had even more to be angry about now. The man was frowning as he climbed down from the car. He was middle-aged, big, thickset. He wore a Barbour jacket, which was tight across his shoulders, heavy leather boots. If there was a fight, Magnus wouldn't stand a chance. Magnus moved away from the window so he couldn't be seen, but Henry didn't even look in his direction. He climbed over the gate and followed the line of footsteps made by the woman. Now Magnus was interested. He would have liked a view of the scene which was being played out at the bottom of the hill. If it had just been the woman he would have gone out to look. He thought she must have waved at the teacher's husband, called for him to stop his car.

And then just as he was imagining what might be happening, the young mother came back, stumbling slightly as she reached the road. He could tell she was upset. She had a dazed and frozen look which Magnus had seen before. Georgie Sanderson had looked like that when he'd had to give up his boat and his mother had been the same way after the death of Agnes. She hadn't been frozen when Magnus's father had died. Then, it had seemed that life would carry on as normal. *It'll just be you and me now, Magnus. You'll have to be a big boy for your mother.* She had spoken briskly, even cheerfully. There had been no tears.

Magnus thought now that the woman had cried, though it was hard to tell. Sometimes the cold wind brought tears to your eyes. She got into the driver's seat of the Land Rover and started the engine, but the car didn't move off. Again he wondered if he should go out to her. He could tap on the windscreen – she wouldn't hear him approaching over the sound of the diesel engine and the windows had steamed up so she wouldn't see him. He could ask her what had happened. Once she was in the house, he could suggest that she might like to come back for a visit with the little girl. He began to plan what he might get for the girl to eat and drink. Those round little biscuits with the pink sugar icing, chocolate fingers. It would be quite a tea party with the three of them. And there was still a doll in the back which had once belonged to Agnes. The fair-haired child might like to play with it. He couldn't give it her to keep, that wouldn't be right. He had kept all the toys which had belonged to Agnes. But he couldn't see there would be any harm in her holding it and tying a ribbon into its hair.

His dreams were interrupted by the sound of an engine. It was another Land Rover, this time a navy blue one – and it was driven by a man in a uniform. The sight of the heavy waterproof jacket, the tie, the cap which the man put on his head when he got out of the vehicle, threw Magnus into a panic. He remembered the last time. He was back in the small room with the shiny gloss paint on the walls, he heard the furious questions, saw the open mouth and the fat lips. There had been two of them wearing uniforms then. They had come to the house for him early in the morning. His mother had wanted to come with them, had hurried away to find her coat, but they'd said there was no need. That had been later in the year, not so cold, but damp, a squally westerly full of rain.

Had only one of them spoken? He could only remember the one.

The memory made him shake so violently that the cup rattled in the saucer he was holding. He could feel his mouth form the grin his mother had hated so much, the grin which had been his only defence to the questions and which had irritated his interrogator beyond endurance.

'Is it funny?' the man had shouted. 'A young lass missing. You think that's a joke? Do you?'

Magnus hadn't thought it a joke, but the grin stuck, petrified. There had been nothing he could do about it. Neither could he reply.

'Well?' the man had screamed. 'What are you laughing at, pervert?' Then he had lifted himself slowly to his feet and while Magnus watched confused, as if he was nothing but an observer, he'd drawn his hand into a fist and smashed it down on Magnus's face, forcing back his head with a jolt that rocked the chair. There was blood in his mouth and chips of broken tooth. The man would have hit him again if he hadn't been stopped by his partner.

Now Magnus thought that blood tasted of metal and ice. He realized he was still holding the saucer and set it carefully on the table. He knew it couldn't be the same policeman. That had been years ago. *That* policeman would be middle-aged by now, retired maybe. He returned tentatively to the window, resisting the first impulse, which had been to hide in the back room with his eyes shut. When he had been a boy he had imagined that if he shut his eyes, nobody could see him. His mother had been right. He had been a very foolish child. If he shut his eyes now, the policeman would still be there, outside his house, the ravens would still be in the sky, tumbling and calling, their claws stained with blood. Catherine Ross would still be lying in the snow.

Chapter Six

Alex Henry had sent her back to sit in the Land Rover. She'd still been screaming when he came up to her. About the birds. She couldn't leave Catherine there with the birds.

'I won't let them back,' he'd said. 'I promise.'

For a while she sat upright in the front seat of the Land Rover, remembering Catherine as she'd last seen her. There'd been a PTA meeting, the AGM, and Fran had asked Catherine to babysit. Fran had given her a glass of wine and they'd chatted before she'd gone down to the school. Catherine had a poise and confidence which made her seem older than she really was.

'How have you settled into Anderson High?' Fran had asked.

There'd been a brief pause, a slight frown before Catherine had answered. 'Fine.'

Despite the difference in their ages Fran had hoped they might become friends. There weren't that many young women in Ravenswick after all. Now it was sweltering in the Land Rover. The heater was pumping out hot air. Fran shut her eyes to push out the picture of the girl in the snow. She fell suddenly and deeply asleep. A reaction to the shock, she thought later. It was as if a fuse had blown. She needed to escape.

When she opened her eyes, the scene around her had changed. She had been aware of car doors banging and voices but put off the return to full consciousness for as long as possible. Now she saw there was drama, a show of brisk efficiency.

'Mrs Hunter.' Someone was knocking on the window of Alex Henry's Land Rover. 'Are you all right, Mrs Hunter?' She saw the face of a man, the impressionist image of a face, blurred by the mist and muck on the glass, wild black hair and a strong hooked nose, black eyebrows. A foreigner, she thought. Someone even more foreign than me. From the Mediterranean perhaps, North Africa even. Then he spoke again and she could tell he was a Shetlander, though the accent had been tamed and educated.

She opened the door slowly and climbed out. The cold hit her.

'Mrs Hunter?' he said again. She wondered how he knew her name. Could he be an old friend of Duncan's? Then she thought that Alex Henry would have told the police who had found Catherine when he phoned them. Of course he would. This wasn't a time for paranoia.

'Yes.' Even here, seeing him in the clear, there was something unformed about his face. There were no sharp lines. A stubble of beard broke the silhouette of the chin, his hair was slightly too long for a police officer, not brushed surely, and it was a face which was never still. He wasn't wearing uniform. Underneath the heavy jacket, she knew the clothes would be untidy too.

'My name's Perez,' he said. 'Inspector. Are you ready to answer some questions?'

Perez? Wasn't that Spanish? It was a very odd name, she thought, for a Shetlander. But then, he seemed a very odd man. Her attention began to wander again. Since seeing Catherine lying in the snow, it had been impossible to focus on anything. They were stringing blue and white crime-scene tape, to block the gap in the wall where she had walked down the hill after stopping on her way back from school. Was the girl still lying there? She had the ridiculous notion that Catherine must be freezing. She hoped someone had thought to bring a blanket to cover her.

Perez must have asked her another question, because he was looking at her, obviously waiting for an answer.

'I'm sorry,' she said. 'I don't know what's wrong with me.'

'Shock. It'll pass.' He looked at her, as she might once have looked at a model during a photo shoot. Appraising, dispassionate. 'Come on. Let's get you home.'

He knew where she lived, drove her there without asking, took her keys and opened the door for her.

'Would you like tea?' she said. 'Coffee?'

'Coffee,' he said. 'Why not?'

'Shouldn't you be down there, looking at the body?'

He smiled. 'I'd not be allowed anywhere near it. Not until the crime scene investigator is finished. We can't have more people than necessary contaminating the site.'

'Has someone told Euan?' she asked.

'That's the girl's father?'

'Yes, Euan Ross. He's a teacher.'

'They're doing that now.'

She moved the kettle on to the hotplate and spooned coffee into a cafetière.

'Did you know her?' he asked.

'Catherine? She came occasionally to look after Cassie when I went out. It didn't happen often. There was a lecture in the town hall by a visiting author I enjoy. A PTA meeting at the school. Once, Euan invited me down to his house for a meal.'

'You were friendly? You and Mr Ross?'

'Neighbourly, that's all. Single parents often stick together. His wife had died. Cancer. She was ill for a couple of years and after her death he felt he needed a change. He'd been headmaster of a big inner-city school in Yorkshire, saw the job here advertised and applied on a whim.'

'What did Catherine think about that? It would be a bit of a culture shock.'

'I'm not sure. Girls that age, it's hard to tell what they're thinking.'

'What age was she?'

'Sixteen. Nearly seventeen.'

'And you?' he asked. 'What brought you back?'

The question made her angry. How could he know that she'd lived here before?

'Is that relevant?' she demanded. 'To your enquiries?'

'You found a body. The body of a murder victim. You'll have to answer questions. Even personal questions which seem to have no relevance.' He gave a little shrug to show that it was part of the system, beyond his control. 'Besides, your husband, he's a big man round here. People gossip. You can't have expected that you could slip back to Shetland unnoticed.'

'He's not my husband,' she snapped. 'We divorced.'

'Why *did* you come back?' he asked. He was sitting in the chair by the window, his crossed legs stretched in front of him. He'd taken off his boots at the door. His socks were made of thick white wool and were bobbled from washing. His jacket was hanging on the hook on the wall, next to one of Cassie's and he was wearing a crumpled red plaid shirt. He leaned back in his chair, a mug in his hand, looking out. He seemed entirely relaxed. She itched to get a large sheet of paper and a stick of charcoal to sketch him.

'I love it here,' she said. 'Because I stopped loving Duncan, it seemed contrary to deprive myself of the place. And it means that Cassie can maintain contact with her father. I enjoyed London, but it isn't a good place to bring up a child. I sold my flat there and that gave me enough to live for a while.' She didn't want to tell him about her painting, the dream that it could support them, the failed relationship which had triggered the move. How she'd grown up without a father and hadn't wanted to do that to her daughter.

'Will you stay?'

'Yes,' she said. 'I think I will.'

'What about Euan Ross? Has he settled?'

'I think he still finds it hard, coping without his wife.'

'In what way?'

She struggled to find the words to describe the man. 'I don't know him well. It's hard to judge.'

'But?'

'I think he might still be depressed. I mean,

clinically depressed. He thought the move would change things, solve things. How could it, really? He's still without the woman he was married to for twenty years.' She paused. Perez looked at her, expecting her to continue. 'He called in the day I arrived to introduce himself. He was very kind, charming. He brought coffee and milk, some flowers from his garden. He said we were almost neighbours. Not quite, with Hillhead in the way, but he lived down the hill between here and the school. I'd never have realized on that first meeting that anything was wrong, that there was any sadness at all in his life. He's a very good actor. He hides his feelings very well. When he saw Cassie, he said he had a daughter too, Catherine. If ever I needed a babysitter she was always desperate for cash. That was it. He didn't mention his wife at all. Catherine told me about that, the first time she came to look after Cassie.

'When he invited me for a meal, I wasn't sure what to expect. I mean, a single woman of my age, sometimes men hit on you, think you're desperate, try it on. You know what I mean. I hadn't picked up any of those signals, but sometimes you get it wrong.'

'You went anyway, even though you were unsure of his motives?'

'Yeah,' she said. 'I don't have much of a life, you know. Sometimes I miss adult company. And I thought, anyway, would it be so awful? He's an attractive man, pleasant, unattached. There aren't so many of those around here.'

'Was it a good night?' He smiled at her, in an encouraging, slightly teasing way. The style was fatherly, almost, though there could scarcely be any difference in their ages.

'To start with. He'd gone to a lot of effort. It's a lovely house. Do you know it? There's that new extension, all wood and glass, with wonderful views down the coast. Lots of photos of his dead wife. I mean they were everywhere, which seemed a bit spooky. I wondered what it must be like for Catherine, growing up with that. I mean, would you think you were second best, that he wished *you* had died instead of your mother? But then I thought everyone deals with grief in their own way. What right did I have to judge?

'We sat down to eat almost immediately. The food was mind-blowing, I mean as good as any I've had anywhere. We managed to keep the conversation going OK. I told him the story of my divorce. Kept it light and amusing. I've had plenty of practice. Pride. It's hard to admit to the world that your husband has fallen passionately in love with a woman who's almost old enough to be your mother. Plenty there to joke about. He was drinking quite heavily, but then so was I. We were both rather nervous.'

She could see the scene quite clearly in her head. Although it had been dark outside he hadn't drawn the blinds, so it was as if they were a part of the night-time landscape, as if the table was set on the cliff. The room was softly lit by candles; one lamp shone on a big photograph of the dead woman, so Fran had almost believed that she was present at the meal too. Everything was slightly elaborate – the heavy cutlery, engraved glasses, starched napkins, expensive wine. And then he started to weep. Tears ran down his cheeks. It had been silent at first. She hadn't known how to react so she'd continued eating. The food after all was very good. She'd thought that given a little time, he might pull himself together. But then he began to sob, embarrassing, choking sobs, wiping the snot and the tears on one of the pristine napkins, and pretence had been impossible. She'd got up and put her arms around him, as she might have done if Cassie had woken suddenly from a bad dream.

'He couldn't hack it,' she told the detective now. 'He broke down. He wasn't ready for entertaining.' The enormity of the tragedy of Catherine's death suddenly hit her. 'Oh God, and now he's lost his daughter too.' It'll push him over the edge, she thought. No one will be able to save him now.

'How did they get on?' Perez asked. 'Did you have any sense of tension, friction? It must be hard for a man bringing up a teenage girl. Just the wrong age. They're rebellious then anyway. And they hate being different.'

'I don't think they ever argued,' Fran said. 'I can't imagine it. He was so wrapped up in his own grief that I think he just let her get on with things. I don't mean he neglected her. Not that. I'm sure they were very fond of each other. But I can't see him making a big deal over the clothes she wore or the time she went to bed or whether or not she'd done her homework. He had other preoccupations.'

'Did she talk to you about him?'

'No. We didn't talk about anything important. I probably seemed as old as the hills to her. She always seemed very self-contained to me, but then I think most young people are like that. They never confide in adults.'

'When did you last see her?'

'To talk to? New Year's Eve, in the afternoon. I'd left a message on her mobile. There's a concert I'd like to go to in a couple of weeks' time. I asked if she'd be able to babysit. She called in to say that would be fine.'

'How did she seem?'

'Well. As animated as I'd known her. Quite forthcoming. She said she was going into Lerwick with her friend that evening to see in the new year.'

'Which friend?'

'She didn't say, but I presumed it would be Sally Henry. She lives at the school. They seem to knock around together.'

'And that was the last time you saw her?'

'To speak to, yes. But I did see her yesterday. She got off the lunchtime bus. She walked down the road with the strange old guy who lives in Hillhead.'

Chapter Seven

The police came to Magnus at the only moment that day when he wasn't looking out for them. He was in the bathroom when they knocked at the door. His mother had got Georgie Sanderson to build a bathroom at the back of the house. It was when Georgie's leg was so bad that he couldn't go to the fishing any more. A sort of favour, because he hated being idle and she would pay him for the work. Georgie was a practical kind of a man, but there would have been better people to ask. The bath had never fitted properly against the wall. The light had fused soon after Magnus's mother died and Magnus had never bothered getting it fixed. What would be the point? He shaved in the sink by the kitchen and he could see the toilet from the light in the bedroom.

He'd been aware for some time of the need to relieve himself, but he'd not been able to leave his post at the window. More people had arrived. Constables in uniform. A tall man in a suit. An untidy chap had gone up to the young woman sitting in Henry's Land Rover and taken her away in his car. Magnus hoped she wasn't in the room with the shiny walls in the police station. At last he hadn't been able to put off the visit to the bathroom any longer, and it was at that moment, when he was standing there, like a peerie boy, with his trousers and his pants round his ankles, because he'd been in too much of a hurry to fiddle with zips and flies, that the knock came. He was thrown into a panic.

'Just wait,' he shouted. He was in midstream. There was nothing he could do about it. 'I'll be there in just a minute.'

He finished at last and pulled on his pants and his trousers all in one go. The trousers had an elasticated waist. Now that he was decent again the panic began to subside.

When Magnus went back to the kitchen the man was still waiting outside. Magnus could see him through the window. He was standing quite patiently. He hadn't even opened the door into the porch. It was the scruffy-looking man who had driven away the young woman. He couldn't have taken her all the way into Lerwick then. Maybe just up to the house by the chapel. Magnus thought the police probably dealt differently with women.

Magnus opened the door and stared at the man. He didn't know him. He didn't live round here. He didn't look like anyone Magnus knew, so he probably didn't have relatives round here either.

'Whar's du fae?' he demanded. It was what came into his head. If he'd thought about it, he'd have used different words, as he had with the girls, so if this stranger *had* come from the south he would have understood. But it seemed he understood anyway.

'Fae Fair Isle,' the man said, echoing the rhythm of Magnus's words. Then, after a beat, 'Originally. I trained in Aberdeen and now I'm working out of Lerwick.' He held out his hand. 'My name's Perez.'

'That's a strange kind of name for a Fair Isle man.'

Perez smiled but he didn't explain. Still Magnus didn't take the hand. The old man was thinking he'd never been to Fair Isle. There was no roll-on roll-off ferry even now. The trip took three hours in the mail boat from Grutness, the harbour in the south close to the airport. He'd seen pictures once of the island. It had a big craig on its east side. The minister who'd lived in that house next to the chapel had been preacher on Fair Isle. There'd been a slide show in the community hall and Magnus had gone with his mother. But he couldn't remember any more details.

'What like is it there?' he asked.

'I like it fine.'

'Why did you leave then?'

'Oh you know. There's not an awful lot of work.'

Magnus saw the hand then and reached out and shook it.

'You'd best come in,' he said. He looked past Perez down the bank and saw a constable in uniform staring up at him. 'Come away in,' he said, more urgently.

Perez had to stoop to get through the door and once he was inside the room, he seemed to fill it.

'Sit down,' Magnus said. It made him nervous, seeing this tall man towering over him. He pulled out a chair from the table and waited for Perez to take it. He'd been expecting the police to come to his house all morning and now he didn't know what to say. He didn't know what to think.

'Sit down.' It was the raven. It stuck its beak through the bars of the cage and repeated the words, running them into each other. 'Sitdownsitdownsitdownsit.'

Magnus took an old jersey and threw it over the cage. He was afraid the interruption would make the policeman angry. But Perez seemed only amused. 'Did you teach it to do that? I didn't know ravens could speak.'

'They're clever birds.' Magnus could feel the smile appearing, could do nothing about it. He turned his head, hoping it would go away of its own free will.

'Did you see the ravens down the hill this morning?'

'They're always there,' Magnus said.

'There's been a death. A young girl.'

'Catherine.' He couldn't help it. Like the daft grin, the words had come out despite his efforts to stop them. *Tell them nothing* his mother had said. Her last words to him when the two policemen came to take him into Lerwick all that time ago. *You've done nothing, so tell them nothing.*

'How did you know she was dead, Magnus?' Perez was speaking very clearly and very slowly. 'How did you know it was Catherine who was on the hill?'

Magnus shook his head. *Tell them nothing.*

'Did you see what happened to her down there? Did you see how she died?'

Magnus looked wildly around him.

'Perhaps you saw the ravens and wondered what had disturbed them.'

'Yes,' he said gratefully.

'And you went out to look?'

'Yes.' Magnus nodded violently.

'Why didn't you tell the police, Magnus?'

'She was already dead. I couldn't have saved her.'

'But the police should have been told.'

'There's no phone in the house. How could I tell you?'

'One of your neighbours would have a phone. You could have asked them to call for you.'

'They don't speak to me.'

There was a silence. Underneath the jersey the raven scratched and scuffled.

'When did you see her?' Perez asked. 'What time was it when you went down the hill to look?'

'After the bairns had gone into school. I heard the bell as I left the house.' Magnus thought that was a clever answer. His mother wouldn't have minded him telling that.

There was another pause while Perez wrote some words in a notebook. At last he looked up. 'How long have you lived here on your own, Magnus?'

'Since my mother died.'

'When was that?'

Magnus tried to find an answer. How many years would it have been? He couldn't guess.

'Agnes died too,' he said, so he wouldn't have to work out the number of years in his head.

'Who was Agnes?'

'She was my sister. She caught the whooping cough. It was more bad than anyone realized. She was ten.' He shut his mouth tight. It was none of the policeman's business.

'It must have been lonely here, after your mother died.'

Magnus didn't answer.

'You'd be glad of some company.'

Still he said nothing.

'Catherine was a friend of yours, wasn't she?'

'Yes,' Magnus said. 'A friend.'

'You met her yesterday on the bus from town.'

'She'd been to a party.'

'A party?' Perez said. 'All night? Are you sure?'

Had she? That was right, wasn't it? Magnus had to think about it. He couldn't remember. She hadn't said much at all.

'She looked tired,' he said. 'She'd stayed out all night. I think she said it was a party.'

'How was she dressed?'

'Not in fancy clothes,' Magnus admitted, 'but then they don't dress up much for going out these days.'

'When you went out to look at her on the hill you'd have seen what she was wearing. Had she changed since you saw her yesterday?'

'I don't think so.' Then he wondered if he should have given a different answer, if the question had been a trick. 'I remember the red scarf.'

'Did she tell you where the party was?'

'She didn't say. She didn't notice me then. Only later when we both got off the bus together.'

'How did she seem?' Perez asked.

'Tired, I said.'

'But sad tired or happy tired?'

'She came into the house,' Magnus said suddenly. 'For tea.'

There was a silence. Magnus knew he'd made a mistake. He continued quickly, 'She wanted to take my photo. For a project. She wanted to come.'

'Did she take the photo?'

'She took several.'

'Had she been in the house before?' Perez asked.

He didn't seem troubled by what Magnus had told him. There was no fuss, no threat, no outrage.

'New Year's Eve. Catherine and Sally. They were on their way home. They saw the light and called in to wish me happy new year.'

'Sally?'

'Sally Henry, the teacher's lass.'

'But yesterday Catherine was on her own?'

'On her own. Yes.'

'Did she stay long?'

'She took some cake,' Magnus said. 'A cup of tea.'

'So she wasn't here all afternoon?'

'No. Not long.'

'What time was it, when she left?'

'I can't say for sure.'

Perez looked around the room. 'That's a fine clock.'

'It belonged to my mother.'

'It keeps good time?'

'I check it with the wireless every night.'

'You'd have noticed what time the girl left, surely. The clock, sitting there on the shelf. You'd have glanced at it when she went out. It would be automatic.'

Magnus opened his mouth to speak, but the words wouldn't come out. His thoughts seemed frozen, sluggish.

'I don't remember,' he said at last.

'Was it light when she left you?'

'Oh yes, it was still light.'

'Because this time of the year, it gets dark so early . . .' Perez paused, looked towards Magnus as if expecting him to change his mind. When there was no response he continued, 'Where was she going?'

'Home.'

'Did she say that was where she was going?'

'No, but that was the direction she was headed in. To that house halfway down the bank where the building work was done. The one with all the glass at the front. She lives there.'

'Did you see her go in?'

Was that another trick? Magnus looked at the policeman. He became aware that his mouth was open and he shut it.

'It'd only be natural,' Perez said. 'You'd watch her go down the hill, wouldn't you? Nothing wrong with watching a pretty young girl anyway. But you must spend a lot of time sitting here looking at the view. This weather, there's not much else to do.'

'Yes,' Magnus said. 'I saw her go in.'

They sat. The silence lasted for such a long time that Magnus wondered if that was it, if the policeman would go now and leave him alone. Suddenly he wasn't even sure that was what he wanted. 'Would you like some tea?' he asked. He frowned, imagining how it would be in the house, with the policeman gone, and only the noise of the ravens calling from the hill outside.

'Yes,' Perez said. 'Tea would be fine.'

Neither of them spoke until the tea was made and they were sitting together back at the table.

'Eight years ago,' Perez said, 'a girl went missing. She was younger than Catherine, but not that much younger. Catriona, she was called. Did you know her, Magnus?'

Magnus wanted to shut his eyes to shut out the question, but knew that if he did, he'd imagine himself back in the police station with the fist pulling back from his face, the taste of blood in his mouth.

He stared into space.

'You did know her, didn't you Magnus? She came to visit you for tea too. Like Catherine. She was very bonny, I hear.'

'She was never found,' Magnus said. He tried to compose the muscles in his jaw to stop the dreadful smile. He fixed his lips tight shut and remembered his mother's words. *Tell them nothing*.

Chapter Eight

Perez drove back to Lerwick after leaving Magnus Tait's house. He wanted to talk to Catherine's father and knew that the man was still at the high school. There might not be much he could do at this stage – the man would be in shock – but it seemed respectful to introduce himself and explain the procedures. He couldn't imagine what it must be like to lose a child. Not really. Sarah, his wife, had had a miscarriage, and that for a while had seemed like the end of the world. He'd tried not to show how much it hurt him. He hadn't wanted Sarah to feel that he loved her any less, or blamed her for the loss of the baby. Of course it had been himself he'd blamed. Himself and the weight of his family's expectations. He'd felt that almost physically, pictured it as a crushing pressure, which made it impossible for the baby to survive. It would have been a boy. The pregnancy had been sufficiently advanced for them to know that. There would have been another Perez to carry on the family line.

Perhaps he'd played the role too skilfully. Perhaps Sarah had thought he really didn't care. Though surely she must have known him well enough to realize it was an act for her benefit. It was from the miscarriage that he charted the breakdown of his marriage. Sarah grew grey and distant. He spent more time at work. When she told him she was leaving, it was almost a relief. He couldn't bear to see her looking so miserable. Now she was married to a GP and living somewhere in the Borders. It seemed she'd had no problems conceiving with her new partner. There were already three children and the Christmas card – it had been a very civilized divorce and they still kept in touch – informed him that there was another baby on the way. He imagined her sometimes living in one of those solid country houses he'd glimpsed from the train south. He'd see her in a kitchen which looked out over woods and a meadow. She'd be giving the kids their tea, a baby on her hip, laughing. Not being part of that seemed a sort of bereavement. Bad enough. What must it be like for Catherine's father to lose a real child?

Euan Ross was sitting in the head teacher's office, on an easy chair, next to a round coffee table. This would be where the head would sit when he came out from behind his desk to put anxious parents or nervous students at ease. The female uniformed officer beside him looked as if she longed to be somewhere else. Anywhere else. Ross was an angular man in his mid-forties, greying. When he saw Perez, he reached into his pocket for a pair of spectacles. He wore dark trousers, a jacket and tie, everything smart, too smart for most of the teachers Perez had come across. If he hadn't known, Perez would have put him down as a lawyer or accountant. There was a tea tray on the table. It was untouched and looked as if it had been there some time.

Perez introduced himself.

'I want to see my daughter,' Ross said. 'I've tried to explain how important that is.'

'Of course. But I'm afraid that will be later. No one is allowed to disturb her now. We have to preserve the crime scene.'

Ross had been sitting very upright, but now he collapsed and put his head in his hands. 'I can't believe it. Not until I see her.' He looked up. 'I was with my wife when she died. She'd been ill for months and we'd been expecting it. But even then I couldn't quite believe it. I kept expecting her to turn her head to me and smile.'

Perez didn't know what to say, so he kept quiet.

'How did Catherine die?' Ross asked. 'No one will tell me anything.' He looked at the policewoman. She pretended not to hear.

'We believe she was strangled,' Perez said. 'We'll know more when the team from Inverness arrives. They have more experience of serious crime than we do.'

'Who would want to kill her?'

He didn't seem to be expecting an answer, but Perez took advantage of the question. 'We're hoping you'll have the information to help us discover that. There isn't anyone who comes immediately to mind? A boyfriend she's recently dumped? Anyone who might be jealous, angry?'

'No. At least there might be, but I'm not the person to ask. You'd think we'd be close. There are only the two of us after all. But she didn't confide in me, Inspector. I know very little of what she got up to. We lived under the same roof, but sometimes I thought we were strangers.'

'I suppose that's how it is with teenagers,' Perez said. 'They resent their parents' prying.' *Though how would I know? I don't have children and when I was that age I was boarding out at the hostel. I'd have loved to have my parents to talk to every night.* 'But you'll be able to give me the names of her friends. They'll be able to help.'

There was a moment of silence before Ross answered. 'I'm not sure Catherine was very close to anybody. She didn't need people. Liz, my wife, was very different. She had so many friends. At her funeral the church was packed, people standing at the back, people I'd never met but who felt close to her, touched by her warmth. I don't know who will come when we bury Catherine. Not many people.'

The statement almost took Perez's breath away. It seemed such a sad and chilling thing to say. He wondered if that was how it had always been. If Catherine had always been compared to Euan's wife and been found wanting.

'Didn't she hang around with Sally Henry?' he said at last.

'The teacher's daughter? Yes, she did. They came into school on the bus together. I didn't usually bring Catherine in. I leave the house too early and get back too late for her.' He gave a little smile which made Perez at last feel some sympathy for him. 'Besides, it wouldn't have been very cool, would it? Getting a lift with your Dad? Sally was often in the house. I was pleased that Catherine had the company. I'm not sure though how close they were.'

'Had she a regular boyfriend since you moved to Shetland?'

'I don't think she's ever had a regular boyfriend,' Ross said. 'And I'm not sure I'd know about it if she had.'

Perez left him, sitting in the head's office, staring into space. He couldn't tell if it was his daughter Ross was grieving for or his wife. Outside the school he looked down at the familiar town. He'd moved back to Shetland after Sarah had left. He'd seen it as a failure, an act of running away. It had been a sort of promotion, but it wasn't real policing, was it? That was what his colleagues in Aberdeen had said. *A bit young for retirement, aren't you, Jimmy lad?* After losing the baby and separating from Sarah, he hadn't really cared. The big cases hadn't excited him any more. He'd stopped caring about the glory. And now he had a big case on his own patch and he felt something of the old thrill. Nothing to make a song and dance about just yet. But something stirring in his guts so he felt a bit more alive. The possibility of getting it right.

Chapter Nine

When Fran arrived at the school to collect Cassie, a
crowd of adults was already there. This was unusual.
Most of the children – even the younger ones – were
allowed to make their own way home. Fran stood apart
for a moment watching the group. There was something intimidating about them, gathered in a circle. It
was almost dark and it was hard to make out individuals. They stamped their feet against the cold and
talked in low, intense voices in a dialect she had problems understanding. Then she thought she had as
much right to be there as they did. And when she
approached them, they welcomed her, said how much
of a shock it must have been to come across the body
like that. They were sympathetic and she was the centre of attention. Inside the school the lights were on.
They shone on the playground, reflecting from the ice
where boys had made a slide and a half-built snow-
man.

At first their curiosity offended her but she thought
none of them had really known Catherine. It wasn't as
if she'd grown up there. They saw the girl as a character, someone they might have seen on TV. They
crowded around Fran asking for details. Was it true
that the birds had ripped out both the eyes? That

Catherine had been naked? Was there blood? Despite herself Fran answered.

'I saw that detective from Fair Isle was in Magnus Tait's house.' Fran didn't recognize the speaker. It was a sharp-faced, pinched little woman. In her forties, she could have been a mother or a young grandmother. She continued shrilly, breaking in on the conversation around her, 'Perhaps this time they'll put him away where he belongs.'

'What do you mean?'

'Didn't you know? It's not the first time it's happened. A girl was killed here before.'

'Now, Jennifer, we don't know she was killed.'

'Well, she'd not have disappeared into thin air, would she? And although it was summer, it was stormy that week. I mind it fine. There were no planes or boats south for days. Not that Catriona could have got on to either without someone realizing it was odd for a young girl to be on her own.'

'Who was she?' Fran told herself this was malicious gossip. She should stand apart from it and not get involved. But it didn't prevent the question.

'Catriona Bruce. Eleven years old. The family lived in the house where Euan Ross stays now. Some coincidence huh? They had to move. How could they stay there with reminders of her everywhere and not knowing for certain what happened to her? I think it was a worse crime than killing her, not letting on what he'd done with the body.'

'But if Magnus was never charged,' Fran's *Guardian* values reasserted themselves, 'you can't be certain it was him.'

'It was him all right. We always knew he was daft

in the head. He was like a child himself. Everyone thought he was harmless. We were more innocent in those days, maybe. People thought they were doing a kindness, letting their children in to talk to him. We know better now.'

I let Cassie talk to him, Fran thought. Nobody warned me not to. She remembered Magnus hurrying out of his house to greet them, almost stumbling in his eagerness to catch up with them, before they'd walked on. She shivered. Inside the school a bell rang and the children ran out.

By the time they arrived home it was quite dark. This time of year once the sun fell below the horizon night came very quickly. She went in and drew the curtains before switching on the lights. She'd hurried Cassie past Magnus's house, tugging on the mittened hand, jollying her along with the promise of treats at home. She'd wondered how she'd react if Magnus came out, but wasn't put to the test. She'd glanced once towards Hillhead, thought she'd glimpsed a pale, staring face and had looked quickly away. Perhaps she'd imagined it; perhaps he'd already been arrested.

Now she imagined what Euan must be going through. The police would have gone to the high school and told him about Catherine's death. Surely they wouldn't expect him to look at the body? Not lying where it was in the field. Perez had told her that it would be there all night. But perhaps he would want to see his daughter. Perez had said a team would come from Inverness and the detectives and scene of crime officers would need to see the body on site. He'd thought it hardly likely they'd make the three o'clock plane from Aberdeen. More likely the six-thirty. But she supposed there would be questions for Euan. Perhaps that would be a distraction of a sort. She thought the worst time would be returning to the big glass house and his dreams of two dead women.

She considered phoning to check if he was home. It wasn't having to confront the image of Catherine's death which prevented her. She hated seeming like the relatives waiting by the school gate. What if Euan thought her prurient and intrusive? What if her motives *had* more to do with curiosity than an attempt to provide support?

There was a knock at the door. Cassie was engrossed in a television programme and hardly looked up. The tension and excitement outside the school seemed to have passed over her head. Usually Fran would just have shouted, *It's open, come in.* Today she hesitated, opened the door a crack, thought in the moment of opening it *What if it's the old man? Would I turn him away?*

Euan stood outside. He was wrapped up in a long black overcoat, but he was shaking.

'I was on my way home,' he said. 'They offered to send someone with me. I told them I preferred to be on my own. But now I can't face going into the house. I don't know what to do.'

She felt she should offer him comfort, put her arms around him as she had when he'd broken down talking about his wife. But now he was too cold and distant. She thought it would be like attempting to hug a formidable headmaster if you were still at school. Impossible.

'Come in,' she said. She sat him by the fire and poured him whisky.

'I was teaching a group of third years. *A Midsummer Night's Dream*. Maggie came in. She's in charge of RE. Maybe they thought that was appropriate. Could she have a word? I could tell it was serious, but I thought one of the kids in my class . . .' He stopped. 'I don't know what I thought. But not that.'

'I'll phone Duncan,' Fran said. 'He's always wanting extra time with Cassie. She can spend the night with him. Then I can come back with you to the house, see you in. I can spend as long there as you need.'

At first she wasn't sure if he'd heard, but eventually he nodded. He sat with his coat still on while she made the arrangements, but after a few moments set the whisky carefully on the table and took off his gloves with great concentration.

Duncan arrived with a flourish, his palm on the horn. She took Cassie out to him although on other occasions this loutish behaviour would have kept her in the house, forcing him out of the comfort zone of his 4x4 to knock at the door.

'Shall we go?' she said to Euan. He had sipped the whisky, but barely touched it.

He stood up without a word. She was reminded of a visit to a psychiatric hospital to see one of her London friends who was being treated for anorexia. Euan had the same stiff gait and immovable features of some of the other patients in the day room, drugged up she'd supposed, to keep them quiet and safe.

Automatically polite, he opened the passenger door for her, and drove slowly down the hill. At his house he braked a little sharply, forgetting the snow and the car skidded for a few yards before stopping.

She walked into the house before him and switched

on all the lights. He hesitated before following. He stood in the hall, apparently bewildered. It was as if this place was strange to him.

'What would you like me to do?' she asked. 'Would you prefer to be alone?'

'No!' he said sharply. 'I'd like to talk about Catherine. If you can bear it.' He turned to face her. 'They said you found her body.'

'Yes.' She held her breath, dreading that he would ask what Catherine had looked like, but he just stared at her for a moment and moved on. She realized she was trembling.

He led her through to the back of the house, to a room she hadn't seen on her previous visit. It was small. The walls were painted deep red and there were a couple of posters for art-house movies. At one end stood a desk with television and DVD player and a rack of DVDs. Against the wall was a small sofa which looked as if it let down into a bed. There was a book face down on the sofa. A paperback anthology of Robert Frost's poetry. Fran supposed it was a school set text.

'This is where Catherine brought her friends,' Euan said. 'She liked her privacy, kept her bedroom to herself. The police have already been in here. I gave them a key earlier. She'd have hated that, the thought of them going through her things.' He looked around him. 'It's not usually this tidy. Mrs Jamieson came in yesterday to clean.'

'Do the police have any idea what happened?'

'They didn't tell me anything. I'm to have someone attached to me to keep me informed. But apparently until the specialist team arrives from Inverness tonight, there's nothing to say.'

'Who did you see?'

'Perez, the local guy. He's in charge until the team from the mainland arrives.' He paused. 'He was sensitive enough, but the questions he asked made me realize how little attention I'd given Catherine recently. I was so wrapped up in myself. Self-pity. Such a destructive emotion. And now it's too late. I could tell the inspector thought I was a dreadful father, that I didn't care.'

She wished she could say that of course he'd been a good father, but he'd have seen through the lies.

'I'm sure Catherine understood,' she said.

'He asked me about her friends. Did she have a boyfriend? I know about Sally, of course. The two of them met up as soon as we arrived here. But I couldn't put a name to any of the others she hung out with. Only the ones I teach. Sometimes there were boys in the house, but I never asked if there was anyone special. I didn't even know where she was the night before she died. It didn't occur to me to worry about her. This is Shetland. It's safe. Everyone knows everyone else. The only crime comes out of binge drinking in Lerwick on a Friday night. I thought I had time. I could allow myself the space to get over Liz's death and then I could get to know my daughter.'

He still spoke in the impassive tone he'd used since he'd turned up on her doorstep. She thought it wasn't real yet. He was trying to convince himself. He needed to feel in his gut that Catherine was dead.

'Have you got anything to drink?' She was finding the tension unbearable.

'In the kitchen. Wine, beer in the fridge. Whisky in the pantry.'

'Which would you prefer?'

He considered as if it was a matter of great importance.

'Red wine, I think. Yes. That's in the pantry too.' He didn't offer to get it. Perhaps he was incapable of moving.

In the kitchen she laid a tray. Two glasses. The bottle, opened. A plate with a lump of Orkney cheddar she'd found in the fridge, a tin of oatcakes, two small blue plates and a couple of knives. She realized she hadn't eaten all day and she was hungry.

When she returned he was sitting in exactly the same position as when she'd left him. She didn't want to squeeze on to the sofa with him and sat on the floor next to a low table. She poured the wine for him and offered the cheese, which he refused. At last, to break the silence – after all, he had said that he wanted to talk about Catherine – she asked, 'When do the police think she was killed?'

'I've told you. I don't know anything.' He must have realized that he sounded rude. 'I'm sorry. It's not your fault. That was unforgivable. It's guilt again.' He twisted the stem of his glass. 'I didn't see Catherine last night. I hadn't seen her for two days. That wasn't unusual. You know what it's like here. Transport is difficult. Last night I was late home. I'd been in school all day, although term didn't start for the kids until this morning.' He looked up at her. 'We'd had a training session. And in the evening all the staff went out for a meal together. It's the first social event that I've gone along to. They've invited me before of course but I've always managed to refuse. This time I couldn't say no. The meal was almost an extension of the training day. Team building. You know the sort of thing?'

She nodded quickly. Now that he'd started talking, she didn't want to interrupt.

'It was actually a very pleasant evening. We sat talking over coffee. It was later than I realized when I got back. There'd been a text message from Catherine sent in the morning. *Don't worry if you don't see me tonight. Might stay out again.* He paused, punishing himself. *'Lots of love. Catherine.* She'd been to a party the night before. When she wasn't home when I got back from Lerwick, I assumed she was staying out again and that she'd go straight to school this morning.'

'Where was the party?'

'I don't know. I never asked.' He stared into his wine. 'But in one sense it doesn't matter. We know she *did* come home at lunchtime. The police told me that much. She was seen on the bus and by that old man who lives at Hillhead.' And by me, Fran thought. I saw them together. Euan continued. 'They seem to think she was killed close to where her body was found. They won't let me see her. I can't bear that.'

'What did the police say about the old man?'

'Nothing. Why?'

She hesitated only briefly. He would hear the rumours eventually. Better that the information come from her.

'There was a lot of gossip when I picked Cassie up from school this afternoon. You know how parents talk. A young girl went missing a while ago. She was called Catriona Bruce and she lived in this house. The old man, Magnus Tait, was suspected of having a hand in her disappearance. People are saying that he killed Catherine.'

He sat very still. He seemed frozen, incapable of moving. 'I don't think it matters who killed her,' he said at last. 'Not yet. Not to me. Later it might seem important, but it doesn't now. All that matters now is that she's dead.'

He reached out and poured himself another glass of wine. Fran wondered at the difference in his mood tonight, and when he'd broken down talking about his wife. She supposed this was shock. It didn't mean that he cared less for his daughter. Had he been this calm in his dealings with the police? What would Perez have made of it?

Soon after she said she would go home. He made no objection, but looked up just as she was about to leave the room. 'Will you be all right? Should I walk up with you?'

'Don't be silly,' she said. 'There are police all over the valley.'

And it was true. As soon as she was on the road she could hear the distant chug of a generator and as she approached Hillhead, she saw that the crime scene was illuminated by big arc lights. A constable standing by the farm gate nodded to her as she walked past.

Chapter Ten

When Sally got in from school her mother told her about Catherine Ross, but rumours had been flying around Anderson High since midday and it was all anyone had been talking about on the bus. Sally pretended it was a surprise though. She spent her life pretending to her mother. It had become a habit. They discussed it, sitting together at the kitchen table, so Sally knew something was wrong. Her mother didn't like sitting without something to do – a pile of mending or her knitting or the ironing. Or preparation for her work in the school. Often the table was spread with shiny white card while her mother wrote out lists of words in thick black felt pen under various headings. *Nouns. Verbs. Adjectives.* Margaret despised inactivity.

It wasn't in her nature to make a drama out of the incident, but Sally could tell she was concerned. As close to agitated as she could get.

'Your father drove past after Cassie Hunter's mother found the body. She was in quite a state apparently. Hysterical. He had to call the police. She refused to move.'

Margaret poured tea and waited for a response

from her daughter. What does she expect from me? Sally thought. Does she think I should cry?

'Your father thinks she was strangled. He heard a couple of police talking.' Margaret set down the teapot, fixed her gaze on her daughter. 'They'll want to speak with you, because you were friends. They'll want to know who she knocked about with, boys. But if it's too upsetting you must say. They can't force you to speak to them.'

'Why would they want to know that stuff?'

'She was murdered. Of course there'll be questions. Everyone's saying that Magnus Tait must have done it, but there's one thing knowing who killed her and another proving it.'

Sally found it hard to focus on her mother's words. She found her thoughts slipping back to Robert Isbister. But that wouldn't do. It was important to concentrate. 'When I speak to the police, will you be there?'

'Of course. If you'd like us to be.'

Sally could hardly say then that it was the last thing she wanted.

'I was never sure about that Catherine.' Her mother stood up. She sliced a loaf and began buttering the bread, making smooth, easy motions with the knife. She had her back to Sally. Margaret could never keep quiet if she felt there was something needed saying. It was a matter of pride with her.

'What do you mean?' Sally felt her face flush and was pleased her mother wasn't looking.

'I thought she was a bad influence. It changed you going round with her. Maybe Magnus didn't kill her, whatever people think. Maybe she was the sort of woman who brings violence on herself.'

'That's a dreadful thing to say. It's like saying some women ask to be raped.'

Margaret pretended not to hear that. 'Your father phoned to say he'd be late. A meeting in town. We'll eat without him.'

Sally thought there'd been more and more meetings in town lately. She wondered sometimes what he was up to. Not that she blamed her father. She hated mealtimes at home and tried to avoid them if she could. It would have been different if there'd been brothers and sisters, if her mother was less intrusive. All she got was questions. *How was school today, Sally? What mark did you get for that English course work?* Her mother picking away at her, probing. Margaret should have joined the police, Sally thought. Really, after fending off a lifetime of her mother's questions she had nothing to fear from a detective.

They ate the meal as always at the kitchen table. No television. Even when her father was with them, even on a special occasion, there was no alcohol. Margaret often said with pursed lips that parents should set an example. How could you blame children for drinking themselves stupid in Lerwick on a Friday night when the parents could scarcely go a day without a drink? Self-control was an old-fashioned virtue, Margaret said, which should be practised more often. Until recently, Sally had presumed that her father shared these views. He never disagreed with them. Occasionally, though, she thought she caught a glimpse of a more relaxed individual underneath. She wondered what kind of man he'd have turned out to be if he'd married someone else.

The meal was over. Sally offered to wash the dishes, but Margaret waved a hand, dismissing the idea. 'Leave them. I'll see to them later.'

Like sitting down before tea was prepared, this was another indication that a seismic shift had taken place somewhere in her mother's consciousness. Margaret couldn't bear to see dirty dishes standing. It was as if she had a physical response to them. Like some people had allergies which brought them out in lumps.

'I'll go and start my homework then.'

'No,' her mother said. 'Your father will be in just now and we want to talk to you.'

And that sounded serious. Perhaps she'd found out about New Year's Eve. This place you couldn't fart without the whole of Shetland knowing about it. Sally wondered what else it could be that kept her mother in her seat, with dirty plates still on the draining board. She steeled herself for questions, began to rehearse the lies in her head.

Then there was a knock on the door and Margaret jumped up to get it, as if she'd been expecting it all the time. There was a blast of cold air and a man came in, followed by a young woman in uniform. Sally recognized the woman, who was a kind of second cousin on her father's side. So Margaret *would* have been expecting the call; Morag would have warned her. That was how things worked with families. Sally tried to remember what else she knew about the woman. She'd joined the police after working in a bank for a while. Margaret had had things to say about that too. *She always was a flighty young madam.* Now she greeted the constable as if she was a bosom pal. 'Morag come away in by the fire. It must be freezing out there.'

Sally looked at Morag critically and thought she'd put on weight. Sally was aware of how people looked. She knew it mattered. Didn't you have to be fit to work for the police? And there was *nothing* flattering about that uniform. The man was very big. Not fat, but tall. He stood just inside the door waiting for Morag to speak. Sally saw him nod towards her, encouraging her to take the initiative.

'Margaret, this is Inspector Perez. He'd like to ask Sally some questions.'

'About yun girl that died?' Margaret was almost dismissive.

'She was killed, Mrs Henry,' the detective said. 'Murdered. You have a daughter the same age. I'm sure you want him caught.'

'Of course. But Sally was a close friend of Catherine's. She's had a bad shock. I don't want her upset.'

'That's why I brought Morag, Mrs Henry. A friendly face. Now, why don't we take Sally into another room, so we don't disturb you?'

Sally expected her mother to object, but something about him, the authoritative, easy tone, the assumption that he'd get his own way, must have made her realize there was no point in putting up a fight.

'Through here,' she said stiffly. 'I'll just put a match to the fire. Then I'll let you get on with it.'

The room was tidy, of course. Margaret couldn't abide clutter. She allowed the music stand and Sally's fiddle to stay out, either to encourage spontaneous practice or to give the impression to guests that they were a cultured family, but everything else was in its place. She never let her marking or preparation for school escape into here. Perez folded himself into a seat with his back to the window, stretched out his long legs. Margaret had already closed the curtains. It was a ritual. One of many. In winter, as soon as she came in from school, she shut the curtains in every room in the house. Morag sat beside Sally on the sofa. Sally thought this was a pre-arranged move. Perhaps she was there to offer comfort. Oh my God, Sally thought. I hope she doesn't touch me. Those fat, fleshy hands. I couldn't bear it.

Perez waited until Margaret had left the room before speaking.

'It must be a terrible shock,' he said. 'The news about Catherine.'

'They were talking about it in the bus on the way home. But I couldn't believe it. Not until I got home and my mum said what happened.'

'Tell me about Catherine,' he said. 'What was she like?'

Sally hadn't been expecting that. She'd thought there'd be specific questions: *When did you last see Catherine? Did she mention a row with anyone? How did she seem?*

She hadn't practised the answer to this.

He saw her confusion. 'I know,' he said. 'It probably isn't relevant. But I'd like to know. It seems the least I can do for her, treat her as an individual.'

Still, Sally didn't quite understand.

'She came from south,' she said. 'Her mother had died. It made her . . . different from the rest of us.'

'Yes,' he said. 'I can see that it would.'

'She seemed very sophisticated. She knew about films and plays. Different bands. People I'd not heard of. Books.'

Perez waited for her to continue.

'She was very smart. At school she seemed way ahead of us.'

'That wouldn't have made her popular. With the teachers maybe, but not with the kids.'

'She didn't care about being popular. At least that was the impression she gave.'

'Of course she cared,' he said. 'Everyone does to some extent. We all want to be liked.'

'I suppose so.' Sally wasn't convinced.

'But *you* were friends. I've spoken to her teachers today and to her father. They all say she got on better with you than with anyone else.'

'She lived just up the bank,' Sally said. 'We got the bus into town every day. There's no one else of my age lives here.'

There was a silence, broken by the clatter of plates in the room next door. The inspector seemed to be giving Sally's words more significance than she thought they deserved. Morag shifted in her seat as if it was torture for her to keep quiet, as if there were questions she was dying to ask.

'I went to the Anderson,' Perez said at last. 'I expect things are different now. Then it was all cliques. We had to stay in the hostel. I came from Fair Isle and us and the Foula kids, we couldn't even get home at weekends. Then there were the people who came in by ferry every week from Whalsay and Out Skerries. The lads from Scalloway were always fighting with the Lerwick boys. It wasn't that you didn't make friends from a different group, but you knew where you belonged.' He paused again. 'As I said, I expect things are different now.'

'No,' she said. 'Not very different.'

'You're saying you two were thrown together then. You didn't hang around because you had much in common.'

'I don't think she was close to anyone. Not to me, not to her father. Perhaps her mother . . . I had the impression the two of them were more like friends . . . Perhaps after that . . .'

'Aye,' Perez said. 'After that, it would be difficult to trust anyone.'

The fire cracked and spat sparks.

'Did she have a boyfriend?'

'I don't know.'

'Come on. She'd have talked to you about stuff like that, even if it wasn't common knowledge. She'd have wanted to tell someone.'

'She didn't tell me.'

'But?'

She hesitated.

'This is confidential,' he said. 'I'll not tell anyone and if it gets back to your parents Morag gets the sack.'

They all laughed, but there was enough of a threat in his voice for Morag to take it seriously. Sally could tell that.

'New Year's Eve,' she said.

'Yes.'

'I wasn't allowed into town. My parents disapprove of bars. But all my friends would be there. I told them I was at Catherine's house but we both went to the market cross. Catherine's father never seemed to mind what she did. We got a lift back. I thought maybe Catherine knew the lad who was driving.'

'Who was it?'

'I couldn't see. I was sitting in the back of the car. There were four of us, all crushed in. You couldn't see a thing. They were all off to a party except Catherine and me. Catherine was in the front with the driver. They weren't talking but it seemed like they knew each other. Perhaps because they *weren't* talking. There was none of that polite conversation you get with strangers. Maybe that's silly.'

'No,' he said. 'I know just what you mean. Who else was in the car?'

She named the student and the nurse.

'And the fourth person?'

'Robert Isbister.' She didn't need to say anything else. Everyone in Shetland knew Robert. His family had made a shedload of money when the oil first came ashore. His father had been a builder, ended up with most of the construction contracts, still owned the biggest building firm in the place. Robert had a pelagic fishing boat – the *Wandering Spirit* – which went out of Whalsay. Tales of the boat were told in every bar on the island. When he'd first bought it he'd brought it into Lerwick and thrown it open for people to look round. The cabins had leather seats and televisions with Sky TV. In the summer he took groups of his friends to Norway. There were wild parties as they sailed up the fjords.

'Robert wasn't Catherine's boyfriend?' he asked.

'No,' she said, too quickly.

'Only, I've heard he has a taste for younger lasses.'

She knew better than to answer.

'Maybe you fancy him yourself?' His voice was joky and she could tell he didn't mean it, but still she felt herself blushing.

'Don't be daft,' she said. 'You don't know what my mother's like. She'd kill me.'

'You really can't remember anything about the car or the driver?'

She shook her head.

'Catherine was supposed to be at a party the night before she went missing. Were you there too?'

'I've told you.' Her voice was bitter. 'I'm not allowed at parties.'

'Did you know anything about it?'

'I wasn't invited. People have stopped bothering to ask me. They know I'll not be going.'

'Didn't anyone mention it at school today?'

'Not to me.'

He sat looking into the fire. 'Is there anything else you think I should know?'

She didn't answer immediately, but he waited.

'That night we came back from Lerwick,' she said. 'Early New Year's Day.'

'Yes.'

'We went up to see the old man. Magnus. We'd both been drinking and his light was on. It was a sort of dare, to knock on the door and wish him happy new year.'

Perez showed no surprise. Perhaps she'd been hoping to surprise him. 'Did you go in?'

'Yes, for a while.' She paused. 'He seemed obsessed with Catherine. He couldn't stop staring at her. It was as if he'd seen a ghost.'

Chapter Eleven

When he left the school at Ravenswick Perez set back towards Lerwick. He thought he might just fit in a visit to Robert Isbister before the plane arrived from Aberdeen. There'd been delays at the airport and the Loganair people weren't sure when it would get in. It seemed he'd spent all day driving backwards and forwards down the same bit of road, but he wanted to show the team from Inverness that he'd made some progress, that he hadn't just been sitting waiting for them to arrive.

Perez never quite knew what to make of Robert Isbister. He'd been spoiled, that was clear. His father was a good man, who had been surprised by his sudden affluence. He was generous to his friends and family in a discreet, almost embarrassed way. Robert worked hard enough at the fishing, but everyone knew he hadn't paid for that showy big boat by himself. Michael Isbister would have given him the money. And then everyone knew too that Robert's parents hadn't much of a marriage. It can't have been easy growing up in that family, despite the wealth. It must have been hard knowing that everyone talking about them had a kind of smile on their face, which was half sneer and half sympathy.

Throughout his life, Robert would be compared to his father. It was lot to live up to. Perez knew something of what that was like. *His* father was skipper of the Fair Isle mail boat. Before any decision was made about life on the Isle he was consulted. But for Robert it was worse. Although he was a quiet and unassuming man, Michael Isbister was famous everywhere in the islands. He was a musician, an expert in the dialect words and traditional songs. He'd been on the Up Helly Aa committee since he was a young man. This year he'd been awarded the honour of being made Guizer Jarl. It meant a lot to him. More than an honour from the Queen. He would lead the procession of the fire festival, appear on television, give radio interviews. For this year, at least, he would represent Shetland to the rest of the world. Robert would be in the Jarl's squad, dressed like a Viking, the same as his father. A sign that he hoped to follow in his father's footsteps. And everyone in Shetland would be watching to see if he measured up.

Robert wouldn't be at home this early in the evening. He might be out with the boat, but Perez didn't think so. When the inspector visited friends at Whalsay earlier in the week, the *Wandering Spirit* had still been there, dominating all the other vessels at the mooring. Perez drove through the town and out towards the docks. He pulled into a side street, parked and got out to a cold which took his breath away, the smell of fish and oil. He hoped Robert would be on his own. He didn't want an audience of the man's cronies for this conversation.

As he pushed open the door to the bar, the warmth hit him. There was a coal fire, banked up hard. Only a small grate, but it was a small room, walls stained brown by tobacco and coal smoke. On the walls there were smeared photos of long-past Up Helly Aa squads, groups of men staring out, self-conscious but earnest. The academics might deride the tradition, but these men were deadly serious. They believed they represented the islands' culture, their way of life. And in the corner of the gloomy bar sat Robert Isbister. His wild white hair seemed to light up the room. He was pouring a bottle of Northern Light into a glass, concentrating as if he'd already had a few. He didn't notice Perez come into the room. Behind the bar a tiny, skinny woman sat on a high stool, reading a paperback book which she'd bent back at the spine and held in one hand as if it was a magazine. She forced her eyes from the print.

'Jimmy. It's early for you. What are you having?' You could tell she wasn't that thrilled to see him. He'd not be good for business.

'Coke please, May.' He paused, looked at Robert. 'I'm driving.'

Neither she nor Robert made any response.

Perez took his glass and sat at Robert's table. May returned to her book. She was lost immediately. Sarah had read like that. There could be a volcano under the house and she'd not notice. Robert looked up, nodded.

'Have you heard about the body they found at Ravenswick?' Perez said. No point in being subtle. Not with Robert.

'May said something when I came in.' The words were slow, careful. Was that the beer or another sort of caution? Robert enjoyed a few pints with the lads but he didn't usually drink heavily this early on a week-day.

'A friend of yours, I understand.'

Robert set down the glass. 'Who was it?'

'A young lass. Catherine Ross. You *did* know her?'

The pause was a beat too long. 'I'd seen her about.'

'Only sixteen. A bit young even for you, Robert.' It was a standing joke that Robert went for younger women. Perez thought it was because he'd never grown up. The big boat was to prove he was a man. He continued. 'New Year's Eve . . .'

'What about it?'

'After the market cross you went to a party.'

'Aye. The Harvey girls' place in Dunrossness.'

'You gave Catherine Ross a lift home. As far as the Ravenswick turn off.'

Robert turned his head so Perez was looking into the pale blue eyes. Bloodshot. Worried.

'I wasn't driving,' Robert said. 'I'm not that stupid.'

'Who was?'

'I don't know his name. A young lad. Still at school.'

'Friend of Catherine's?'

'I don't know. Maybe.'

'Any idea where he comes from?'

'Somewhere in the south. Quendale? Scatness? The family haven't been in Shetland long.'

'You said you'd seen Catherine around. Where had you seen her?'

'Parties. Bars in town. You know how it is.'

'She was the sort of girl you'd notice then. The sort of girl you'd pick out in a crowd.'

'Oh yes,' Robert said. 'You'd notice her. She didn't say much. She was always watching, weighing you up.

But you couldn't help noticing her.' He picked up his glass, took a drink. Suddenly he seemed more relaxed. 'How did she die?' he asked. 'Hypothermia, was that it? Too much to drink and passing out in the cold?'

'Did she drink a lot?'

Robert shrugged. 'They all drink too much, don't they, those young girls? What else is there for them to do in the winter?'

'It wasn't hypothermia,' Perez said. 'It was murder.'

Chapter Twelve

Magnus had thought the police would come back for him. He sat all evening waiting stiff and upright in his chair. Five times cars went past but none of them stopped. The blue and white tape still fluttered across the gap in the wall. The headlights caught it as they dipped down the hill. And Catherine was still there, lying under a tarpaulin. He hated to think of it. What would her body be like now? At least the ground would be frozen, he thought. There would be no decay. No animals or insects to tear into the flesh. Last time it had been summer. He knew how quickly a dead lamb began to rot when the sun was on it. The earth soon warmed.

The next car did stop. He waited for the knock on his door, but the men stood by the side of the road, their hands in their pockets, chatting, waiting for something to happen. Then there was a Transit van. It pulled right on to the grass to let other cars past. They manhandled a small generator out of the back and lifted it on to a trolley to pull it across the field. There were cables and two big lights on stands. They all disappeared over the hill and out of Magnus's line of vision. He could imagine what Catherine would look like, pale and frozen under those powerful white lights. He looked at his mother's clock. Eight o'clock. The plane from Aberdeen would have landed by now. The team from Inverness would be driving north from Sumburgh. They had sent a special team last time, but they'd achieved no more than the local men.

There flashed into his mind the image of a little girl's face, clear as a photograph. *Catriona*. He said the word out loud because it came into his head. She had long hair, tangled by the wind, dark eyes narrowed in laughter as she ran up the hill. She'd opened the door without knocking and in one hand held a bunch of flowers picked from the garden. That would have been the last day he'd seen her.

He stood up, suddenly restless, and looked out of the window. The police were out of sight. He presumed they were nearer to the body. A patch of cloud shifted and he saw there was a full moon. His mother always said a full moon made him dafter than usual. Its light formed a path on the still water. He realized he hadn't eaten all day and wondered if that was what was making him feel confused. It would be that or the moon. In his mind he saw Catriona dancing on the road outside his house. It was a strange sort of jig with her hands held above her head, her arms curved like a ballet dancer's. He imagined that she tilted her head in his direction and gestured for him to follow her.

He knew that it must be his imagination. Even if she'd lived, Catriona would be a young woman now, older than Catherine. But he couldn't stay in the house. It was the moonlight on the water and waiting all day for the police to come back. It was listening to his mother saying *Tell them nothing* and the memory of the little girl. He put on his boots, fumbling with the laces in his rush to be out. He had a woollen hat which his mother had knitted, and the big jacket she'd bought for him in Lerwick just before she'd died. It was as if she'd known she'd die soon, and she didn't trust him to buy his own clothes. She'd brought back a pile of underpants and socks from the same trip and he sometimes still wore those too.

Out of the house he climbed away from the track until he reached the Lerwick road. In the house by the chapel there was no light. There was a gap at the bedroom window where the drawn curtains didn't quite meet, but he could see nothing through it, only a ghostly reflection of his face in the glass. Reluctantly he turned away and started off again on to the hill.

In the shadow of a dyke he stopped and looked back. The police hadn't seen him leave Hillhead. In the moonlight he saw them surprisingly clearly in the field where Catherine lay. The scene spread out below him and he could recognize individuals by the way they stood and the way they moved. They were blinded by the fierce white lights and their concentration on the small body covered by the tarpaulin shroud. When they turned away from the crime scene it was to look out for headlights from the south. Soon the team would arrive from Sumburgh.

Magnus continued his climb. He walked slowly. He knew he had to pace himself. He'd had a winter of laziness since he'd last been up here. He felt the strain in his knee and a wheezing in his chest. The sunshine during the day had melted the snow in patches, so he could see the peat and the dead heather through it. He reached the top of the bank and ahead of him there was nothing but bare hillside. They'd told him at school that once, Shetland had been covered with trees. He couldn't picture it. Now the only trees were in folks' gardens. He thought this must be what the moon must look like, if you were standing on it, not looking at it from the earth. He stopped for a moment to catch his breath and looked behind him again. The figures in the field looked less important from here. Beyond them he saw the silver ice on the voe and the houses of Ravenswick. If he had any sense he'd go back to his bed, but something kept him moving. Was this how Catriona had felt when she couldn't stop dancing?

He hadn't been sure he'd know the place, but now, approaching it even in this strange light, it was familiar. He'd spent much of his youth up here, working with his uncle, his father's elder brother, who had run the croft. Magnus had helped count the hill sheep, collect them into the cru for clipping and bring them down the hill ready for slaughter. And in the early summer, this was where they'd come to cast peats. Hard work that had been, peeling back the turf from the bank and cutting into the dense dark earth. The digging had been back-breaking work and even worse was wheeling the peats down to the road in a barrow. Now, if they dug peat, and not so many did, they used a tractor and trailer. His uncle had been proud of him. He'd said Magnus was stronger and a better worker than his own sons. In those days Magnus had had a father and a mother, an uncle and cousins. Then, he'd had a sister. Now he had nobody.

He came to a small loch, where his cousins had come in the winter to shoot geese. You'd hear the birds flying in from the north, calling, a long line of them following each other so closely you could believe they were attached, like the ribbons on a kite tail, and the cousins would be out then with their guns. Magnus had never been allowed a gun, but afterwards his mother would cook the goose and they'd all come together to eat it. Out on the freezing hillside, he had a picture of them gathered round the table in the Hillhead kitchen and it was so real he could smell the goose fat and feel the heat from the range on his face. Magnus wondered if he had an illness. All these daydreams reminded him of the scenes which play through your mind in a fever.

At the edge of the loch he stood for a moment to get his bearings. The ice was thick. In some places it was clear so he could see the grey water underneath. In others it was white and lumpy and looked a bit like the sweeties his mother had made with dried coconut, sugar and condensed milk. He wondered why it had happened like that, why the water hadn't frozen evenly. The thought distracted him for a moment and he worried away at the puzzle without coming to any conclusion. His mouth was open in concentration. Then the need for movement came on him again and he set off up the hill.

He had a map in his head. Like the treasure map in a story they'd read to him at school, though he'd never drawn it or written down directions. What would the directions say? *Walk west from the loch until you reach the Gillie burn. Follow the burn up the hill to the gully where the land always slips after heavy rain.*

And it was just as he pictured it. When the thaw came the burn would be full of peaty water. Now it was deep with soft snow. And he came to the peat bank and the mound of rocks which looked like a small landslide. It wasn't unusual for this to happen on the hill, especially after a dry summer followed by heavy rain. The water seeped into the cracks in the dry earth and loosened it, sending rocks and soil and peat spilling down the bank. Even in the snow he recognized the place. At last he lost the urge to continue moving. He stood with his face to the sky and let the tears run down his cheeks.

He might have stayed there all night, but a distant explosion – a lifeboat maroon which seemed unusually loud in the still night – brought him to his senses. What would his mother say? *Don't du be a baby Magnus.* He made his way home because there was nothing else to do, crossing the steep peat banks crabwise, sure-footed despite the icy surface.

The constables were still standing guard over Catherine's body, but the other man was sitting in his car, waiting, his eyes closed. The plane from Aberdeen must have been delayed. The van which had brought the lights and the generator had gone. As Magnus watched, one of the constables unscrewed the top from a vacuum flask, poured out steaming liquid, handed it to his colleague. They'll be pals, Magnus thought. Working together like that, up all night, it would make you close. He felt a vague nostalgic longing which became almost unbearable. He wondered how it would be if he took his bottle of Grouse out to them and offered them a dram. They'd welcome that as it was so cold, and wouldn't they talk to him as they were drinking it, just to be polite?

If it hadn't been for the detective from Fair Isle, he might have gone out to them. But drinking on duty probably wasn't allowed. He thought the constables would turn him down with their boss watching. Then he remembered the police station and the room with the shiny walls. He'd probably be better drinking on his own. He'd find it hard not to tell them everything.

He was in the house, with a small glass of whisky in his hand, when a small convoy of cars turned up. He didn't want to think what they might be doing to the girl with the hair the colour of a raven's wing. He took his drink with him to bed.

Chapter Thirteen

Sitting in the car with his eyes shut, Perez heard the silence. He was listening for the vehicles coming from the south, although he'd already confirmed that the plane from Aberdeen was running late. He didn't mind waiting. He was glad of the time to think, to consider the events of the day. Usually he had to focus on procedure. Even in Shetland there were targets to meet and forms to complete. Now he had nothing to do but wait and think. He could allow his thoughts to follow a path of their own.

He wondered how it must have been for Catherine Ross, coming to Shetland as an outsider. He understood something of that, with his Spanish name and his Mediterranean features, but his family had lived on Fair Isle for generations, for centuries if you believed the myths. And he did believe the myths. After a few drinks at least. Really, it hadn't been like Catherine's experience at all.

It had been hard for him to leave home to come to school in Lerwick. The town had seemed so big and full of noise and traffic. The street lights made it seem that it was never dark. For Catherine, living here after the Yorkshire city, it would be the quiet she'd notice the most.

Again his thoughts slid away from the murder investigation back to Fair Isle and the legend of his family name. The story was this. During the Spanish Armada a ship, *El Gran Grifon*, was blown off course, far off course from the English mainland which had been her destination. She had been wrecked off the island. And this at least was true. Divers had found her. There were records. Archaeologists had recovered artefacts. Some people claimed the wreck was the source of the famous Fair Isle knitting. It had nothing to do with the Scandinavians, they claimed. The Norwegians knitted too, of course, but their patterns were regular and predictable, small square blocks, restrained and boring. Traditional Fair Isle knitting was brightly coloured and intricate. There were shapes like crosses. It was the sort of design a Catholic priest might wear splashed across his robes.

These patterns, people said, had arrived with *El Gran Grifon*. More specifically, they had arrived with a Spanish seaman, a survivor of the wreck. By some miracle, Miguel Perez had managed to swim ashore. He had been found on the shingle of the South Harbour, scarcely alive, the tide still licking at his ankles. He had been taken in by the islanders. And of course there had been no escape. How could he get back to the heat and civilization of his native land? In those days it would have been an adventure to set off for the Shetland mainland. He had been stranded. What had he missed most? Perez wondered sometimes. The wine? The food? The smell of oranges, olives and baked dust? The distilled sunlight bouncing off old stone?

Legend had it that he'd fallen in love with an island

girl. There was no record of her name. Perez thought the sailor had just made the best of it. He'd been at sea for months. He'd be desperate for sex. He'd pretend to be in love if that was what it took, though surely love would have hardly come into it, even when it came to island couplings. Women wanted strong men who could manage a boat. Men wanted housekeepers, brewers and bakers. Whatever the attraction between the two of them, they must have had a boy child. At least one. Because since that time there had been a Perez on Fair Isle, working the land, crewing the mail boat, finding the women to provide more male heirs.

Jimmy Perez shifted in his seat. The cold brought him back to the matter in hand. Catherine Ross hadn't been brought up in a small community of less than a hundred people, many of them related. It would be new to her, this sense of living in a goldfish bowl, everyone knowing her business, or thinking they did. Her mother had died after a long illness. Her father, wrapped up in his grief, had been distant to the point of neglect. She must have been lonely, he thought suddenly. Especially here, surrounded by people who knew each other. Even with Sally Henry down the bank and some boyfriend they still had to trace, she must have felt terribly alone.

That led him to think about Magnus Tait, because mustn't the old man be lonely too? Everyone was convinced that Magnus had killed the girl. The only reason he wasn't in custody already was that, once in the station, they'd only have six hours to hold him. It wasn't like in England. And no one knew when the team from Inverness would arrive. What if there'd been a fault with the plane and it didn't turn up until the morning? They'd have to let Magnus go in the middle of the night.

At dusk, Sandy Wilson, one of his constables, had asked if they should have a man posted at Hillhead.

'Whatever for?' Perez had demanded. Sandy always provoked in him an unreasonable impatience.

Sandy had blushed, chastened at the sharpness of the tone, and Perez had pushed home his advantage. 'How's he going to get off Shetland at this time of night? Swim? His house is surrounded by open hill-side. Where do you think he's going to hide?'

Perez didn't know if Magnus was a murderer or not. It was too early to say. But the easy assumption of his colleagues that Tait had killed the girl annoyed him. It was a challenge to his professionalism. It was the sloppy thinking, the laziness which irritated him most. So a young girl had disappeared before and Tait had been a prime suspect? As Perez saw it, the cases had very little in common. If Catriona Bruce had been killed, her body had been hidden. Catherine's had been displayed, exhibited almost. Catriona had been a child. Perez had seen photographs still held on file. She'd looked younger than her age. Catherine was a young woman, sexy and defiant. Perez hoped that the team from Inverness would come with open minds. He planned to get at them before they were infected by the Shetland gossip and the locals' distrust of an old man who'd become an outsider.

The silence was broken by the buzz of the small generator they'd brought in to power the lights. For some reason Sandy must have started the engine. A couple of minutes later Perez's phone rang. It was the constable who'd been sent to Sumburgh to meet the plane. 'It's landed. We'll be on our way shortly.' Perez was amused, but not surprised, that Sandy Wilson had been informed of the news before him. Brian at the airport and Sandy had been brought up on Whalsay together. It was how things worked.

There were six of them in the team from Inverness. One crime scene investigator, two DCs, two DSs and a DI, who would act as senior investigating officer. The same rank as Perez, but with more experience, so he'd take charge. They came in two cars. Perez felt momentarily resentful at the intrusion on his daydreams. He felt soporific. It was an effort to move. He opened his door and stepped out. In the warmth of the car, he had forgotten how cold it was. He was still feeling half asleep as the DI introduced himself, was aware of a loud, eager voice and a knuckle-squeezing handshake. There wasn't a lot to do until the crime scene investigator went in. Jane Meltham was a cheerful, competent woman with a broad Lancashire accent and a dry, black humour. They watched her open the boot and bring out her case.

'What'll you do with the body when you've finished with it?' she asked.

'It'll go to Annie Goudie's mortuary,' Perez said. 'She's the undertaker in Lerwick. We'll keep it there until we can ship it south.'

'When'll that be?'

'Well, it's missed the ferry tonight. We can't get it on a plane. It'll be tomorrow evening now.'

'No rush then.' She was climbing into a paper suit. 'I hope this is big enough to get over my jacket. If I have to take off my coat, I'll freeze and it'll be the pair of us you'll be shipping to Aberdeen.' She pulled on the hood, clipping back stray hairs. 'Don't the other passengers mind sharing the boat with a body?'

'They don't know,' Perez said. 'We use an old Transit van. It's kind of anonymous.'

'Who's doing the post mortem?'

'Billy Morton at the university.'

'Great,' she said. 'He's the best in the business.'

Perez thought she was a woman of sound judgement. He rated Billy Morton too. Jane looked up at him.

'You realize I probably won't get done tonight. I'll have to come back at first light.'

'I was hoping,' Perez said, 'we wouldn't have to leave the body. That's a school down there. The kids have to come past. And it's been out here for a full day already.'

'OK.' He could tell she was considering the matter carefully. She wasn't one of those officials who make problems just for the sake of seeming important. 'If there's any way we can manage it, we'll shift her tonight.'

She went through the gap in the wall. They watched her circle the field to approach the body from a different angle, avoiding all the footprints in the snow. When she was almost at the body, she shouted back at them.

'What's the weather forecast for tomorrow?'

'Not much change. Why?'

'If there was going to be a sudden thaw I'd work on these now. There seems to have been a lot of tramping backwards and forwards. Nothing's very clear. It's possible that we'll get something, but I'll leave it until the morning, concentrate on the body.'

She looked very odd in the fierce light. Everything was white. It made Perez think of a horror movie he'd seen once, about the world after nuclear fallout, all mutants and monsters. And he realized they were all staring at her, the locals and the incomers. They were fascinated by her progress over the hard ground. They watched her in silence. She held their attention completely. There was no weighing up of personalities, no discussion of the case. That would come later.

It came when they were all crammed into a bedroom in a hotel in the town. It had been allocated to the two DCs and the inspector from Inverness had commandeered it for them all to come together to talk about the case. There were two twin beds, but still it wasn't that big and it was slightly shabby, with dusty curtains and a threadbare carpet. For some reason, Perez felt slightly embarrassed by it. Was this the best they had to offer the incomers? What would they think? Roy Taylor, the DI, had opened a bottle of Bell's and they were drinking out of whatever came to hand – tea cups, plastic mugs from the bathroom, a polystyrene mug which had held airport coffee. Perez was sitting on the floor, watching. Taylor held centre stage from one of the beds. Perez hadn't decided yet what he made of him. He was young to be a DI, mid-thirties. His hair was shaved very close to hide premature balding. It made his head look like a skull. This could even be his first case as SIO. He was certainly driven. Perez could tell that. Naked ambition? Perhaps, but Perez thought there was more to it. From the moment he'd pulled the bottle of whisky from his holdall, the man hadn't stopped asking questions. And at first it was hard to make out what he was saying. He might work in Inverness now, but that wasn't where he was born. 'I'm from Liverpool,' he said when Perez asked. 'The greatest city in the world.'

Taylor listened to the answers as ferociously as he fired out the questions. He didn't take notes but Perez thought the replies must be branded on his brain. It was as if he felt cheated because he hadn't been on the island early enough to carry out the initial investigation. Perez could imagine him pacing backwards and forwards in the terminal at Dyce, counting the seconds to take-off, swearing under his breath when he learned the plane would be late.

Now Taylor got off the bed and stretched. He was standing on the balls of his feet and reached up towards the ceiling. Perez was reminded of an ape he'd seen in Edinburgh Zoo on a school trip. It had pushed against the bars of the enclosure, needing more space. Taylor was a man who'd always need more space, Perez thought. Stick him in the middle of an African savannah and it still wouldn't seem enough for him. The boundaries must be somewhere inside his head. A stupid thought. He'd drunk the Scotch too quickly.

He realized they were all talking about bringing in Magnus Tait, about how they'd handle it, who'd do the interview. One local and one member of the Inverness team, they decided. And they'd play it gently. Taylor had looked at the Catriona Bruce notes. There'd been an implication that Tait had been roughly handled, he said. No one was going to play silly buggers like that this time. He wasn't having the case thrown out because one of his team lost it. And they were all one

99

team now. He was including Shetlanders too. He looked around and seemed to embrace them in a sweep of his arm. Perez could tell that he meant every word of it. Anyone else talked like that and it would make you feel like puking. Taylor could get away with it. He had them eating out of the palm of his hand.

'I don't think we should jump to the conclusion that Magnus Tait is a killer.' Jimmy Perez hadn't meant to speak. Perhaps he'd been infected by Taylor's fervour. He sat in his corner, swirling the oily whisky in his glass.

'Why?' Taylor stopped stretching. He crouched, a hand on each side of his body on the floor to steady himself, reminding Perez again of an ape. His face was level with Perez's now.

Perez listed the concerns, the problems he'd been worrying over as he sat in the car. The victims were different. If Tait was a killer, why had he waited this long to do it again? Catherine Ross was a streetwise girl from the city. She was physically strong. She wouldn't stand there waiting for Magnus to murder her.

'If not Tait, who then?' Taylor demanded.

Perez shrugged. All the circumstantial evidence pointed to Magnus, but he didn't want to sleepwalk into an arrest without considering the alternatives.

'I don't have any theories,' he said. 'I just want to keep an open mind.'

'Was there a boyfriend?'

'Maybe. She stayed with someone the night before she disappeared.'

'And we don't know who that was?'

'Not yet. I've been asking around. He shouldn't be too hard to trace.'

'A priority to find out, wouldn't you say?'

Nobody answered.

Suddenly Taylor stood up again. 'I'm off to my bed,' he said. 'Tomorrow's going to be busy. I need my beauty sleep and so do you.'

Perez thought that Taylor wouldn't be one for sleeping much. He imagined him awake all night, walking backwards and forwards, caged in his room.

Chapter Fourteen

Jimmy Perez walked to his house. It was only five minutes from the hotel. He stopped once to look across the harbour to a huge factory ship. The vessel was lit up but there was no sign of anyone working. The narrow streets were empty. In the cold he felt sober and clear-headed.

He lived on the waterfront in a tiny house crammed between two bigger ones. There was a tide-mark on the external stone wall and in rough weather the salt spray whipped against even the upstairs window. The house was cramped, damp and impractical. There was no parking. If his parents stayed he had to sleep on the sofa. He'd bought it on a romantic whim after Sarah had left and he'd moved back to Shetland. He couldn't quite regret it. It was like having a home on a boat. Inside it was much like a boat too. Very tidy. Everything in its place. He didn't care about his appearance but he cared how the house looked. The walls of the living room were lined with horizontal wood panels, neatly fitted carvel-fashion, painted grey. An attempt, he realized now, to hide the effect of the damp. Wallpaper would be impossible. The only window was small and looked out over the water. He could stand in the middle of the galley kitchen and touch each wall.

It was precisely midnight when he stepped through the door. Taylor had said he wanted everyone in the Incident Room an hour before first light the next day, but Perez wasn't ready for sleep. As he switched on the kettle to make tea, he remembered he hadn't eaten since lunchtime and stuck sliced bread under the grill, fished margarine and marmalade from the fridge. He'd have breakfast now, save time in the morning.

As he ate, he read the previous morning's mail – a thin airmail letter from an old Fair Isle friend who'd decided in her thirties that she needed to see more of the world than the north isles. She was working as a teacher for VSO in Tanzania. With her words she conjured up dusty roads, exotic fruit, smiling children. *Why don't you come to visit?* When he was fifteen he'd loved her. He thought he probably still did. But then he'd loved Sarah when he'd married her. *Emotionally incontinent.* A phrase he'd picked up from somewhere. It was the sort of thing Sarah might have said. Horrible but probably appropriate. He leaked unsuitable affection. Already, in this investigation, he felt protective towards Fran Hunter and her child and an almost overwhelming pity for Magnus Tait, whether he was a murderer or not. And police officers were supposed to be detached.

He rinsed the cup and plate and set them on the draining board, filled a glass with water to take with him to bed. But still he didn't go upstairs. He lifted the handset on his phone and heard the signal which meant there were messages. The first was from his friend John and was timed at eight-fifteen. John was in The Lounge, a bar in town, and was calling from his mobile. In the background Perez heard fiddle music and laughter. *If you're free come along and I'll buy you that pint I owe you. But I guess you're probably tied up. Catch up with you soon.* That meant news of the murder must be common knowledge.

The second message was from his mother. She didn't bother to identify herself.

I thought you'd be interested to know that Willie and Ellen have finally decided to leave Skerry. They're moving south to be closer to Anne. Phone me sometime.

He recognized a suppressed excitement in her voice. He knew what that was about. Willie and Ellen were an elderly couple who'd been farming on Fair Isle since they were married. Willie had been born on the island, was a sort of relative through Perez's grandmother. Ellen had come in as a young woman to be a nurse. Once they left, a croft would be free.

What was his response to the news? Panic? Depression? Delight? He found it impossible to decide. Instead he had a clear visual memory of his last visit to Skerry. The house had recently been renovated and Ellen was showing it off. There'd been a new roof, they'd made the window in the kitchen bigger and there was a view all the way down to the South Light. Ellen had made griddle scones. He'd stood by the window munching and thinking that the fields around the croft were sheltered enough for barley. If ever he came back, he'd thought, he'd like to return to the days when the farming was more mixed.

And now the matter was more than speculation. Perez could take over Skerry if he wanted to. The

National Trust for Scotland which owned the island always gave priority to applicants from Fair Isle families. So he'd be forced to face the decision which he'd hoped to put off for a while longer. If he moved back to the island his future would be settled. Tradition was still important. His father was skipper of the mail boat. Perez would automatically join the crew and eventually he would become skipper in his father's place. At one time he'd thought that was what he'd wanted – the continuity and security of island life. Now that he was faced with the possibility, he wasn't so certain. Wouldn't it bore him rigid?

Perhaps he would think differently if he wasn't in the middle of the most exciting investigation he'd ever worked on. He knew he'd been influenced by the passion of the Inspector from Inverness. It was probably another romantic whim, but tonight it seemed important to be a policeman. Would he feel the same when his workload consisted of petty theft and traffic violations?

His family longed for him to be home though they would never say so. It was his choice, they said. He should do whatever made him happy. They were proud of the work he did. But the pressure was there, subtle and unspoken. He was the last Perez. His sisters had married and were living on the Isle, but he was the only one to carry the name. When he'd told his mother about his separation from Sarah, there'd been one brief unguarded moment and he'd known she'd been thinking, *So. No grandchildren. At least for a while.* Sarah must have felt the pressure too. Throughout the pregnancy and after the child was lost.

He carried his drink upstairs. He was in no state to

make any rational decision tonight. He looked out of the window and closed the curtains. Usually he fell asleep to the sound of water, almost imperceptible, not consciously noticed. Tonight the sea closest to the shore was still frozen and there was silence, except for the occasional strange creak. He had thought the image of the dead girl, her face pecked by birds, might keep him awake, but he was haunted by the view down Fair Isle from Skerry, sunlight over the South Harbour and cloud-shaped shadows racing over Malcolm's Head.

When he arrived at the station the following morning Taylor was already waiting for him. He called him into one of the meeting rooms and already seemed to know his way about the place. Perez thought he couldn't have had much sleep.

'Just a quick chat,' Taylor said. 'Before we meet the troops. Talk me through what steps you took yesterday, who you met. We know about the old man. Who else did you speak to?'

Perez told him. It felt strange. It had been a long time since he'd answered to another detective.

'I need to get the timetable clear in my mind. The order of events.' Taylor tore a sheet of paper from a flip chart, laid it on the table and started to scribble in thick black marker pen. Perez hoped nobody else would be expected to read it. It was unintelligible.

'The early hours of New Year's Day she and her best mate fetch up at Magnus Tait's place. A sort of dare. The night of the 3rd she tells her father she's at a party and not to expect her home. Then there's the text on the 4th saying she might stay out again.' He looked up from the paper. 'Didn't he ask where she was? Who was having the party?'

Perez shook his head. 'His wife died not long ago. He still seems to be suffering some sort of depression. I think the girl was allowed to get on with it.'

'OK. A place like this, we shouldn't have any trouble finding out. Late morning on the 4th and she's catching the bus back home. Tait is on the same bus and asks her in for a cup of tea. He says she leaves his place before it gets dark, but that's the last time anyone admits to seeing her. The next morning, the 5th, her body is found on the hill not far from Hillhead. Is that right?'

'Yes.' He almost said *Sir*, stopped it just in time. This was his patch.

'Let's go and see what the rest of them have got for us then.'

Perez had asked Sandy to manage the Incident Room. The constable had an instinct for computers and was good at routine and Perez preferred him in the office, safely out of the way of the public. Sandy was fit for drunken scraps in town on a Friday night, but not for anything requiring more subtlety or tact. He stood now, scratching his bum, waiting for Taylor's response to the layout of the room, making Perez think of a cub scout waiting for Akela's inspection. That was Sandy's problem. He still thought like a peerie boy.

'Will it do?' He was freckled and eager. 'Of course we've never run an investigation on this scale before. Not in my time. The PCs are up and running.'

'Fantastic,' Taylor said. 'Really, fantastic.' It was over the top and Perez could tell that his mind was elsewhere, but Sandy was taken in. Here, with an audience, Taylor had lost none of the energy of the night before, but Perez could see blue smudges like bruises under his eyes. Outside it was still dark. Now, the room was lit by desk lamps. There were pools of light and shadows in the corners. Perez was reminded suddenly of a wartime ops room from an old movie. There was the same tension and expectancy.

Taylor was still talking. 'I take it we've got a specified outside line with a number we can give to the public.'

'It's just been connected.'

'I want it manned 24/7. Someone has the information which will lead to a conviction. I don't want a witness finding the courage to ring, only to get an answerphone. They get through immediately to a real person. Understood?'

'There'll be lots of folk pointing the finger at Magnus Tait,' Sandy Wilson said.

'Pointing the finger's not enough. We're polite but we make it clear we need evidence.' Taylor paused for a minute to check that he had their attention. 'I've decided to use the Inverness team to work the phone. They can take it in shifts. This is a unique situation and we have to be sensitive to it. Our callers might want to stay anonymous. Fat chance of that if there's someone they know answering the calls.' He looked quickly round the room. 'Everyone agree?'

The question was a formality. They all knew the decision had already been made. Taylor perched on a desk at the front of the room.

'I take it the body's been moved?'

'It's at the undertaker's. The CSI was happy enough

to release it. It'll go south for the post mortem on this evening's boat. Jane Meltham will go with it to be there for the pm.'

'What did the girl have on her? A bag, keys, purse?'

'No bag or keys. A purse in her coat pocket. Morag searched her bedroom yesterday and found a small handbag. No keys there either.'

'That's weird isn't it? That she didn't take her keys with her. How would she get back into the house?'

'People don't always lock up here. Not unless they're going to be away for a while. Perhaps she did have them, but they dropped out of her pocket when she was killed.'

'I'd like a fingertip search of the fields around the scene. How do we manage that? Do we have to ship in more personnel?'

'In the past we've organized a search through the coastguard,' Perez said. 'They made the cliff rescue team available. I'm not sure if it was officially sanctioned . . .'

'Bugger official sanctions. We know how long it'll take to get more people up here. A gale or a blizzard and we've lost any evidence which might be there. Can I leave you to sort that? Get them out on the hill as soon as practicable.'

'Sure.' There was no other possible answer, though Perez wasn't sure how long it would take to call the team members in.

'Then I want you to go to the school.' In full flow Taylor talked very quickly, the words tripping over themselves. Sometimes he couldn't find the right phrase but continued anyway. 'Ask to speak to all the sixth year. I don't know. Perhaps a special assembly if you can organize it, something formal. To emphasize how important their help would be. Do it today, while they're still in shock, before they have time to get used to what's happened.' He was sitting on the desk in front of them, swinging his legs like a child who couldn't keep still. 'There should be a lot of sympathy for the father. I know, pupils and teachers, they don't always get on. But in a case like this. I mean, for Christ's sake. Give them the number of the special phone line. Tell them they'll get through to an outsider if they call it, but make it clear they can talk to you if they prefer. That way we're giving them a choice. We want to know where Catherine was the night before she died, who she usually hung out with, boyfriends, wannabe boyfriends.' He stopped for breath. There was a brief moment of silence. Looking beyond the SIO Perez saw, through the long window, that the darkness wasn't so dense. Soon it would be light.

'There's one lad I want to trace,' Perez said. 'He drove the girls home on New Year's Eve. I know where he lives. It should be easy enough to find him through the school.'

'What about Magnus Tait?' It was Sandy Wilson. He could never hold his tongue and Taylor's appreciation of the Incident Room had made him overconfident. 'I mean, if he killed the girl, do we need to bother with all this?'

Taylor jumped down from the desk and swung round to face him. Perez expected an explosion. He had the inspector down as a man who wouldn't suffer fools gladly and there were times when he thought Sandy was the biggest fool in Shetland. But Taylor kept his temper. Perez thought it was taking an effort, but the SIO would know it wouldn't help relationships between Inverness and Lerwick if he ballocked one of the Shetlanders in front of his colleagues.

'We can't close off any options at this stage of the case,' he said evenly. 'You know how it works, Sandy, when you get to court. Some slick lawyer, out to make a name for himself. *What other lines of enquiry did you follow, Inspector Taylor? What other actions did you take? Or were you so convinced by my client's guilt that you didn't try to look any further?* It's my responsibility to obtain a conviction, not just to get a man in front of a judge. And you didn't even manage that when Catriona Bruce went missing. Someone like Magnus Tait needs careful handling. Do you understand what I'm saying, Sandy?'

Perez thought that hoping for understanding from Sandy Wilson was like waiting for piggies to float over Sumburgh Head, but by now Taylor was carried along by the flow of words and seemed not to notice the lack of response from the constable.

'We keep an eye on Tait. We'll be working on the crime scene for a few days and he lives close by, so that won't be hard. We can do it unobtrusively. If he goes out, we follow him. I don't want another murder. But overnight I was thinking about what Jimmy said. You disturbed my sleep Jimmy, but you were right. We explore the other options first. We only bring in the old man when we're absolutely sure.'

Great, Perez said to himself. *So now it's my responsibility if things go wrong.* He thought Taylor was cleverer and much more devious than he'd realized.

Chapter Fifteen

Sally got the bus to school as usual. Waiting for it to arrive, the implication of Catherine's death hit her properly for the first time. Until now the events of the previous day had been like a drama, so exciting and different from everyday life that she hadn't been able to take it in. It had been like watching a video. Soon the film would end and she'd go back to the real world. Now, standing at the bus stop in the dark, her feet frozen already and no one to keep her company she realized *this* was the real world. The absence of Catherine was more solid than the presence had ever been. In life Catherine's mood changed every minute. You never knew where you were with her. Death was constant. Sally felt if she reached out her hand she'd be able to touch the hole where once Catherine had been. It would feel hard and shiny like ice.

Sally could have stayed at home if she'd asked. Her mother wouldn't have minded and had almost suggested it. She'd turned from the cooker, where she was stirring porridge when Sally came down for breakfast.

'Are you OK to go in?' she'd asked, dead sympathetic. It would have only taken Sally to hesitate for a moment for her to add *Why not stay at home? I'm sure they'd understand.*

But Sally had answered firmly and immediately 'I'd rather be with the others. Take my mind off things.'

And her mother had nodded approvingly, thinking probably how brave her daughter was. It was ironic. There'd been hundreds of times when Sally had dreaded school, had dreamed up vague illnesses, headaches and stomach aches. Her mother had never shown the slightest sympathy then. She hadn't understood what it was like to grow up as a teacher's daughter, so there was no escape from school. The piles of exercise books on the shelf in the kitchen, her mother's painstaking writing of lists on the shiny card, all that was a reminder of what would happen when they walked across the yard and into the classroom. The calling of names, the sly pinches, the blank stares. And none of that had changed much when she moved to the high school. The kids were more subtle in their torture, but it was still a nightmare. Not even Catherine had understood that.

Today her mother had asked if she fancied porridge for breakfast. Would she rather something else? An egg, maybe? When Sally had been bothered that she was putting on weight again and suggested fruit instead of porridge some days for breakfast, her mother had only sniffed and said she wasn't running a restaurant. She hadn't understood the agonies of needing to fit in.

Sally's father had already gone to work by the time she got up. She wasn't sure what he made of Catherine's murder. She never knew what he thought about anything. She thought sometimes that he had a life that none of them knew anything about. It was his way of surviving.

After breakfast her mother had begun to pull on her coat. 'I'll wait with you until your bus arrives. I don't like the thought of you standing out there on your own.'

'Mother, there are police all over the hill.' Because the last thing she wanted was her mother fussing over her, appearing concerned, but prying and poking for information. Robert Isbister took up so much room in Sally's head, it'd be hard not to let something about him slip. She couldn't bear her mother knowing about him. Not yet. Margaret would go on and on about him, about what a waster he was and nothing like his father. Sally could picture her right in her face, mocking and jeering. Sally had never been able to stand up to her mother. She might end up believing some of the things she said. And it was only the dream of being with Robert which kept her going.

So now she was standing by the bend in the road, waiting. Every now and again her mother's head appeared in silhouette at the kitchen window, to check that she hadn't been raped or murdered. She tried to ignore it. Her mind was suddenly filled with memories of Catherine. Although she tried to think of other things – the old romantic fantasies of Robert – pictures of Catherine wouldn't go away. She could see the two of them on New Year's Eve, first of all in Lerwick, then stumbling into Magnus Tait's house. Catherine had been so in command of herself that night, hard and bright and invulnerable.

The caretaker had put salt on the paths leading into the school, turning the snow into a slushy mess, which they carried on their shoes into the corridors. In the fourth year area a bunch of kids sat on the pool table, shoving and giggling. She thought they seemed very young. The radiators were full on and condensation ran down the windows. The place smelled like a laundry, with all the drying coats and gloves. The first person she met was Lisa, tarty Lisa, whose boobs were so big you wondered how she managed to stand upright.

'Sal,' she said. 'I'm so sorry.'

In school it seemed everyone was still in the phase of considering Catherine's death a drama laid on for their own entertainment. Walking to the house room to dump her coat Sally could hear them whispering in corners, passing on rumours and gossip. It made her sick.

When she pushed open the door there was a brief silence, then suddenly they all crowded round, wanting to talk to her. Even the posse who'd taken over the table in the middle of the room and were usually too aloof to mix with anyone outside their own crowd. She'd never felt so popular. She'd never had a proper friend at school. Catherine had been the closest to it and Catherine was far too wrapped up in her own concerns to bother much about Sally. Now she was the centre of attention. They gathered around her, covered her with mumbled commiseration: *It must be dreadful. We know how close you two were. We're really so sorry.* Then came the questions, tentative at first, becoming more excited: *Have the police talked to you? Everyone's saying it was Magnus Tait – has he been arrested?*

Before, floating around the edge of several groups, not really accepted by any of them, she'd tried too hard. She'd talked too much, laughed too loud, felt big and clumsy and stupid. Now that they wanted to hear what she had to say words failed her. She stumbled through some answers. And they loved her for that. Lisa put her arm around Sally's shoulder.

'Don't worry,' she said. 'We're all here for you.'

Sally knew that if Catherine had been here, if she'd heard, she'd have stuck two fingers down her throat and pretended to be sick.

Sally was tempted to tell Lisa and all the others that she could see through them. They weren't sorry Catherine was dead at all. Certainly they hadn't particularly liked her when she was alive. Lisa had called her a stuck-up southern cow only last week, when Mr Scott had read out a chunk of her essay on Steinbeck. They were enjoying every minute of this. They weren't in the least sorry that Catherine would never take her place again in the front row for English.

But she didn't say that. She had to survive in school without Catherine. And she was enjoying all the sympathy, the arm around the shoulders, the loving whispers. It didn't matter any more what Catherine thought of them. Catherine was dead.

A bell rang and they wandered off to first lesson, leaving the posse in the house room gagging for more. She and Lisa had English and they walked together. Sally hated the English department. It was housed in the oldest part of the school and the high-ceilinged rooms were always freezing. They had to pass a glass case with a load of stuffed birds inside. Catherine had loved those birds. They'd made her laugh. She'd brought in her camera specially to record them, though Sally had never been able to see the joke. Catherine had said the whole English department would make a brilliant set for a Gothic movie.

In the classroom too, there was a ready audience. Lisa acted as her agent, protective, encouraging, helping her to put the most exciting spin on the story. Sally was in the middle of describing her interview with the detective from Fair Isle when Mr Scott came in. The girls who'd made up her audience slipped reluctantly from the window sill where they'd been warming their legs on the radiator and into their seats. There was no urgency in this manoeuvre. Even in ordinary times he wasn't a teacher who inspired fear or respect. Today, they knew they'd get away with anything.

Mr Scott was a young man, straight from college, unmarried. Everyone said he'd fancied Catherine. That was why she'd got good marks, why he raved about her work. It was because he was trying to get into her knickers. And perhaps there was some truth in the rumours. Sally had seen him staring at Catherine when he thought no one was looking. She knew about unrequited lust. She'd dreamt of Robert Isbister for months following the dance when they'd first met up. It had been enough just to see him out in the town to make her blush. She recognized the signs.

Mr Scott was a pale, thin man. *A stick of forced rhubarb* said Sally's mother, who had seen him at a parents' evening. Today, in the snowy grey light he seemed more pale than usual. He blew his nose over and over. She wondered if he had been crying. Catherine had always been scathing about him. She'd said he was a crap English teacher and a pathetic human being. But Catherine had talked about everyone in that cold, hard way and she hadn't always meant it. Looking at him now, as he tried to speak without breaking down, clutching on to the big white handkerchief, Sally thought there was something cute about him. With her new popularity she could afford to be generous.

After taking the register, Mr Scott stood in front of them in silence for a moment. He looked very serious, and so faintly ridiculous. Sally wondered if Catherine could have led him on, just for the fun of it. He seemed to have difficulty speaking.

'There will be a different timetable this morning. We'll have normal lessons up till break and then there will be a special assembly just for the sixth year. It'll be an opportunity for us all to come together to remember Catherine and her father. One of the detectives working on the investigation will speak to us too.' He paused, looked bleakly, rather theatrically around the class. 'I know everyone will be deeply upset by this tragedy. If you need to speak to someone today or in the future, the staff will be available to talk to you. Specialist counselling can be provided if we think that would be helpful. You don't need to be alone in your grief. We're all here to support you.'

Sally imagined Catherine pulling a face, rolling her eyes towards the ceiling. She realized with astonishment that next to her, Lisa was enjoying a good cry.

There were a lot of tears at the special assembly. Even some of the boys seemed to get caught up in the emotion of the occasion. Some must have been genuine. Apart from Sally, Catherine had found it easier to get on with boys than girls. But even the dead heads – the thugs, the footballers and the bullies – seemed moved. At one point Sally thought she was the only person in the hall with dry eyes. In the end she dabbed at her cheek with a tissue, just so she wouldn't seem hard-hearted. She wondered if there was something wrong with her. Why couldn't she cry? But she knew Catherine wouldn't have cried either. She would have mocked the hypocrisy and the sentiment.

'Maudlin rubbish!' she'd said one evening when they'd been watching the telly in her little living room and there'd been a fuss about a rock star who'd been killed in a car crash.

Sally hadn't known what maudlin meant and had looked it up in a dictionary. Now, refusing to be taken in by the false grief, she muttered the same words under her breath like a chant.

The policeman who'd come to talk to her at home was sitting on the stage next to the head teacher. Sally had seen him as soon as she had walked in. She found his presence disturbing and although she tried not to, she kept flicking her eyes towards him. He'd made some effort to dress for the occasion, he was wearing a grey shirt, a sober tie and a jacket, but the overall impression was still one of untidiness. It was as if he'd had to borrow the garments and had thrown them on at the last minute. She couldn't tell if he'd recognized her in the crowd of faces turned up towards the stage.

She didn't hear the head make the introduction because she was watching the policeman prepare to speak. He was straightening his tie, collecting up the papers he'd put on the floor by his seat. She sensed his nervousness, felt a tightening in her own stomach. He stood up, looked out at them and said how sorry he was about the way Catherine had died. It was a double tragedy for them because they all knew Catherine and her father. Sally thought he was one of the few people in the room who *was* genuinely sorry. That was strange because he'd never met Catherine. Then she thought it was easier for him to be sad just because he'd never met her. In his mind she could be anything he wanted her to be.

But now he was saying how important it was for the police to know the real Catherine. 'Now, when we're suffering such shock, we can't imagine why anyone would want to kill her. We just want to remember her kindly. But this isn't a time for kindness. It's a time for honesty. It's important for me to understand everything about her. Perhaps there were parts of her life which she would have preferred to keep secret. She doesn't have that choice now. If you know, or suspect, that she was involved with activities which might have led, even indirectly, to her death, you have a duty to share that information with me. If you had any sort of relationship with her, I need to speak to you. I'll be in school all day. Mr Shearer has allowed me to use his office. If you prefer to speak anonymously to an officer who doesn't usually work in Shetland that can be arranged too.' He was just about to leave the stage when he turned back to them. 'Come and talk to me,' he said. 'All of you know more about Catherine than I do. All of you have something important to contribute.'

Then he was gone and throughout the room came the hiss of subdued whispering. There were none of the cynical comments which were the usual response to an adult's lecture. Sally had no doubt they would queue up outside the head's office to talk to him. They would want to play their parts in the theatre. She wondered what he would make of what they had to say.

Chapter Sixteen

Standing on the stage in the overheated hall, looking down at them all, Perez thought this was a waste of time and effort. Sandy Wilson was probably right. They'd get Magnus Tait for the killing in the end and he'd have wound up these kids for nothing. They'd already be shocked by the murder. Why persuade them to bring their grubby little secrets about Catherine to him? Why not leave her in peace?

He'd been a pupil here and perhaps that had something to do with his discomfort. He would rather be back at Ravenswick supervising the search of the hill. He'd feel cleaner out in the open air. It wasn't that he'd actively disliked school. He'd never been academic but he hadn't struggled like some of the others. He'd been desperately homesick. He'd missed his parents, the croft and the Isle. He'd been happy in the small school there. It had just one teacher and he'd been related to most of the kids. To arrive here at twelve to live in the hostel had been a shock. It wouldn't have been so bad if they'd been allowed home at weekends, but Fair Isle wasn't like other places. The boat couldn't always make it and if the weather was wild or foggy the plane couldn't land on the airstrip at the foot of Ward Hill. He'd been here for six weeks the first time, feeling abandoned despite his mother's regular phone calls and although he'd known there was no alternative. This was the way things had to be. Would he want it for his own children?

Sitting behind the headmaster's desk he remembered his first home visit. October half-term. He'd worried all week that a storm would blow up, but it had been one of those still dry autumn days, with a taste of ice in the air. They'd been allowed off on the Friday morning because that was when the boat went. A bus had taken them to Grutness and they'd arrived in time to see the *Good Shepherd* approach from the south. His grandfather had been skipper then and his father had been one of the crew. Squashed beside his father in the wheelhouse, Jimmy had decided he would never go back to Lerwick. They couldn't make him. He sat eating his grandmother's date slices, which seemed to taste somehow of salt and diesel, quite determined. Though of course when the time came and he'd stood with the other children in the dark early morning at the North Haven, he'd got on to the boat without a fuss. He couldn't show his parents up.

He knew it was the awareness of the imminent vacancy at Skerry which triggered the memories, not just the noise and the smell of Anderson High. He'd have to speak to his mother about it this evening. She wouldn't expect a decision immediately, but he'd have to work out what tone to take. He couldn't raise her hopes if there was no possibility of his applying for the croft.

That was still at the back of his mind when there was a knock at the office door. He felt out of place behind the headmaster's desk, impudent for being there. There was a pause. He realized a response was expected. 'Come in,' he shouted, again feeling like an impostor. 'Come in.'

He'd prepared himself to greet a student, to be informal and welcoming, but an adult hesitated inside the door. Just an adult, he decided. There was something about this man which was still unformed. He looked as if he might grow further, fill out, at least. His clothes hung on him. At the same time he had an air of someone prematurely middle-aged. There was a stoop and his dress – a shirt with a roundneck sweater topped by a cord jacket – was the uniform of a teacher close to retirement. Perez rose from his chair and held out his hand. The man approached.

'My name's David Scott. It's about Catherine.' His voice was English, the sort of accent Perez thought of as public school.

Perez said nothing.

Scott looked around him as though he was searching for a seat, although there was a chair just in front of him.

'I taught Catherine English. I was also her form teacher.'

Perez nodded. Scott lowered himself into the chair.

'I wanted to talk to you before any of the students . . . I'm aware there've been rumours.'

Perez waited.

'I admired Catherine. She had a wonderful grasp of language, a fine mind.' He pulled a large handkerchief out of his jacket pocket.

No other words were forthcoming and Perez asked,

'Did you ever see her outside school?' He suspected the fine mind wasn't the only attraction.

'Only once.' Scott looked wretched. 'It was a mistake.'

'What happened?'

'She read widely outside the set texts. Contemporary fiction. It was very refreshing. For most of my students the object is to pass an examination. They're not interested in the books themselves.' He paused, realizing he wasn't answering the question. 'I wanted to encourage her, build on her enthusiasm. I didn't get the impression that Euan did much of that, though of course he teaches English too. I suggested we go for a coffee after school one evening and I'd go through a list of recommended reading with her.'

'What was her response?'

'She said that coffee wasn't conducive to literary debate. Why didn't we buy a bottle of wine and go back to my flat? I said that wasn't a good idea. She'd miss her bus and the chance of a lift home with her father. She usually got the bus to and from school. Euan is something of a workaholic. He's in early and works late.'

Perez thought that Scott seemed to know a lot about Catherine's daily routine.

'She said it didn't matter. I could give her a lift home. It didn't matter how late she got in. Her father was used to it. Or if I didn't want to do that she could stay over with friends.'

'And did you agree? To the wine and the intellectual conversation?'

'I didn't think there would be any harm in it.' Which of course was nonsense. He'd been tempted, because she was pretty and bright and he hadn't wanted to appear stuffy like the other teachers. But he'd known he'd been playing with fire. That must have been part of the attraction, the thrill. But what had been the attraction for Catherine? Surely she wouldn't have fallen for this dry, pretentious young fogey. And Perez had an impression of her which didn't include kindness to foolish and naïve teachers.

'Did she explain her plans to her father?'

'Certainly. She sent him a text message, saying she'd be late.'

'Saying she was with you?'

He blushed. 'I don't know. I didn't see the text.'

'Was it a successful evening?'

'No, I've already told you.' His voice had become irritable. Perhaps he was regretting his impulse to speak to Perez. 'It was a mistake. I should never have agreed to it.'

'Why?' Perez asked. 'There'd be nothing more satisfying, I'd have thought, than helping a responsive student.'

'That was why I went into teaching.' Scott broke off and looked up sharply, suspecting he was being mocked. 'But there are so few students who care, who really want to learn.'

'Tell me about the evening.'

'It was the last week of term. Everyone was in festive mood. At any other time I don't think I would even have considered her suggestion, but just before Christmas, that's when rules can be relaxed. It was already dark when we left the building of course and it was very foggy. Perhaps you remember those few days in the middle of December when the fog never lifted and it never seemed to get light. She'd waited for me outside the staff room. What I'm saying is that there was nothing furtive or secret about our movements. Anyone could have seen us.'

Now that he'd started talking more freely, Scott seemed to find some relief in sharing the experience. It was as if he'd forgotten Perez was a policeman.

'She seemed in a very good mood. Elated even. I put that down to the end of term too. It's a frantic time – preparation for the Beanfeasts, our Christmas dances – but everyone enjoys it. She was singing something under her breath as we walked. I didn't recognize the tune, but it stayed with me afterwards, haunted me. She offered to buy the wine. I said I had some at home, there was no need. Of course I didn't want her going into an off-licence and breaking the law and I hoped that when we got home she might forget about the idea, make do with a coffee. My flat's in the town, near the museum. The fog seemed even thicker there. Even with the street lights it would have been easy to lose our way.

'When we got to the flat she seemed completely at ease. She looked at my bookshelf, then chose a CD. She was an only child. Perhaps she was more used to adult company than her peers. She was nearly seventeen, but in our conversation I didn't feel that I was talking to someone younger than me. There was, after all, only eight years between us. If anything I was the one who was nervous. She talked a lot about film. She was raving about a director I'd never heard of. She made me feel unsophisticated and ignorant. It seemed quite natural then to open the wine and offer a glass to her. I was even worried, I remember, what she'd make of it. I suspected she'd be much more of an expert than me.' He fell into a silence.

'Did you discuss books?' Perez asked at last, gently. He didn't want to break the mood. He wanted Scott still to imagine himself in that room, the curtains drawn against the fog outside, the beautiful girl and the wine.

'Oh yes. She'd just finished Sarah Waters's *Affinity*. She was hugely impressed by the writing, the Victorian voice. I was so pleased because I'd recommended it to her. It's such a compliment, isn't it, when another person becomes passionate about a book you love. It gives you a connection, a sort of intimacy.'

'Is that what you said to her?'

Scott blushed. 'I'm not sure. Perhaps not in those words.'

'Because it's the sort of idea which might be misinterpreted. That's why I ask. Perhaps Catherine got the wrong impression . . .'

'Yes,' Scott said gratefully. 'Yes, I'm afraid she might have done.'

'In what way?'

'It wasn't then. It was as she was leaving. We were in the middle of a conversation about crime fiction. We'd discovered that we shared an affection for the early English women writers, though I was championing Dorothy Sayers and her favourite was Allingham. She received a text message. She said she had to go. I thought the message must have been from her father and immediately I offered her a lift home. I'd been very careful about what I'd had to drink, so there would be no problem about my driving. You see, Inspector, I wasn't entirely irresponsible. But she said she wasn't going home. The message was from a friend. They'd meet up in Lerwick. I'll admit I was quite relieved. The weather was dreadful and I didn't like the idea of driving to Ravenswick.

'It was as she was at the door. I was helping her into her coat. I kissed her. It seemed the right thing to do. I was saying goodbye to a friend. There were no sexual connotations. Not really. She overreacted. As you say, perhaps she misinterpreted my intentions. She pushed me away, held me for a moment at arm's length, looking at me as if I disgusted her. Then she turned round and walked out before I could apologize. She didn't seem upset. I mean there were no tears, nothing like that. She just walked off. I was going to run after her, then thought it would be better to let her go. It was better not to make too much of it. I could talk to her in school the next day. But for the last two days of term she avoided me. She didn't come into class for registration. I was glad when the holidays arrived. I thought this term we'd have a new start. But of course, now that's not possible.'

'Why did you come to Shetland to teach?'

The sudden change in tone seemed to bring Scott back to the present. He smiled wanly. 'I suppose,' he said, 'I wanted an adventure. I thought there'd be so much scope . . . It would be ground-breaking work.'

Ah, you thought you were bringing culture to us ignorant natives.

'And I wasn't sure that I'd be able to hack it in a city school.'

'If Catherine hadn't been your student, how would things have been different between you?' Perez threw out the question as Scott was preparing to leave.

The teacher stood for a moment, considering. 'I'd have been honest with her and told her how I really felt. That I was devoted to her and I was prepared to wait.' He gathered up his bag and left the room.

Perez knew the answer was a piece of self-dramatic nonsense, but he couldn't help being moved. There'd been a dignity in Scott's words. He told himself it was the emotional incontinence at work again. Really, there was no reason for him to feel sympathy.

Another knock on the office door broke into his thoughts. It opened and a slender boy with an anorak bundled under one arm came in. Another English voice. 'Excuse me Sir. They said you wanted to see me. I gave Catherine a lift back to Ravenswick on New Year's Eve. My name's Jonathan Gale.'

As he took the chair, Perez saw how upset he was. His eyes were red. Another man who had fallen for Catherine. It seemed she had made fools of them all.

Chapter Seventeen

Fran waited until mid-afternoon before going to fetch Cassie from Duncan's house. When she woke up the police were still in the field where the body had been. Men in waterproofs were walking across the moor behind her house in a straggling line. She didn't want her daughter asking questions about what they were doing. She wasn't ready yet to explain. She phoned Margaret Henry to tell her that Cassie wouldn't be at school.

'She stayed at her father's last night. I thought it would be best . . .'

'Of course,' Margaret said. 'It must be a worry for you living so close to Hillhead. We'll all be glad when it's over, when the man's behind bars.' As if there was no question about the identity of the culprit.

Duncan was the nearest thing there was to a crown prince of Shetland, Fran thought. She hadn't realized that when she married him, hadn't realized it would be like a commoner marrying into royalty. His family had lived in the islands for generations. They owned land and boats and farms. He lived in a big stone house which was almost a castle. A ruined castle until the oil had come and the family had leased access land for the pipelines to the oil companies at prices which meant that Duncan would never have to work again. He *did* work, though Fran had never been sure exactly what at. He called himself a consultant.

Never mind the oil, he'd said soon after they met. The islands' future would depend on tourism, eco-tourism. He set himself up to represent Shetland all over the world, advising local businesses, encouraging indigenous arts and crafts. He had an office in Lerwick and he went out to meetings with important people in Glasgow, London and Aberdeen. He seemed to have power and that was part of the attraction. There was a sexual charge in the speed of his driving and the inter-national calls on the mobile phone. She'd been seduced by all that.

She'd met him when she'd been sent to Shetland to take photographs for an article on a young designer from Yell who was selling her exciting knitwear to exclusive shops in New York and Tokyo. Not to London. London wouldn't take them, though soon after the article appeared the designer started to receive beg-ging letters from a number of British fashion houses too.

Duncan had pitched the original idea of the story – in his role as consultant, Fran presumed – and had been there to meet her at the airport. She'd been charmed by him. It had been mid-summer. He'd bought her a meal in town then driven her west. They'd walked along the cliffs and seen the Foula lighthouse in the distance. They'd made love in a loft bed in a converted boathouse in Scalloway, the windows open to let in the sound of the water and the perpetual light. She had thought that he lived there, hadn't realized then it was only one of the buildings he owned and let out to tourists, only part of his empire.

She'd thought that was it, had never believed she'd see him again. She'd flown home the next morning exhausted and a bit ashamed. It had been her first one-night stand. Then he'd turned up at her office in London with champagne and one of the beautiful sweaters made by the young designer, which she knew would have cost her almost a month's salary. *You'll need something warm to wear when you come to live with me. But that doesn't mean you can't be glamorous* . . .

And eventually she had gone back to live with him, because she'd been as much a sucker for the grand gesture as the next woman, and anyway she'd loved the islands even on that first visit. Had it been Duncan she'd fallen for, or the place? Would champagne and a jumper have persuaded her to move to Birmingham?

They hadn't married until Cassie was on the way. Cassie hadn't been planned exactly and Fran had been surprised by Duncan's ambivalent attitude. She'd expected him to be as thrilled as she was. Pregnancy was a drama, wasn't it, and he did so like dramas. 'I suppose we should marry then,' he'd said tentatively, almost as if he was hoping she'd suggest another option. 'Why?' she'd cried. She was an independent woman after all. 'We don't *have* to get married. We can stay as we are. Only there'll be a child.' 'No,' he'd said. 'If there's a child then we should marry.' It was a proposal of sorts. She had dreamed of his proposing to her but had imagined something wonderful. Paris, at least.

Then, when Cassie was six months old, Fran had caught him in bed with another woman, an older woman, another Shetland aristocrat who could trace her family back to Norwegian rule. She too was married. It seemed the relationship had being going on for years, certainly before Fran had arrived to take her photographs. Most of their friends had known about it, taken it for granted. Fran had known the woman, Celia, well, had considered her a friend. Celia was the sort of woman Fran would have liked as a mother – strong, independent, unconventional. She had a style which was unusual among the island women – she wore a lot of black and bright red lipstick, long earrings made of silver or seashells or amber. She'd married against her family's wishes.

Fran had collected together the baby's things and taken the first flight south. She refused to listen to Duncan's explanations. She thought he was pathetic. What was it with the Oedipus complex? She could see that he would never give up Celia. Fran would make her own life again in London. She told herself she was more hurt by the betrayal of a woman whom she'd admired than by her husband.

Then, when Cassie was approaching school age, Fran had experienced some sort of crisis of her own. There'd been a bruising end to a relationship. The usual thing. Nothing noble or uplifting. She'd just felt the need to run away and hide. Pride again. She hated the thought of having to relive the humiliation in conversation with her friends. Shetland was as far as she could go, and it wasn't fair on Cassie, after all, to deprive her of her father's company. He might be a screwed-up little shit but he loved his daughter. She'd never known *her* father. He'd separated from her mother when she was a baby, started a new life and a new family and had wanted nothing to do with her. It still hurt. She wanted better than that for Cassie.

She was rerunning all this in her mind as she drove very slowly over the icy roads north across the huge bare expanse of the peat moor. As always it came down to this – what was it that Duncan saw in Celia? She might have a sort of quirky attractiveness but she had a grown-up son. Her hair would have been grey if she didn't dye it. Surely Fran should have been able to compete with that? The question, which still provoked a sense of anger and insecurity, took her mind off Catherine Ross's death and the mad old man at Hillhead.

Usually when she collected Cassie she didn't spend any time with her ex-husband. She said enough to be polite, to present a united front for the little girl. Today she was inclined to linger. She didn't want to go back to the house in Ravenswick immediately. Even with the police and the coastguard on the hill she didn't feel safe there. In London there had been muggings and rapes in her neighbourhood, a shooting once in her street. Yet she'd never felt this exposed.

Duncan's house was built on low ground close to a wide sandy bay. It was huge, a four-storey, granite and slate Gothic heap, a house from a fairy tale with a turret at one corner. It was built into the slope of the hill and sheltered from the prevailing winds. There was a walled woodland on one side of the house, mostly scrubby sycamores growing in the shelter of the valley, but the only trees for twenty miles. She remembered when she'd first seen the house. Duncan had made her keep her eyes shut until they came to this point, then she'd opened them and it was all part of the fairy tale. She'd imagined herself living there when she was old and surrounded by grandchildren.

Here, in the shelter of the hill, the road was clear of snow. The sun was coming out. Driving towards the house, Fran saw that Duncan was on the beach with Cassie. They were collecting driftwood, pulling it above the tideline. Duncan always lit a big bonfire for Up Helly Aa. She realized that the festival was almost upon them. It was held in Lerwick on the last Tuesday of January every year. For some people in the south that was all they knew of Shetland – the pageant of men dressed as Vikings and the longboat paraded through the streets before it was burned. Postcard images promoted by the tourist board to boost the number of winter visitors. The main event was in town but other communities held their own celebrations over the winter too. As she drove through the big stone gateposts she lost sight of her husband and child on the beach. She parked by the front door.

Celia seemed to spend as much time at the Haa as she did in the house on the edge of Lerwick which she shared with her husband. It seemed she didn't object to Duncan's many flings. She indulged him as she did her grown-up child. Fran still found it hard to be civil and, to avoid her, walked around the house to the beach. The garden was held back from the sand by a whitewashed stone wall. Beyond the wall someone had collected a pile of seaweed to rot down for compost.

They had given up the search for wood. Duncan was skimming stones over the shallow water. Cassie was drawing with a stick in the sand, frowning in concentration. She heard the sound of Fran's boots on the shingle and turned round with a squeal of joy. Fran looked at the picture in the sand, already blurring at the edges where the water was seeping underneath.

'Who is it?' It was the drawing of a person, a stick figure with enormous fingers, carefully counted, and spiky hair. She hoped Cassie would say it was her. She knew there should be no competition for their daughter's affection, but it always crept in. The old insecurity. She couldn't bear it if Cassie had been drawing Celia.

'It's Catherine. She's dead.' The girl squinted down at it. 'Can't you tell?'

Fran looked furiously over Cassie's head towards Duncan. He looked exhausted. His eyes were red and his face was drawn. *He's getting too old for the lifestyle*, she thought. He shrugged. 'I didn't say anything. We were in the shop in Brae this morning and people were talking. You know what it's like.'

Cassie chased away, arms outstretched zigzagging back towards the house. They followed her more slowly.

'What were they saying?'

He shrugged again. She could have hit him. 'Everyone's very shocked. It's like when Catriona disappeared. The whole community holding its breath, waiting for the nastiness to go away, so they can get back to real life.'

'Catriona was never found,' she said.

'People forget. Life goes on.'

'They won't forget this. Not two girls.'

'Why don't you come and stay here for a bit?' he said suddenly. 'Both of you. I'd be happier. We could still get Cassie to school in the morning and pick her up. It's not so far. Just until it's over.'

'What would Celia make of that?'

'She's not here just now,' he said. He paused. 'There's some domestic drama with the boy. She's gone home.' Something about his voice made her wonder if there was more to it than that.

'Feeling lonely, are you?' she said spitefully. 'Need a bit of company in the evening?'

'I can get company whenever I like,' he said. 'You know that. This house has had more parties than anywhere else in Shetland. I worry about you. I want you to be safe.'

She didn't answer.

They caught up with Cassie by the kitchen door. She was trying to pull off her wellingtons, balancing on one leg. Duncan took the girl into his arms and threw her into the air, catching her again at the last minute. Fran stopped herself shouting at him for his recklessness. Cassie was giggling.

He made her tea. Cassie disappeared for illicit television. Duncan let her get away with anything.

'Does it feel odd?' he asked. 'To be a stranger in your own house?'

'It's not my house. Not any more.' She looked around the kitchen. She wondered how long Celia had been gone. The room had a cold, uncared-for air. There were dirty plates waiting to go into the dishwasher and spills on the worktops. Celia was tidier than her.

'It could be.'

'Don't be silly, Duncan. Do you expect Celia and me to take turns to make supper?'

'She's not coming back.' He had his back to her, but

she could feel his pain, found herself feeling a moment of pity before the satisfaction. He could still get to her.

'What was it? One bright young thing too many? I suppose Celia's too old for partying.' Though she couldn't really believe it. Duncan and Celia had fallen out before. She'd always come back.

'I wish I knew. Something like that I suppose.' He opened a blue cake tin which stood on the workbench and seemed surprised to find it empty.

'Sorry,' she said. 'You'll have to find yourself another live-in housekeeper.'

'Come on Fran, you know it's not like that.'

'That's just how it seems.'

He was standing with his back to the window. She could see the bay beyond him, was briefly intensely tempted. *All this could be yours. The house. The beach. The view.*

'I'd met the girl,' he said suddenly.

She was distracted by her desire for the place, confused. 'Which girl?'

'Catherine. The girl who was murdered.'

'How did you know her?'

'She came here.'

'What was Catherine Ross doing here?' She thought of Catherine as a schoolgirl. Not the sort of person Duncan would usually mix with. But then, in Shetland, Duncan knew everyone, even the kids.

'She came to a party,' he said slowly. 'It wasn't long ago. A couple of days after new year.'

'Was she here with her father?'

'Nothing so respectable. She turned up one night . . . I thought Celia knew her, so I let her in. You know what it's like. Open house. Not that I'd have turned her away. At one point I was talking to her. About film. That was her ambition, she said. To be the first major female British film director. In ten years everyone would have heard of Catherine Ross. That was how I remembered the name. They have such confidence at that age, don't they?'

'She must have come with someone.' *He fancied her* she thought. *Only sixteen but that didn't matter to him. Fifty or fifteen, he didn't care.*

'Perhaps. I really don't remember, or didn't notice. It was the end of the evening by the time we had that conversation. I'd had a lot to drink. Celia had just told me she was going and wouldn't come back.'

'Did Catherine spend the night here?'

'Probably. Most of the guests did.' He looked up at her sharply. 'But not with me, if that's what you're thinking. She was only a child.'

'I saw her the next day, getting off the bus. And the morning after that I found her body. You'll have to tell the police. They're trying to trace her movements.'

'No,' he said. 'What would be the point? What could I tell them?'

He didn't ask her to stay again and when she rounded up Cassie to collect her things, he made no protest.

Chapter Eighteen

Sally Henry saw Inspector Perez leave the building. She was just coming out from a classroom on her way to get the bus and he was there, standing just inside the main door. He seemed lost in thought. She'd seen some of the sixth year queuing up earlier in the day to speak to him. She'd have liked to ask him if it had been useful, sitting in the head's office, listening to stories about Catherine. But she didn't have the nerve, and anyway he was hardly likely to tell her. He must have realized eventually that he was in the way, just standing there, blocking the flow of the kids who were on their way out, and he walked off. He had a padded jacket over his suit and most of them seemed not to recognize him. She wondered if she should follow him to his car. He was more likely to talk to her when there was no one else listening in. She was Catherine's friend. She had a right to know what they'd discovered.

Her phone rang and there was the usual scramble to get it out of her bag, so she didn't see which way he went. She didn't get a chance to look at the display before she answered so it was a surprise, a delight to hear Robert's voice. She'd only seen him once since new year, a brief fumbled meeting one afternoon when she was supposed to be in town shopping. She'd plucked up the courage to phone him and suggested they get together. She hadn't been sure he'd known who it was at first. 'Sally,' she'd said 'Sally. You do remember New Year's Eve?' He'd been in the pub at the time, so perhaps that explained why he'd seemed so muddled. Since that meeting she'd texted him a couple of times, but there'd been no reply. That didn't mean anything though. If he was out in the boat, he could be out of range and there were places in Shetland where reception was crap. Most of the smaller islands were impossible.

'Hi,' she said. She knew better than to ask why he hadn't been in touch. She'd read the magazines. There was nothing more likely to put off a man than a nagging woman. She tried to keep her voice low and husky. She turned away from the crowded lobby into a corridor which was empty, except for a cleaner with a bucket and mop right at the other end. She shut her eyes to block out the boring details of school life, pictured him.

'Any chance of meeting up?' He kept his voice light but he really wanted to see her. She could tell that.

'When?'

'I'm in town,' he said. 'Ten minutes?'

'I don't know . . .' How could she explain about the school bus and her mum calling out the police if she wasn't on it, because she'd always been paranoid but after Catherine's death she'd turned seriously weird? How could she explain all that without sounding like a six-year-old? 'It might be awkward.'

'Please, babe. It's important.' And then he seemed to guess the sort of problem she might have, which proved to Sally just how sensitive he was, how he wasn't at all the boorish lout everyone made him out to be. 'Just one drink and then I'll give you a lift home. You'll still be back ahead of the bus.' And that was probably true, because the bus zigzagged all over the place to drop kids off and Archie, the driver, was about a hundred and four and drove so slowly sometimes she thought it'd be quicker to walk.

'OK,' she said. 'Why not? One drink.'

They met in the back bar of one of the town centre hotels, not in the bar near the docks where he usually drank. Upstairs in the dining room there was a funeral tea. Through the open door she saw a trestle table covered with a white cloth and plates of sandwiches curling at the edges, elderly people dressed in black. The voices were becoming loud and a little desperate. One of the women was weeping.

Robert was waiting. She was pleased. Her only visits to pubs had been with Catherine on occasional illicit visits to town. She wouldn't have had the nerve to go in by herself. Before setting out, she'd stopped to put on some slap, just a bit of powder to hide the spot which might be starting by the side of her nose, and some mascara. But all the same you must be able to tell that she'd come straight from school. She had her bag with all her books and files in. She looked into the room. It was narrow as a corridor, wood-panelled, four grubby tables, a variety of unmatched chairs. You could smell lunchtime's fry-ups and cigarette smoke. He stood up as soon as he saw her.

'What'll you have?'

She thought of her mother, standing by the stove, stirring pans. X-ray eyes and X-ray nose for smelling alcohol.

'Diet Coke.'

He nodded and went straight to the bar, without touching her. She supposed he was thinking of her, being discreet, but there was no one else in the room except a little grey man slumped asleep in the chair by the fire. Robert came back with the Coke and a whisky for himself. Then he did reach out and touch her hand. She grasped his, rubbed the fine gold hairs with her thumb.

'How're things?' he asked. He seemed anxious. Usually he walked into a bar as if he owned the place. That's what Sally loved most about him, that confidence. It sort of rubbed off on her. It cancelled out all the snide remarks from the kids at school about her being the teacher's girl. When she was with him she ought to feel she owned the place too.

'Strange,' she said. 'You heard about Catherine Ross?'

'Aye.'

'She was my best friend, lived near me. You remember, she was there in the car on New Year's Eve.'

'I mind that,' he said.

'Did you know her?' Sally looked at him over the Coke. 'I mean apart from then, had you met her?'

'I'd seen her around. You know, parties.'

Sally was going to press for more details but decided against it and continued.

'They found her on the hill just up from the school, lying in the snow. A detective came to the house last night to interview me, and he's been in school all day, talking to the kids.'

'How was she killed?' he asked. He had pulled his

hand away gently and was playing with the glass, twisting it round and round on the table.

'No one's saying. It said on the radio they had to do forensic tests, but they're treating the death as suspicious.'

He lit a cigarette, narrowing his eyes as he flicked at the lighter. Suddenly she wondered what she was doing there. It was different from the fantasies, the romantic books she'd escaped into when things at school got really rough. Once her father had taken her to the cliffs at the north end of Unst. It had been spring, the air full of wheeling screaming seabirds and the sharp stench of their untidy nests. Looking over the cliffs, even at a safe distance, she had felt dizzy and breathless. She could see the waves breaking on the boulders below, but couldn't really believe in them. It was like staring down into nothing. She'd thought she was at the end of the world and there was nowhere else to go. Now, sitting opposite Robert Isbister, she had the same feeling of panic. What, really, did she want to come out of all this? To be loved by him? Oh that, certainly. It was what she'd been dreaming of. The small gestures of affection – his hand on her neck, stroking her hair – the gifts. But that he should *make* love to her? On the way home tonight, perhaps, in the back of his van? Then that she should stroll into her mother as if she'd just got off the bus to answer questions about her day at school? Was she expecting that? She felt out of her depth. Really out of her depth as if the water was coming over head and she was gasping for breath.

She realized that he'd asked her a question. 'Sorry?'

'Everyone's saying Magnus Tait did it. What did Perez tell you?'

'Nothing about that,' she said. 'He wouldn't, would he? He just wanted to know about Catherine.'

'What about her?'

'Everything. Did she have a boyfriend? Who her mates were. He was trying to find out where she'd been the night before she came back to Ravenswick on the bus.'

Robert leaned back in his chair. The little man by the fire snored, a rush of air through his nose, so loud that it woke him up. He looked blankly around him then fell immediately back to sleep.

'And did she have a boyfriend?' Robert asked.

'Not that I knew.'

'And you would know, wouldn't you?'

'I'm not sure,' she said. 'I don't know what to think any more.' She wished then he would put his arm around her and hold her, comfort her, tell her it was all right, that it was natural for her to be upset. In a film that was what a hero would do. She wanted to tell him how hard it was for her to be here. Someone might come in who knew her parents. She wasn't like the other young girls he knocked around with. She'd thought he'd been able to tell she was different and that was why he liked her.

'Did she tell you where she was the night before she died?'

'How could she? I didn't see her that day.'

'Who do you think did it?' he asked. 'I mean, did she say anything to you before she died? About any weirdos who might have been hanging around?'

'No,' she said. 'Nothing like that. Anyway, you

couldn't believe everything she said. She could be pretty weird herself. She was screwed up after her mother died. I don't think she lived in the real world.'

'Oh.' She thought he was going to ask something else, but he just added 'Right,' and stared at the old man sleeping by the fire.

'Look,' she said, 'I should go. My mother will expect me back on the bus.'

'Oh. OK.' He drank his whisky but made no move.

'You said you'd give me a lift.'

'So I did.' He smiled. It was something of the old smile, gallant and a little mocking at the same time, but she thought his heart wasn't in it. She thought then that he hadn't wanted to see her at all. He'd arranged to meet her simply to find out what she knew about Catherine's death. He was no better than the kids in her class.

His van was parked near the harbour. They walked down the steep lane to get to it. He put his arm around her. She looked around anxiously in case some friend of her mother's should be out watching, but it was very dark, slightly milder with a damp mist in the air, and anyway there was no one about. Before he opened the van door for her he kissed her and, feeling an ache between her legs and the tightness in her breasts, she could remember why she'd dreamed about him since new year. But since that moment of panic in the pub she found it harder to delude herself. He didn't fancy her, did he? Not really. She'd just be another conquest. She pulled gently away.

'I should get back.'

'Yeah?' He stood for a moment, deciding whether he should push it and decided she wasn't worth it. The new clear-sighted Sally could see him weighing up the possibilities, coming down on the side of common sense. Better just get her back to Ravenswick without a fuss. She wasn't his type anyway. That, at least, was how Sally interpreted the small shrug, the resigned 'OK then, if you're sure.'

They passed the bus just before the Ravenswick turn-off, near the old chapel. Without asking for directions Robert took the van slowly down the hill past Hillhead. Sally saw that the old man had pinned a sheet of cardboard up at the window. Perhaps he'd been bothered by people looking in.

'Where do you want me to leave you?' Robert said.

'By Catherine's house. That's where the bus stops and my mother will see it come down the hill.'

Was it a test? If so, he passed. 'I don't know where that is, do I?'

'Just here.'

He pulled in beside Euan Ross's car. 'Nice place,' he said.

More than anything in the world she didn't want to be talking now about Catherine, or Euan Ross. She didn't care if her mother saw her standing outside Catherine's house before the bus arrived. She opened the door of the van. 'Thanks for the lift.'

He leaned across to kiss her, but she was already on her way out.

'Will I see you again?' This time, she couldn't tell from his voice what he really wanted.

'I'm sure we'll bump into each other,' she said. 'A place like this . . .' Proud of herself for not being too eager and this time it wasn't a game. She didn't know what she wanted any more. Things weren't simple. For the first time since Catherine had died, she felt like weeping.

He didn't say anything. He pushed the van into gear and drove off. She stood shivering, staring up at the window of the room where once Catherine had slept, until the bus rattled down the hill.

Chapter Nineteen

At home that night, Sally kept thinking of the first time she'd met Robert. Really met him. Of course she'd known who he was and seen him about before that. Everyone knew who he was. His father was leader of the council and this year would be Guizer Jarl during the Up Helly Aa celebrations. Robert would be in his squad following close behind him in the procession. Everyone said Michael Isbister was a natural choice. A good man. Robert had talked about it and she knew he was proud of his father. Proud and a bit jealous. One day, he said, he'd be Jarl himself. Imagine what it would be like, walking through the streets, all the folks looking at you.

She'd first met Robert to talk to, to touch, in the autumn at a dance in the hall to support some charity *her* father was working with. Something to do with rare plants. Or dolphins. It was always a cause like that where her father was concerned. She hadn't wanted to go. *What* would they say at school when they found out? They didn't give her such a hard time now Catherine was on the scene, but even so, they could make her life pretty miserable. Her mother hadn't been keen either, but although you always thought of Margaret as being the strong one, when it came down to it her father usually got his way, and Margaret had turned out anyway. In martyr mode.

Sally hadn't made much effort getting ready. She'd been wearing that dreadful dress her mother had bought her from the catalogue last Christmas. No make-up. She hadn't even bothered with concealer on her zits. And it had been as boring as she'd suspected it would be. A couple of old men sawing away on fiddles. A fat lass squeezing an accordion. The pooled supper. She'd eaten more than she should, couldn't help it. There'd been nothing else to do.

Then Robert had turned up. Slightly drunk obviously. Ready for a laugh. What would he have been doing there otherwise? It had been the first cold night of the season and every time the door of the hall opened a blast of cold air came in. And one of the blasts had blown in Robert, red-faced, laughing, with a couple of his mates. Big and beautiful like a huge Norse god. The old people hadn't liked it. She could hear them tutting about the state he was in, and what a shame it was letting his father down like that. But what could you expect, they said, the way his mother carried on.

She'd watched from her hard wooden chair, tilting it back to rest against the wall. Her parents were dancing, her mother enjoying herself despite all the moaning that had gone on beforehand, looking OK actually for her age. She was a good dancer, light on her feet, although she had a square, solid frame. A bar had been laid out at the end of the hall and that was where Robert ended up. Sally hadn't been drinking, though she'd been tempted to sneak one when her parents weren't looking. Her father looked over her mother's shoulder and smiled at her. Sally thought he seemed happy. She wished she understood him better and could tell what he was thinking. She smiled back briefly, but it was Robert she had her eyes on.

That was when he moved away from the bar, launched himself off from it and came across the floor to Sally. He leaned against the wall beside her. Despite the draughts from the door she felt suddenly very warm, sweating even.

'Do you want to dance?' And he'd reached down and taken her hand and pulled her to her feet, just as one of the fiddlers called folks up for an eightsome reel. She still remembered the feel of his hand, strong against her back, guiding her through the steps, though she knew the dance as well as he did. And seeing him so close, the heavy shoulders and the twist of muscle in his arms, his legs flexed slightly as if he were balancing on the deck of a ship, she'd thought he was what a man should look like, not like the skinny boys in the house room at school or the flabby teachers. Later, when her parents were caught up in a dance of their own, Robert had pulled her outside, and he'd kissed her, holding her buttocks and pressing her into him. She hadn't been able to enjoy it properly because she was worried that her mother would appear at the door and see her, and as the music slowed she'd hurried away inside, rubbing her lips with the back of her hand.

Since then Sally had dreamed of him. After a bad day at school it had only been the thoughts of him which kept her sane. And now the dreams returned. It didn't matter that in the pub she'd had doubts about him; she needed the fantasies more than ever. She arrived home at exactly the time she would have done if she'd caught the bus, drank tea with her mother as she did every afternoon. Then, when her mother marked primary six's arithmetic, she sat in her bedroom, pretending she was doing homework, and dreamed about Robert.

When she went through into the kitchen her father was home from work. He'd taken off his boots and stood just inside the door in his stockinged feet. Her mother was in the same room, but they weren't talking or even looking at each other. Perhaps they'd been arguing and had stopped when they heard her coming from her room, although that was unlikely. Sally had never heard them raise voices to each other. Usually her mother did as she pleased, but if Alex was insistent Margaret gave in quickly. She knew there was no point in putting up a fight. In matters which meant a lot to him he was stubborn, immovable as rock.

What meant most to him was his work. That was what Margaret said occasionally, muttering it under her breath like a defiant schoolgirl, not quite brave enough to say it out loud. Sally had heard her though. Perhaps Margaret had meant herself to be heard. Anyway, she sensed Alex's work as a presence, forcing her parents apart, like the experiment they'd done in physics in the first year, when the magnets couldn't come together no matter how hard you pushed them.

Now, Sally's mother was doing her best to be pleasant.

'Good day?' she asked, speaking to Alex, not to Sally. Sally had already had the questions about her day at school.

'All right,' he said. 'There's been some oil found on

a beach near Haraldswick. Some skipper washing out his hold. You'd think by now they'd know . . .'

'This time of year, there's not much harm it can do. By the spring when the birds come back to nest, it'll all have gone.' Margaret couldn't help herself. She thought he overreacted where his work was concerned. All those seabirds. Did it really matter if one or two were lost?

'That's hardly the point.' He scowled, shook himself out of his jacket, hung it on the hook in the porch. Sally wondered sometimes why he'd married at all. Without Margaret he'd be able to work all the time, glued to the computer in winter, out on the islands when the light days came.

She supposed they loved each other, or had done once. She didn't think they'd have sex now of course. At their age you wouldn't expect it. They probably hadn't done it since she was born. But she thought her father probably missed it. She saw the way he looked at women. Younger women. And sometimes he touched Margaret, slid his hand over her body, and Sally thought there was something desperate in the gesture. Desperate and a bit pathetic.

Her mother had cooked a chicken for tea, a treat midweek. 'Something to cheer us up a bit,' she'd said when Sally came in. Sally had smelled it cooking when she was in her bedroom, had been looking forward to it, but now she was sitting at the table she couldn't face it. Usually her mother would have made a fuss, spoken about good food going to waste, but today she just seemed concerned. Sally excused herself from the table and left her parents there, eating in silence.

Chapter Twenty

Jimmy Perez knew he should go back to the narrow house by the sea wall and speak to his mother on the phone. When Sarah had left, all that he'd wanted was to scuttle back to Fair Isle where he'd always been safe. The promotion in Shetland had been the next best thing, but he'd told himself he was just waiting until a croft became vacant at home. It was typical that now he was being offered what he'd dreamed of he couldn't make a decision. The drama of the investigation was confusing him. He couldn't see straight any more.

As he approached Fran Hunter's house on the way to Ravenswick, Robert Isbister's van was coming up the hill. The van had to stop at the junction and Perez saw the personalized number plate, caught a glimpse of Robert's mane of hair in his headlights. Everyone knew Robert. What had he been doing there? Where had he been visiting? Hillhead? Euan Ross's place? The school? Could he be the friend Scott had talked about? But Catherine, surely, would have better taste than to knock about with him. He was good-looking enough if you liked the macho, Viking type, but he thought Catherine would want more than that.

There was a light on in Fran's house. Perez didn't stop, though he had a fantasy about what it would be like inside. Very warm. The mother and the little girl curled up together in the big chair which sat by the fire, reading a picture book together. The child would be sweet-smelling after her bath, her hair still damp, the mother relaxed at last, almost asleep. He thought, That's what I want. Then almost immediately after, But would it be enough?

He was still considering this as he drove down the Ravenswick road, and he passed Hillhead without noticing if Magnus was around. Euan's car was parked outside the big house, but there was no sign of life, the enormous windows were blank and uncovered. When he rang the bell at first there was no response. He thought some acquaintances must have come to collect the teacher, to take him away from all the memories of his daughter. He must, after all, have some friends at the school.

Then a light appeared at the back of the house – Perez saw it through the glass as a wedge through an open door – and there were footsteps, slow, old footsteps. Then the front door opened.

'I'm sorry to disturb you,' Perez said. 'Could I have a word?'

Euan stood for a moment, blinking as if he didn't recognize the inspector, or as if he'd just woken and wasn't quite sure where he was. Then he made an effort to pull himself together and when he spoke he was as courteous as always.

'Come in,' he said. 'I'm sorry to have kept you waiting.'

'Did I wake you?'

'Not exactly. I find it difficult to sleep. A sort of daydream, perhaps, reliving old times, trying to capture something of her, while there's still a flavour of her in the house. It's real, you know. A perfume. The shampoo she used, I think. Something else I can't pin down. I know it won't last for long.' He turned and led the way into the house. Perez followed.

They ended up in the kitchen, though this wasn't where Euan had been sitting. He switched on lights, filled the kettle, made an effort to pull himself back to the present. 'Are you all right in here?'

The kitchen was a workplace, modern, lots of stainless steel and marble. There wouldn't be many memories of Catherine here, little for Perez to contaminate with his questions.

'Of course.' Without waiting to be asked, Perez sat on one of the tall chrome stools by a workbench.

'Coffee?'

'Please.'

'Have you come with information,' Euan asked. 'Or questions?'

'Questions, mostly. We won't have any details from the post mortem until tomorrow.'

'I'm glad she's going south on the ferry,' Euan said. 'She loved the boat and never really enjoyed flying.' He looked up. 'What a foolish thing to say.'

'I don't think so. I prefer the ferry too, going to sleep in one place, waking up somewhere different. It makes you realize how far away from anything we are.'

'I thought she'd be safe here. I did think it was different.' He turned away sharply to make coffee. 'Now, what questions do you have?'

'The officer who searched her room found a handbag, but we've still not found Catherine's house keys. Was it usual for her to go out without them?'

'I'm not sure. I always lock the house. Habit, I suppose. Perhaps she was more careless about it.'

'I've been at school all day, talking to the staff and the students. I spoke to a boy called Jonathan Gale. He gave Catherine a lift home on Hogmanay. Do you know him?'

'I don't teach him, but I know of him. A bright English lad. He's been to the house once or twice. I always thought he had a soft spot for Catherine. You don't think he killed her?'

'Not at all. Just checking out his story.' He paused. 'Does the name Robert Isbister mean anything to you?'

Euan frowned. 'No, should it? There are Isbisters in school, but no Robert, I think.'

'It's probably nothing,' Perez said. 'He's older than Catherine, but someone she might have bumped into at parties. I saw him drive up the road just now. I wondered if he'd come to visit you.'

'Some colleagues came earlier in the day. They were very kind, brought food, a casserole of some description. I suppose I should eat it sometime. But since then, no, I've had no visitors.'

He still hadn't taken a seat. He'd poured the coffee and was drinking his where he stood. Perez could tell he was desperate to have the house to himself again, before the elusive scent of his daughter faded altogether.

'That's all then,' he said. 'I'll come back tomorrow when we have some news from the pathologist. Do you have any questions for me?'

He wasn't expecting anything. He thought Euan would see him gratefully and quickly to the door. But the teacher paused, his mug in his hand. 'The old man at Hillhead . . .'

'Yes.'

'People are saying that he was responsible. That it wasn't the first time. That he'd killed before . . .'

'There were rumours. He was never charged, let alone convicted.'

'When I first heard it hardly seemed to matter. Catherine's not alive any more. What else is there to care about? But if it's true, it means that Catherine's death could have been avoided.' He looked directly at Perez. Through the spectacles his eyes seemed unnaturally large, staring. 'I would find that unforgivable.'

Then carefully he set down his mug and showed Perez to the door.

Perez was sitting in his car, thinking about that, when his phone rang. It was Sandy Wilson from the Incident Room. 'We've had a call from Fran Hunter, that wife who found the body.' *Wife? When does a woman stop being a girl and become a wife?*

'What did she have to say?'

'I don't know. She wouldn't talk to the chap from Inverness who was manning the phone. She'll only speak to you.'

Perez ignored the snigger in Sandy's voice. It was automatic, meant nothing. 'When did she ring?'

'Ten minutes ago. She said she'd be in all evening.'

'I'm in Ravenswick now. I'll call on my way home.'

He knocked quietly because he thought Cassie might be in bed, but she was still up, just as he'd imagined in dressing gown and slippers, sitting at the table. She was drinking hot chocolate and there was a mushroom-coloured moustache on her upper lip. Fran had looked out of the window before opening the door to him. All over Shetland people would be doing that. Here more than anywhere, he thought, that poem by John Donne they'd had to read in school, was true. One person's death affected them all, made then see the world differently. And perhaps that wasn't a bad thing. Why should they be protected? What made them special?

'I wasn't expecting you just yet,' Fran said. 'I hope you didn't rush over here on a wild goose chase. It's probably not important . . . Look, can you wait just a minute, while I sort Cassie out?'

He sat in the big chair, where he'd imagined her sitting. She brought him a glass of red wine, which he knew he should refuse, but didn't, and a slice of cheese and spinach flan. 'I don't suppose you've had a chance to eat,' she said, not making a big deal of it.

He heard the two of them chatting, in the bathroom, and singing a silly rhyme about a fox in a box, then the murmured words of a story, which were too soft for him to make out.

'Sorry about that.' Suddenly she was behind him and she'd poured her own glass of wine. He realized he'd probably dozed off.

'You wanted to talk to me.'

He stood to give up the chair, but she shook her head and sat on the floor, looking into the fire, so he couldn't see her face.

'It's probably nothing. You probably already have the information.'

'Tell me anyway.'

'Cassie stayed with her father last night. I went to collect her this afternoon.' She hesitated. 'I know where Catherine was the night before I saw her get off the bus with Magnus Tait. Duncan told me.'

'He hasn't been in touch,' Perez said, non-committally, 'not as far as I know.'

'He wouldn't. He'd see it as an inconvenience. Having to go into Lerwick, maybe make a statement. That's what he's like. Always busy. Always hustling.'

'We've only put out a general request for information so far,' Perez said. 'There'll be a big press conference tomorrow. Everything takes much longer to organize than people realize.'

'She was at a party at the Haa. One of Duncan's open houses. Half of Shetland will have been there. You'll be able to confirm it.'

Perez had been to Duncan's parties. They were legendary. No invitations, nothing formal ever. Word would get out. *A do at the Haa tonight*. The parties never got going until late. When the bars started to think about closing, then you'd get a taxi, or a friend not quite as pissed as everyone else, and drive up the island. You never knew who you were going to see there. Often musicians. Duncan liked to encourage local talent. That was how he described it, though Perez was never sure what the kids with their fiddles and guitars got out of the event beside a hangover and a sense that they'd brushed against celebrity. Because occasionally you'd bump into a minor star as you passed round Duncan's bottle of Highland Park. An actor on holiday, or a politician up for some conference, a small time director or producer only the arty set had ever heard of. Duncan liked to encourage the arty set. And sophistication. Perhaps that's what the kids felt they got out of it. The guests dressed differently, talked about different things. It wasn't like going to a dance in the village hall.

'Did Duncan say who she was with?'

'He didn't seem to know. I think he was even more out of it than usual. He'd had a row with Celia.'

Celia Isbister. Robert's mother. That was the way things worked in Shetland. It wasn't necessarily significant. People were related in complicated and intimate ways. Coincidence couldn't be allowed to appear sinister.

'Do you know if Robert was there?'

'I don't know. Duncan didn't say. Quite often he was.' Her voice was dry, slightly hostile.

'You don't like him.'

'He's a spoilt rich kid. Hardly his fault, I suppose.'

'Not a kid any longer.'

'Shame he still acts like one.' She turned round, brushing Perez's knee with her shoulder. 'Look, take no notice. I hardly have an unbiased view of that family. His mother wrecked my marriage. At least, Duncan wrecked it. She was complicit. Only it seems she's had enough. She's walked out too. Gone back to Michael full-time. Convenient, just before Up Helly Aa. She'll be there to support him in front of the cameras. Everyone will say what a lovely family they are. Duncan's on his own again. Poor, lonely Duncan.'

For the first time he thought she must have started drinking before he'd got there.

'Did Catherine ever mention knowing him?'

'Robert? No.'

'And Duncan?'

'No, but then she wouldn't, would she? She must have known he was my ex. Even new to the place, she'd have picked up that bit of gossip. And you can't imagine Duncan would have had a fling with Catherine? She was only a child.'

But as she spoke he saw that she was considering the possibility and not dismissing it out of hand. Perhaps she'd considered it before.

'Can you tell me anything else about the party? Did Duncan mention any of the other guests?'

'No. But I had the impression he was in such a state about Celia, that Posh and Becks could have wandered in and he'd not have taken any notice. Not like him at all.'

Perez stood up reluctantly. Different circumstances and he'd have stayed to share the rest of the bottle with her, suggested that they might go out sometime. The film club. She was an arty woman. It might be the sort of thing she'd like. By the end of the week, knowing him, he'd probably have told her he loved her. It was probably just as well that she was involved in a murder case and he couldn't even kiss her on the cheek as he walked out.

Chapter Twenty-One

Magnus sat upright in his chair and listened. He couldn't see outside the house. That was his own doing. During the day there had been people looking in and by the afternoon he hadn't been able to bear it. The first caller had been a young policeman asking for his boots.

'What boots?'

He hadn't understood. Was it a trick to stop him going out?

'The boots you were wearing when you saw the girl,' the man said. 'You told Inspector Perez you crossed the field and saw her.'

'Aye.'

'We need them. To compare with the footprints we found.'

Still Magnus didn't really understand, but he'd pointed to the boots, which were standing on a piece of sacking in the porch. The policeman had stooped, lifted them into a plastic bag and carried them away.

Soon after there'd been another sharp knock. Magnus had opened the door, expecting more police, but it had been a woman from a newspaper with a notebook, talking so quick – clack, clack, clack – that he couldn't make out what she was saying. She'd scared him with her squawking voice, her pointed nose pushing into his face, the pen she poked towards his chest. After that he didn't answer to their banging. He sat at the table pretending to read an old magazine which had been lying around since his mother had died. Why had he kept it? He thought once there had been a reason, but he couldn't remember now.

They'd seen him through the window, peering at an angle to make him out and rapping on the glass to catch his attention, scaring the raven in its cage. That was when he acted. He flattened out a couple of boxes and nailed the cardboard over the window. Now nobody could see in, but he couldn't see out and that made him feel like a prisoner already. He couldn't tell what the weather was doing, or if the coastguard team had finished walking over the hill. It must be dark. He could tell that from the time on his mother's clock.

In his head there were still people waiting for him outside the house, waiting to shout filth and push their faces right against the glass and their shoulders to the door. He hadn't heard anyone outside for some time, but they could be there, silent, waiting to surprise him, like the monsters in a nightmare he'd had as a boy.

After Agnes died, the nightmares became worse.

In his dreams he'd seen her, pale and thin as she'd been when the whooping cough turned to pneumonia and they finally took her to the hospital. Spitting out blood when she coughed. Arms and legs white and bony so they reminded him of a sheep's bones, when the carcass has been left out in the weather and picked over by animals and birds. But in his dreams she was still at Hillhead, doing the things she always did, helping his mother with the cooking – peeling tatties or baking, milking the cow that they'd had then in the byre by the house, squatting beside the animal, pulling and squeezing the teats, murmuring a little song to herself as she worked. And all the time getting thinner, so at the end of the dream, just before he woke up sweating, all that was left of her was her smile caked in blood and her slanting grey eyes.

Now, sitting in his mother's chair, watching the hands of her clock, those nightmares returned. The people he imagined waiting outside weren't strangers. He had a vision of his sister, banging on the window, rattling the door, surprised that it was locked.

He stood up and poured himself a tumbler of whisky. His hands were shaking. He was going daft, sitting here. Anyone would be the same, locked in a room with no view out, just waiting for the police to take him. He shook his head to clear it of the foolishness, and tried to remember Agnes as she was when she was well. He'd always been ungainly and slow, but she was dainty as a bird, flying across the fields on the short cut to school, her hair streaming behind her. 'Look at your sister,' his mother would say, trying to shame him. 'She's younger than you and she doesn't break everything she touches. She's not a big, clumsy fool. Why can't you be more like her?'

He pictured her in the schoolyard skipping. Two other girls were holding the ends of a long rope and Agnes had been jumping, not chanting the rhyme, but frowning in concentration, counting the steps in her head. He'd watched, proud of her, so proud that the grin had spread across his face and had stayed there all day. She'd been wearing a cotton print dress, faded from too much washing and so short now that when she jumped you could almost see her knickers.

Had Catriona been one for skipping? It bothered him that he couldn't be certain. He'd seen her sometimes in the schoolyard, when he'd found reason to walk down to the shore, to pull out a useful piece of driftwood, some netting or a barrel. Mostly she'd been standing, surrounded by two or three of her chums, chatting and giggling. Those had been different times, he thought. It wasn't like when he and Agnes were children. When Catriona was growing up, she had television in the house and there'd been catalogues to buy modern clothes from. There'd been more to play with than an old piece of rope. The oil had come to the islands and there'd been money for computers and fancy games and the teachers had taken the children on trips south. Once there'd been a school trip to Edinburgh. A couple of the mothers had gone, all dressed up for the adventure, and Mrs Henry, the teacher, standing there with her sheet of paper when the bus came to take them to the airport, ticking them all off, though surely she must know them all. Catriona had loved the city. She'd talked about it for days when she got home. She came up to Hillhead specially to tell Mary Tait about it and he'd broken off from his work to listen. He'd never left Shetland and asked so many questions – about the buses and the big shops and what like it was to travel on a train – that Catriona had laughed at him and said one day he should go to Edinburgh. It was only an hour on the plane.

The next time she'd come to Hillhead was the day she disappeared. It had been dreadful weather, an awful wind for the season, not cold, but fierce, blowing from the south west. And her mother had sent her out and she'd been bored, so she'd landed up here, teasing and tormenting, wicked as if the wind had got inside her and made her flighty and wild.

But he didn't want to think of that day. He didn't want to think of the peat bank and the pile of rock on the hill. It would bring the nightmares back.

Chapter Twenty-Two

Roy Taylor had called the meeting for mid-morning, not first light. He'd hoped to have some feedback from the pathologist by then, though he knew he was pushing it and now it was ten-thirty and he was still waiting. He'd asked Billy Morton to ring him from Aberdeen as soon as he had anything useful to report. They had the crime scene investigator's report at least. Nothing back from the lab yet. That took bloody days, even fast-tracked.

Jimmy Perez sat quietly on a desk at the back of the room, listening to Taylor explaining about the delay and how frustrated he was by it. You had to listen carefully because of the unfamiliar Scouse accent, the strange, mangled vowels. The inspector had grabbed their attention from the beginning. He had the stage presence of a fine actor or a stand-up comedian. He was compulsive viewing. Perez wished he had that sort of presence, the same ability to motivate his team. Outside the weather was milder and there was the beginning of a thaw. In the lulls in conversation Perez thought he could hear the dripping of melted snow. The clouds which had been lurking out to sea all night had rolled inshore and the room was almost as dark as during the last team meeting at day-break.

Taylor was going through the evidence of the crime scene investigator. 'Besides the constable who was first called to the scene there are three sets of footprints,' he said. *Constable*. He was being more polite than most. Perez thought on his home patch Taylor would have a different name for the uniformed men who did the routine work. Here, he was careful not to offend. 'The snow was deep enough to get good impressions and it didn't melt during the day so the crime scene investigator was lucky. She's a bit of an expert on boots and shoes. Apparently.

'One set belonged to Mrs Hunter. Size six welling-ton boots. Of course really there are two tracks in each case – one going into the scene and one coming away. Another, more recent, in places crossing the prints of Mrs Hunter came from Mr Alex Henry, the teacher's husband from Ravenswick. Size nine walking boots. Again, only to be expected. We know that Mrs Hunter waved at him, he crossed the field to join her and he used his mobile to call us. The third set belongs to Magnus Tait. His prints aren't very clear. It's hard to tell how long he was there and what he was up to. That's because the other sets are laid on top of his. He was there before either of the others. Our examiner is quite clear on that.'

Sandy Wilson gave a cheer, punched his fist in the air, then fell silent when everyone else just sat and watched him.

'You think this is a cause for celebration, Sandy?' Taylor asked. The voice deceptively mild, but with an edge of sarcasm which Perez and the Inverness team recognized. He could be polite only for so long.

'Well it means we've got him,' Sandy said. 'Doesn't it?'

'He's already admitted to being at the scene,' Perez said. 'He didn't attempt to hide it. He told me on my first visit. It's in the day log, Sandy. But maybe you've not had a chance to look at it.'

'Well, he would, wouldn't he? He'd know that we'd find his prints and he'd come up with a reason . . .'

'I'm not sure he's capable of that sort of thinking,' Perez said. He wished Sandy would admit defeat, not show himself up in front of the others.

'Besides,' Taylor said, 'if he killed Catherine, how did she get there, Sandy? There are none of her prints. Tell me, did she fly? Did those bastard birds pick her up in their talons and carry her?'

'Maybe Tait did.'

'Catherine was a tall young woman. He's an old man. Strong once, perhaps, and still used to some physical work, but I don't reckon he'd have been able to hoist her over two fields without putting her down for a breather. Even if she was already dead.'

'Then how did she get there?'

The question was directed to Taylor, but the inspector from Inverness only looked at Sandy for a long time in silence. 'Tell him, Jimmy,' he said at last. 'You've worked it out, haven't you?' Perhaps he didn't feel he could explain to Sandy without really losing it, saying something he'd regret later.

'She walked,' Perez said. 'She walked in with whoever killed her. Then it snowed and her footprints were covered up. There was a heavy squall at about midnight. I phoned Dave Wheeler the meteorologist on Fair Isle. There was snow on part of the body, though according to the crime scene investigator it had been stroked carefully away from her face and upper torso. That's why Fran Hunter could see her from the road.'

'So Tait could still be the murderer? No reason why not. He could have gone back later, early the next morning. He could have swept the snow from her face.'

'He could be the murderer,' Taylor said, interrupting, finding it impossible now to restrain himself. 'Of course he could. Still most likely prime suspect. But let's picture the scene. It's dark. He took the girl into his house for tea early in the afternoon. We know that. He's admitted it and they were seen getting off the bus together. Let's suppose, just for a minute, that he managed to entertain her all afternoon. How did he persuade her to go out on to the hill with him in the pitch black? She was an intelligent young woman. Brought up in the big city. Not naïve. Streetwise. Even if she hadn't heard the rumours about him and Catriona Bruce, do you think she'd just wander off into the night with him? That's what the defence lawyers will say. And it worries me too.'

Taylor turned quickly, so he had his back to Sandy, as if he wasn't worth further attention. 'Jimmy, what do you think?'

'I don't think she was the sort to be easily scared. And here, in Shetland, there's a sense of security isn't there? Bad things don't happen here. Not the sort of things that happen elsewhere. We let our kids wander round on their own. We might worry about them getting a bit close to the cliffs, but we don't worry about them getting abducted by perverts.' *Except now. Now we're just like everywhere else. All over the islands children are being kept indoors and being told to beware of strange old men.* 'So I think she might have gone with him. If she thought he had something interesting to show her. Or for a challenge or a dare. A story to entertain her friends with the next day.' He paused. 'But she wouldn't just have stood there and let him strangle her. She'd have fought him back. And there's no sign of that. No scratch marks on his hands or his face. They'll take a sample from under her fingernails. Perhaps we'll know more then.'

'So how do you see it, Jimmy?' Taylor asked. 'Set the scene for me. Tell me what you think happened?'

'I think she walked out there with someone she knew and was comfortable with. Someone she'd stand close to, arm in arm maybe, to keep out the cold. When the attack came it was without warning. The scarf she was wearing pulled hard around her neck. She'd still try to fight, but perhaps it was so sudden that she didn't stand a chance. Either that or someone with sufficient strength to catch her off guard.'

'You're thinking a boyfriend then?'

'Aye perhaps. Probably. But not necessarily.'

'Fill us in on the wannabe boyfriend you've tracked down, the lad who gave them the lift back New Year's Eve.'

'Jonathan Gale. Family's English, moved to Quendale not very long ago. He's a year older than Catherine. At the high school too. He came to see me while I was there. Father's a travel writer. Anyway, they were both outsiders so you'd expect them to get on. And he'd certainly fallen for her. Big style. I could tell, though he wasn't saying a lot. Apparently she didn't reciprocate. According to Sally Henry, Catherine hardly spoke to him in the car back from Lerwick. And Euan said she didn't seem interested. But Gale couldn't have killed her. Not according to his parents. He was with them all evening on the 4th. They watched a video.'

'Until midnight?'

'No, but they claim he couldn't have driven away from the house without them hearing.' He wanted to say he'd talked to the lad and liked him, but didn't think Taylor would be impressed by that. Instead he went on, 'It wouldn't have had to be a boyfriend. It could have been anyone she'd not be scared of.'

'Her father?'

'I suppose he'd fit the bill. But wasn't he in Lerwick all evening? And what would be the motive?'

'God knows. But we've checked with his colleagues and he was a bit out with his timings. It wasn't as late as he said in his statement when he left town. It isn't necessarily suspicious, but he could have killed the daughter before the snow set in.' Taylor began his habitual pacing. Perez wondered irritably if they couldn't give him something to slow him down. Valium? Or those little cannabis cookies Sarah used to make when she was at college? What did she call them? Hash brownies.

'I know where Catherine was the night before she fetched up on the bus with Magnus Tait. That might help.'

Taylor stopped abruptly.

'For God's sake man, why didn't you say so before? Where?'

Perez was tempted to say that he hadn't been able to get a word in, but let it go. 'At the Haa. One of Duncan Hunter's parties.'

There was a mutter of recognition, almost of amusement, from the Shetlanders. Taylor, though, was not amused. 'Is this supposed to mean something to me?'

'Duncan's a sort of local playboy. Businessman. Entrepreneur. He throws famous parties. We've all been to them at one time or another. Though few of us can remember much of what went on.'

'Isn't the woman who found the body called Hunter?'

'Duncan's her ex-husband.'

'Any significance there?'

'Only in the fact that it was she who told me the girl was at the Haa that night. Duncan wasn't going to bother letting us know.'

'Hard to keep it quiet, I'd have thought.' Taylor was scowling, trying to make sense of it. Perez thought he was like an anthropologist, coming to terms with some remote tribe's rituals and mores. 'I mean I take it she wasn't the only person there. We'd have got to hear of it as soon as we put out a request for information at the news conference.'

'I don't think we need assume Duncan was trying to keep it quiet,' Perez said. 'He's the sort who thinks rules are for other people. Like I said, he just couldn't be arsed to pick up the phone.'

'An arrogant bastard?'

'Aye, something like that.'

'Should one of us go to speak to him?' *One of us.*

One of the outsiders. The team spirit hadn't survived long.

'Let me speak to him first,' Perez said. 'If I think he's messing me about one of you can have a shot.'

They sat for a moment in silence. Even Taylor's thinking was showy, energetic. Looking at him, frowning, you could imagine the synapses jumping and fizzing. A phone rang. Sandy answered it.

'Boss?' Diffident now, though he still wasn't entirely sure what he'd done wrong. 'Professor Morton from Aberdeen.'

The inspector took the call in his office and while they were waiting there was an edgy silence. Perez wandered over to the window and looked out at the town. The straight lines of the grey houses were blurred by the rain which was coming down now in hard straight lines. When Taylor returned he was carrying an A4 writing pad. He'd made notes, very detailed, Perez saw, the writing small and cramped.

'Caroline Ross *was* strangled,' he said. 'Not manually, but with the scarf we found with her. Just as we thought. No sign of struggle. Time of death? Not very helpful. Between six pm and midnight the night of the 4th. She'd had quite a bit to drink soon before she died. Very little to eat. Almost certainly she was killed where she was found.' He looked towards Sandy. 'And if a scientist says *almost certain* that means 110 per cent definite. Otherwise she was a healthy and fit young woman.' He paused. 'Any questions?'

'Any trace of recent sexual activity?' Perez asked the question before Sandy could find another, less delicate way of phrasing it.

'No,' Taylor said. 'Nothing like that.' He paused again. 'She was a virgin.'

The two of them met up together after the rest of the team had dispersed. Taylor's idea. 'Anywhere we can get a decent coffee in this place?' Perez had taken him to the Peerie Café in the narrow lane up from the harbour. Downstairs was full with middle-aged women in anoraks taking a break from shopping and the weather. A couple of young mums were deep in conversation in a corner. One of them was discreetly breastfeeding. The child's head almost hidden by a baggy sweater and Perez wondered how it could breathe. Upstairs they found a table. There was so much background noise that no way could they be overheard.

'So,' Taylor said. 'What do you think? I mean, I'd always assumed that if Tait was involved the motive would be sexual. But there was nothing.'

'Doesn't mean he didn't kill her.'

'Perhaps he liked them innocent,' Taylor said. 'We thought Catriona and Catherine had nothing in common, but there was that. Both untouched.'

'You wouldn't know, though, to look at Catherine.'

'First names both starting with C,' Taylor was getting into his stride. 'Both living in the same house. That's some coincidence.'

'Maybe,' Perez said. 'Still doesn't mean it was Tait.'

'What's he like, this Duncan Hunter?'

Perez shrugged. 'I can't stand the man. Doesn't mean he gets his kicks killing lasses.'

'Would he have been around when Catriona Bruce disappeared?'

'He's always been around. Big fish in a little pond. His ego'd not survive in the big world outside.'

Taylor's smile was mocking. 'So, what's he done to you?'

'We were at school together. Big mates at one time.'

'And then?'

Perez shrugged again. 'I'd best go to see him. See what he's got to say about Catherine.'

'Do you want me to do it?'

'No. He'll say nothing to you.'

Taylor looked slightly wistful. It was like a recent non-smoker taking in the fumes. He liked being senior investigating officer, but he missed being out there talking to people, getting a feel for the case. 'Come and see me when you get back,' he said. 'Let me know how you got on.'

Perez nodded, eased himself from the chair and out into the street.

Chapter Twenty-Three

At the time Perez thought Duncan had saved his life. That was what it felt like. He was thirteen. It was September, the start of a new school year, and it was like having to get used to Anderson High all over again. Classes, and living in the hostel, and only being able to talk to his family on the phone. After a summer of being on the Isle, helping his dad with the sheep and the boat, it was like being in prison. Worst of all was being back with the two Foula lads who'd made his life a misery during the first year and who hadn't forgotten what fun that was over the holidays. During the week it wasn't so bad. There were other kids who boarded weekly, there was a bit of a buzz about the place. More staff on duty. Weekends were a nightmare. Other kids looked forward to the weekends. Jimmy Perez hated them. He anticipated them with dread. He imagined himself at the wheel of a small boat and a huge wave rising up on the horizon and bearing down towards him. Inevitable. Unavoidable. And when Friday night did arrive he counted off the minutes until it was Monday morning, doing the schoolboy sums in his head, working out the percentage of misery time passed and the nightmare still to come.

Then Duncan Hunter took a liking to him. How

had that happened? Was there one moment of recognition, the realization that they might be friends? Perez couldn't remember. He had one image in his head. A breezy, sunny day. The water in the harbour whipped against the tide into tight little waves. He and Duncan would have been nearly fourteen and there'd been a joke. Perez couldn't remember which of them had told it, but he remembered the pair of them laughing. Duncan had been laughing so hard he'd had to put his arm around Perez's shoulder to stop himself falling over. Perez had tipped back his head and it seemed the sky was wheeling around him, because the clouds were blown so fast. And when he'd straightened up, spent and dizzy, there were the two Foula boys, sullen and resentful, because he had a friend, an ally and they'd have to find someone else to torment.

Then Perez started looking forward to weekends too. On Friday nights he'd go with Duncan in the bus to North Mainland and they'd walk together down the long drive to the Haa. When he'd first seen the house he couldn't take it all in. It was bigger than anything he'd ever seen. 'Which part do you live in?' he asked. Duncan didn't quite understand. 'The rooms near to the shore are so damp. We don't use those much. And there's no staff. Not really. So no one sleeps right at the top.' And in those days, at the peak of the oil rush, Duncan's father was too busy or too dazed by the possibilities or too cautious to spend much on the house, and it was still very dark and primitive. Often the generator didn't work and there was no power. Then they ate supper by candlelight at the long table in the dining room. Perez first got drunk in the Haa and touched a girl's breasts for the first time. That was when

Duncan's parents were away in Aberdeen. To celebrate having the place to themselves, they held a party, Duncan's first party. It was mid-summer and light nearly till dawn. Perez took the girl on to the beach. She was called Alice, an English girl on holiday. They sat watching the sun not quite set, leaning against the whitewashed wall around the house and Perez slipped his hand under her shirt. She let him stroke her for a few minutes, then pushed him away with a laugh.

Once he asked Duncan, 'Don't your parents mind me being here every weekend?'

Duncan had seemed surprised by the idea. 'No, why should they? They know I like it.'

Perhaps that was the first time Perez had been aware of the gulf between them. Whatever Duncan liked, he got. He considered it his right. The gap was more noticeable when Duncan spent a few days with him on Fair Isle. There was nothing you could put your finger on. Duncan was charming, polite to his parents. There was a dance at the hall and he joined in, swirling the middle-aged women off their feet, so they giggled and said he was a rascal and should come back another time. But occasionally Perez saw that he was bored. Some of the comments were patronizing. He knew the whole of the family, himself included, were relieved when they waved Duncan off on Loganair.

And now? Now, as he'd told Roy Taylor, he couldn't stand Duncan Hunter. He hated the fake shows of friendship when they met, the remembered incidents from their childhood which were always discussed, because in the present they had nothing in common to talk about. That wasn't the only reason for the dislike.

There was something more concrete too. Blackmail. But that was never discussed.

He knocked at the front door of the Haa, not expecting to find Duncan in. These days Duncan spent as much time in Edinburgh as he did in Shetland. Perhaps Celia would be back. Duncan had a way with women. Most of them returned in the end. Perez hoped it would be Celia who opened the door. He'd always liked her and she could fill him in on Catherine Ross and what the girl had been doing there. He wouldn't have to go through that business of pretending to be old mates before he found out anything useful.

He thought at first that the place was empty and he'd have to come back. The blanket of cloud seemed to hold in the smell of salt and rotting seaweed from the beach. The rain was heavier than ever and standing at the front of the house, banging on the door, he got soaked. Water spilled from the gutter and splashed out of the drain. Then there was another sound. The slap of slippers against the flag floor. The turn of a key in a lock. Duncan stood there. Hangover personified. Unshaven, sour-smelling, blinking against the light. 'For Christ's sake man. What do you want?'

At least, Perez thought, he was spared the usual male hug and reference to the old days.

'It's business,' he said quietly. 'Police business. Can I come in?'

Duncan didn't answer. He turned and shuffled back towards the kitchen. By the range there was an Orkney chair, with the high, hooded wicker back to keep out draughts. Perez remembered it had always been there. Duncan sank back into it. Perez thought he'd probably spent all night there, once the bottle of Highland Park by his feet was empty. The policeman filled a kettle and moved it on to the hotplate. 'Tea or coffee?'

Duncan slowly opened his eyes. He gave the smile that made Perez want to hit him. 'Good old James,' he said. 'Always there to save the day.'

'This is murder. Nothing I can do to make that go away.'

It was as if Duncan hadn't heard him. 'Tea,' he said. 'A good strong cup of tea.'

The kitchen looked as if half a dozen students had been camping out in it for a term. Duncan saw Perez looking at the mess. 'You can't get the staff these days,' he said.

'No Celia?'

'She left.' The smile and the flippancy disappeared. 'I thought she was besotted.'

'So did I.'

The kettle boiled. The tea bags were where they'd always been. Perez rinsed two mugs. There was just enough milk in the fridge.

'Catherine Ross,' he said. 'How well did you know her?'

'I didn't.'

'But she was here, at your party, the night before she was killed.'

'You've been speaking to Fran.'

'Mrs Hunter found the body.'

Duncan finished the tea, then got out of his seat and poured himself a pint of water. He stood, leaning against the draining board for support.

'I should have made it work with Fran,' he said. 'I

really loved her, you know. There was no reason why it shouldn't have.'

'Only Celia.'

'Well, Celia. That was different. No question of me marrying her. She would never have left Michael. Appearances count here. You know that. Really there was no competition. I'd *married* Fran, hadn't I? We had a child. Anyway, now I've lost Celia too.'

Perez allowed himself to be distracted. 'What happened there? I thought you had that worked out. A relationship of convenience on both sides.'

'So did I. But recently she's been a bit possessive. Insecure. Her age, maybe. She suddenly started getting heavy about other women. A pain in the arse, actually.'

He took a mouthful of water, stared gloomily outside. The rain splashed against the window.

'But you didn't ask her to leave. She left you. Why?'

'Honestly? I'm not sure. It was all very sudden. It happened the night the girl was here for the party. I wasn't doing anything I hadn't done dozens of times before. Chatting. Flirting, maybe. Harmless stuff. We were in the middle of a conversation. Nothing heavy. Her saying *You know you're too old for this. Why don't you get rid of them? Let's have the house to ourselves.* Stuff she'd said a hundred times before. And I promised like I always did. *This is the last time. The last Haa party. You're right. I should be thinking of settling down.* Then she said she was leaving and wouldn't be coming back. She didn't make a big scene. That's not her style. Dignified. Celia's always been dignified. She packed a bag and then I heard her car. I knew she meant it. I knew I'd really blown it.'

'Did anything happen while you were talking to make her leave suddenly?' *Was this relevant? Why was he so interested after all? Because he was taking a delicious pleasure in Duncan's misery. It served the man right.*

Duncan shook his head. He'd closed his eyes again for a moment as if a wave of pain from the hangover was hitting him. Then he opened them.

'She had a text message. She read it while I was still talking, then announced that she was leaving.' He looked across at Perez, suddenly horrified. 'Do you think it could have been from another man? That she had a lover all the time she was with me?'

'Did she often get text messages?'

'Only from her son. Robert can't wipe his bum without clearing it with her first.'

'Wasn't Robert there that night?'

'I think he was earlier. Not when Celia ran off. He hates my guts but he still comes to my parties.'

'Did he arrive with the girl who died?'

'Hey man, you know what it's like at my parties. The door's open and people wander in.'

'You told Fran you let Catherine stay because Celia knew her.'

'Did I? I'd have let her stay whatever. She was bloody gorgeous.'

'You did talk to her then?'

'Yes, I talked to her.'

'Before Celia left or after?'

'Both probably. Yes, both.'

'Was she with anyone? I mean a boyfriend.'

'No.'

'Did you ask her?'

'Maybe. But you notice, don't you? There's an attractive young woman, you look to see if she's with anyone.'

'She wasn't with Robert?'

'Not in that way. I mean, I think I saw them talking when she first got here. Anyway, please! Robert Isbister! This was a beautiful girl with a brain. What would she be doing talking to Robbie? I mean all he wants in the world is to be as famous as his father.'

What would she be doing talking to you?

'You did speak to her though. What about?'

'Film. I told Fran that. She was a film freak. She even had a camcorder with her. She showed me how it worked.'

'She was filming the party?'

'I don't know. Maybe. She was talking about the film club. Why was it that all they had were block-busters? Why couldn't we get some European stuff occasionally? She said that was the one thing she missed about living in Shetland. A good art-house cinema. She was pretentious, you know, in the way bright kids are, but she didn't take herself too seriously.'

'Did you try it on?'

'Not seriously.'

'What does that mean?'

'She made it clear she wasn't interested. You know me. I don't need to work at it. There are lots of women out there.'

But Perez remembered other conversations with Duncan, the effort he'd put into charming Fran. If he'd been really taken with Catherine, he'd have worked at it.

'How did she seem? I mean what sort of mood was she in?'

'She was buzzing, really elated. I told her, whatever you're on, I want some of it.'

'Do you think she *had* been using?'

'No. She was young, that was all. Young and pleased with herself. The way I used to be.'

'Did she stay the night?'

'Apparently. According to Fran she was seen on the bus from town at lunchtime the next day. But she wasn't with me. I was feeling sorry for myself, got maudlin drunk and passed out. It's been happening a lot recently. I only held it together yesterday because Cassie was here.' He paused. 'Did you see her at Fran's? My beautiful Cassie?'

'Yes.'

'I wasn't sure I wanted a child when Fran told me she was expecting. I didn't think I was ready for it. Now I can't imagine life without her. I couldn't bear it if Fran took her away again.'

'Is there any danger of that?'

'I'm not sure. She seems settled enough here, but you can never tell, can you? She'll meet someone else eventually. Now you have to go. I need to shower and change. I'm taking the afternoon flight south. Work.'

Perez stood up. 'When will you be back?'

'Tomorrow evening. You don't need to worry. I'm not planning on running away.'

Before going back to his car and despite the rain, Perez walked round to the back of the house, which faced towards the shore. He stood for a moment, try-ing to find some shelter under the wind-stunted sycamores, and looked down at the beach where he'd sat with Alice. He'd been convinced that he loved her and couldn't understand why she didn't reply to his letters once she got home.

Chapter Twenty-Four

It was Saturday. No school, but no rest. Usually on Saturday Sally went into Lerwick for youth orchestra practice. Her father often gave her a lift and stayed in town to do some work in his office. At least that's what he said. Sally wasn't sure. Saturday was Margaret's day for cleaning and laundry and nobody wanted to be around when she was in the middle of that. This morning Sally woke up feeling light-headed and strange. She'd had a disturbed night. Too much dreaming. Sometimes she worried that was all her life consisted of. Dreams. Nothing in it was real. The family life her mother had created – kirk on Sunday, sitting down to tea together every night, everything placid and ordered and calm – all that was a sham. Sally went along with it for a quiet life. She pretended to be a dutiful daughter, yet there were times when she wished her mother was dead. Even her friendship with Catherine hadn't been what it seemed and it had been a real effort to keep the resentment and jealousy from floating to the surface. Sometimes the effort of all that acting made her feel weird, cut off. Like she was looking down at herself. She'd tried to explain it once to Catherine, who hadn't understood it at all.

At breakfast she still didn't feel like eating. She

could tell her parents were anxious and she quite enjoyed the idea that they were worried about her. It made a change. All that time when the kids at school had been picking on her, she'd tried to explain to them what was going on, but they hadn't really taken it in. 'Take no notice,' her mother had said. 'Sticks and stones.'

'Why don't you give orchestra a miss today?' Margaret was putting the pans to soak in soapy water. Even at the weekends she didn't believe in a leisurely breakfast and the plates were snatched away as soon as you'd finished. 'It's delayed shock, I expect. Maybe we should ask the doctor to take a look at you. Have a day at home.'

But that was the last thing Sally wanted.

'I'll probably feel better if I'm out.'

Her father poured himself a last mug of tea from the pot. 'Why don't you come with me? It's my day for the beached bird survey. Fresh air and a bit of exercise. That might do the trick.'

She couldn't come up with any reason to refuse him. She could tell he really wanted her to go, and like her mother she found it hard to stand up to him. She went into the bedroom and changed into jeans and an old sweater, then stood in the porch to pull on her wellingtons. He was already waiting for her. Margaret came out with a flask and a packet of sandwiches and stood to wave them off. Sally could tell she was eager to have the house to herself. They only made it untidy.

The rain had cleared overnight and it was a little warmer. A false promise of spring. Sitting high up in the front seat of the Land Rover there was a view across the fields to where Catherine had been lying.

One of the pieces of police tape had come loose. The ravens were sky-dancing in the thermals at the top of the cliff.

'What did she look like?' Sally asked.

He knew what she was talking about, but there was a moment's silence while he considered. She thought he was going to tell her not to think about Catherine, that she should put all thought of the murder from her mind. At last he said, 'She looked dead. I'd never seen a dead body before. You think it'll just look like someone sleeping, but it doesn't. You mustn't worry about what happened to her out there. The birds. All the rumours that are flying around. Whatever made her Catherine had gone by then. Long gone.' He paused. 'Do you understand what I mean?'

'Yes, I think so.'

Every month Alex walked a stretch of the coast looking for birds which had been washed up dead. He wasn't the only one. All around the islands there were people walking their own patch, Pete from the RSPB, Paul, Roger, all the volunteers. It was a census, a snapshot of the health of the islands' bird population. He explained this to Sally as he manoeuvred the Land Rover down a narrow track towards a small farm. She listened, glad of the distraction. There was something comforting about her father's obsessions. They were always the same. The house at the end of the track was freshly whitewashed and a line of nappies blew behind it. As they approached a young woman came out and scattered grain to the chickens which pecked around the garden. She waved at Alex before disappearing inside.

'A young couple's just taken it over,' he said.

'Incomers. At least they're living there. It was a holiday let for a few years.' She was surprised that he knew about the new family. She'd thought he didn't notice much about people.

He led her past the house on to a pebble beach. It shelved steeply into the water and there was a line of seaweed, piled up, which marked the high tide. She could smell it from where they were standing. 'We might find a few oiled birds,' he said. 'There was some pollution further north.' He was talking to himself. She scrambled down the beach after him, almost tripping when the shingle shifted underneath her boot. He turned and caught her elbow just in time to stop her falling. His grip was strong and the physical contact shocked her. Even when she was young she couldn't remember him touching her. He'd never been one for giving a cuddle. Once he realized she was firm on her feet he pulled his hand away and walked ahead of her, his head bent to look at the shore. Almost imme-diately he found a long-tailed duck, freshly dead, and held it out, stretching the wing carefully, so she could see the individual feathers.

'It's been oiled,' he said. 'Not badly, but enough to kill it.'

She didn't know what to say. She couldn't pretend to be sad about a dead sea duck. She wandered down to the water, let it wash over her wellingtons, until he'd moved on. She stood looking out over the grey sea, letting her mind go blank.

When she caught up with him he had another corpse in his hand. 'Guillemot,' he said. He turned it over, felt along the bone between its wings. 'There's no fat at all. Precious little muscle.' She expected him to drop it into the black bin bag and continue walking, but he couldn't help explaining about it. About climate change; the melting polar ice, the effect it seemed to be having on plankton and sand-eels. 'The food for seabirds is disappearing,' he said. 'Last summer puffins, red-throated divers, arctic skuas, raised no young at all.'

Sally understood why her mother resented his passion. He cared too much about it. And it was all too big. How could they compete with his concern for the whole planet? Even the brutal murder of a schoolgirl seemed insignificant in comparison. Sally remembered then that Catherine had wanted to interview her father. She'd heard him speak on Radio Shetland and been impressed by him. And she hadn't been impressed by many people. They'd been sitting in the little living room at the back of the Ross house, doing some homework, the radio on in the background, when his voice had suddenly filled the room. Sally had been excited despite herself. *That's my dad.*

She couldn't remember now what he'd been talking about. Overgrazing maybe. That was his party piece. And Catherine had said, 'He's so committed. He really cares about that stuff, doesn't he? Do you think he'd let me interview him?' And she'd sounded as passionate as him. Very alive. It was difficult now to think that had gone.

It seemed as if Alex had read her thoughts. 'You must miss her. The Ross girl.'

Sally remembered how lonely she'd felt, waiting for the school bus. 'Yes,' she said. 'I miss her a lot.'

'I didn't know her. Not really. But she seemed a strange kind of girl.'

'I liked her.'

'You mustn't be scared,' he said. 'I wouldn't let anything bad happen to you.'

It was the first time she'd thought there might be anything to be scared about.

'Did she ever interview you for her project?' Sally asked. She'd have expected Catherine to tell her if she had, but with Catherine you never knew. She had her own secrets.

He frowned. 'What project would that be?'

'Something we were doing for school. About Shetland. Her impression of it as an outsider, I think. She wanted to talk to you about your work.'

'No,' he said. 'She never did that.' Something about his voice made Sally think that he would have liked that and he was sorry it had never happened.

Robert phoned her when they got back to the Land Rover. She was sitting in the passenger seat on her own, fiddling with the radio, trying to get some decent music. Alex had gone to chat to the woman in the farm. The new people were interested in natural history, he said. He'd get them to look out for more oiled birds on the beach. She watched him walk up to the front door. He opened it without knocking and took his boots off, leaving them on the step. And that was when Robert phoned. It couldn't have been better timing. Almost as if he'd been watching, waiting until she was on her own.

'Do you want to come out tonight?'

'I can't.' She didn't have the energy to make up an excuse to get away from her parents. It would be a nightmare without Catherine to cover for her.

'When then?'

'I don't know,' she said. 'Give me a ring next week. During the day. If I'm in class I'll call you back later.' She wanted to ask what he'd been doing, to chat, to make ordinary conversation.

But he said, 'I don't know when it'll be. I'm taking the boat out.' Then he hung up.

It was a quarter of an hour later when her father got back and by then she was very cold. She wondered what he could have been up to in the house with the young woman. She was proud of herself for not falling in straight away with Robert's plans, but she wished she had something more definite to look forward to.

The following morning she went to the kirk with her parents, because she didn't have the energy to make a fuss. While they were praying for peace in the world she was thinking about Robert Isbister. Of course. He was always there, distracting her, worming his way into her head. Why hadn't she gone with him when he asked her? Why hadn't she fixed a definite date for later in the week? The familiar words washed over her and she joined in the responses but she didn't hear a thing. She wondered if her father, dressed in a suit, scrubbed and polished, was listening or if his mind was elsewhere too. Afterwards, while her parents stood chatting, the minister came up to her and patted her hand. He was an obese man, so fat that the effort of walking made him wheeze. 'If you need anyone to talk to, you know where I am. This must be a very difficult time.' She could hardly say he'd be the last man in the world she'd confide in, so she just thanked him and hurried off to wait outside.

Sundays followed the same pattern. After the service came Sunday lunch. Margaret always put the joint in the oven and peeled the potatoes before they set out for the kirk, so when they got back there wasn't too much to do. They were driving back down towards the school after the service and Sally was lost in thought when Margaret said, 'Should we ask Mr Ross to have the meal with us? It must be dreadful for him sitting on his own in that great house. There'd be plenty of food.'

Sally was horrified. She tried to imagine Mr Ross, sitting at their kitchen table while her mother hacked at the overcooked meat and picked away at him with her questions.

'I think it's too soon,' Alex said. 'He'd see it as an intrusion. Maybe later.'

Her mother seemed to accept that and they ate, as usual, on their own.

They were sitting by the fire when the phone went. Margaret was knitting but had her eyes glued to the omnibus edition of a soap, which she pretended to despise but always watched. Sally had just finished the washing-up. Her father had changed out of his suit and was reading. He got up to answer the phone but her mother set down her knitting and said, 'It's all right. I'll go. It'll probably be a parent.' Margaret liked speaking on the phone even better than she liked watching bad television. She felt in control with the receiver in her hand. Important. She had a special voice, calm and a touch patronizing for parents. But she came back almost immediately and seemed a little put out.

'It's for you,' she said to Alex. 'That detective.'

Chapter Twenty-Five

Perez met Roy Taylor for lunch in the bar of the hotel where the Inverness boys were staying. Taylor had suggested it. 'Just a chat,' he'd said. 'You can fill me in on your meeting with Hunter. We can think where we want to go from here.' Perez didn't mind. Sunday was his mother's day for a long phone call and he still didn't have an answer for her. He stuck his head round the door of the Incident Room on his way through town. Taylor had done the news conference and the phones had been ringing ever since. There was nothing useful though. Not at this stage. Mostly it was people reporting cars they didn't recognize on the road south from Lerwick on the night of the 4th. Some people who'd seen Catherine at the party at the Haa.

The bar was full of people eating Sunday lunch. Most of them recognized Perez, but they could see he was busy and didn't bother him. Taylor seemed depressed. He listened to Perez's story of the interview with Duncan Hunter in silence. He'd bought drinks as soon as they'd come in, but most of his pint was left untouched. They were sitting in a gloomy corner where no one could overhear them.

'I've phoned Mr Ross and asked him to find the camera for us,' Perez said. 'If Catherine was filming the party we might be able to identify more of the people there.'

Taylor looked up from his beer. 'I thought we'd have made more progress by today. I'd hoped it would all be cleared up by this weekend. It's turned out to be more complicated than I'd hoped.'

Perez saw the Englishman had come to Shetland thinking it would be a simple case, that he'd sort it quickly and return home in glory.

Taylor took a quick gulp from his pint. 'Is there anything we've missed?'

'Alex Henry,' Perez said. 'The teacher's husband. We got a statement from him because he was second person on the scene, but nobody's really talked to him. If we *are* linking the murder of Catherine Ross with Catriona Bruce's disappearance, maybe we should. He stays right beside the house where both girls lived.'

'He was living there when Catriona went missing?'

'Margaret Henry has been teacher at Ravenswick for years. She taught the girl. There's a statement in the file. She might even have been the last person to see her before she vanished. She claimed to see Catriona run up the track towards Hillhead that afternoon. It was a Saturday. No school.'

'Was *he* interviewed at the time too?'

'Only briefly. Everyone was convinced Magnus Tait was the killer.'

'Tell me about him.'

'There's not a lot to tell. He's a scientist. Conservation Officer for Shetland Islands Council. It's his job to monitor the natural history, consider planning applications. The post was created with oil money originally. He seems conscientious. He's made a few enemies – you know the sort of thing. Objecting to house building on the grounds that a marsh with rare plants in it would be drained. The fishermen hate him because he's threatened to prosecute them for shooting seals. He's quiet. A family man. A bit of a loner maybe.'

'We'll go and see him then, shall we?'

'You want to come?'

'Go on Jimmy. Let me.' And Taylor smiled, pretending to be a kid, begging to be let into the big boys' gang. Perez didn't say that as he was the SIO he could do what he liked.

'I'll phone him. This afternoon OK?'

'Don't you have a life, Jimmy? Someone you want to spend your Sunday afternoon with?'

'Nothing that won't wait.'

Alex Henry had an office in the museum, a solid grey building close to the library, up the hill from the harbour. He said he'd meet them there. When they arrived the light was on and the door was open. He was standing by a tray in the corner with a kettle in his hand. 'I was making tea,' he said. 'Is that all right? There's only powdered milk.'

He was a squat, thickset man. Perez could see him on a boat. He'd have a low centre of gravity and he'd keep his balance in a storm. He was wearing a hand-knitted sweater and baggy jeans bought through a catalogue without trying them first.

'You didn't mind not coming up to the house, Jimmy,' he said. 'It's been a difficult time, especially for Sally. Everywhere we go there are reminders.'

'Not at all.'

His office was very small and they sat in the

museum itself, surrounded by exhibits, models of brochs and Viking boats, chairs and spinning wheels. There was a special display about Up Helly Aa. That wouldn't be long, Perez thought. It was always a nightmare to police. The islands full of visitors. The fire. The booze.

'How can I help you?'

'It's possible that Catherine's death is linked to the Bruce girl,' Perez said. 'We're talking to every man who lives in the Ravenswick area. You know we have to cover all the angles.'

'Of course.'

'Can you tell us what you remember of Catriona?'

'Now, after all this time, very little. Then it was such a terrible thing. So shocking. We had Sally by then, though she was only little, and I couldn't imagine what the Bruces could be going through. When it happened you thought it was impossible you'd ever forget. It was all people talked about.'

Perez was surprised that the man was so forthcoming. He didn't know him well, but Alex had never been one for volunteering information. When the Henrys went out as a couple it was Margaret who did the talking. The only time you couldn't shut him up was when he got started on the islands' wildlife.

'What did people say?'

'That Magnus had killed her. His father had died. It was just him and his mother. It was Mary, the old lady, that kept the croft together. She was gone eighty when she died, tiny, but strong as an ox. Formidable. He did most of the work around the place, but just what she told him. She wouldn't hear a word spoken against him. I remember one day there were people gathered outside the house, calling for Magnus to give himself up and tell where the girl's body lay. The old lady came out. She screamed at them. *My Magnus is a good boy. He hasn't hurt anyone.* They admired her for sticking up for him, but it did no good. They still thought him guilty.'

'And you? What did you think?'

'I find it hard to have firm views on anything, unless I'm given proof. Too much the scientist, I suppose. I didn't think there was the evidence to convict him. I thought if he *had* killed her, in a moment of rage maybe, or more likely by accident, then he'd have admitted it. I couldn't see him lying. But I have no other explanation about what happened to the girl.'

'Did Catriona ever come into your house?'

'Aye, occasionally. We were friendly with her parents. Not in and out of each other's houses every day. Margaret and I don't live like that. But special times. They used to come in for Boxing Day tea. We'd go to them New Year's Eve, take Sally with us, put her to bed upstairs, then carry her out still asleep when we went home. You know how it is.'

Oh yes, Perez thought. I know how it is. Is that how it'll be for me on Fair Isle? Everything planned and the same for years to come.

'What were they like, the parents?'

'Quiet people. Kind. Kenneth's father had farmed that land and that was all *he'd* wanted to do since he was a lad. But after Catriona went, he couldn't face it. They sold off the house and the land separately and then they moved south.'

'There were no problems? You never suspected that the parents might be involved?'

'Never once. It always crosses your mind, doesn't it, when you see fathers on the television and there's a child gone missing. *I wonder if it could be you, if this is all an act.* That's what we've come to. We can't trust anyone. But with Kenneth and Sandra, no, we never thought like that. Not once.'

'Were there any other children?'

Perez knew, of course. He'd read the file over and over. But he was getting more of a feel for the family by listening to Alex than he had from pages of witness statements.

'There was a peerie boy. Brian. Two years younger than Catriona. Margaret taught them both.'

'Where were you that day, Alex? The day Catriona went missing?'

'I was working here, preparing papers for a planning committee. I didn't go home. I had a meeting the next day in Kirkwall and went straight down to Sumburgh to get the plane out. I didn't hear that Catriona was gone until I phoned Margaret that night. She said everyone was out searching. I was sure they'd find the girl, either dead at the bottom of Raven's Head, or alive on the hill, lost and scared. I never thought she'd just vanish.'

'Couldn't the tide have taken her? If she'd fallen from the cliff?' Taylor spoke for the first time.

'Only on a high spring tide with a strong wind behind it. There's a shelf of rock and a shingle beach which only gets covered twice a year. The weather was bad but it was a neap tide and the wind was offshore. If she'd have fallen she'd still have been there when the cliff rescue team looked the next day.'

'What sort of child was Catriona?' Perez asked.

'Margaret must have talked about her. Was she the sort who might wander off?'

'Perhaps that's why I wasn't too worried when I heard she was missing. She was a minx by all accounts. A bit precocious anyway. Always showing off in class, Margaret said. She thought Sandra spoiled her. But they were an older couple, her and Kenneth. They'd had to wait a while for kids to come along.'

'Catriona wasn't easy then?'

'Lively,' Alex conceded. 'She was certainly that.'

'Had she run away before?'

'Not run away. But she caused a bit of a stir the week before she vanished. Nobody could find her. Kenneth was down at the schoolhouse looking for her. They discovered her in Hillhead. Mary Tait was baking and Catriona wanted to wait until the scones came out of the oven. Mary said she insisted. Just refused to leave. That's why everyone assumed she was there when it happened again.'

'Where do the family live now?'

'I don't know. Margaret might remember. We had a Christmas card the first year, but nothing after.'

'And what did you make of Catherine Ross?'

There was a long pause. 'She was a young woman,' Alex said. 'Not a child.'

'Only the same age as your daughter.'

'Well maybe she's a young woman too, only we don't want to see it. Margaret doesn't at least. Sally's never had much confidence. She's a pretty lass, just not skinny like some of those stars they all read about. She's always been worried about putting on weight. Catherine was different though. More sure of herself. More sophisticated. Margaret didn't like it. She thought

Sal was overpowered by her, that she was leading Sal astray.'

'And what did you think?'

'I was pleased that Sally had a friend of her own age living so close. At first we both were. It can't have been easy for Sally being the teacher's daughter. It sets you apart right from the beginning. She found it hard to make friends with other children. I was worried about her, thought at one time she was being bullied. Margaret didn't think there was too much to worry about and we let it go. We hoped it would be better when she moved to the Anderson, but she never seemed happy there either. It was worse if anything. Sally didn't seem to have any friends at all. Not until Catherine arrived. Perhaps she just tried too hard to belong and that put the other kids off.'

'And Catherine made a difference?'

'Sally wasn't on her own so much. I'm not sure how close they were.' He paused again. 'Perhaps Margaret was right and Catherine was only using her. But I didn't see it that way. I thought she was unhappy. She wasn't good at making friends either. And she was a teacher's kid.'

'Is there anything else you can tell us about her?'

'I don't think so. She wasn't an easy girl to know. She was always polite. You could tell she'd been well brought up. But she was never relaxed. She wanted to make an impression. Perhaps her father could tell what she was thinking. I'm not sure anyone else could.'

Perez thought the girl had fascinated him. Those weren't the sort of things you'd normally say about your daughter's friend. Alex had wanted to understand her. 'Did you ever meet her on your own?'

Alex looked shocked. 'No, of course not. Why would I?'

'What were you doing the evening before Mrs Hunter found her body?'

'It was another late night. A meeting of the natural history society. Their visiting speaker had let them down so I gave a talk.' He looked up. 'There were thirty people there. It wasn't a brilliant speech, but they'll remember it.'

'What time did you get home?'

'I went for a drink with them after. One drink. So it was probably about ten-thirty when I got in. Perhaps a bit later.'

'Was it snowing then?'

'No. There was even a gap in the clouds, a bit of moonlight. The snow came later.'

'Did you see anything unusual when you drove down the hill?'

'A body in the field, do you mean? I'm sorry, I've thought about it. I didn't notice anything but that doesn't mean it wasn't there. The road was very icy. I was concentrating on getting down the bank in one piece.'

'Was there a light on in Hillhead?'

He thought. 'I'm sorry, I don't remember.' He paused. 'There was light in Euan's house. There's that big glass extension. The blinds weren't drawn.'

'Did you see anyone inside?'

'No. No one.'

'Is that all, Mr Henry? Or is there anything you think we should know?'

Alex paused again, so Perez thought this time the open question might come up with something. Occasionally it worked. But the man just shook his head slowly. 'No,' he said. 'I'm sorry I can't help.' Which, Perez thought, didn't quite answer the question.

Chapter Twenty-Six

Fran had acquired a dog. One of the mothers at school had turned up with it the evening before. She'd been tentative. 'We don't want to intrude but we thought she might be a comfort. There's no harm to her, but she makes an awful lot of noise when she's disturbed. We thought, being on your own, and so close to where the body was . . .'

Fran had invited the woman in, offered her wine which she refused and tea which she accepted. Fran had intended this as a polite introduction to refusing the gift. In London she'd always hated dogs. They crapped on the pavements and whined. The woman talked about their respective children, about the school. 'Oh, she's a great teacher, Margaret Henry. She stands no nonsense.' Fran didn't offer her own opinion. Neither did she discuss the murder. But when the woman stood up to go, the dog stayed. Fran had the sudden superstitious feeling that if she rejected the offer she would be setting herself up for something dreadful to happen. An attack on the house, on her and Cassie. She imagined the parents talking about it afterwards in the playground. *It was her pride, you see. We offered her the dog to look after her and she turned it down.*

So Fran had a dog called Maggie. A mongrel with a lot of collie in her. Black and white. Cassie was delighted – she had pestered often for a pet – and spent the evening tormenting the animal, who accepted the treatment with such equanimity that Fran thought it unlikely she would be much good as a guard dog.

Now it was Sunday afternoon and Cassie was at a school friend's birthday party. She'd dressed in her favourite dress, all pink frills and glitter, working herself almost into tears when her hair wouldn't stay up as she'd wanted it. *What will the others think of me, looking like this? Other people's mothers have straighteners and curling tongs.* By implication Fran was a terrible parent. Fran tried to understand the tantrums. It would be Cassie's first proper sleepover. A rite of passage. She'd been given a lift to the party and Fran had stood at the door waving her off, but Cassie didn't notice. She was already giggling and gossiping with the other girls in the car. Maggie was lying asleep in front of the range.

Fran began work again on a pen and ink drawing she'd started earlier in the week. It was inspired by Raven Head, the patterns on the rock face, the shingle beach below. She'd begun with a clear vision of how she hoped the design would work, but now she found it impossible to concentrate. There was a prickly restlessness which felt like caffeine overload. She'd caught Cassie's frenetic mood. In a moment of frustration she screwed the paper into a ball and threw it on to the fire.

She felt she'd been trapped in this one room for days. If I was in London, she thought, I'd call someone.

We'd meet in a bar for a late lunch, a couple of glasses of wine. There'd be people around, noise, gossip. If I'd found a body there, I'd talk it out of my system. The image wouldn't sit in the back of my mind, contaminating every thought. It wouldn't float in front of my eyes when I was trying to draw.

She pulled on a pair of wellingtons and a coat and opened the door. The dog followed. An astonishing change in temperature had occurred outside overnight. It was as if Ravenswick had become a different place, softer, less hostile. The police were still on the road down by Hillhead, but there weren't so many of them on the hill now. From this distance the men looked like children's stick drawings, like the drawing Cassie had made in the sand on the beach at the Haa.

She could see Euan's house too. His car still stood outside. She thought on impulse she should visit. If she was feeling stifled, how much more difficult must it be for him? She walked down the hill with the dog yapping at her ankles. When she knocked at the door, Euan opened it immediately and glared out at her. She took a step back in surprise.

'I'm sorry' he said. 'I thought you were a reporter. The police stop them at the top of the bank, but one or two have got through. It's not the locals. The nationals must have got wind of the case now too.'

'I wasn't sure if you'd want a visitor. I'm quite happy to go if you like . . .'

'No. I should be looking through Catherine's things. The police have asked to see her video recorder. But I'm not sure I can face it yet. Let's have some tea, shall we?'

She left the dog in the garden and followed him.

When he took her into the space-age kitchen, she saw what an effort it was for him to hold it all together. His hand shook as he held the kettle under the tap.

'I want to know about the other girl,' he said, his back still towards her.

'What other girl?'

'Catriona Bruce. The other girl who lived here. The other girl who disappeared.'

He turned and lifted two mugs from a shelf. 'At first it didn't matter who'd killed Catherine. Not really. It was being without her. Her absence. Very selfish, I'm sure, but that was all that mattered. Then you told me about the other girl and I realize it makes things different.'

'How?'

'If Catherine's death is part of a pattern, it could have been avoided. You do see what I mean?'

Fran wasn't sure she understood at all, but she nodded slowly.

'So I have to know what happened to the girl eight years ago. It's a way of making sense of things. A way of understanding why Catherine died.'

'Catriona's body was never found.'

'I know that.' The electric kettle had boiled but he ignored it. His tone was impatient and the anger had returned. 'Of course, I know that.' He walked past Fran. 'Come here,' he said. 'Come here.' He seemed about to grab her arm, but stopped himself. He led her through into a small utility room, with a sink, washing machine and drier. It was a dark little room which had escaped the improvements in the rest of the house. It smelled damp. 'This must have been the old kitchen,' he said. 'And this must have been the larder.' He opened a cupboard door. 'Look.' His voice had risen to a shrill squeal. 'Look.'

The inside of the larder door hadn't been painted for years. He pushed it wide open so she could see the marks in felt-tip pen drawn inside showing the height of the children who'd lived there. By each mark there was an initial and the date. He pointed to the lower mark. 'B,' he said. 'That's for Brian, her younger brother. I asked the detective. He told me his name. This is Catriona.' The mark was pink. 'This is how tall she was a month before she died.'

'She was small for her age,' Fran was moved despite herself. Cassie would only be a couple of centimetres shorter.

Euan seemed to have forgotten that he'd offered her tea. He wandered back to the kitchen and sat on a stool with his head in his hands. She stood for a moment, helplessly, but realized there was nothing she could do for him. When she said she should go, he seemed not to notice.

Fran set off up the bank. She needed to walk away from the vision of the educated man crumbling in front of her, looking for an explanation in patterns and old pen marks on a wall, becoming obsessed with another child. Was it guilt which drove him? The guilt of knowing he'd not been much of a father? The dog danced beside her then ran on. She came to an area of flat ground before the land started to rise steeply. Everything here was soggy, the ditches full of melted snow, the peat soaked and spongy. There was a pale sunshine which reflected from the standing water, the pools and puddles which had appeared overnight.

They ran together into one wide, shallow lake. She splashed through it, thinking, Cassie would love this.

I don't think I can handle this on my own, she thought. It wasn't just the big things, like Catherine and her father. There was other stuff she'd have liked to discuss with friends. Men, for instance. She missed having a man in her life, would have liked to have admitted that, joking, weighing up the possibilities. Here, it was impossible to talk about it. People wouldn't understand. She missed even the trivial conversations about clothes, diet, holidays, the stuff she'd despised when it was a part of her life. She'd always thought of herself as an independent woman. Strong. Now, for the first time since moving back to Shetland she longed for the company of her women friends.

Here, she'd always be an outsider. Always. Cassie might grow up with a Shetland accent, marry a local man, but people would never forget that her mother was English. It would have been different if Fran had stayed married to Duncan. There would have been acceptance of a kind then. Now she couldn't see how it would work out.

Of course there were other incomers, expat English. Hundreds of them, like Euan and her, trying to forge a life for themselves in the islands. Some of them tried so hard to be local that they made themselves ludicrous, with their spinning lessons, their music and attempts at dialect. She saw them gathered in the cafés and restaurants in town, in their elaborate Fair Isle cardigans and handspun woollen sweaters. She met them at the film club and the book festival. Other incomers preferred to keep themselves apart. For them Shetland was a temporary exile and soon they'd return to civilization with tales of the cold and the isolation. Both groups mixed mostly with their own kind. She couldn't see herself fitting in with either of them. So, is this how it'll end? she thought. I'll become pathetic, lonely and middle-aged, living only through my art.

But already the exercise was lifting her mood. There was a childish pleasure in kicking out at the water as she walked through it. The last thought was self-mocking. And what was wrong, after all, with living through her art?

She began climbing the hill, following a drystone wall. She'd never been this far before. Usually on walks she had Cassie with her and the girl couldn't walk at this pace. She grizzled and whinged to return as soon as they were out of the house. Here, high on the moor, the effect of the rain and the melted snow was more dramatic. It ran in waterfalls down gullies in the rock and through the peat, picking up the soil and shale, scouring out a path down the hillside. It would take only one heavy rainstorm to cause more severe landslides. She'd heard Alex Henry talk about it on the radio. Part of the problem was overgrazing, he'd said. There were just too many sheep, loosening the root structure of the grass, pulling away the fabric of the land. It was a good thing the system of subsidies would change and there'd no longer be a payment for every animal. She'd thought it had been a brave thing to say. It wouldn't make him friends among the farmers. He was a local and perhaps he was more isolated than she was. She'd heard the parents muttering about him in the school playground and wondered if he had any real friends at all.

The dog had run on, unaffected by the gradient. Now she stopped and was barking. Fran called to her, but she refused to return. Fran followed her across the hill, sliding occasionally where the ground was bare and muddy. Maggie was at the top of a steep peat bank. The rain seemed to have loosened a pile of rocks and boulders exposing the black peat below. The dog was scrabbling into the debris. Fran called her again. She turned, but still she didn't move. The sun came out from behind thin cloud and shone more brightly than it had all day. It was low against the hill now and the light seemed unnatural, sulphurous. The dog and the boulders and the hillside seemed hard-edged, drawn by a heavy hand.

Breathing heavily, Fran reached the dog. She began swearing at her and told her she'd never wanted her in the first place. Then she stopped and caught hold of her collar and pulled her away. There was something under the pile of rock. A shoe. The leather was discoloured and the buckle was tarnished. It was a child's shoe. The dog was going crazy, barking and jumping, and Fran thought she would strangle herself. She was still trying to keep hold of the collar. There were a few tatters of clothing. Yellow cotton. And then the waxy outline of a small foot, pale against the black, fibrous peat.

Chapter Twenty-Seven

Perez's mobile rang when he was on the landline to his mother. He'd just got in from talking to Alex Henry and decided he couldn't put it off any longer. He didn't know what he'd say to her, but she deserved a call. He poured himself a beer and dialled the number.

'Well?' she said, not asking first about the case, though she must surely know all about it, at least have heard about it on Radio Shetland. 'What about Skerry? Have you decided?' Her voice was calm. She wouldn't want to put him under pressure, but he could sense her excitement. More than anything she wanted him back at home. Perhaps she wanted that even more than grandchildren.

If she'd asked first about the case, if she'd realized how important his work was, not only to him but to the victims' families, he would have responded differently. But he felt a stab of resentment because her world was so restricted. Its limits were the edge of an island three miles long and two miles wide – the North Light and the South Light, Sheep Craig and Malcolm's Head. So when the mobile rang and he saw Fran Hunter's number come up on the display, he said, 'Look I'm sorry Mum, that call's urgent. Something to do with the Ross case. You can imagine what it's like here. Manic. I'll have to take it.'

'Of course,' she said, contrite, because she *could* imagine it. 'I'm sorry. I know you've other things to think of.'

'I'll ring you back. This evening if I can make it.' Already he regretted being so abrupt. 'We'll talk about it then.'

'There's someone else interested,' she said quickly, fitting the words in, while his mobile played its ludicrous tune in the background. 'In Skerry. Willie's grandson. The one who went away to agricultural college. He wants to come home.' Then she put down the phone. She took a starring role in the panto every Christmas. She knew how to do dramatic endings.

'Hello!'

Automatically he'd pressed the answer button and he could hear Fran Hunter, but his mind was elsewhere and it took a couple of seconds of her shouting *Hello, hello*, like a passenger on a train as it hits a tunnel, before he answered her.

'I've found the other girl,' she said, when she realized he could hear her. The words came singly. They dropped one by one into his ear, pebbles thrown from a cliff into water. *I've / found / the / other / girl*. By then he was sufficiently aware of how serious this must be, he could tell by the dull flat tone of her voice, so he didn't have to ask her what she meant.

Perez found her on the road outside her house, looking out for him. She'd shut the dog inside and she was jumping up at the window. It was almost dark. There was just a light grey strip above the horizon to the west.

'I'll take you up,' she said. 'It'll take you ages to find it on your own.'

He thought she looked like a child herself, huddled inside her jacket, the hood pulled right down over her forehead and zipped up over her chin, so all he could see were the eyes.

'I have to wait for a colleague.' He'd left a message at the hotel for Roy Taylor. His phone had been engaged. Perez knew his life wouldn't be worth living if he went on without the English detective. 'He'll not be long.'

'Oh.' She looked very pale. 'Shall we wait inside?'

'Are you OK?'

'What do you think? I've just found a body. The second in a week.' He was surprised by the sharpness in her voice and wasn't sure what to say.

'I'm sorry,' she said. 'It just seems weird. I mean, why me? Again.'

'Where's Cassie?' The coincidence of the first name struck him and he was astonished that he hadn't realized it before. Another girl whose name started with C.

'At a party. Otherwise she'd have been with me.' She turned to him, to make him understand what a nightmare that would have been.

He wondered if he should say something, warn her never to let the girl out of her sight, but then Taylor turned up, driving the car so hard that they could hear it long before it came into view. Perez found himself disappointed by the arrival. He liked the inside of Fran's house. He wouldn't have minded waiting there with her, by the fire in the warm.

Taylor's first concern when he jumped from the car was for Fran. He bounded towards her, very solicitous in an eager, clumsy way, which was patently sincere. He took one of her hands in two of his. 'How dreadful,' he said. 'What a terrible shock all over again.' There was no trace of suspicion. Nothing to indicate he thought finding two bodies in less than a week was more than an unfortunate coincidence. Perez realized that he was looking at his boss almost as a rival. Perez wanted Fran to like him best, to think him most considerate. Did Taylor have a partner? He had never mentioned a wife or a regular girlfriend. But perhaps there was someone. He had been talking on the phone for a long time while Perez was trying to get through to him.

Perez thought his own response to Fran must have seemed mean and uncaring in contrast and tried now to put that right.

'Mrs Hunter has offered to show us the place on the hill,' he said. 'I don't think that's necessary, do you? We'll pull in some other men, cover the hill ourselves.'

By now it was completely dark, but the sky had cleared and there was a moon. Taylor seemed to consider the matter very seriously. He turned to Fran. 'If you really don't mind,' he said. 'It would be a tremendous help.'

Even in the dark, Perez could tell she was smiling. A child was lying dead on the hill and Roy Taylor could make her feel good about herself.

'Actually, I don't mind at all. It's much better than sitting on my own and waiting.'

The expedition across the hill was an experience at once bizarre and strangely companionable. Later, he would remember it as a series of scenes. Fran led the way and the men followed one after the other. He was at the rear. At one point he looked up and saw that all three of them must be silhouetted against the moonlit sky. From the road they would look like characters from a children's cartoon. Something strange produced in Eastern Europe when he was a boy, he thought. Three eccentrics in search of hidden gold. Those films always had a quest at the heart of them.

The next moment to stick in Perez's memory was when Taylor stood in the Gillie Burn. He must have seen it, milky in the moonlight, but there was no way round. He wasn't wearing wellingtons and the cold water seeped almost immediately over the top of his boots, oozing through the thick woollen socks to the skin. He didn't swear, though of course he would have done if Fran hadn't been there. Perez took a delight in his discomfort, then thought that was childish. He was no better than the boys from Foula.

Then, just as they reached the landslip which had exposed the girl's body, the moon went behind a cloud, and the hill was suddenly dark. Perez shone his torch and that was how they first saw Catriona Bruce, caught in the torchlight. Very theatrical. The star, centre stage, lit by one spot. Her clothes were in tatters, but she was perfectly preserved. Perez thought of the fairy story – *Sleeping Beauty*. That had ice and blood in it too. If I kiss her, he thought, she'll wake up. She'll turn into a princess.

Chapter Twenty-Eight

Magnus Tait knew that they would come for him as soon as he saw the cars on the Lerwick road and the pinpricks of light moving over the hill. He wouldn't have known the police were there if he hadn't gone outside. He hadn't heard any unusual noise. He'd woken suddenly from one of his nightmares, panting and sweating, and had climbed out of bed because he couldn't bear the thought of going back to sleep and living the dream again. Then he thought there would be nobody outside his door, not at two o'clock in the morning. He could see the time on his mother's clock. The journalists would be in their beds now, surely. It would be a chance to go outside. He needed to remember what it looked like out there. He was going mad locked up in the house. It was making him upset and the nightmares were always worse when he was upset.

He went back to the bedroom and pulled on some clothes. Then he went out. He couldn't remember the last time he'd spent so long indoors. Even when he was ill with the sore throat and cough which came sometimes, he still liked to be in the open air. Then he thought it was probably the day after Catriona went missing. That was the last time. He'd been shut in all day then too. People had gathered outside the house and they'd all been angry, more angry than the folks there yesterday, because Catriona belonged, didn't she? Kenneth was a Ravenswick man. His family had always been in the valley. It wasn't like Ross who'd only moved in six months before. That day they'd been crowded around the windows, banging on the panes, until his mother had gone out and shouted at them to leave him alone.

He's a good man.

That was what she'd said. She'd shouted it very loud and even cowering in the bedroom, he'd heard the words. He wondered if she'd say the same thing now.

He opened the door slowly, just a crack at first, so if there were people there, he'd be able to shut it very quickly and put the bolt across. There was a car parked on the track below his house but he took no notice of that at first. He filled a tin bucket with peats and thought how clever he was to remember that. If the people came back at daylight he'd still have fuel. He put the bucket into the porch, then stood outside, just enjoying the air, thinking how mild it was. He didn't even have a jacket on and he hardly felt the cold.

That was when he saw there was a man in the car. He was in the driver's seat. Magnus could see the shadow of his head. *He must be watching me. He's been sat there all night just watching me.* And despite himself that made him feel important, that a man had been kept up all night to look out for him. Were they scared of what he might do? Were they frightened of him? Were they?

He walked a little way down towards the track. Not so far that he couldn't run back into the house if he needed to. Perhaps halfway to the car where the watcher was sitting. He thought of him as the watcher, though he couldn't tell what he was up to. He walked there to see what the man would do and to stretch his legs.

Then something made him turn round. He looked up to the hill beyond the Lerwick road and saw the cars outside the Hunter wife's house, which had lights on in all the windows. And he saw the big van, which had been parked outside *his* house when they found Catherine, and the sparks of light from torches moving across the hill. And he knew then that they'd found Catriona. And soon they'd be coming to get him.

When they came he was ready for them. He had a suit, which was hanging up in the painted cupboard in the bedroom. He'd worn it to chapel when he'd gone every Sunday with his mother. The last time he'd been, the last time he'd worn the suit, was the day of her funeral. Laying it out on the bed he remembered the service. That smell of damp was there and the smell of polish they used on the seats. He'd sat on his own at the front. All the relatives were dead. His uncle and his cousins. The place was full though. There were neighbours, people she'd grown up with. He'd heard the whispers, spoken just loud enough to be sure he *would* hear. *He was the death of her. She couldn't stand the shame. Mary was always a proud woman.*

He found a white shirt. It was frayed at the cuffs but clean. He'd promised his mother he'd keep himself clean and most fine days he had washing on the line behind the house. He'd thought he had a tie, but he couldn't find one. In the top drawer of the dresser he saw the ribbons he'd taken from Catriona's hair. Quite

often he took them out. Not to remind himself of her –
he would never forget her – but because he could picture her better when he had the ribbons running
through his fingers. The silky feel of them excited him,
made him think of the pink silky petticoat she'd worn
under her dress.

The shirt and the suit were too big for him. The
jacket hung off his shoulders and he had to find a belt
to hold up the trousers. He must have been a big man
then, he thought, surprised. A big, strong man. He had
nothing else to wear, so he kept them on, thinking his
mother would have approved. Only decent, she would
have said. A mark of respect. He put the ribbons on
the table. He wasn't sure what to do with them. He'd
stolen them. Perhaps Kenneth and Sandra would want
them back. Then he made himself tea and sat in the
chair by the fire to wait. He got up twice, once to use
the toilet and once to put water out for the raven. It
occurred to him that he should shave, but somehow he
was too tired to make the effort.

It was still dark when the policeman came for him,
but it was morning. The clock said seven thirty-eight.
As on the last occasion, the man knocked and waited.
He didn't attempt to come in until Magnus opened
the door to him. He looked exhausted. Magnus was
reminded of men who used to go out all night for the
fishing and came back with their hair stiff with salt
and their hands red and cracked. When they got home
all they wanted was their bed. They were too tired
even to undress.

'Come in,' he said, 'and warm yourself through.
You'll be chilled out there on the hill all night, even
though it's not freezing any more.' A thought came to

him. 'Did you go fishing around Fair Isle? It would be good there for fish.'

'Not bad,' the policeman said. 'We had a few pots for lobsters. You can get a good price.'

'Are we in a rush?' Magnus asked. 'Will I make some tea?'

The policeman smiled sadly and Magnus saw that there was no rush at all, rather he wanted to put off the time when they would have to leave. 'We just have some questions to ask,' he said. 'About Catriona. And I would love some tea.'

'We could put a dram in it.'

'Aye, why not? Just a small one though. We don't want me driving you off the road.'

'Are you on your own? Last time they sent two men.'

'There's another chap waiting in the car, but we wouldn't want him driving. Safer me drunk than him sober.'

Magnus saw that was some kind of joke and smiled to be polite.

'Would he want tea too?'

'No, he's asleep. We'll just leave him be, shall we?'

Magnus put water into the kettle and put it on the hotplate. Turning, he saw that the policeman had seen the ribbons.

'They belonged to Catriona,' he said. 'I took them from her. I thought her hair was prettier loose. Finer that way, I thought.'

'We shouldn't talk about Catriona. Not here. Not until we get to the police station.'

'I don't like the police station,' Magnus said.

'They won't hurt you. I'll be there and I won't let anyone hurt you.'

'Do you think they'd let me keep the ribbons?'

'No.' The question seemed to annoy the policeman. 'No, of course not.' He changed his mind about the tea and said they should get off after all, because soon it would be light and the children would be on their way to school and the reporters would come.

'Will I be coming back?' Magnus asked, just as they were at the door.

'I don't know. Perhaps not for a while.'

'Who will feed the raven?'

There was a silence. Magnus was hoping the policeman would say *he'd* take care of that, but he said nothing. Magnus stood there, waiting for the policeman to speak.

'If no one will care for the raven,' Magnus said at last, 'you must kill it. The best way is to hit its head against a wall. You can't let it starve in its cage. And if you release it, it will still starve. It has no way of finding food.'

Still the policeman was silent.

'Will you do that?'

'Yes,' the detective from Fair Isle said. 'I'll do it.'

'It eats dog food. If you can find someone to look after it, that's what it eats.'

The room had been painted since he'd last been there – so recently painted that Magnus could smell it – but it was still the same colour on the wall. The colour of the top of the milk when it separated in the churn. That made him think of Agnes with the cow again.

There was a big radiator and that was cream too. It was very hot. On his way in Magnus had heard the constables behind the desk talking about it. One of them said there must be something wrong with the controls, but the other thought nobody had bothered to turn the heating down since the freeze. He would have liked to take his jacket off. He could hang it over the back of his chair so it wouldn't crease. But he wasn't sure that would be respectful. So he left it on.

The detective from Fair Isle was there and a woman, younger, who wasn't a Shetlander. The detective introduced her but Magnus didn't remember the name. If he'd been given the first name he would probably have remembered that. He liked women's first names. Sometimes when he found it hard to sleep he repeated them in his head. The detective introduced himself with the strange foreign name which Magnus had heard before and which now stuck in his mind. And there was a lawyer, who looked as if he had a bad head from the drink, wearing a suit much smarter than the one Magnus was wearing. It was a crush the four of them sitting round the little table. Magnus knew he should keep the grin from his face. Sometimes he missed what they said to him because he was trying so hard to keep his face straight.

'We're not charging you,' Perez said. 'Not yet. We'll just be asking you some questions.'

The lawyer had told him he didn't need to answer all the questions and again Magnus remembered his mother's words *Tell them nothing*.

'When did you get the ribbons from Catriona's hair?' Perez asked. 'Did she give them to you?'

Magnus thought for a moment. 'No,' he said at last.

'I asked her if I could keep them, but she wouldn't let me.' He shut his eyes remembering the teasing voice *Why would you want ribbons, Magnus? You've hardly any hair.*

'You took them then?'

'Aye, I took them.'

Should I have said that? He was suddenly confused. Perhaps that was something to keep quiet about. But when he looked at the lawyer, his face was blank.

'Was Catriona alive when you took the ribbons, Magnus?'

This time he knew exactly how to answer. 'No, man. If she'd been alive I'd not have taken them from her. She'd have needed them. She was dead then. What use would she have of them?'

'Did you take anything from Catherine Ross, after you'd killed her?'

He was bewildered and for a moment he didn't know who they were talking about. Then he realized. Catherine. His raven. 'I didn't kill her,' he said, rising in his seat to make them believe him. The idea was so shocking that he stopped thinking about his face and he could feel the grin sliding back. 'She was my friend. Why would I kill her?'

Chapter Twenty-Nine

At breakfast, Sally's mother was full of the fact that they'd taken away Magnus Tait.

'What a relief,' she said. 'My nerves have been on edge all week, knowing that he's been staying there, just up the bank.'

Sally supposed that it was a relief for her too, though of course it couldn't bring Catherine back.

'Did you see them arrest him?'

'No. Maurice saw them take him away as he drove down this morning. He said there were so many cars all over the top road he could hardly get through.' Maurice was the school caretaker and cleaner.

Alex came into the kitchen. He'd just come out of the shower and his hair was wet. He had on a short-sleeved T-shirt and carried his sweater over his arm, so he could put it on before he went outside. Sally thought he looked good like that, with the jeans and white T-shirt, younger and fitter. As young certainly as Mr Scott from school. Margaret ladled porridge into a bowl and put it at his place on the table. He poured milk on to it and started to eat. Margaret stopped talking about Magnus Tait and started complaining about one of the kids in school who wouldn't behave. Everything was so normal and ordinary that Sally thought she must have been imagining all the crazy things that had happened. When she walked up to the bus stop outside the Ross's house, Catherine would be waiting for her. Her father would look himself again, boring and middle-aged. Soon she'd wake up.

The phone rang. They let Margaret get it. Sally thought the story of Magnus's arrest would have got out and everyone in Ravenswick would be wanting the news. It wouldn't do to spoil her mother's fun. She put her plate on the draining board and began gathering together her things for school. Alex was still at the table, slowly buttering toast. When Margaret came back in her face was flushed. She stood just inside the door and waited for them to look at her.

'That was Morag,' she said. 'She thought we should know. It'll be all over the news soon anyway.'

In the past, Sally thought, Alex would have asked his wife what she'd found out, but today he just sat, chewing his toast, waiting for her to come out with it. He wouldn't give her the satisfaction of asking. Sally was curious but she didn't say anything either.

Margaret seemed driven to the verge of tears by their lack of interest. 'It's Catriona,' she said. 'They've found her body in one of those peat banks on the hill. Morag said it was perfectly preserved. You'd have thought she'd only died yesterday.' She paused for a moment. 'That's why they arrested Tait. They've got the evidence now. Who else could it be?'

Alex put down his knife. 'How did they find her?'

'The rain and the melted snow must have caused a bit of a landslip. Catriona had been lying in a peat bed and the landslip shifted it. Cassie Hunter's mother was up there with that dog of the Andersons. It was she who raised the alarm.'

Sally was watching her father's face. She couldn't tell what he was thinking. 'Poor woman,' he murmured. 'What a terrible coincidence to fall over a dead body twice.'

Sally thought that sounded terribly funny. It conjured up a ridiculous picture in her head, Cassie Hunter's mother tripping up, falling on her arse. But she knew she couldn't laugh.

'At least Kenneth and Sandra will know what happened to the girl now,' Margaret said. 'They might even feel able to come home.'

At school Sally was the centre of attention again, because nobody else had heard the news about Magnus Tait and the dead little girl. In registration she told Mr Scott that Catherine's murderer had been arrested. His reaction surprised her. It was as if she'd given him a present. He thanked her, not in that polite, dry way that he might if she was handing in a piece of work, but as if he was really grateful. 'It was good of you to let me know so quickly. I wouldn't have liked to have heard it in the staff room.'

It occurred to her that Robert Isbister might not have heard the news yet either. It would be a good excuse to phone him. He'd been interested after all and it would mean she wouldn't have to wait for him to ring her. She didn't think she could stand the strain of waiting. First lesson was French. She couldn't bear French. She told Lisa that the news had made her think all over again about Catherine, she wouldn't be able to concentrate. Would Lisa tell the teacher? It was the first time she'd skipped a lesson without a proper excuse. She went into the toilets, locked the door of a cubicle and phoned Robert.

He answered quickly. The reception wasn't much good and his voice sounded like a stranger's. She didn't have the usual physical response to hearing him.

'Magnus Tait's been arrested,' she said. 'For Catherine's murder. They've found the body of the other little girl. I thought you'd be interested.' Why did she know he'd be interested? She wasn't sure why he was so fascinated. Just ghoulish, she thought. Like all the others.

'Any chance of meeting up? Can you get away?' He sounded dead eager and she thought she had him hooked. He wanted all the details, though really she had nothing more to tell.

She ran through the day's timetable in her head. Nothing important. Lisa would tell them all she was upset. They'd assume she'd gone home. 'Sure. Why not?'

He met her in his van on the harbour. She had to wait a quarter of an hour for him, with the gulls screeching around her head, and she was suddenly nervous. She thought he wanted more from her than chat and tea. More even than information about the murders. Was she ready for him? She'd made no effort before setting out that morning, hadn't even been in the shower because the talk about Tait had made her late. She saw herself as he would see her – a slightly scruffy schoolgirl, a bit overweight, with a bag full of books.

When she got in beside him, he put his hand on the back of her neck, pulled her gently towards him and kissed her. She sensed something different about him.

Relief. Perhaps that was what all the people who'd been touched by the drama were feeling. Not just relief because a murderer had been locked up, but because it would stop the police prying into their lives. They all had secrets. Mr Scott, Robert. Perhaps even her parents. Now the policeman from Fair Isle would leave them alone.

He drove north without speaking. She stroked the fair hairs on his wrist and he played with her hand, rubbing her palm with his thumb. She wanted him to kiss her again, but was too shy to ask, and anyway there was an excitement in waiting.

'Where are we going?'

'I thought we'd go to *Wandering Spirit*. Would you be interested in seeing her?'

His boat was moored in Whalsay. That meant getting the roll-on roll-off ferry to the island. She tried to think if she knew anyone who worked on the ferry who might tell her parents, but Robert seemed so keen that she had to go along with it.

They were at the front of the queue for the ferry and sat in the van on the quay holding hands watching it approach, squat and flat-bottomed and pitching forward with each wave. There were a couple of trucks and just one other van. They sat in the lounge for the crossing. Robert bought her coffee from the machine. He knew the man in the other van, who was sitting there too, but he didn't introduce her. While the two men were chatting about fish and some party there'd been at one of the bars on Whalsay, she looked out of the window and watched the island getting closer. She couldn't remember if she'd been there before. Not for years certainly.

ANN CLEEVES

The boat was just as grand as everyone said it was, gleaming white and bristling with aerials and radar masts, much bigger than she'd imagined. Robert was very proud of it. You could tell how much it meant to him. It wasn't just a way of making a living. It defined him. It was who he was. When Sally thought that, she decided it was something Catherine might have said, and that made her proud too.

He took her below and showed her the room where the crew sat when they weren't working. It had leather seats and a big television. There was a fridge. He took out a couple of tins of beer and offered one to her. She took it. She could feel the movement of the boat under her. It sat low in the water and the grey sea was very close through the glass. The horizon tilted, a regular, mesmeric beat.

'Did you fancy Catherine?' she asked suddenly. 'I mean I can understand why you would. She was stunning to look at.'

'No,' he said. 'Honestly? I wouldn't have wished that sort of death on her. Of course not. But I thought she was a stuck-up cow. All that stuff about films and art. All that talking.'

'Will you take *me* to one of the parties at the Haa one day?'

'I didn't take her,' he said quickly. 'She was there. We were chatting. That was all.'

'But will you take me?'

'Aye, why not?'

She'd drunk the lager quickly and it was stronger than she was used to. The movement of the boat disorientated her. He fetched her another can. They talked. About his work, his family. Later she would

232

remember him describing his mother. *People don't understand her. It's all Hunter's fault. She's so soft she can't say no to him.* And his father, though that wasn't like hearing about a real man. More like some hero you'd read about in a book. But her mind wasn't engaged. She was aware of her body under her clothes, her tongue against her teeth, the skin of her feet against the undersole in her trainers. Everything held in, tied up. She bent down and unlaced the shoes. She kicked one off and prised off the other by pushing down its heel with her foot. She pulled off her socks and rolled them into a ball. There was a carpet on the floor with a rough texture, almost as hard as coconut matting. She flexed her feet against it. Robert, who had still been talking, about a gale which had blown up out of nothing when they were off Stavanger, fell silent.

'Sorry,' she said. 'It's a bit hot in here.'

He bent down and took a foot in his hand, twisting her body as he did, so she was almost lying along the bench seat. He rubbed the sole of her foot with his thumb, as he had been playing with her hand in the car. She thought she might faint.

Later, she thought, Is this how it is for everyone? Is it the same for old people? She wondered about her father and mother, if they did occasionally get it together. Part of her thought it might be better for them, not so hurried and scrabbled. Her father would be more patient. Not quite so rough or demanding. But she dismissed that idea as disloyal and ridiculous. What could she expect for her first time? Robert was lying back and smoking a cigarette. Now she would have liked him to speak, but he seemed lost somehow in his own thoughts. Perhaps all men were like that afterwards. She would have liked to ask, *Was that all right? Did I do the right things?* But she knew it was wiser to stay quiet.

At last she said, 'I should go back or I'll miss the bus.' She had plenty of time but she was starving. Now she wasn't dreaming of sex, but Kit-Kats and crisps, maybe a bacon sandwich.

He roused himself slowly and she saw again what she'd found attractive in him. She watched his broad shoulders and the muscles in his arms and his back. It hadn't been a big mistake after all. In the lounge on the ferry she found herself smiling. He sat next to her with his wide hand on her leg and when he dropped her off at the school he kissed her. They still hadn't discussed what had happened.

It was too early for school to finish and she went to the shop on the corner and bought chocolate and a magazine. She turned straight to the problem page, but none of the letters there could help her.

On the bus on the way home her phone rang. She answered it immediately, certain that it would be Robert. He would say something sweet and reassuring. He would tell her how much he'd enjoyed being with her. But it was a woman's voice, unfamiliar at first.

'Sally? Is that you? Your mother gave me your number. I'm so sorry to disturb you. This is Fran Hunter. You know, from the house by the chapel.'

Duncan Hunter's ex-wife, she wanted to say. But of course she didn't. How rude that would be!

'I wondered if you'd be able to babysit. I've been asked to teach a couple of evening classes at the college. The teacher's going to be off sick for a few weeks. Maybe you'd feel awkward, because Catherine used to . . . But your mother said to ask anyway . . .' The voice tailed off.

'No,' Sally said quickly. 'Really, I'd be pleased to.' She was thinking it would be one way to meet Robert without her mother knowing. Risky, but better than being out in Lerwick with him. 'Any time.'

Chapter Thirty

The Bruces arrived from Aberdeen on the same plane as Jane Meltham, the crime scene investigator. They looked small and bewildered as they walked across the tarmac from the plane, older than Perez had expected. He'd expected them to be the age they'd have been when Catriona died. That's how they were in his head. But of course they hadn't been preserved in the peat like her. You would never have thought they were coming home; they were more like refugees arriving in a strange country. The boy with them, Catriona's younger brother, was taller than they were. Roy Taylor took the family in one car and Perez drove Jane in another.

'Interesting stuff, peat,' she said as they passed the Sumburgh Hotel. 'What did the girl look like?'

'Undamaged,' he said. 'You'd have thought she'd been kept alive somewhere and buried only hours ago. There was a faint brownish tint to the skin and her hair had turned a kind of chestnut colour. That was all. She'd been wearing a cotton dress and that hadn't rotted at all.'

It was impossible to shift the image of the girl from his mind. They'd cleared some of the mud from her face, knowing they shouldn't touch anything at the

scene, but wanting to identify her, so there'd be something definite to tell the parents. After all these years
of waiting it would be intolerable not to give them an
identification. She'd been lying on her back. Her fair
hair, filthy now, was arranged loosely around her face.
Had Magnus done that? Had he thought it looked prettier? Or had he wanted the ribbons for himself? Perez
couldn't make sense of it. Was that the only reason
he'd killed her?

The procurator fiscal had decided they had enough
evidence to charge Magnus. For the murder of
Catriona Bruce at least. And of course he was right.
There were the ribbons. A confession of a sort, though
after that first interview Magnus had stopped talking.
He'd sat there with that nervous grin on his face, just
shaking his head. Even in private discussion with his
lawyer he'd said nothing, apparently. They would get
a conviction. Manslaughter perhaps because of dimin-
ished responsibility. There'd be medical reports to
show he had a low IQ, possible brain damage, but
Magnus Tait would certainly go to prison. He'd leave
Shetland for the first time in his life to be locked away.

That wasn't enough for Jimmy Perez. He wanted to
know what had happened that day when Catriona had
run up the track to visit Hillhead. He wanted to know
what had prompted Magnus to stab her. Because she
had been stabbed. Even before the crime scene investigator's arrival they could tell that. The body was so
well preserved that you could see the wound in the
girl's chest, the fabric of the dress marked with rust-
coloured stains. And more than anything, Perez
wanted to know why, after eight years, Magnus had
decided to kill again. Why Catherine Ross? Just

because she'd wandered quite by chance into his house on New Year's Eve and he'd taken a fancy to her? Was it because of her name? If she'd been called Ruth or Rosemary, would he have left her alone? And why, this time, had he strangled?

Jane was talking about the bog bodies found by archaeologists. 'They were thousands of years old and still intact,' she said. 'It's hardly surprising you get the same result after eight years. Fascinating.' He could tell she was itching to get to the scene and have a look. She hardly gave a glance at the magnificent coastal landscape passing the window.

He left her with the team on the hill and went back into Lerwick. He couldn't face the Incident Room, Sandy with his *I-told-you-so* smirk, the jubilation. They'd already be drinking probably, celebrating the arrest and the Inverness boys' imminent return to civilization. Both camps would be celebrating that. He needed a sleep and a shower.

At home his answerphone was flashing. His mother of course. He'd not had a chance to phone her back on Sunday night. He was tempted to ring her now, without any more thought. *Yes, I'm coming home. I'm fed up here. Let the factor know I'm interested in Skerry.* But he ignored it, stood mindlessly under the pathetic dribble of his shower, fell into bed and went immediately asleep.

When he woke it was late afternoon and dark outside. He didn't feel rested. He woke as he'd fallen asleep, troubled by the anxiety that was eating away at him. About Fran and Cassie. About Magnus. A fear that they'd cocked up the whole bloody case. The old man might have killed Catriona. But Catherine? He checked the phone messages. A sort of penance or punishment. There *was* one from his mother but it was short and apologetic. *Sorry to bother you. I know you're busy. I don't mean to nag.* That didn't make him feel any better.

The next was from Duncan Hunter. *I've heard the news about Magnus Tait. Good work. I don't suppose this is relevant now, but I've remembered something about that party at the Haa. Give me a ring. I'll be in the office all day.* No number. As if he assumed everyone would know the number of Hunter Associates. That you couldn't possibly manage in Shetland without it.

Perez looked it up in the directory and dialled. A young woman said Mr Hunter was in a meeting and unavailable. Could she take a message? Perez could picture her. She'd be young and skinny, long red nails and thin red lips, a tiny skirt hardly covering her bum.

'I'm returning Mr Hunter's call,' he said. 'Inspector Perez. He did say it was urgent.'

'Just one minute.'

There was a blast of music. Not the usual bland electronic noise for Hunter Associates. This was something contemporary with the sort of beat young people bounced to in nightclubs. Duncan had probably paid for it to be composed specially. It stopped as suddenly as it had started, mid-phrase.

'Jimmy. Thanks for getting back to me. Look, maybe you're not interested any more.'

'I'm interested.'

'I can't talk now. Let's meet later. Monty's. I'll buy you dinner. It'll be quiet on a Monday night. Around eight.'

The line went dead before Perez had a chance to reply.

Monty's was probably the best place to eat in Lerwick. It was where the tourists went every evening once they found it, along with the expat English, who raved about the local produce to their friends. It was a bit pricy for the locals if it wasn't a special occasion. The room was small and the tables were close together, but as Duncan had said, a Monday night in January, it was quiet. He was already there when Perez arrived. He'd ordered a bottle of red and was one big glass in. When he saw Perez, he stood up and held out his hand. 'Congratulations.'

'It's not all over yet.'

'That's not what folks are saying.'

Perez shrugged. 'What did you have for me?'

Duncan was looking better than the last time they'd met, but not a whole lot better. He was shaved and smartly dressed and he'd had a haircut, but Perez thought he wasn't getting much sleep. He'd lost the old Hunter arrogance.

'I've been thinking about that party at the Haa.'

'The one Catherine Ross came to?'

'Yes.' There was a pause while the waitress took their order. 'Look, I was out of it, OK?'

'But you've remembered something?'

'You were asking about Robert. He didn't come with Catherine. He'd been there earlier, talking to Celia before anyone else turned up. I'm not sure what it was about. Family stuff I suppose. Pretty intense, at least—' He broke off suddenly. 'Perhaps he was persuading her to go home with him. He never liked me and he could always twist her round his little finger.'

Perez looked at him, wondering what this was *really* all about. It had nothing to do with helping the police with their enquiries, that was for sure. Duncan wouldn't see the point. With him, there was always a hidden agenda. He could manipulate for Shetland.

'Catherine and Robert knew each other,' Duncan said. 'I mean, when she walked in, you could tell.'

'How?' Perez was losing patience.

'He was talking to Celia in the kitchen. She'd been putting together some food. That was where the drinks were. So that was where I was. Catherine came in with a group of other people and Robert saw her. It was a shock. He wasn't expecting it. He broke off his conversation with his mother and just stared at her. Like thunderstruck. Like there was no way she should have been there.'

'Was he pleased to see her?'

'I think so. Pleased but a bit nervous perhaps. Anxious.'

'How did she react to him?'

'She didn't. She gave no sign that she knew him, not then. She poured herself a drink and started chatting to me. Flirting, I suppose. She was one of those women who make you feel special. They can make you believe you're interesting, funny. Fran could never do that. She could never be bothered to make the effort. But Catherine, oh, she was very good.'

'She was only sixteen.'

'But sophisticated,' Duncan said. 'Experienced.'

And a virgin.

'Is that all you have to tell me? Hardly worth a dinner at Monty's.'

'While she was flirting with me, she had one eye on

Robert. I don't know why. I mean, I can't imagine for a minute that she fancied him. But at one point they disappeared together. At least, I think so. I mean, I'm pretty sure. It was before Celia hit me with the news that she was leaving. But you know how it is with parties. Good parties, at least. You get into an interesting conversation and everything around you fades into the background. You hear the music but you're not really listening. You know there are other people there, but you're not aware of what they're doing. They're just bodies moving, dancing'

'Throwing up?'

'Not that early in the evening.' Duncan said crossly. He paused. 'No need to take the piss, man. I'm trying to help. Honestly. There was one point when I noticed neither of them was there. I'd enjoyed the girl's company. OK, I was looking for her. I looked all over for her. She'd got to me somehow. She had style. And when I've thought about it since, I've realized Robert wasn't there either. I told you it might not be important.'

The waitress came with their food. Perez didn't recognize her, although she was about his age and she sounded local. He was preoccupied for a moment trying to place her. Duncan started eating immediately, sulking because Perez wasn't more grateful for the information.

'Where did they go?'

'I'm not sure. I didn't search the whole place. It wasn't *that* important.'

'But they were in the house?'

'For fuck's sake I don't know. Maybe they went for a drive. Had wild and passionate sex in the back of

Robert's van. Only I don't see it. Like I said before, she was an attractive young woman. Robert's a thug. A spoilt mummy's boy. Good looking I suppose if you like the blond Viking type, but she was too bright to be taken in by that.'

And what are you? Perez thought. You're a bully.

It wasn't such a big deal, the event which had made him see Duncan in a different light. It might have happened anywhere. Here, where the web of relationships caught you and held you and wouldn't let you go, it was the sort of thing you had to deal with every day. Duncan had been speeding. Crazy speeds down the road from the north. Sandy Wilson had stopped him. He'd realized he'd been drinking and said he'd have to test him. But Sandy Wilson's dad worked for Duncan's company. He was a joiner, who could turn his hand to anything, and he worked on the renovations of the buildings Duncan bought. Duncan threatened to sack the father if Sandy did him for drink driving. Perez wasn't sure he would have done it; good craftsmen were hard to come by. But Sandy believed him and Duncan got away with just a spot fine for speeding. Blackmail. Perez found out about it later. Sandy got drunk one night and blurted out the whole story. Perez kept it to himself. Sandy was a pea-brained bigot, but he didn't deserve to be dumped on. And anyway Perez owed Duncan, didn't he? He'd saved his life when they were at school, saved him from the Foula boys, at least. But the debt was paid and he felt he didn't owe him any more. That was why he hated Duncan. Not because he was a bully, but because he'd forced Perez to see him as one. Because when he was fourteen, he'd been Perez's best friend.

ANN CLEEVES

'How long were Robert and Catherine away?' Perez
asked.

Duncan shrugged. 'An hour? No more than that.
Less maybe. It wasn't that late. Before Celia said she'd
had enough, at least. I was still sober enough to stand.
And I remember Catherine coming back. Maybe they
had been outside. She looked flushed, red-cheeked, as
if she'd been in the cold. And she seemed elated. I told
you. That was when she told me she wanted to go into
film. She had so many dreams, she said, so many projects in her head she wasn't sure she'd have time to
work on them all . . .' He broke off and for a moment
Perez could believe that he was sad. For the girl. Not
just sorry for himself.

'And how was Robert Isbister?'

'I don't know. I didn't see him again. He didn't
come back.'

After the meal they stood together outside the
restaurant, in a narrow alley at the bottom of steep
steps.

'Why don't we go on somewhere,' Duncan said.
'Have a few drinks. Like the old days.'

Perez was tempted. It would have been good to get
very drunk with someone who didn't work for the
police. But Duncan was too eager and Perez wondered
again what the evening was all about. It couldn't be,
surely, that Duncan was lonely too, that at school he'd
needed the shy boy from Fair Isle as much as Perez
had needed him?

Chapter Thirty-One

He watched Duncan walk away down the lane towards the market cross and his car. It was early and Perez wasn't ready to go home. Word of Tait's arrest would be all over the islands by now. The people would feel safe again, settle back into the knowledge that this had been a crazy aberration and violent crime only happened elsewhere. They'd sleep. Except for the families of the victims.

The Bruces were staying with relatives in Sandwick. He supposed Euan Ross would be alone in the big house close to the shore. Perez had sent a constable to inform him that Tait had been taken into custody, but thought now he should go himself. Ross had been bitter that Tait had been released after Catriona's disappearance. It seemed cowardly not to face him and answer his questions. The police owed him that much at least.

Driving past Hillhead, he remembered the raven. Should he kill it now and get it over with? The CSI must have finished with the place because the police tape had been removed and the house was in darkness. When he found the door locked he was relieved. One of the team would have taken the key. They might even have found a home for the raven. He remembered that there was a woman in Dunrossness who cared for sick and injured birds. Maybe they'd taken it there. He'd have to check. He'd go back later.

Euan Ross was angry. His face was flushed and it showed in the violence with which he opened the door. Perez thought he had been waiting all day for someone to speak to him.

'Inspector,' he said. 'At last. I've lived here long enough to realize that there's little sense of urgency in Shetland, but I'd have thought it would have been courteous to respond to my request more quickly than this. It was your phone call which started it all off after all.'

He turned and walked away into the house, leaving Perez to shut the door behind him and follow.

They sat in the big room, with the glass wall, looking out towards Raven's Head. Euan hadn't turned on the central light. The space was lit by a couple of spots attached to the wall. There were big areas of shadow. At some point over the winter he must have collected driftwood, because there was a chunk of pitch pine on the fire. The smell of it must be covering the last trace of Catherine's perfume.

For a moment Perez was confused. He couldn't think what the man was talking about. 'I'm sorry. No one told me that you'd asked to see me.'

'What are you doing here then?'

'I thought you might have questions after the old man's arrest. I didn't want you to hear all the details from the press. They quite often get things wrong.' He was going to add that he'd considered it would be courteous to visit, but stopped himself. This was a bereaved father. He was entitled to be angry and rude.

There was a moment of silence. Euan Ross struggled to regain his composure.

'They should have passed on your message,' Perez said quietly. 'Perhaps you could explain why you wanted to see me.'

'You asked me to look for Catherine's camcorder.'

'I did. You've found it then?'

Euan didn't answer directly. 'Do you have proof that Tait killed my daughter?'

'Not yet. There is evidence to connect him with the death of Catriona Bruce. At this point he's just been charged with the first murder. Of course we'll do all we can to get a conviction on both counts.'

'I hadn't thought it mattered,' Euan said. 'But I don't think I could bear it if I never found out what happened to her. It isn't anything to do with revenge. It's just about not knowing.' He paused. 'And something about justice for Catherine perhaps. Doing right by her at last.'

'Can I see the camcorder, Mr Ross?'

But still he seemed reluctant to come to the point. He said he would make tea. Inspector Perez had time for some tea, didn't he? He disappeared into the kitchen, leaving Perez looking out into the night. At last he came back with two mugs on a tray and immediately he started talking. They sat facing each other in armchairs close to the big window, but Euan didn't look at Perez. He had his face turned to the dark space outside.

'She wasn't an easy child. One of those babies who hardly seem to need sleep. Liz found it very difficult. I tried to take my turn, but I was working all the hours there were, marking, planning, out-of-school activities.

Generally making myself indispensable. I was ambitious in those days. It seems ridiculous now. Liz couldn't face having any more children. I said we'd get a placid one next time, but she wasn't willing to take the risk. It wasn't a big deal. We didn't argue about it. I adored Liz. I'd have gone along with anything she said. Now I wish we had considered it. When Catherine was a bit older perhaps. Not for me, but for Catherine. She missed out when Liz died and I went to pieces. It would have been company for her.'

Perez said nothing. He drank his tea and listened. He thought Ross had forgotten all about the camera. He just needed to talk.

'Catherine was very like me,' Ross went on. 'Very driven. Perhaps because she was an only child she didn't find it easy to make friends of her own age. She was too honest, too direct. She didn't realize she might be hurting the other children's feelings. She loved projects. Even when she was very young she'd become completely absorbed in her work and rather competitive in it. It didn't always make her popular. She liked to win.' At last he turned and faced Perez. 'I'm not sure why I'm telling you this. It probably isn't relevant. I just want to talk about her. To tell the truth, as she would have done. She would have hated people to say sweet and misleading things about her, just because she's dead.'

'I'm interested. It helps.'

'When we first moved here she was very bored. She said she had nothing in common with any of the other young people. That wasn't true but she didn't make much of an effort. She came across as patronizing, full of herself. I heard teachers talking in the staff room about her when they didn't realize I was listening. They resented her attitude too. I was worried she'd become very lonely, a target for bullying. Of course much of it was my fault. I depended on her after Liz died. I didn't treat her as a child.'

'She became friendly with Sally, though.'

'Yes, Sally was kind to her and Catherine really enjoyed her company. They were unlikely friends but they got on well.' He paused. 'The friendship with Sally was important, but it wasn't that which helped her make an effort to belong here. That was something quite different. She found a new project . . .' He lapsed again into silence, the mug of tea untouched on the floor by the chair. He seemed so lost in thought that Perez realized he'd forgotten for a moment that he had a guest.

'What was the project, Mr Ross?'

'Film. And that's where the camcorder comes in. I'd given it to her for her birthday. She loved film. It was her ambition to become the first great female British director. She was a natural observer, perhaps because she found it hard to engage with people of her own age. She was delighted by the present. At first she played around with it, working out, I suppose, how to use it, just how much it would do. I have a film of her. I took it on her birthday and we saved it on her computer. I'm so glad I did that. It'll always be there . . .' He seemed to realize that he was moving from the subject again. 'Then she began to take her filming more seriously. As I say, it was a project. She hoped to submit it as part of her university entrance application. The course she'd set her heart on was very hard to get in.'

'What was her film about?'

'Shetland. The place and its people.'

'A documentary?'

'Of a kind, I suppose. She said she wanted to subvert the stereotype. It wouldn't be about the beautiful landscape, the harsh way of life. At least that would provide the backdrop. But she wanted to show that people are the same wherever they live. At least, I think that was it. She did talk about it. I didn't always give her my full attention.'

'Did she have a chance to finish the film?'

'I think so. Almost at least. She was editing it in the weeks before Christmas. Sometimes I'd hear her talking in her room and think Sally was in there with her, but it would turn out to be her, doing the voice-over.'

'So you'll have that too. Something else to remember her by.'

'No! That was what I wanted to tell you. You asked me to look for the camcorder but I couldn't find it. It's disappeared. But the Shetland disk is missing too. It's been stolen.'

'Are you sure?'

'Catherine was an obsessive, Inspector. In the weeks leading up to her death this film was the most important thing in her life. She'd put hundreds of hours of work into it. Nobody was allowed into her bedroom. I explained when you were here before that privacy was very important to her. It was the one room Mrs Jamieson didn't clean, yet it was always tidy. She kept the disks in a rack by her computer. The Shetland film is definitely missing.'

'Perhaps it's still on her computer.'

'I've checked. It isn't on the hard drive.'

'Has the house been broken into?'

'No, but the murderer wouldn't need to break in. If Catherine had her keys on her, the murderer could have taken them. Perhaps that's why they were never found.'

'Have you had a sense that anyone has been in the house?'

'Oh, Inspector, I've seen ghosts wherever I've looked. But it's never occurred to me that a real person could have been here.'

'Would you show me her room?'

'Of course.'

The room had been searched the day Catherine's body was discovered, but not by Perez. It looked, he thought, more like an office than a bedroom. It had a pale laminate floor, a work station and PC, a small filing cabinet. The single bed was covered with a black cotton throw. The wardrobes were fitted and matched the computer desk. Everything was clean and uncluttered. There was one picture on the wall, a large framed print of a fifties French movie poster. Black and white.

'She designed the room herself,' Euan said. 'It was where she felt most comfortable. When she was younger she didn't really enjoy human contact. She never liked to be cuddled as most children do. We did wonder, Liz and I, if she might be slightly autistic. I don't think she can have been, or if she was, she managed it very well. But she needed to be alone for long periods before she could go out and face the world again.'

'What did she keep in the filing cabinet?'

'School work mostly. Look for yourself.'

Perez pulled out one drawer. The files were

labelled according to subject. It was very different from his own jumbled desk at work.

'You talked about her reading a voice-over,' he said. 'I wondered if there might be a script.'

'Of course!' Euan was more animated than he'd been all day. 'The thief might not have thought of that. I'll look, shall I?'

'Shall I help?'

'No, Inspector. If you don't mind this is something I'd rather take care of alone.'

In the hall they stood for a moment. Perez put on his coat and prepared to go out. Euan reached out awkwardly and shook his hand 'Thank you for taking me seriously, Inspector. Since Fran Hunter found her body, I've been searching for an explanation for Catherine's death. The discovery of Catriona's body on the hill provided one of a sort. Not a very satisfactory one. A madman who enjoys inflicting violence on young girls. It's not something I can make sense of. Too random. Too arbitrary. It seems to me that the missing film could provide another explanation. If Catherine had filmed something which the murderer would rather keep hidden, that might provide a motive. But perhaps I'm deluding myself. Perhaps I'm going mad too.'

He opened the door and held it wide for Perez to pass through. Walking down the path to his car, Perez remembered a conversation he'd had with Magnus early on in the investigation. Magnus had said Catherine had taken his photo on the day she'd come to tea. The day after the party at the Haa. Perhaps it wasn't a photo. Perhaps she'd wanted Magnus to be in her film.

Chapter Thirty-Two

When Jimmy Perez got to the police station the next day, he saw most of the Inverness boys had gone but Taylor was still there. Perez could hear him as he walked up the stairs. He'd taken over a desk in the Incident Room and was sitting at it, the chair tilted back, his legs outstretched, shouting into the phone. He was the only person in the room, which had an empty, leftover feel about it, like the Northlink ferry once the passengers had disembarked. There were scraps of rubbish on the floor, used polystyrene cups on the desks. It was mid-morning and outside the sun was trying to get through. Two gulls perched on a nearby roof were screaming at each other. Perez stood, waiting, until Taylor replaced the receiver.

'They want me to sign off the case and go back to Inverness. I can't. I'm not satisfied Tait killed Catherine, certainly not sure we'll get a conviction. There's nothing forensic to link him with her. They weren't even killed in the same way.'

'Circumstantial though. Two girls murdered in the same place . . .'

'I've told them I'm staying. If they push it I'll take a few days' leave.' He looked up, grinned. 'I've always wanted to be here for Up Helly Aa.'

'It's a show for the tourists,' Perez said. 'An excuse to get drunk.'

'It's an excuse not to go south just yet.'

Perez wondered again if Taylor had anyone to go home to. Maybe after a couple of beers he'd pluck up the courage to ask. 'There is something else . . .' He began explaining about his visit to Euan's house, the missing film and immediately he sensed Taylor's scepticism. 'It could be a motive,' Perez said, wondering why it mattered to him so much. 'Perhaps the girl filmed something she wasn't supposed to see.'

'Is the guy sure it's not there?' Taylor rocked forward so the chair was firm on the ground. 'I mean he must be upset. It'd be easy to overlook.'

Perez shrugged. 'He seemed pretty positive. The camcorder's gone too. Magnus said Catherine took a picture of him the day before her body was found. Perhaps he talked to her about Catriona. It might be worth getting her computer south to the experts. See if there's some way of retrieving the deleted material.'

There was a silence then Taylor looked up suddenly from his desk. 'What do you think? Do you think Tait killed them both?'

Perez wanted to say it didn't matter what he thought. All that mattered was getting a conviction. But Taylor was still looking at him. 'I don't know,' he said at last. 'Really, I don't know.' He could tell he'd disappointed Taylor with his answer and went on, feeling for the right words, 'I think I understand Catherine better now. After talking to her father. She was lonely. She saw life through film. That was how she survived here. That was how she got her pleasure, her kicks.'

'A female voyeur?'

'An observer, a commentator.' Perez paused, remembering what Duncan had said of her. 'A director.'

'Doesn't a director make things happen? That's being more than an observer, surely.'

'Perhaps she tried to make things happen. Perhaps that's why she was killed.'

Celia Isbister lived in the house her husband Michael had built once he started making money. It was on the edge of Lerwick, with a view of the town and down to the sea. At the time of the wedding, gossip had it that he was a lucky man. He was marrying money. Certainly she'd carried with her an air of affluence. She'd been sent south to an expensive school. There was a big house on Unst. But the school had been paid for by a rich aunt and when their parents died, the big house went to her elder brother. There was nothing else to share out but debt.

If Michael had been disappointed by his new wife's poverty he hadn't blamed her for it. He'd carried through his life an astonishment that she'd ever agreed to marry him and took on the task of making himself worthy of her. He developed a transport and haulage business. When the oil came, his lorries carried cement and pipes and beer to the terminal at Sullom Voe and his taxis collected executives from Sumburgh Airport. If he knew of Celia's affair with Duncan – and surely he must have known – he never challenged her about it. She always stood at his side at civic functions. When he introduced her to visitors, to the ministers and civil servants who came occasionally from London and Edinburgh, he glowed with pride.

Celia had let Michael have his own way with the house. Perhaps it was a penance. Certainly, it couldn't have been to her taste. It was a sprawling ranch-style bungalow with an open-plan lounge. She only drew the line at gold taps for the ensuite bathrooms. Jimmy Perez wondered again what Robert had made of his parents' marriage. He moved in both their worlds. He was the youngest man on the Up Helly Aa committee and he went to the parties at the Haa. He must know that Celia's affair with Duncan was public knowledge. In Shetland information about other people's lives was assimilated subconsciously, a form of osmosis. For as long as Perez could remember people had been expecting Celia to leave Michael and to move into the Haa with Duncan Hunter. But she still lived in the bungalow with her husband and Robert. Running these facts in his head, Perez thought he was stupid to believe that Catherine had been killed because she'd filmed some secret. So little in Shetland *was* secret. It was simply unacknowledged. There was something Victorian in this need to put on a good show.

He'd phoned beforehand to check that Celia would be in. She'd said she would be, all day. She didn't ask what she wanted from her. Perhaps she assumed he was there to speak on Duncan's behalf.

Celia was on her own in the bungalow.

'Michael not about?' Perez asked. He'd have liked to talk to Michael too.

She shook her head. 'He's in Brussels. Some European conference on fringe communities. Followed by a meeting in Barcelona on endangered dialect. He went on the third and won't be back until just before Up Helly Aa.'

She led Perez into the kitchen and started making coffee without asking first if he wanted any. He thought she seemed pale, distracted. She was a handsome woman, approaching fifty, with fine cheekbones, a generous mouth. He understood what Duncan found attractive about her, caught himself watching her as she stretched to reach mugs from a high shelf.

'I don't suppose this is a social call,' she said.

Of course not. I never called on you, even when Duncan was still my friend. You were a secret everyone knew about, but we couldn't acknowledge you.

'But it can't be about the dead girl. That's all over, isn't it?'

'Still a few loose ends to tie up. Is Robert around?'

She looked at him carefully, then shook her head. 'He's out on *Wandering Spirit*. A long trip beyond Faroe. I'm not sure when he'll be back.'

Was that too much information? 'He was friendly with Catherine Ross, wasn't he?'

Celia bent to take milk from the fridge. She was wearing jeans, a black sweater. 'He never mentioned her.'

'He was with her the night before she was killed. At Duncan's party.'

'Was he? I didn't notice. I had other things on my mind.'

'Does Robert have a girlfriend at the moment?'

She laughed briefly. 'Robert always has a girlfriend. At least one. He can't stand being on his own. And he's a good-looking man.'

'So who's he hanging around with at the moment?'

'How would I know? He never brings his women home.'

Perez pulled out a chair from the kitchen table, sat down. 'What had Duncan done that night to upset you?'

The question shocked her. She considered it bad manners. But she decided to answer it anyway. Perhaps she felt the need to explain. She wanted him to understand.

'It wasn't anything specific. I realized that if I didn't leave then I'd never go. At this age I can just about carry it off. The relationship, I mean. Being the older woman. But when I'm sixty? It would be ridiculous. And I can't bear the idea of looking ridiculous.' She stopped for a moment then continued, 'I've left him before, but I've always gone back to him. I'm an addict. It must be the same for alcoholics, trying to give up drinking. You think you've got it cracked, one glass won't hurt, then you're hooked again. This time it has to be for ever.' She gave a little laugh. 'Sorry to sound melodramatic. He's just been on the phone. The third time today. It's very hard not to give in.'

'He's upset.'

'He'll get over it. He'll find someone young and pretty to console him.'

She turned away, so he couldn't tell how she wanted him to respond to that. She poured coffee then faced him again. 'I would leave Shetland,' she said, 'but I don't think I could bear that either. It wouldn't be fair to Michael. And it would kill me.' Perez sipped coffee and waited. Eventually she continued. 'I married too early. I thought I loved Michael. My family considered him unsuitable, which made him more appealing of course. He's a very kind man and there wasn't much kindness in our family. In the end kindness isn't enough, but it was my mistake. I have to live with it.'

Perez said nothing.

'I would never have made the decision to break things off with Duncan if it hadn't been for the girl,' she said abruptly.

'The girl?' said Perez, though he knew exactly who she meant.

'The dead girl. Catherine.'

'What could she possibly have said to make you leave Duncan?'

'She didn't say anything. But I saw myself suddenly through her eyes. A middle-aged woman giving up her life for a younger man who took her for granted. A fool.'

'How did she do that?' The question came out as polite interest. He gave the impression he was sustaining the conversation. Nothing more.

'She was filming us. It was very discreet. She didn't hide the fact that she was doing it, but after a while everyone stopped noticing. You know those fly-on-the-wall documentaries on television? You look at people making idiots of themselves and you think, What are they doing? They must know the camera's running. But I could understand how that happens.'

'Duncan mentioned the camera.'

'Did he? He certainly featured in the film. He made an absolute fool of himself. Perhaps as the evening went on he forgot what she was doing. Or was too drunk to care what a spectacle he was making. I was aware of her all the time because I kept imagining how I would look in her film. Ridiculous. In the end I couldn't stand it. I told Duncan that it was over and walked out.'

'Was that the only reason?' Perez's voice was tentative, apologetic. 'I thought you had a text message.'

'Did I?' She was stalling for time.

'According to Duncan. He said you received a message on your mobile, read it and left immediately after.'

'I'm sorry. I don't remember that.'

'Who else was Catherine filming?'

'She was filming the party. All the folk who were there.'

'Robert then?'

Celia frowned. 'I suppose so. Along with everyone else.'

'But they disappeared together for a while. Catherine and Robert.'

She set down her mug. 'Who told you that?'

'Does it matter?' She held his gaze and finally he conceded. 'Duncan. He said they went off together. She came back looking flushed and excited. Robert never returned. Soon after you had a text message and left.'

'Well,' she said. 'Duncan's just making mischief. You shouldn't believe what he says. He can't stand Robert. Never has been able to.'

'Why not?'

'Who knows what goes on in Duncan's head? The boy was a nuisance to him when he was younger, because he was my responsibility. I put him first. Duncan sulked about that. It'll be interesting to see how he copes when Cassie's old enough to make demands on him. He adores her now that she's no trouble.'

'And now that Robert's older, more independent?'

She flashed a smile at him. 'Now he just reminds him of the age gap between us. He's much closer in age to Robert than he is to me.'

'Does he have any other reason for disliking Robert?'

He saw then that he'd pushed her too far. She stood up, formidable and articulate in her anger. 'What is all this prying for, Jimmy? I've always thought it was an unpleasant way to make a living, setting yourself in judgement over your friends. Are you still jealous of Duncan? Is that what this is about?'

Perez had no answer for her. He felt shy and awkward, the boy from Fair Isle facing the Lerwick sophisticates in the Janet Courtney hostel at Anderson High.

She put him out of his misery. 'You'd better go,' she said, dismissing him. 'I won't answer any more questions without a lawyer.'

When he walked back to his car he sensed her looking after him.

Chapter Thirty-Three

Sally had a free period and sat in the house room. A group of boys had pulled benches at an angle around a low table and were playing cards. There was music she didn't recognize coming out of the CD player. At one time she'd hated coming in here. She'd preferred to spend her free time in the library. Now it was hard to remember what it was that had so scared her about the place, why the stares and scowls of the insiders could cause such panic. She'd tried to explain to Catherine. *They hate me.* 'Of course they don't hate you,' Catherine had said. 'They need you. They wouldn't feel superior without someone to despise. They're inadequate.'

Catherine hadn't cared. She'd walked over the posse's bags, taken their favourite seats, put her own music on the CD. She'd walked right up to them protected by her camcorder, pushing it into their faces, enjoying their hostility, catching it on film. Then she'd turned to Sally as if to say, *See. The world hasn't ended. What can they do to you?* And it had helped. Sally had been able to face them too. But it had never been easy.

Now Sally felt almost at home in the sixth-year house room. She looked with pity at the outsiders who lingered in the corridor without finding the nerve to come in. She bitched to Lisa about them. Lisa was an easier friend than Catherine. She told Sally what she wanted to hear. Sally was tempted to tell her about Robert. They were sitting on their own in the corner of the house room, Lisa big and comfortable and sympathetic, lying back in the battered armchair. She'd been out the night before and was moaning about her hangover. It was on the tip of Sally's tongue. *Guess who I'm going out with?* She knew Lisa would be dead impressed, longed to see her face when she heard. But whatever Lisa was, she wasn't discreet. It'd be all over the school in minutes. Sally couldn't risk it. She'd tell her parents in her own time, when she was ready.

Instead, she rooted in her bag and switched on her phone. There was a text message. Robert was back from the fishing and wanted to meet. She turned away from Lisa and hit the buttons. *Babysitting for Fran Hunter 2nite. See me there?* She felt a sudden thrill. It made it even more exciting, agreeing to meet Robert at Fran's house.

'Anything interesting?' Lisa asked. She had her eyes shut to show how rough she was feeling.

'No. Just about babysitting tonight.'

She supposed she should feel guilty about arranging to meet Robert like that. Her mother would be horrified. She didn't think Fran would mind though. Or her father. It came to her suddenly that perhaps he had a secret lover, that he arranged meetings like this of his own. She smiled at herself for being ludicrous. Even if he had the nerve for an affair, someone would know about it. Word would have got out. As it would about her and Robert eventually.

At lunchtime the weather seemed to lift and she

thought she'd go out into the street to get something to eat. Perez was standing in reception. He saw her coming down the corridor and waved at her.

'They've just sent someone to find you,' he said. 'I was hoping for a chat.'

'Why? I thought it was all over.'

'Just a few more questions.'

'I was on my way to lunch.'

'I'll take you,' he said. 'Let's go into town. My treat.'

He bought her fish and chips and they sat on a bench looking out over the harbour eating them. When he suggested it, she thought it wasn't much of a treat, but the fish tasted good and it wasn't so bad, being there, talking to him. Better than being in the house room, at least. The new Sally didn't get shy with strangers any more. She thought she'd been transformed, like the frog kissed by a princess in the fairy story. Though Robert made a pretty weird princess.

'You must miss her,' Perez said. 'Catherine, I mean.'

It was what her father had said too. She didn't like everyone thinking she'd been dependent on Catherine. She tried to choose her words carefully and to be as honest as possible. 'I'm not sure how much longer we'd have been close friends. I felt a bit overshadowed by her. She was too intense for me.'

'In what way intense?'

'She questioned everything people said or did, dug around for the meaning behind it.' She shrugged. 'At first I was impressed by that. After a bit it gets tedious. You just want to get on with your life.'

'Is that what the film was about? Digging around?'

'Yeah, I suppose.'

'Why didn't you mention the film she was making?'

'It was just a school project. No big deal.'

'Important to her though?'

'You could say that. It mattered to her more than anything.'

'Tell me about it.'

'Why? I thought you'd arrested Magnus Tait.'

'We have.'

She waited for him to go into more detail, but he said nothing. He screwed up the chip paper into a ball and threw it into the bin.

'The film was like her comment on us. On Shetland.'

'A documentary? I mean not a story. Factual.'

'Her view of the facts.' Sally knew she shouldn't sound so critical of a dead friend, but she couldn't help it. 'I mean, hardly objective.'

'What was in it? Did she show you?'

'Bits.'

'It wasn't finished then?'

'Just about.'

'But you didn't see it all?'

'No. Like I said, just bits as she was making it. Shots she was specially proud of.'

'Such as?'

'There was one scene filmed in the house room – that's like the common room at school.'

'I know,' he said. 'I went there, don't forget.'

'There are these two lads talking. They can't have realized she was filming them. People got used to her wandering around with the camera. Sometimes it was switched on. Usually it wasn't. We stopped taking any notice of her after a bit. These lads were talking about foreigners. You know sometimes in the summer we get visitors . . . Not white people . . .' She could tell she was flushing, felt as awkward as when Catherine had played the film to her. '. . . And they were talking about how they hated foreigners and how Shetland's no place for them and what they'd like to do to them. It wasn't so much what they were saying as how Catherine made them look on the film. I mean they looked really violent and mad.' Sally paused. 'She said something like, *I'll have to get this to Duncan Hunter, won't I? Get him to include it in the latest tourist campaign. Show what a welcoming lot you Shetlanders are.* She thought we were all like that. Ignorant, prejudiced, stupid. That was what the film would have showed.'

'Did you see anything else?'

'I think there might have been a piece about Mr Scott in it. I think she might have filmed that secretly. She talked about how she might do it. She'd put the camera into a bag with a gap in the seam. Then she said what a laugh it would be when she played it back in class. I'm not sure she would have done that though. You could never tell with Catherine. Sometimes she spoke in that really cruel way, but she didn't mean it. It was a weird kind of humour. I don't think she deliberately set out to hurt people.' Sally shook her chip paper and they were surrounded for a moment by gulls.

'Did she tell you what the scene with Mr Scott contained?'

'No. She said she didn't want to spoil the surprise.'

Perez stood up to show that the meeting was almost at an end. Sally wondered what the conversation had really been about. At the car he paused. 'We can't find the camera or the disk. Do you know where it might be?'

Sally thought back to the last time she'd been in the big house in Ravenswick. 'She always kept the disk in a metal pencil box in her bedroom. She said if the house caught fire, it would have a chance of surviving. If it's not there, I don't know what she would have done with it.'

When Sally got off the bus that evening, her mother was still in the school. She saw Sally walking across the yard and waved her to come in. Inside, there was the familiar smell of plasticine, floor polish and powder paint.

Sally hadn't enjoyed her time in the little school. From the moment she started a couple of the older lads had made fun of her. They'd made her cry and she'd gone to her mother, who'd told her not to be a baby, but had shouted at the boys all the same. After that, every time her mother made an unpopular decision, somehow it was her fault. *Snitcher Sally* they'd called her. Her work got trashed when she wasn't looking and they tripped her up in the playground. She'd been a round dumpling of a girl in those days and that hadn't helped. Now, though, even Anderson High didn't seem so bad. She felt more in control than she had since starting there.

The children had been working on some painting to tie in with Up Helly Aa. A Viking longboat in corrugated cardboard lay across several desks. They did the same display every year – Sally remembered it from her time in primary seven. Margaret Henry didn't have much imagination when it came to art.

'I need to get it up on the wall. Give me a hand will you?'

'You should get them to make torches to go with it. Collage. Anything red, orange or yellow they can cut out of magazines. Or something more shiny. Cellophane, wrapping paper.'

'Aye. Maybe I should.' Margaret stepped back to check that the boat was straight. Sally could tell she *wouldn't* get the kids to do anything different.

'Will Dad be home on time tonight?'

'No. A meeting in Scalloway.'

'I'm babysitting for Mrs Hunter.'

'I'd not forgotten.' Margaret wiped her hands on a paper towel. 'Let's hope the child doesn't play you up. She a handful, that Cassie Hunter. Full of herself.' Her attention was still on the longboat and she was talking almost to herself. 'There's something about her that reminds me of Catriona Bruce.'

Sally arrived at Fran's house carrying a bag with some books in and some make-up. This time she'd make a bit of an effort for Robert. Cassie was already in bed.

'She's knackered,' Fran said. 'Sometimes she gets a bit restless at night, but that's usually later. You shouldn't have any bother.'

Although Fran was only wearing jeans, you could tell she'd made an effort of her own before going out. She'd put on lipstick and Sally could smell perfume. She was wearing a silky top, close fitting, low cut. Sally would never have been able to get away with it, the size of her belly.

'It was good of you to come,' Fran said. 'I don't feel so bad asking now they've made an arrest, but it must make you think of Catherine.'

'I've been thinking about her all day. The inspector came to school at lunchtime to talk to me about her.'

'Oh?' Fran had been brushing her hair, looking at herself in the mirror over the mantelpiece. She stopped, the hand holding the brush poised over her head. Sally could tell she was dying to ask what he'd wanted, but didn't want to appear too nosy.

'Something about the film she was making. Apparently it's gone missing,' Sally said.

Fran pushed the brush into a drawer and straightened her collar. 'She talked about the film. A project wasn't it? A shame it's lost; it would be something to remember her by.'

'Aye.'

'There's a bottle of wine open in the fridge,' Fran said at the door. She appeared suddenly reluctant to go. 'Help yourself. And to something to eat.' Then she seemed to convince herself that it would be safe to leave her child, grabbed hold of her bag and was gone. The house was quiet.

Sally was seldom alone in her own home at night. Margaret didn't have any real social life and if she was out, it was usually at a meeting in the school, so close that Sally could hear the raised voices or polite clapping through the walls. The school seemed to insinuate itself into everything they did. She had spent time in Catherine's house, but had never imagined herself living there. It was too big. Too grand. This place was different. She prowled around the room looking at the photographs and the sketches, checking out the music, imagining what it must be like to have your own place. Imagining what it would be like to live here with Robert.

In the fridge there was fancy French cheese, a plastic tub of black olives, a bag of salad. She poured herself a glass of white from the bottle in the door. If her mother noticed drink on her breath, she'd say Fran had insisted.

She drank it very quickly and the glass was almost empty when there was a gentle rap on the window. She turned in her chair and she saw him, his face squashed up to the glass, pulling a ridiculous face so he looked like a cartoon monster. She opened the door. He stood, filling the space between the door frame, holding the plastic tie round four beer cans.

'Where have you parked?'

'Don't worry. Round the back. There's a pull-in between the hill and the house. No one will see.'

She liked the fact that he understood her need for secrecy, that he didn't mock her for it. 'Come in, come in,' she said. Much as the old man had done, when he'd invited her and Catherine into Hillhead at New Year.

Chapter Thirty-Four

Fran thought, when she arrived home, that Sally had had a man in the house. There was an unfamiliar smell. Nothing unpleasant. Certainly he hadn't been smoking, she wouldn't have allowed that. Perhaps it was aftershave. Did young men wear aftershave these days? She didn't mind that Sally had invited a boy in – it must be a nightmare to be young here, no privacy, everyone knowing your business – but she wished the girl had had the nerve to ask. She was quite entertained by the notion that she might act as a sort of fairy godmother. And she hoped they'd been discreet. It wouldn't do for Cassie to wander in when they were having full-blown sex on the sofa.

Fran wouldn't have minded an early night with a large glass of whisky – she had a lot to think about – but Sally didn't seem eager to go.

'Cassie was fine,' she said. 'Not a peep. I stuck my head round the door once just to check she was OK. She's a lovely girl. You must be very proud.'

And just because of that, Fran found herself opening another bottle of wine and offering a glass to Sally and settling down to chat. Catherine had never said anything flattering about Cassie.

'Did you have a good evening?' Sally asked. Her

eyes were very bright as she looked over the rim of her glass, and Fran remembered suddenly and quite vividly what it had been like to be sixteen. The irrational mood swings between elation and despair, the sense that no one older could possibly understand the intensity, the passion, the terror. She realized that Sally was staring at her, waiting for an answer.

'Very good, thank you.' And then, because obviously more was required, 'Because I went to art school, they thought I'd be able to fill in for the teacher. It was OK. Some of the students were very good.'

'Oh yeah, right. Well, anytime . . .'

'Next week, same day.' Now Fran had had enough. She fumbled in her purse for a ten-pound note. 'Will you be OK walking down the hill by yourself? I'd drive you back, but I can't leave Cassie. I'll lend you a torch and watch you down from here. Make sure you get in safely. Or you can phone your dad for a lift if you like, if you think he'll still be awake.'

'I'll walk,' Sally said. 'I'm not sure about Dad. He had a late meeting in Scalloway, but that should have finished hours ago. And don't worry about me. We're all safe, aren't we, now they've got Magnus locked up?'

But Fran stood in the porch and watched her down the hill. She had never worried about Catherine and wondered why she was bothering now. As Sally had said, Magnus was locked up. She told herself that she had a right to be nervous. She'd discovered two bodies. Here, in Shetland, where she'd believed nothing bad could happen. Anyone would be nervous.

It was a clear night and although the moon was thin, she could see Sally's silhouette until it was lost behind Hillhead. Then she followed the spark of the torch all the way down the bank, saw it swinging around the bend in the road in front of Euan's house and disappear into the school. She saw a light go on in the schoolhouse kitchen window and at last she turned to go back inside.

Cassie was standing in the doorway to her room. She was white and shaking, still half asleep. Fran put her arm around her and led her back to bed. 'It's all right,' she said, over and over. 'Just a nightmare. It's all right.' She lay beside her daughter on the bed and waited until her breathing was easy and regular again.

The next morning Cassie showed no sign that the nightmare had upset her. When Fran mentioned it casually she seemed not to know what she was talking about. But some clue to its cause came on the way to school when they passed Hillhead.

'That's where the monster lived,' Cassie said.

'What do you mean?'

'The monster who likes to kill little girls.'

'Who told you about that?'

'Everyone. Everyone's talking about it at school.'

'Magnus lived there. You remember Magnus. He gave you sweeties sometimes. The police think he killed Catherine. And a little girl called Catriona. He's an old man who's done terrible things. But he isn't a monster.'

Cassie seemed slightly confused. 'The police think Magnus killed Catherine?'

'Yes.'

'But Catherine wasn't a little girl.'

Fran was starting to feel out of her depth. 'You mustn't think about it.'

'But—'

ANN CLEEVES

'Really, you shouldn't worry about it. Magnus has been locked up. He can't hurt anyone any more.'

In the schoolyard Fran wondered if she should have a word with Mrs Henry, explain about the nightmare, the stories which were being passed around. But she suspected that the teacher already had her down as an over-anxious and neurotic parent. It was probably best not to make a fuss, she thought. She'd be able to help Cassie deal with it herself. Besides, she was looking forward to a day of uninterrupted work. The image of the ravens in the snow was still potent, perhaps because of the tragedy with which it was now linked in her head. The fire of the rising sun, the brilliant white snow and the black ravens, had haunted her since she'd first seen it. The picture contained the elements of traditional fairy story and primitive sacrifice. She hoped she'd make it as strong on canvas as it was in her imagination.

As she turned to walk back up the hill, she saw Euan through the big glass window at the front of his house. He was standing, looking out. He was wearing his spectacles, and had a dishevelled look which gave him the air of an absent-minded professor from a children's book. She thought he was too preoccupied to notice her, but she must have penetrated his thoughts, because suddenly he waved wildly at her. She climbed the path to his door.

'Come in,' he said. 'I was just taking a break. You'll have some coffee with me.' His depression seemed to have lifted. Now he seemed overtaken by a sort of manic need for activity. Close to she saw his face was drawn and his eyes were red. He hadn't shaved. Perhaps he hadn't slept all night.

'Taking a break? Are you working?'

'I'm going through Catherine's things.'

'Oh Euan, do you need to do that now?'

'Absolutely,' he said. 'It's vital. I've only stopped because I felt I was losing concentration. Besides, I promised Inspector Perez that I would. Come along. I'll pour you some coffee, then we'll go upstairs.'

He led Fran along a corridor at the top of the house to the room where Catherine must have slept. It was square, unnaturally tidy, except for files arranged in heaps on the bed. One of the drawers of a small filing cabinet was open and empty. A plain white blind covered the window and he was working in the light of an anglepoise desk lamp. Fran felt uncomfortable there. It made her think of a room in a private hospital. A mental hospital perhaps, where the doors would be locked.

'Do you mind?' She pulled up the blind and let in the cold morning light. There was a view down to the school and beyond to the bay. She could make out Mrs Henry through the schoolroom window, but the children were out of her line of sight.

She'd expected that he'd be going through the girl's clothes. This systematic search of her papers made no sense. What did her school work matter now?

'What are you looking for?'

'The script to Catherine's film. At least, that was what I started looking for. It soon became clear that was missing too. She would have kept it with the disk, I think. She was a very organized young woman. Perhaps that *was* something I was able to teach her. The need for order. So anyone stealing the film would have taken the script too. But there might have been notes, the scrap of an idea or a theme. Something which would point us in the right direction.'

'I'm sorry,' Fran said. 'I don't quite understand.'

'Catherine was making a film, a sort of project for school, a documentary.'

'And you've lost the film?'

'No. Not lost. Definitely not that. The film has gone missing certainly. But it has been stolen. Not mislaid.'

'How can you be sure?'

He looked up. 'I explained. She was an organized young woman. She never lost things. Certainly nothing as important to her as this. And the film has been wiped from her computer.'

'Is it important?'

'Of course it's important. It provides a motive for her murder. It gives some sense to her death.'

'You think Magnus Tait stole it?'

'Ah,' he said. 'Now you realize how important this is. It seems unlikely doesn't it? Possible perhaps that he stole the hard copy and the script. But I really can't see a man of his age and education wiping the material from her PC.'

Already his eyes had strayed back to the mound of paper arranged on the bed. She could tell that he was itching to get back to it. She thought if he was left here to go through it alone, he would lose all sense of perspective. And if she abandoned him, she would think about him all morning. It would be impossible to concentrate on the painting.

'Would you like me to help?'

'Would you?' He put his mug on the window sill and looked down at the bed. 'The police have just rung. The Bruces would like to visit. I suppose they hope to catch some sense of their daughter here. Especially if they've looked at her body, they'll need to be reminded of the girl she really was. I can understand that. But I don't want to be still working on this when they arrive. You do understand? They think they know what happened to their child. Perhaps they're right. At least it must give them some peace. I'm planning to work through the files one drawer at a time. I'm fairly sure the script isn't here. I looked for that last night. But I thought there might be something. Her original notes perhaps, something which might give us some sort of clue.'

'Didn't she talk to you about it?'

'Not really in any detail. Not that I remember. I don't think I was a very good listener. Not after Liz died.'

There was a silence broken by gulls calling outside.

'I think I'll sort the files out here,' he said, suddenly brisk and matter of fact. 'The project was only set in the second half of last term. Any work written earlier than that won't be relevant. The rest we can take downstairs and work on in more detail. Does that seem sensible?'

'Yes, very.'

So they sat together on the narrow bed and went through the essays and the lesson notes, returning the early ones to the filing cabinet. It helped that Catherine had been meticulous. Every piece of work was dated. The rest they piled into a yellow plastic box, which Euan brought from a spare room and which might once have held her toys.

They were about to take it downstairs when the bell went in the school. Fran stood at the window for a moment and watched the children run out into the yard. She could see Cassie in her pink anorak. She seemed to stand alone, looking around her, then chased up to a pair of girls who were holding hands, and began to join in their game.

Chapter Thirty-Five

The yellow box stood in the centre of the kitchen table. Euan was filling the kettle, waiting for her to join him before he began the search. She thought it would be a complete waste of time, but didn't know how to tell him. In the brief glimpse she'd seen of the essays upstairs there'd been nothing relating to a film.

'Did Catherine have a school bag?' The thought had come to her suddenly. 'I mean, kids don't have satchels any more, but there must have been something she'd carry all her books in. Wouldn't the stuff she'd been working on most recently be in there?'

'It must be somewhere. Just a moment. I'll look.'

He disappeared. He was gone for so long that Fran wondered if she should go to find him. At last he returned with a leather bag which looked very like an old-fashioned child's satchel, but which had been painted green, with a huge yellow flower stencilled on the flap. 'I'm sorry about that. I couldn't find it. In the end I phoned Mrs Jamieson. She'd tidied it away in one of the cloakroom cupboards.' He sat for a moment looking at it. 'I remember when Catherine bought it. Before we moved. It was from one of the little second-hand shops in the Corn Exchange in Leeds. I thought it was a bit of tatty nonsense, but she spent nearly a day painting it up.'

He unbuckled the flap and began taking out the contents an item at a time. There was a plastic Simpsons pencil case, three envelope files, a short-hand pad, a box of tampons and a few scraps of paper. His breathing was very laboured. Fran looked at him, was about to ask if he was feeling ill, but she could tell from his face that he probably wouldn't even hear her. He opened the pencil case. He tipped out a fountain pen, a couple of biros and some coloured pencils. A fine pen for drawing. Then he lay the shorthand pad in front of him and lifted the cardboard front cover.

At the top of the page was written in Catherine's fine hand *English Assignment: Non-fiction/documentary. Film? Check that would be OK.* Below, in spiky letters large enough to cover the rest of the page: *FIRE AND ICE.*

'That was what she was going to call it,' Euan said. 'Of course.'

'Isn't it a poem?'

'From Robert Frost. Just a minute.' He disappeared from the room but this time came back much more quickly. 'The book was on the table in her room downstairs. I'd seen it there.' He riffled through the pages until he found what he was looking for.

'It's a good title,' Fran said. She thought it would be a brilliant title for a painting as well as a film, had in her head again the ravens in the snow, with the big red ball of the sun behind them. 'What else is there in it?'

She reached out to take the notebook from him, but he set it back on the table out of her reach. 'Perhaps we could go through it together later,' he said. 'The idea that there might be something important in there is an incentive. A reward for going through the rest of her files. We can't afford to miss something. You do understand?'

She wasn't sure she did understand such control, but she nodded and lifted a pile of paper from the yellow box. She could tell how hard he was finding it to hold himself together and didn't want to push him over the edge. She started with detailed notes and three essays on *Macbeth*. It would be, she supposed, a sort of education. An hour later she had read everything in front of her. Besides *Macbeth*, she had struggled through Catherine's history notes on the Counter Reformation and psychology essays about gender stereotyping and peer pressure. Her Shetland film was mentioned nowhere. Only an obscure visual reference showed that she was thinking about it all the time. In the margin of a set of notes and an essay plan there was the same recurring doodle. The first time Fran had dismissed it as an attractive pattern with no representational significance. When it was repeated she looked more closely. The design was so similar to the first that it looked like a logo. It showed an eight-sided crystal superimposed on a tongue of flame. *Fire and Ice*.

She showed it to Euan. He scrabbled back through his own pile of papers and came up with three more examples of the same design. 'I'd missed them altogether,' he said. 'I don't have your visual imagination, obviously. I was concentrating on the words.'

'Did you find anything?'

'No,' he said slowly, reluctant to admit defeat. 'Nothing.'

'Wouldn't anything she was working on recently be in her bag? In the notebook which had the title or one of the envelope files.' She was starting to lose patience with him. Why didn't he just look in the more obvious places? Was he waiting for her to go, so he could look at them by himself?

'Perhaps,' he said. He looked up from the table. 'Or perhaps I'm deluding myself and we'll never find out why she died.'

She stretched out and scooped up the scraps of paper which had been crumpled in the bottom of the bag. The first was a ferry ticket. She gave it to him. 'She took the roll-on roll-off to Whalsay just before Christmas. Did she have a friend there?'

'I think I remember that. There was a party. Some lad from school, she said. I can't see that it has any significance.'

'Then there's this. A supermarket till receipt.' She stretched it out on the table, stroked it with her thumb to flatten it. 'Safeway's in Lerwick. Dated the day before her body was found. Did she do any shopping that day?'

'Not for me.' He took it from her, frowning. 'None of those items turned up in the house. She wouldn't have bought sausages or the pie. She was practically a vegetarian and certainly never ate processed meat.'

He turned the paper over. Fran saw writing on the back, but from where she was sitting couldn't make out what it said. He slid it along the table to her. 'Look what's scribbled on the back. It's Catherine's writing.'

Fran read: *Catriona Bruce. Desire or hate?*

'What does it mean?'

'It's a reference to the same poem.' He picked up the anthology again and read out loud, his voice shaking as if he'd suddenly aged, 'From what I've tasted of desire/I hold with those who favor fire./But if it had to perish twice,/I think I know enough of hate/To say that for destruction ice/Is also great . . .'

'What is Catherine saying then?' Fran had forgotten her irritation with him. She was hooked by the puzzle. Suddenly this had little to do with the reality of two dead girls. 'That Catriona was killed because someone desired her or hated her? Those emotions must lie at the root of most violence. And what does it have to do with the film?'

'Surely there's a more fundamental question.' He sat upright in his chair. His voice was clipped, almost academic. 'Why was she interested in Catriona Bruce at all? I'd never heard of the girl until Catherine died. I think I knew that a family called Bruce lived here once, but not that the daughter had gone missing. Had Catherine discovered something about the girl's disappearance? If so, that might provide a powerful motive for her murder.'

Fran sat looking at him, trying to grasp the enormity of what he was saying. It seemed absurd to read so much from a scribbled note, but he was right.

'Can we look at the rest of the notebook now? The other files from her bag?' She realized, too late, that she must sound very eager. He mustn't think she was treating his daughter's death as a game. She turned to Euan, hoping she hadn't offended him, but a noise outside had caught his attention.

'A car,' he said. 'It must be the Bruce family. I wasn't expecting them just yet.' He slipped the receipt

into the notebook, pushed them both into the green
leather bag and went to open the door. She put
Catherine's books and essays back into the plastic box
and stuck it under the table.

Chapter Thirty-Six

Kenneth and Sandra Bruce had expected the house to be the same as they remembered it and it was so different that they seemed lost. They wandered into the big room, looking around them like unsophisticated visitors to an art gallery, not sure exactly what response was expected of them.

'It's very nice,' Sandra said. 'Yes, very nice.'

Fran could tell that Euan's mind wasn't really on the encounter. He was still thinking about the receipt from Safeway's, the unread notebook. Perhaps that was his way of feeling close to the daughter he had lost. It was as if he thought Catherine was still trying to communicate with him. But to the visitors he must have appeared aloof, rather arrogant. Fran found herself playing the part of host, offering coffee, taking coats. There was a woman with them, a police officer in plain clothes. Perhaps they'd known her when they lived in Shetland, because they called her by her first name, Morag.

'Why don't you just look around by yourselves,' Fran said at last. 'That will be all right, Euan, won't it?'

He looked up, startled. 'Yes, yes, of course.'

The son, Brian, had followed his parents in and had answered Fran's questions about coffee or a soft drink in monosyllables. He was a tall, ungainly boy who seemed embarrassed by his size, the uncertain pitch of his voice. Now, when they went off to look upstairs, he stayed where he was, sitting by the fire, cradling his can of Coke in his huge hands, looking at his feet. Euan, standing by the big window and staring down to Raven Head, seemed not to realize that he was still there. Fran couldn't bear the silence.

'I don't suppose you remember much of this,' she said. 'You must have been quite young when you left.'

He looked up at her. His chin was spattered with acne.

'I remember some of it very well,' he said. 'The day Cat went missing. I remember that.'

She waited for him to continue but he tipped back his head and took a swig from the can.

'It's the small details you remember, isn't it?' she said. 'Like, what you had for tea and what you were wearing.'

He smiled and she saw that one day he might be good-looking. 'I was wearing a Celtic shirt. I don't know why, but I always supported Celtic.'

'It was the summer holidays, wasn't it? No school.'

'I hated school.'

'Did you?' She would have liked to ask why, but didn't want to frighten him back into silence.

'Maybe that was down to Cat. She *really* hated it, put me off before I started.'

'Why did she have such a bad time there?'

He shrugged. 'Mrs Henry didn't take to her. That's what my parents said. You know they talk about stuff and they think you're not listening or you're too young to understand. My Dad wanted to move her to a different school. He said she'd never get on at Ravenswick, with Mrs Henry on her back all the time. Mum said it would be awkward. How would they explain it to her?' He looked up at Fran. 'They weren't like friends, not really. But neighbours, you know, calling in on each other. You can see it would have been difficult, moving Cat. Like saying, *We think you're a crap teacher*. After, when Cat ran off, Mum blamed herself. She thought if she'd found a different school Cat would still be here. Dad said that was daft. It was the holidays. The last thing she'd be thinking of would be school.'

'Why didn't Mrs Henry take to her?' *And what happens if she takes against Cassie?*

'Dunno. Cat was always kind of fidgety. Like she'd never sit still or do as she was told. She always wanted people to look at her.'

'That must have been a bit difficult for you.'

'Not really. I didn't want anyone looking at me.' He paused. 'Mrs Henry thought she should see someone. I dunno. A psychologist. Someone like that. Dad was furious. He said there was nothing wrong with Cat. She just got bored easily. Mrs Henry couldn't handle a bright child.' He smiled again. 'That was something else I wasn't supposed to hear.'

The Bruces had moved upstairs. Fran could hear their footsteps on the ceiling, faint voices. They must be in Euan's bedroom now, the bedroom where they had slept, had conceived their children. She thought Brian had finished speaking, but despite all the changes, the house must have triggered memories for him. 'That day she went missing she was getting under Mum's feet. It was a sunny, blowy kind of day and

Mum was washing curtains. I remember her in here standing on a chair, taking the curtains down. The window was smaller then, but it was still an awkward job. Cat was running around and knocked into the chair. Mum fell and the fabric ripped. Mum screamed at us both to go outside and play.' He paused. 'She'd already put one load of washing on the line. Towels and pillow cases. I can see them in my head, the wind sort of tugging at them. Weird isn't it how pictures stick in your head?'

'Like a film,' Fran said, thinking of Catherine.

'Aye. Just like a film.'

'Is that when Cat ran off?'

'No we played for a bit. Some game. Cat would have been in charge. She always was. Then she started picking flowers from the garden. There were a few growing in the shelter of the house. Mum's pride and joy. I told her she'd get into trouble. She said they were for Mary and Mum wouldn't mind. She'd told her to be kind to Mary.'

'Mary was Magnus's mother? Lived at Hillhead?'

'She was really old,' he said. 'I thought she must be like a hundred years old, because Magnus was old and she was his mother. But I guess he was about sixty and she would have been in her eighties. Then Cat tied one of her ribbons in a bow round the flowers and ran up the hill with them. I went down to the beach. There were some other kids there. Mum must have thought Cat was with me, because she came down to call us up for our tea.' He paused. 'The rest of it is all a blur. That's all I remember clearly.'

They heard Sandra and Kenneth Bruce come downstairs, their feet loud on the bare wooden steps.

They hovered in the doorway, Morag standing behind them. Sandra was holding a handkerchief to her eyes.

'Come on, son,' Kenneth said. 'We're away now.'

Brian stood up, nodded to Fran and to Euan who had turned back to face the room, and followed them out. Euan didn't see them to the door. Fran walked with the family to the car and felt she had to apologize for his rudeness.

'It's been a terrible shock for Mr Ross,' she said. 'I'm sure you can understand.'

When she returned to the house Euan was already sitting at the kitchen table. He'd placed the green bag in front of him and had taken out the notebook. It lay, unopened on the table. He was staring at it. He waited until she'd joined him then reached out to open it. His hand was trembling. She was sitting very close to him, so she could read at the same time. Under the smell of coffee, his breath was slightly sour.

The first page they'd already seen. *FIRE AND ICE*, not written as much as drawn, very big, designed as if the letters had been formed from icicles. On the next page it was written again, but this time each word was linked to other words and phrases, a sort of brainstorming chart. From *Fire* came *passion, desire, madness, midnight sun, Up Helly Aa, sacrifice. Ice* was linked to *hate, repression, fear, dark, cold, winter, prejudice.* The lines joining the words were thick and strong.

'Her themes for the film, I suppose,' Euan said.

'Perhaps she hoped to link visual images with some sort of exploration of those emotions,' Fran said. 'Something to do with the extremes of landscape and light? An ambitious project.'

Euan looked up from the paper, sensitive to any

implied criticism. 'She was sixteen. You're allowed to be ambitious when you're sixteen.'

He turned the next sheet of paper. There was nothing there. He flicked through the remaining pages. They too were empty. He threw the book away from him and smashed his hand palm down on to the table. The violence of the response scared her. 'That doesn't give us enough,' he said. 'I need to know what happened to her.'

Fran didn't know what to do. This was a grown man in the middle of a temper tantrum and she could hardly tell him to snap out of it and pull himself together. 'We haven't finished,' she said. 'There are the envelope files from the bag. Why don't we look at those?'

He stood up and she thought he was going to walk out and leave her there alone. She'd heard the patronizing tone in her own voice and wouldn't have blamed him. Instead, he went to the sink, ran the tap, cupped cold water in his hands and threw it on to his face. Still wiping his hands on a towel, he returned to the table. 'You're right,' he said. 'Of course, you're right.' He was quite calm. The outburst had shocked her, but now it was hard to believe it had happened. 'Let's look in the files.'

There were three of them. One was labelled history, one psychology and one English. Fran let Euan make the choice. He flicked through the first two and discarded them quickly. They were recent lesson notes, handwritten. The English file was very thin. She was worried that it would be empty. Then she saw on the outside of the cardboard a series of the *FIRE AND ICE* doodles. He opened the envelope file and pulled out a single sheet of paper. It was A3 size, folded into two so it fitted in the file. He spread it out and stood beside her, so they could look at it together.

At first Fran could make nothing of it. She thought this must just have been a first attempt to capture random thoughts and ideas on paper. The sheet was divided up into small boxes. Each rectangle had a series of sketches in black ink. There were scribbled words. It seemed unlike Catherine's usual, organized way of working. The writing was cramped and almost unintelligible.

'What do you think?' Euan said. Then, becoming more desperate. 'This is all there is. This is all we have to work on.'

'It could be a storyboard,' she said. 'Each scene drawn out visually. Not exactly that, because sometimes she uses words instead, but a plan for how she'd like the film to turn out.'

'A master plan. So she'd know what scenes she needed to shoot.'

'Perhaps.'

She focused on one square at a time, blocking out the others around it with her hands and a blank sheet of paper torn from the back of the pad. 'How does it start? This is a sketch of the ravens. Really they're very good. So the film would start here, at home. At least I guess that's it.' She moved on to the next one. 'Does this mean anything to you?'

'It says "house room". That's what they call the sixth-form common room at school. A scene there, I suppose.'

'And this?'

He shook his head. 'A couple of stick figures which

could have been drawn by a child. It obviously meant something to her. A sort of shorthand perhaps. It doesn't say anything to me. But this plan gives us something to go on. It should be possible to work out what she intended.'

Fran thought it unlikely they'd ever be certain what Catherine had in mind, but didn't say so. She was pleased that Euan's mood seemed to have lifted. She moved slowly on. In one square they made out representations of sheep, in another seals. Perhaps those images were to provide a background for her voice-over. She couldn't see how they fitted with her themes of ice and fire.

There were initials scattered throughout the grid. Most meant nothing to her. Then she came across *RI*. She didn't expect Euan to pick up on it, but he did. 'Robert Isbister,' he said. 'That could be Robert Isbister.'

'It could be lots of other people too.'

'But Inspector Perez asked me about him. He asked if I knew him. He'd seen his van out here one night. But that was after Catherine died so I suppose it's hardly relevant.'

Unless he'd come here to steal the film and the script, Fran thought. That could have happened after the murder. Euan didn't start looking for the film until several days after that. But she kept her thoughts to herself. She didn't want to explain how she knew Robert. What would she say? He's the grown-up son of my husband's middle-aged lover? In the same box as the initials something else had been scribbled.

'What do you think this is?' In the storyboard, Catherine's writing was much less clear. It was as if she'd wanted to get down her ideas very quickly, before she lost track of them.

Euan turned the page so he could see it more clearly. 'A date. January 3rd. It looks as if it's been added. Isn't it in different ink?' He straightened, stretched. 'We must be missing something. I can't see anything here which would lead someone to murder her.'

'Perhaps there is nothing.' It sounded brutal, but she didn't know how else to say it. 'Perhaps Magnus Tait was responsible all the time. Perhaps the film and the script aren't in the house, because she'd finished it. She took it into school at the end of last term and left it there. Perhaps we should have checked before putting you through all this.'

'No,' he said 'I can't accept that. If the film was edited and complete in the middle of December why the date, the third of January? Why the reference to Up Helly Aa in the notebook? That doesn't happen until the middle of January.' He picked up the receipt with its own message. 'Why the interest in Catriona Bruce?'

'This isn't for us to decide.' Fran thought he would go quite mad if he kept on with it, imagined him sitting up for another night, reading conspiracies and hidden messages into words which had been thrown down almost carelessly. 'You have to show this to Jimmy Perez. He'll know what to do with it.'

His reaction shocked her again. He stood up so suddenly that his chair tipped behind him. 'No,' he said. 'This is my business. It has nothing to do with the police.' Then he must have realized that he'd frightened her. He picked up the chair, sat down and became again the courteous and controlled teacher. 'I'm sorry. Of course you're right. But I'll have to take a copy before I give it to them. It seems so intimate, this writing. I can't bear the thought of people going through it. It's another sort of violation.'

Chapter Thirty-Seven

Magnus sat in the police cell. There would be one more court appearance before he was transferred to the prison on the Scottish mainland, though he hadn't quite grasped that. He knew sometime he would be moved and every time an officer approached, the keys rattling on his belt, boots firm on the tiled floor, Magnus thought the time had come for him to leave Shetland. Sometimes he thought the future was like an enormous black wave waiting to drown him. But it was worse than that. A wave he could understand. He couldn't swim so he would never survive, but he could understand it. This was unknowable, blank. He was so terrified about moving that when the door opened for his food to arrive, or for his lawyer to visit, he began to shake. No one could get any sense out of him and they'd given up talking to him.

Outside it was raining. He could hear the rain on the window, but it was too high for him to see outside. In his head, it was summer, and he was cutting hay, using a scythe in the old way, because they had so little land that it wasn't worth the fuss of asking a neighbour with a machine for help. He stopped to catch his breath and wipe the sweat from his forehead with his sleeve. There was a stiff westerly, blowing the waves beyond

Raven's Head into white peaks, but the effort of bending and cutting had made him hot. He could see a small child dancing up the hill. She was carrying flowers tied with a ribbon, which streamed out behind her. He leaned the scythe carefully against the wall. He'd been working since breakfast. He'd thought he'd get the field done before he stopped, but now he decided he'd take a short break, have a cup of tea and one of those griddle scones his mother had baked the day before.

Outside in the passage there were shouts. He couldn't make out the words – he'd been lost in his daydream. Two constables calling to each other. He held his breath, grew dizzy with panic, but it must just have been a bit of fun. There was a sudden burst of laughter and he heard them move away into the office. He began to breathe again.

He'd talked to Catherine about Catriona, that last time she'd come to visit, the day he'd gone to Safeway's and he'd seen her on the bus. He hadn't meant to. He'd just asked her in for tea. She'd wanted tea. Not a dram, it had been too early for that, she'd said. But she was dying for a cup of tea.

She'd taken his picture. First outside, with him standing by the house and looking down towards the school. Then in the house, swinging the camera all around and stopping for a while next to the raven, pointing it very close to the bars of the cage. Since they'd locked him up, Magnus had thought every now and then about the raven and about how maybe it would have been better to kill it as soon as he'd found it injured. Maybe that would have been kinder than keeping it shut in.

Catherine had shown him the pictures she'd taken,

pointing to them on a little screen. 'Look Magnus, you're on television.' But his eyesight hadn't been good lately and he hadn't been able to make out the images. They seemed to be jumping up and down in front of him, and how could photos do that? He pretended he could see, though, because he didn't want to hurt her.

He'd thought she would go then, but she sat down in his mother's chair, lying back as if she was exhausted. She'd taken off her coat and thrown it on the floor beside her. She was wearing trousers, black trousers, very wide at the bottom. His mother had never worn trousers in her life, but in the warm there as the light started to go outside, it was almost like talking to his mother.

Why had he started talking about Catriona? Because the girl had been in his mind a lot since new year when Sally and Catherine had tumbled into his house. They were older than Catriona, more like women than girls with their shiny lips and the black lines around their eyes, but they made him feel the same. It was the giggling and the fast way of talking and the way they played with their hair. Catherine's tiny feet and skinny wrists, Sally's soft plump arms, their bangles and beads. But now Catherine sat in his mother's chair, with her legs crossed and her stockinged feet stretched towards the fire and she didn't giggle. She asked gentle questions and listened to his answers. He forgot his mother's words *Tell them nothing* and he described what happened that day after Catriona came to call.

Later, of course, he regretted it. Later, he knew he'd done wrong.

Chapter Thirty-Eight

They sat in Jimmy Perez's house. Somehow Taylor was still in Shetland. Perez wasn't sure how he'd managed to get out of returning to Inverness. He'd avoided phone calls, talked vaguely about taking a few days leave, said his back was playing up, made excuses about details of the case. *Still some loose ends to tie up.* The same excuses Perez made when he tried to explain what he was doing still looking into Catherine Ross's murder. Because that was all over, wasn't it? The old man was in custody. Any day now he'd be sent south and they could forget all about it until the case came to court.

Only Perez couldn't forget it. And neither could Taylor. Which was why they were sitting here, in Perez's house, and not at the police station, where Taylor might be caught lying down the phone to his superiors in Inverness. And it was why any resentment Perez might have had about an outsider coming in and taking over the case had evaporated. Rank didn't matter any more. They were allies.

Outside the weather had changed again, brightened up a bit. The rain had stopped and the wind had eased. The forecast for January 25th was for high pressure and frost. That would be fine for Up Helly Aa –

a clear night so you could see the bonfire for miles. In town that was what the talk was about – the boat, the procession and who would lead it – and already the tourists had started to arrive.

They were sitting in the wood-panelled room and a milky sun was reflected from the water. Perez had made coffee, a big cafetière which was supposed to last them, but which was already nearly empty and anyway was cold. The cafetière and two mugs stood on a tray on the floor. On the low coffee table lay the notebook, the big sheet of paper with Catherine's plan for her film and the crumpled Safeway's receipt.

Euan Ross had brought them in the night before. He'd come straight from the library where he'd taken copies. *I know her writing better than you do. Something might suddenly make sense to me.* The paper and notebook had been in a clear plastic A4 envelope, which he'd held away from his body, gingerly, like a bomb. He'd refused to hand it over to anyone else in the police station.

When Taylor picked up the receipt Perez wanted to take it from him. The Englishman's hands were so big that Perez was afraid he might damage it and already the print from the till was faint. Taylor looked at the note in Catherine's writing. *Catriona Bruce. Desire or hate?* Then he turned it over.

'It's dated January 4th and timed ten fifty-seven,' Perez said, trying to keep his voice calm, hoping Taylor would replace the scrap of paper. 'The purchases are listed: oatcakes, milk, tea, biscuits, economy pork sausages, a steak pie for one, two tins of peas, two tins of beans, a white sliced loaf, a ginger cake and a bottle of Famous Grouse. I've been to Magnus's house . . .' Not for the first time. He'd been there the day after the old man's arrest, carried out the raven in its creaky old cage and taken it to the woman in Dunrossness to care for. He hadn't told his colleagues about that. They thought him daft enough as it was. But he couldn't just leave it there to starve and he couldn't hit it on the head either. He returned his attention to the receipt. 'There were two sausages of the same brand in his fridge along with the pie, one tin of beans is in his pantry, the other, empty, is in his rubbish bin—'

'OK,' Taylor interrupted. 'So the receipt belonged to Magnus.' Finally he replaced the paper on the table. Perez felt himself relax.

He continued, 'The date, of course, is most significant. January 4th. The day before Catherine's body was found. The day they met up on the bus. Catherine scribbled a note on the receipt when she was in Magnus's house. Something she wanted to remember. We'll come back to that. She took it with her, must have done because Euan found it in her room. That means she must have been alive when she left Hillhead.'

'It doesn't mean Magnus didn't kill her,' Taylor said. 'He could have followed her to the Ross house. Or arranged to meet her outside. We always thought it most likely she was killed where she was found. Almost certain, the pathologist said.'

'Aye,' Perez said. 'Maybe. But why would he follow her? Why kill her?'

'Because he'd talked to her about Catriona Bruce. He must be a lonely man. Living all on his own in that house since his mother died. Suddenly he had company, someone sympathetic, wanting him to talk, listening to him. Perhaps she had her own reasons for encouraging him to speak. She wanted his stories for her film. Perhaps she was just a nice kid who felt sorry for him. And the temptation was too much for him. Perhaps he'd had a whisky or two and that loosened his tongue. Whatever.'

'I can see that,' Perez said. 'I can even see him killing her afterwards to keep the whole thing quiet. But I can't see him going into the Ross house, searching her room and finding the disk, finding the script and wiping all trace of it from the PC. I don't get that.'

They sat looking at each other for a moment in silence. Taylor stretched, shuffled in his chair. He'd told Perez he had a bad back, disc trouble, that was why he couldn't sit still, but Perez wasn't convinced. It was the man's mind that didn't know how to rest, not his body.

'So what do we do about it?' Taylor said. 'Time's running out for me. I've promised I'll be back at the end of the week. Any longer than that and they'll start talking about a disciplinary.'

'I'm going to take another trip to the Anderson,' Perez said. 'Check she didn't hand the film in early, give it to a friend to look at. If the film is safe we have to let the whole thing go. Like you said, the note on the back of the receipt incriminates Magnus. It shows he talked to her about Catriona. Euan says there's no other way she could have known about the girl.'

Taylor stood up, lifting the plan with both hands on his way. He carried it to the window, where the light was better. 'This is crazy,' he said. 'I mean, submit this as evidence and they'll think she was psychotic. What does it mean? Some sort of secret code? It's like that writing the Egyptians used. Hieroglyphs.'

'Euan thinks it was a way of planning the film, of laying out the scenes in the right order.'

'Can you make anything of it?'

'They think she was using the Robert Frost poem 'Fire and Ice' as a framework for the film.'

'They?' Taylor frowned.

'Mrs Hunter was with Euan when he went through it.'

'For Christ's sake! She found both bodies! If the case was more open she'd be a fucking suspect.'

He prowled away from the window. Perez knew he was right to be disturbed, but couldn't see Fran killing anyone. He thought of her sometimes, late at night, when the wind blew rain against his window. He imagined her curled up by the fire, Cassie on her knee, reading stories.

Perez got to his feet and went to the bookshelf. There was a collection of verse he'd had since school. It was stolen, still had the Anderson High stamp inside. He hadn't meant to steal it, he just hadn't got round to taking it back when he left. It had been packed into boxes with all his other books when he left home. Would it get packed again and sit on a shelf in Skerry, in the room with the big window looking south over Fair Isle?

He looked at the index and found 'Fire and Ice', handed it to Taylor. 'Well, what do you think?'

Taylor was unusually still for several minutes. He stood by the window, hunched over the book, ferocious in his concentration on the poem. At last he straightened. 'I don't know which is most destructive,' he said. 'But ice is worse.'

'What do you mean?'

'I can understand violence coming out of fire. Passion, lack of control. I'm not saying I condone it. But it makes sense to me. Someone suddenly losing their temper. That blind rage. But violence which is cold and calculating, planned in advance. Icy. That must be worse, mustn't it?'

Perez was going to say that the result for the victim would be much the same, but Taylor was still gripped in some thought or memory, and he realized he'd be wasting his words.

When Perez got to the high school, the bell had just gone for afternoon lessons. He stood at the main entrance until the crowds had cleared and the corridors were empty. At the office he asked if Mr Scott was teaching. He didn't have to identify himself. The secretary had worked there since he was a boy. She looked at him over the glasses with blue plastic rims which she'd always worn, then checked a timetable pinned to the wall. 'No. Free period. You should find him in the staff room.' She'd never been friendly.

Scott was sitting at a desk with his back to the room marking exercise books. When Perez had knocked at the door a woman had shouted angrily, 'Yes, what is it?' She'd expected a child to be standing there and seeing Perez she was embarrassed. She said something about talking to the head and left Perez and Scott alone. Scott put down his red pen and half stood.

'Inspector,' he said. 'What can I do for you?' He seemed more at ease than when Perez had last been in the school. Perhaps he'd had time to get over his grief at Catherine's death or perhaps he thought Magnus's arrest meant that there would be no more awkward questions about his relationship with the girl.

'Just a few loose ends.'

'Of course. Tea?'

Perez nodded and sat on one of the low orange chairs. Again, he had the sensation of being an impostor. He shouldn't be here. He *should* be waiting outside, a piece of late work in his hand.

'It's about Catherine's film.'

'Last term's project. I'd set the group a piece of documentary writing. They had to capture the spirit of contemporary Shetland. She asked if she could make a film instead. She said she would produce the script to go with it, so I agreed.'

'Last term's project. She handed it in before Christmas, then, did she?'

Scott handed Jimmy a mug of tea. It looked very pale. Perez knew before trying that it would have no taste.

'Not exactly.'

Perez thought he had preferred the English teacher when he was nervous. This new pompous confidence was more irritating. He waited and eventually Scott continued.

'She asked for an extension. Usually she was good about meeting deadlines and she'd obviously been enthusiastic about the film, so I was surprised.'

'Did she make the request before your romantic encounter or afterwards?'

Scott looked suddenly furious, which was what Perez had intended, but the teacher kept control. When he spoke his voice made it clear he thought Perez's comment unworthy of a response.

'It was just before she came to my flat. I'd already agreed to give her more time. There was no possibility that she was putting pressure on me to fall in with her request.'

'What reason did she give for needing an extension?'

'She wanted to include a piece about Up Helly Aa. To outsiders the Viking fire festival is emblematic. I could see that it would be an interesting addition to the film. I did insist though that she let me have a synopsis before the end of term. There was already some petty jealousy around Catherine. I didn't want more accusations of favouritism.'

'And did she give you the synopsis?'

'Not in person, no. I've already explained that I didn't see her during the last few days of term. She must have come into the staff room when it was empty, or given it to another member of staff. I found it in my pigeon hole in here.'

'Could I see it please?'

He thought for a moment the teacher would refuse, but Scott only sighed deeply at the interruption, and asked Perez to follow him to the English department. His classroom was in the old part of the building. It seemed colder in there despite the pale sunshine coming through the dusty skylight. Perez followed him downstairs and into an empty room. Scott opened a cupboard and pulled out a thick box file. 'I've been collecting together all Catherine's work. I thought Euan might like to have it.' He set the file on a table at the front of the room and looked at it for a moment before opening it.

For some reason Perez had been expecting the

synopsis to be in the same cramped handwriting as the editing plan, but it had been typed on a computer. There was the same title, *Fire and Ice*, in bold at the top. He read it slowly, aware that Scott was watching him.

This film uses the stereotypical images of Shetland landscape and history and subverts them to comment on contemporary life on the islands. There is no narrative line; rather the pictures and real conversations are cut to allow the viewer to come to his or her own conclusion about the values which shape this unique community. The story is told by real Shetlanders, native and incomers, in their own words. My voice-over sets the scene and the tone. It makes no moral judgement.

'Is this all there is?' Perez said. 'Not much of a synopsis is it? I mean there's not much detail.'

'Quite,' Scott said. 'A point I intended to make to Catherine when I saw her. Unfortunately I didn't have that opportunity.'

Walking out of the main gate, Perez caught a glimpse of Jonathan Gale, the lad who'd given Catherine and Sally a lift on New Year's Eve. He increased his pace and caught him up.

'Hi. How are things?'

The boy shrugged. 'I'll be glad to leave. University next year. I've got a place at Bristol. I can't wait.'

'You're bound to be upset about Catherine. Losing someone you cared about.'

'I don't know why. She just set out to make a fool of me.'

Perez thought suddenly he knew what Jonathan meant. 'New Year's Eve. Was Catherine with Robert

Isbister?' He thought she'd been flaunting herself with Robert to make a point.

Jonathan gave a bitter laugh. 'No. It was nothing like that. Robert was all over Sally in the car, not Catherine. It was horrible actually. I didn't know where to look.'

So then Perez wondered if it had been Robert who'd been making the point. Some attempt to make Catherine jealous perhaps? Surely he hadn't been so obsessed by the girl that he'd been driven to kill her.

Chapter Thirty-Nine

Cassie wanted to spend January 25th with her father. He always celebrated Up Helly Aa on the same day as the festival in Lerwick. There was a big bonfire on the beach then everyone went back to the Haa. It wasn't like the big show for the tourists in Lerwick. It was a community gathering. Fran rejected the plan out of hand. Up Helly Aa at Duncan's place was a piss-up. The party to end all parties. How could Duncan take responsibility for a child, especially without Celia to keep him on the straight and narrow?

It was Sunday afternoon and Duncan had taken Cassie to Unst to visit an elderly uncle. Now they stood on Fran's doorstep arguing but trying to keep their voices civilized because Cassie was inside watching television.

'Come on,' he said. 'She'll love it. It'll take her mind off everything that's been going on here.'

'You must be joking.' Fran had a nightmare vision of Duncan's Up Helly Aa from a small child's perspective. She imagined Cassie abandoned on the beach looking up at the towering strangers around her while Duncan was playing with his mates. The flames would throw odd shadows on to their faces. Cassie already dreamt enough about monsters. 'She'd be terrified. And you'd be too drunk to look after her properly.'

His face paled and he blinked violently as if he'd been slapped. She stepped away, expecting an angry outburst, but when he spoke it was almost in a whisper. 'Do you really think that badly of me?'

Then he turned and walked away without a word, not even calling in to Cassie to say goodbye. Fran watched him go with a stab of guilt. Perhaps she'd misjudged him. Should she call him back and tell him Cassie could go with him if he promised to take care of her? But then he'd always found ways to manipulate her. Perhaps guilt was just the response he'd been working for.

He must already have promised Cassie she'd be spending Up Helly Aa with him, because back in the house that was all she could talk about. He'd have talked it up. He had a knack of conjuring magic with his words. When Fran made it clear the trip wasn't going to happen Cassie had a major tantrum. She threw herself on to her bed, sobbing, gasping for breath, scaring Fran into thinking she was having some sort of seizure. There were words too, tangled, pushed out hysterically between the sobs. *I'll never be able to go to school again. Everyone else is going to Up Helly Aa. We painted the galley. Jamie's uncle is in the Guizer Jarl's squad. What shall I tell them? What will they think?*

The hair around her face was matted with tears. Fran stroked it from her cheeks and her forehead. 'We'll go into Lerwick,' she said. 'We'll look at the procession and see the boat being burned. That's the real

Up Helly Aa. More exciting than a bonfire on the beach at the Haa.'

The crying stopped abruptly. There were a couple of dramatic shudders. Fran found herself wondering if a skill to manipulate was carried in the genes, transferred of course through the paternal line.

It seemed Euan Ross had been thinking about Up Helly Aa too. The next day Fran called in on him after she had dropped Cassie at school. He made her coffee and took her into the living room with its huge pointed window looking over the bay.

'According to the police Catherine hadn't finished her film. She'd asked for an extension so she could include the fire festival. It would fit with the theme, wouldn't it?'

Fran saw that he had thought of nothing else since he'd found the notebook and the storyboard. Ideas about his daughter's death were fizzing in his brain, stopping him sleeping or eating, driving him slowly crazy. He'd stuck the plan on the kitchen wall and while he was making the coffee he couldn't take his eyes off it. She was about to ask if he'd seen a doctor, but he started talking again.

'I knew Catherine had been to the library to research the history of Up Helly Aa. She was very scathing about it. All men, of course, in the squads, which must have seemed impossible today to an independent young woman. The festival started off, it seems, as some sort of game. In the eighteenth century they rolled burning barrels of tar through the streets of Lerwick to celebrate midwinter. It sounds remarkably dangerous. Catherine would have been there tomorrow. We discussed it, though I didn't realize it had anything to do with her film. She would have been more interested, I suspect, in the ridiculous incidents surrounding the event than in the spectacle itself.' He seemed caught up again in his own thoughts, then turned from the window to look at Fran. 'I'll probably go into Lerwick tomorrow night. I told Catherine I'd be there. It was one of the last conversations we had. It must sound foolish but I feel as if I made some sort of commitment. It wouldn't have mattered to her either way, but I said that I'd be there so I think I should.'

'You're welcome to come with us. I've promised Cassie I'll take her. The other kids at school are so excited about it she'd feel left out if she wasn't there.'

'No,' he said slowly. 'That's very kind but I don't think I'd be good company.'

There was an awkward silence. She thought he was in a mood when he'd prefer to be alone, but she didn't think it would be good for him to be left with his obsession. Besides, she still had half a mug of coffee left and wasn't sure how she could leave without embarrassing them both.

'What are your plans?' she asked at last. 'For the future I mean. Will you stay here? Or will you sell up and move south?'

'I can't think that far ahead.' His attention seemed caught by a small boat crossing the bay and she saw he couldn't think of anything else at the moment. He could only focus on prising meanings from his daughter's writings which might explain her death.

'Do you think Inspector Perez is an intelligent man?' he asked suddenly.

She considered for a moment. 'I think I'd trust him to get things right. He seems to have an open mind at least.'

'I showed him all the information we discovered about Catherine's film. The receipt and the jotter. The plan. He has everything. I only have copies.'

She saw how hard it must have been for him to relinquish the scraps of paper.

'*Fire and Ice*,' he went on. 'I hope the detective picked up its full significance. I tried to explain . . .'

She didn't know what to say. How could she speak for Perez? Anyway she wasn't sure she understood entirely what Catherine had wanted to achieve with the film. It probably had no significance at all. Ross was constructing an elaborate theory from a poem and a piece of homework.

He continued, almost to himself. 'There was ice the night Catherine was killed of course. Ice. Cold hatred. Destructive. And tomorrow night is the fire festival. Fire for passion . . .' She waited for him to go on, but he seemed to realize he was rambling. 'Probably nothing,' he said. 'Nothing sinister at all. An excuse for men to dress up in silly costumes and show off. And then drink too much.'

When she said she would show herself out, she wasn't sure whether or not he had heard her.

Chapter Forty

It was Monday morning and Sally woke up in the dark, switched on the bedside light, felt for her alarm clock and looked at the time. From the kitchen she heard her mother, the shutting of a cupboard door, the rattle of a spoon in a mug. Her mother seemed to get up earlier every morning, though there was nothing more for her to do. Preparation for school was completed every night before bedtime – the pile of orange exercise books marked and neatly arranged. Why couldn't she chill occasionally? Sometimes Sally even felt sorry for her. She had no friends after all. Only the parents who were frightened of her.

In the bathroom Sally looked at herself in the mirror over the sink. Smiled. The zit on the side of her nose had gone. Monday morning and she felt OK. The stomach cramps, the migraine, the panic of the old days had gone. Now she almost looked forward to going to school and meeting everyone. She stood in the shower and tilted back her head so she could wash her hair.

Over breakfast her mother seemed distracted. She'd allowed the porridge to stick to the pan and there was no bread left in the freezer for toast. Sally poured muesli into a bowl, added milk, dreamed of Up Helly

Aa. It would be a great night for Robert, supporting his father as the Guizer Jarl, following him in the procession through the streets of Lerwick and around the community halls. She should be with him.

Of course she'd be in town for the procession and the burning of the galley. That wasn't a problem. Her parents had taken her into Lerwick to see the spectacle since she was a baby. But as soon as the fire died down they would want her to leave town and go home with them. Tomorrow night there was no way she'd be back in Ravenswick, tucked up in bed in the school house by ten o'clock. No way.

'I'm babysitting for Mrs Hunter again tonight.'

'Oh?' Margaret was at the sink, scrubbing the burnt pan. Her bare elbows looked red and bony like uncooked chicken thighs. Sally wasn't even sure her mother had taken in the words. Radio Shetland was on in the background. An excited voice, male but high-pitched, was giving the weather forecast for the following night.

'She asked if I could stop in straight from school, give Cassie her tea while she gets ready to go out. She'll leave me something to eat. Is that OK with you?'

'I don't see why not.'

It was unexpectedly easy. There were no questions, no sarcastic comments about Fran's parenting skills. It crossed Sally's mind that there might be something wrong with her mother. The menopause maybe. When did that happen? Was her mother the right age? She didn't dwell on the possibility for long. She had other things to think about. Although it was early for the bus she left the house before her mother could change her mind.

First lesson was English with Mr Scott. They were still doing *Macbeth*, reading it out loud in class, everyone taking a different character. Since Catherine's death, Sally had found lessons easier too. Teachers had been more patient, more ready to explain. They'd noticed her. She talked less, thought more carefully about what she had to say. That was because she wasn't so nervous.

They'd had to write an essay for Mr Scott about Lady Macbeth and her relationship with her husband. Last term she'd have been a wreck waiting for it to be handed back, gabbing away about nothing to whoever would listen to her, just so she wouldn't think about what he would say. Now there was just a sort of curiosity about what the teacher had made of it. It wasn't as if he'd lay into her about it even if it was crap. Scott wasn't so bad, she thought. Not sexy like Robert, but gentle, sensitive. Catherine had been hard on him.

Now he sat on her table, just as he'd used to sit on Catherine's. His hand, rested flat on the wood supporting himself, was very close to hers. He was wearing the old man's jacket and she could smell the wool. 'An excellent piece of writing, Sally. Some very interesting points. You really seem to have found your voice this term. Perhaps I can recommend some extra reading.'

Beside her she knew that Lisa was smirking. They'd all take the piss at break in the house room, but she couldn't help being flattered. 'Thank you, Mr Scott. That'd be great.'

All day the school felt different, like they were small kids again in the build-up to Christmas. That slightly manic air. Everyone with too much energy and not being able to concentrate. It was all about Up Helly Aa. The sixth years mocked the whole thing, but even in their house room there was a suppressed excitement, a collective silliness. At lunchtime they had a go at her as she'd expected. 'Scottie really fancies you,' Lisa said. 'You can tell.' Then someone said. 'You want to watch it. He really fancied Catherine and look what happened to her.' And the room went quiet for a moment until James Sinclair threw the remains of his sandwich at Simon Fletcher and chaos broke out again.

Sally didn't have a lesson last thing and walked into town, to the hall where they were putting the final touches to the galley. Robert was already there. He looked as if he'd been there all day. He had splashes of varnish in his hair. Although they had arranged to meet, he seemed briefly shocked to see her and she wondered what was the matter with the people she knew at the moment – her mother, Robert, even her father. They all seemed wrapped up in their own dreams or preoccupations so the demands of everyday life seemed to come as a surprise.

She thought the galley looked stunning. It was enormous and the dragon's head at the prow reared up over her, its flared painted nostrils and fiery eyes somehow hypnotic, pulling her attention. Robert grinned. He took a horned helmet from a shelf beside him and put it on, then held the shield across his breast.

'Well? What do you think? My dad gets back later. I want everything perfect for him.'

She thought he was like a little boy showing off. A picture of Mr Scott reading Shakespeare to them came into her head and she wondered in a fleeting, disloyal moment if perhaps Robert wasn't the right person for her after all. Then she saw how magnificent he looked, with his blond beard and blond hair. How could Scott compete with that?

He held the shield high above his head and she thought how strong he was. He'd be able to lift her aloft just as easily, snap her wrist with one of his hands.

'I'm babysitting again tonight. Will you be able to make it? I told you. Remember?'

She saw from the moment of confusion on his face that he'd forgotten all about it.

'I'm not sure,' he said, keeping his voice low. 'There's a last-minute meeting of the squad. The official photograph. My dad will need me. He trusted me to look after things while he was away. But we can be together tomorrow. I've got you a ticket for one of the halls. But tonight? You know how it is. I have to be there.'

No, she thought. I don't know how it is.

'Please.' She reached up and touched his face, then kissed him quickly on the mouth, pushing the point of her tongue between his lips. She saw him look over her shoulder at the two men working on the galley. They were crouched in the hull fitting the base of the mast into its casing and didn't see. What does it matter to him? she thought. I have my parents to worry about, but he's an adult, free. Why does he want to keep this secret?

'I'll try to get there later,' he said. She couldn't tell if he'd really try or if he would have promised anything then to get rid of her.

In the end she was back at school in time to get the

bus home, and she didn't need the cover she'd made up that morning to explain her absence. But she couldn't face her mother, who would be even more bad-tempered after a day of hyperactive children. Sally could remember what it was like in the primary school just before Up Helly Aa – all the kids going wild, beating each other up with cardboard swords. Her mother would be in a foul mood. She got off the bus on the main road and went to Fran's anyway.

'I thought I could give Cassie her tea and you'd have the chance to get ready in peace,' she said, standing on the doorstep, a model babysitter, eager to please. 'If you'd like me to. I haven't much homework tonight.' This was the story she'd given her mother. Sally was a good liar, knew the importance of sticking to the same untruth. And of getting corroboration whenever possible. 'But I can come back later if you want.'

'No,' Fran opened the door to let her in. 'That'd be great. Cassie's as high as a kite. I've promised to take her into Lerwick tomorrow for Up Helly Aa. Her first time. Will you be there?'

'Oh, I'll be there.' She was going to say, boasting, *My boyfriend's in the Guizer Jarl's squad,* but something stopped her. Standing just inside the door, an idea came to her. A story which would keep her mother off her back, give her the chance of a proper night out. *Mrs Hunter has asked me to go with her tomorrow. Help her keep an eye on Cassie. She says, can I sleep over so she can go to a party in the hall? That's OK, isn't it?* Of course Margaret would find out about Robert sooner or later. But Sally wanted time to get her story right, to decide exactly what to say.

Cassie was still awake, fractious and difficult when

Fran went out. Sally thought she'd never met a child so full of questions and imaginings. How could you keep your patience and answer all that? As soon as her mother had gone Cassie was up, restless and fidgety, wanting water and a book to read, talking all the time, wearing Sally down. Sally found it hard to keep her temper, understood for the first time why her mother was so sharp to the kids in school. Robert could turn up at any time and she wanted Cassie asleep by then. At last she got the child to bed and watched until she fell into a light and fitful sleep.

When Robert arrived Cassie must have been woken by his knocking or by the strange man's voice because she appeared again at the bedroom door, her hair tousled, her pyjamas untucked. Sally thought the interruption would make him angry, but he'd drunk just enough to make him mellow, and he sat in the big chair by the fire and took the little girl on to his knee. She resisted for a moment then gave in. Sally couldn't tell if the big stranger in her house had frightened her into silence or if she was enjoying it. Cassie stayed on his knee until she fell asleep. He carried her to her room and laid her gently on the bed. In his arms she looked as floppy and lifeless as a doll.

When Fran came home, Sally thought she should tell her that Robert had been there. It wouldn't do for it to come from Cassie.

'I hope you don't mind. A friend called in. He didn't stay long.'

Sally was waiting for questions. She had her story prepared. But Fran too seemed preoccupied and lost in her own thoughts. 'Right,' she said. 'OK. No problem.'

Chapter Forty-One

Fran hadn't thought there could be this many people in Shetland. All of them, every person from the country and from the north isles and from Bressay, Foula and Whalsay, must be crammed into town tonight. It wasn't just Shetlanders filling the streets either. There were tourists from all over the world. The hotels, guest houses and B&Bs must be full. In the crowd she heard American voices and Australians and languages she couldn't understand. Only now the pipe band leading the procession was coming closer and she couldn't hear much except the music and the cheering, and all the voices seemed to swell together to make one overwhelming sound.

Cassie stood beside her, fidgeting because she couldn't see. Some of the children had squeezed through to the front of the crowd, but Fran was afraid that if Cassie let go her hand, they would never find each other again. Cassie had been in a strange mood all day, full of some secret she'd been told at school. She'd been in turns silent and mysterious, not answering her mother's questions, then suddenly excitable, letting out a stream of words which hardly made sense. Now she was restless, watching for the distant torches. The Guizer Jarl appeared, magnificent in his costume, the shield and the horned helmet gleaming, followed by his squad of Vikings. Fran lifted Cassie on to her shoulders so she could see him, but something about the spectacle – the Vikings, so fierce and warlike, or the following squads of guizers dressed in carnival costumes or the fire – seemed to scare her, because soon she squirmed to be let down. Fran could see that there was a nightmare element to the scene. A dozen Bart Simpsons followed a dozen James Bonds, followed by a dozen cartoon donkeys with enormous flashing teeth. All the men were rowdy, those faces not covered by carnival masks were flushed by the torches and by drink.

The procession took longer to pass than she'd expected. It had to file through the narrow street, trapped on each side by tall grey houses.

'Have you seen enough now?' She bent to yell into Cassie's ear. 'Should we go home?'

Cassie didn't answer immediately. Fran thought she was ready to leave, but knew that the next day she'd have to face the children at school, boasting about how late they'd stayed up, teasing her for having missed the climax of the evening.

'We have to see the galley being burned,' she said at last, stubbornly, expecting a fight. But Fran knew how cruel children could be.

So they stayed, and they were swept along by the crowd towards the King George V playing field, where the galley would be set alight. And again Fran thought the whole of Shetland must be here because everywhere she looked there were people she knew. Sometimes she just glimpsed people in the distance, at others she travelled along with them for a little way until they were separated by the pressing mass.

She saw Euan Ross standing in a doorway. He was at the top of a small flight of steps, observing events without being a part of them. Just like Catherine, Fran thought. Just as Catherine would have acted if she'd been here. She pulled Cassie with her out of the stream and approached him. It was quieter here. The band had moved on. She could talk without shouting.

'What do you make of it?'

He didn't answer immediately. He joined them on the pavement, crouched to say hello to Cassie, knotted her scarf more snugly around her neck. Watching him, Fran thought, He's remembering Catherine at that age. When he had a wife and a child.

'It's rather fun, isn't it?' he said, straightening. 'One knows it's a Victorian invention, but so much time and effort have gone into making it a success that it would be churlish to criticize. It brings people together after all. I hope Catherine would have recognized that in her film.'

'Will you come to watch the galley being burned?'

'Of course,' he said. 'I'll have to see it through now. But don't wait for me. I'll get there in my own time.'

Singing had started. Loud, boisterous men's singing. Like a rugby song or a football chant. Fran left Euan standing there in his doorway, but when she turned back, he'd already gone. Cassie hurried her away, worried that they'd get left behind and they'd miss the action on the field, but back on the street the procession continued, a stream of grotesque grinning faces. There they met Jan Ellis, the Ravenswick woman who'd given them the dog, and her daughter

Shona. Jan seemed pleased to see them, began to ask about Maggie, but Fran didn't get a chance to answer because Jan's husband marched past, dressed like the rest of his squad as a baby in a romper suit and nappy, a pink knitted bonnet on his head. The crowd laughed and cheered.

'It drove me crazy knitting that outfit,' Jan yelled. 'What is it with men and dressing up?'

And then she was gone too, pulled along by Shona, who wanted another glimpse of her father looking ridiculous.

Fran stood still for a moment. The noise made her feel giddy and a bit sick. She worried that she might faint and she bent her head and breathed in deeply. As she straightened, she thought she saw Duncan on the other side of the road, in intense conversation with a large woman in a red anorak. She knew it couldn't *be* Duncan. He would already be at the Haa with his drinking cronies, preparing to light his bonfire on the beach. She wondered if she was secretly hoping to see him. Tonight in her imagination anything was possible. The whole evening was like an elaborate sleight of hand. A Victorian invention dressed up as a Norse midwinter festival, a boat which would never sail, men as babies. This was fantasy masquerading as reality, a conjuror's dream. It made her head spin.

Up Helly Aa at Duncan's house before Cassie's birth had been very different. It had been carried off with a certain style. Duncan had always been a good showman. He had made the festival romantic. She almost wished that she was there, away from the crowd, standing on the frosty beach. The flames from the bonfire would be reflected in the sea. She stared back at the man she'd mistaken for Duncan, but now there was no sign of him or the woman in red amongst the crowd on the opposite pavement. *I'm going mad. Is this how it is for Magnus Tait? Has he lost touch with reality too?*

That was when she realized Cassie was missing.

It took her a few moments to believe it. She looked around her, expecting Cassie to appear with the same ease with which the Duncan lookalike had vanished. Then she forced herself to think clearly and logically. Cassie had dropped her hand when they'd bumped into Jan and Shona. Only babies held hands with their mothers. Fran had understood that, hadn't insisted. Now she peered frantically through the crowd trying to catch a glimpse of Cassie's blue hat. Nothing. She tried to remember if she'd seen Cassie once Jan and Shona had moved on. Her attention had been distracted by the image of Duncan. She'd assumed her daughter had been by her side.

She told herself Cassie must have followed Shona. They were probably all together making their way to the field to watch the burning galley. Jan would keep an eye on her. This panic was ridiculous. It was just as well Margaret Henry couldn't see her now. She pulled her mobile phone from her pocket then looked at it helplessly. She didn't know Jan's number. The crowd in the street was thinning. A group of lads stood, tins of McEwan's in their hands, shouting a bawdy version of the galley song. She pushed past them following the direction of the procession.

At the park the different squads with their torches circled the galley. There was no other light. The street lamps had been turned off at seven-thirty. It was very cold. There was a smell of smoke and crushed grass. She pushed through the laughing people, the families and the gangs of teenage kids, looking for Jan. Everyone was having a good time. They all wore anoraks, scarves and hats, and were as difficult to tell apart as the guizers in their masks. In the flickering light they looked shadowy, exactly the same. Occasionally she would convince herself that she could see Cassie in the distance, but when she approached she saw it was a different child. Someone else's daughter.

The moment of burning had arrived. *They did this to witches. Strange women who had visions.* Someone was counting down from ten. Still searching she thought she saw Celia, a tall straight figure in a long black coat, her head tilted to one side. Of course she'd be there to support her husband. *I thought you were a witch.* Celia might have seen Cassie. She would at least be a familiar figure, if Cassie was wandering around, afraid and lost, someone else to look out for the girl. Fran started making her way through the crowd towards the woman. But then the Guizer Jarl held his torch aloft and threw it on to the galley. All the others followed. There was an explosion of light and in the moment before it faded she saw Jan, standing on the edge of the crowd. Fran walked towards her, pushing past the stewards, too close to the fire. She could taste the burning paint and varnish at the back of her throat. Jan was engrossed in conversation with another mother.

'Have you seen Cassie?'

The panic in her voice made them stop immediately and turn towards her.

'I've lost Cassie. Is she with Shona?'

'No,' Jan said. 'I've not seen her since we were together earlier.'

The galley collapsed in on itself. The long planks bowed and cracked and were engulfed in flame. All that remained was the dragon's head, held by its rib cage of charred timber, rearing high above the crowd.

Chapter Forty-Two

'Another girl missing.'

They were out on the street, walking away from the market cross towards the pier, where it was a bit quieter. On the water the ferry was on its way south to Aberdeen, a moving frame of light. They'd watched the procession like ordinary tourists until the call came through on Jimmy Perez's mobile. It should have been Taylor's last night and they'd had a few beers. Not celebrating. Neither had felt like doing that. But needing to mark the occasion in some way.

Now they could speak without shouting and looked down on the black oily water.

'Another girl whose first name begins with C.' They'd both been thinking it. Perez put it into words.

'Could be a coincidence. She could just have wandered away from her mother. A night like this, how many missing kids do you get reported?' Taylor's Liverpool accent seemed stronger, more edgy. Who's he trying to convince? Perez thought.

He tried to keep his voice even. 'Fran Hunter's hysterical of course. She found both bodies. Hard enough to take. Now this . . .' Perez thought he was close to losing it himself. He could feel the fear like liquid in his stomach, imagined it rising in his throat until it was drowning him. It was foolish to think about Fran, put himself in her skin. He'd only panic like her, then he'd be no good to anyone. He had to hold himself together, think rationally. 'The crowd's clearing a bit now as everyone moves on to the halls and community centres for dancing. If the kid's wandered off and is out on the street, she'll be found in the next hour. I've got people looking. After that we can assume she's been taken. But I don't think we can wait that long. I don't think we can afford to.'

'What about the rest of the team? What do they say?'

'They think I'm overreacting and that the mother's panicking over nothing. After all, the murderer is in custody, isn't he? How can he be back on the street, abducting another child?'

'We can be certain now that Mrs Hunter had nothing to do with Catherine's murder,' Taylor said.

'I never thought she was involved.'

'Where is she now?'

'With Euan Ross. He's taken her back to her house. That was where she wanted to be. In case a neighbour from Ravenswick has picked up the child and brings her home. Morag's there too.'

'What was Ross doing in Lerwick? I'd hardly think he'd be in the mood for a party.'

He was looking for the ghost of his daughter, Perez thought. A slim, dark figure bent over a camcorder on a tripod. What would she be filming now, if she was here? And what can that have to do with Cassie's disappearance? Fire and Ice. We got caught up with the father's obsession with a puzzle. We must have missed something more obvious. 'Fran thought she saw her ex-husband on the street, just before the girl went missing,' he said, leaving Taylor's question hanging, unanswered.

'That's where she is then. That explains it. She'd not wander off with a stranger, would she? Not without a fuss. Maybe you are overreacting lad. You've tried to contact the father?'

'Of course. Landline and mobile. Nothing.'

'That doesn't mean he hasn't got her. Maybe there was some mix up with arrangements. A breakdown in communication . . .'

'Not according to the mother. Duncan had wanted Cassie at his place for Up Helly Aa. Fran refused. Made it quite clear it wasn't going to happen. There was a bit of a row about it.'

'So he took her out of spite?'

Surely, Perez thought, not even Duncan would be that cruel. But he couldn't rule it out as a possibility.

'Do you want me to go out to the kiddie's dad's then?' Taylor was getting impatient. He couldn't understand what Perez was about, standing here, day-dreaming.

'No. I know the way and I'll be quicker. You stay here and coordinate the search on the ground.'

The traffic was heavy coming out of town, nose to tail past the power station, then it cleared suddenly and he could put his foot down. Speeding. Probably just on the limit if they checked for drink. He slowed up a bit through Brae, then he was on his way down the hill and he could see the bonfire already lit on the beach and the black figures silhouetted against the flames. If Duncan was out there, he wouldn't answer his phone. That part of the coast was a black hole for mobiles. There was no reception at all.

There seemed to be lights in all the downstairs windows of the house. He was reminded of the old days before Duncan was married, when everyone young and bright wanted to be here for Up Helly Aa, leaving Lerwick to the tourists and the old folk. Perez had been glad enough of an invitation then. He'd brought Sarah with him from Aberdeen, her first visit to Shetland and she'd been impressed. Duncan had flirted with her of course and she'd responded in a polite, friendly way. Flattered but not taken in by him. She had always been a woman of sound judgement. She'd divorced Jimmy Perez, hadn't she? That showed some sense.

He drove into the walled courtyard and parked the car. Despite all the lights there was no sound from the house. He could see into the kitchen from the court-yard, the stack of cans and bottles on the table, but the room was empty. Everyone must be on the beach.

Perez tried to rehearse what he'd say to Duncan if Cassie was here. If Duncan had taken her from a busy street to make a point. To suggest that Fran wasn't a vigilant mother. Or as Taylor had said, just out of spite because Fran hadn't wanted him to have the girl at the Haa. Perez knew it would be important to keep his temper. He was involved with the family, but he couldn't let it show. He might even have to let Cassie stay here. He'd just call Fran and let her know the girl was safe. Leave it up to her to decide what to do next. But even while he was running through the scenarios in his head, he couldn't allow himself to believe that Cassie was really here, safe and well. That would be tempting providence. He wanted it so much, he couldn't let himself believe it was true.

The first person he saw on the beach was Celia. What was she doing there? The addiction to Duncan must have been too much in the end. She was standing apart from the others, drinking beer straight from the bottle. Her head was tipped back and she emptied the last quarter in one go, then threw the bottle on to the fire. It smashed into pieces on the big smooth pebbles containing the embers. Perez didn't want to get into a discussion about whether she and Duncan were back together. She heard his footsteps on the shingle behind her and turned suddenly. When she saw who it was, she seemed disappointed. Nobody else, amid the drinking and laughing, noticed his presence.

'Where's Duncan?'

'God knows,' she said. 'I've only just arrived. Perhaps he's hiding from me. He might be in bed with one of the pretty young things he always invites to these dos, but it's a bit early for that even for him. He usually stays dressed long enough to welcome his guests.'

'Have you seen Cassie?'

'No. Is she here?' She took another bottle from the crate which stood at her feet, pulled an opener from her coat pocket and flipped off the top. 'Perhaps that's where he is, then, playing happy families. Cocoa and a story before bedtime, a reformed character.'

He was surprised at the bitterness in her voice.

'Haven't you seen him?'

'No,' she said. 'I was in town watching Michael in his moment of glory as Guizer Jarl. Robert following him in the squad, counting the years till he's old enough to do it himself. He's wanted it since he was a boy. He used to act it out, parading through the house with a saucepan on his head.' She was talking to herself, the drink making her reflective, sentimental. 'I'm not sure why it means so much to him. Perhaps sometimes you need someone to tell you that you belong.'

'Was Duncan in Lerwick?'

'No,' she said. 'Why would he be? He never goes to Lerwick for Up Helly Aa. He's above all that. He couldn't bear dancing with the middle-aged housewives in Isleburgh or the high school. He doesn't realize that he's almost middle-aged himself.'

'Cassie's missing,' Jimmy said.

But Celia drank more beer and stared bleakly into the fire. She seemed not to have heard him.

Perez walked over to the crowd by the fire but he could see at once that Duncan wasn't among them. A young man in a long grey coat was sitting on an upended beer crate and playing the guitar very badly. The others gathered round pretending to listen, posing. When he asked about Duncan and Cassie they shrugged. He couldn't tell if they were stoned or drunk or they just didn't care.

He went into the house and started searching, frantic now. Someone had tidied up since his last visit. Duncan had a team of women in Brae he called in to clean for him, in return for a handful of notes and his lost little boy's smile. When the guests had arrived they must have gone straight from the kitchen to the beach, because the long drawing room was quiet and ordered, still smelling of wood smoke and beeswax. The fire was low and automatically he took a piece of driftwood from the bucket and threw it on. It must still have been damp because there was a hiss of steam before it caught.

He continued looking, because he didn't know what else to do and he couldn't go back to town with the job half done. He didn't expect to find anything. He went into rooms he'd never seen before, not even on the weekends when he and Duncan had escaped from Anderson High and had the run of the place. Right at the top of the house there was a whole floor which seemed to be unused. It was cold there, unheated. The floor was bare and many rooms were unfurnished, unsettling in the harsh light of the single bulbs, illuminated briefly as he switched on the light for a flash before moving on. Some were completely empty, some piled with junk. Then he heard a sound and he stood still. There were voices in conversation, a little laugh. The noise came from the last door on the landing.

'Duncan!' His voice was cracked and breathless.

The voices fell silent, so he wondered if he had imagined them, mistaken the breeze which had picked up outside for human whispers. But the door didn't fit properly and light spilled under it. He walked quietly up to it and threw it open. Inside was an attic with a ceiling vaulted like the roof of a cathedral. A long window was covered by a piece of muslin so flimsy that it moved in the draught from the ill-fitting glass. There was a bed as wide as it was long with carved wooden posts at each corner and heaped with faded quilts and rugs. And in the bed sprawled two young people, a man and a woman, not cold, apparently, although they were only half dressed and not covered wholly by a quilt. They were sharing a post-coital cigarette. They were very young – sixteen? Seventeen? His entrance had shocked them but they looked out at him with a smug warmth which made him envy them. He gave a wave of apology, then shut the door behind him. He ran down the three flights of stairs and outside.

At the bonfire, the scene had changed. The guests were making their way back to the house, walking along the tideline. At their head strode Duncan. He wore his coat slung over his shoulders, caught with a single button so it fell behind him like a cloak.

Perez rushed up to him, blocking his process.

'Have you seen Cassie?'

'She's with Fran. The witch wouldn't let me have her tonight. Why?'

'She's missing, she got separated from Fran on the street in Lerwick.'

Perez knew he should stay and explain in more detail. Duncan was her father and had a right to know. But he was aware of time slipping from him. Ignoring Duncan's shouted questions, he left them to their ridiculous ritual and slithered over the shingle to the house and his car. He slammed it into gear and drove too fast back to the town.

Chapter Forty-Three

Sally went out of the community hall to get some air.
The door swung shut behind her and the music grew
fainter. Above her the sky was flecked with stars. The
drink had gone to her head and she bent over, not
thinking she was going to be sick exactly but wanting
to stop that whirring sensation, the feeling that the
earth was shifting and she had to concentrate to keep
her balance, otherwise she'd tip over. She wasn't wearing a coat. She'd only be out for a minute and anyway
it was roasting inside the hall with the heating full on
and all those bodies, everyone dancing.

    She hadn't seen her parents all night. Not to speak
to at least. She'd caught a glimpse of Alex while she
was watching the procession, and she'd wondered
what he could be up to because there'd been no sign of
her mother. Her parents had believed her story that
she'd spend the evening with Fran Hunter and Cassie.
When she'd told them, they'd seemed almost relieved
at the prospect of a night to themselves. If they'd been
around to watch the burning galley, she hadn't seen
them on the playing field. She supposed they'd be
home by now. Margaret would be making a nice cup of
cocoa before bed, filling their hot water bottles. Sally
stood up and tilted back her head to look at the sky. It

made her dizzy again, then the cold started getting to her and she went back inside.

In the hall it was like the first time she'd got together with Robert. A bit rowdier maybe. Some of the girls from school were there, making fools of themselves and she could tell they were dead jealous that she was with Robert. All thoughts of secrecy were over now. In this mood she wanted the world to know. She was feeling good. Not so self-conscious. She'd lost a bit of weight since Catherine had died and that helped. Maybe she could sell the idea to the teenage magazines – *The best friend's murder diet.* She knew it wasn't funny but she couldn't help smiling to herself. She went up to Robert. Her friends were all around him, but he wasn't taking any notice of them. Not flirting anyway, even after she'd left the hall. He hadn't seen her come back in and she'd watched him for a moment to check. Lisa was desperate to get his attention, but he just ignored her. He was still wearing part of the costume but had dumped the helmet and the shield somewhere. The dagger was in its sheath on his belt. When they'd danced that slow dance earlier, she'd been aware of it against her thigh. It had made her feel sexy. She'd never felt quite like that before.

She stroked his neck. He must have had a bit to drink too, but you wouldn't have been able to tell. He'd taken the whole Up Helly Aa thing seriously. She liked that about him. He wasn't like the lads at school who saw everything as an opportunity to take the piss. Now, with the music in the background, she felt she was floating above the scene in the hall, looking down at it from a distance. All the dreadful things that had happened, with Catherine and the hassle with her parents and the stuff that had gone on at school, all that was over. At last she could believe that anything was possible. The music stopped for the band to have a drink. Robert bent down to talk in her ear.

'I was thinking of going back to Brae. There's a party at the Haa. Do you want to come?'

'Why not?'

'I think I've done my bit in town, don't you?'

'Sure.' She was thinking she had nothing to lose. Her parents weren't expecting her back until the morning and anyway it might be safer away from Lerwick. She didn't want her parents turning up and making a scene if anyone had told them what was going on. 'Are you OK to drive?' Maybe he would teach her, she thought. That would make her useful to him. She could stay off the drink and drive him home after parties. He wouldn't dump her then.

'No problem,' he said, though when they went out to the van, he forgot that he hadn't locked it and dropped his keys and started swearing. She wondered why he was so edgy. The whole evening had gone well and she knew he'd been looking forward to it. He hadn't admitted it of course, but he was like one of the kids in her mother's school, taking the starring role in the Christmas show. Perhaps now it was over it was an anticlimax. For the first time she thought she was the strong one in the relationship. When it came down to it, she'd be the one to look after him.

Driving north, he didn't say much. He was driving very fast and on one of the bends nearly lost control. The gritting lorries had been out earlier in the day, but now the roads were slippery. She was tempted to tell him to slow down, but the last thing she wanted was to end up like her mother, always nagging and carping. And anyway there was something exhilarating about driving so fast in the dark along an empty road. He'd pushed a CD into the player and really loud rock music was playing. It gave her the same sensation as staring up at the sky. She wasn't timid Sally any more. Everything had changed. She reached out and put her hand on his knee, rubbed her thumb along the inside of his thigh.

In Brae there were still lights in some of the houses but the place was quiet. Sally had heard about the Haa. Catherine had told her about a party there, though Sally had never understood how she'd managed to get herself an invitation. She was thinking about that, trying not to drag up the old resentments, when Robert braked sharply to turn off the main road. The van skidded and spun. Sally had her eyes shut, imagined it sliding off the road or crashing into the wall in the corner, the boot smashed in, one or both of them dead. But somehow Robert managed to keep it upright. It was just facing in the wrong direction.

'Shit,' he said, 'that would be all I'd need. The cops sniffing round, taking breath tests.' He gave a nervous little giggle which made her realize he'd been a bit frightened himself. Again, she thought she was probably stronger than he was. He reversed slowly until he was facing the right way and took the hill down towards the beach more slowly. As they approached the house, they could see the bonfire on the beach was still smouldering.

He introduced Sally to his mother. Perhaps that was why he'd brought her. He'd known Celia would be here and he'd wanted them to meet. Sally hoped that was how it was. It made her feel like a real girlfriend, Robert wanting her to get to know his family. Now though, she wasn't sure it was going to work. She didn't think she'd get on with Celia. It was like she was in some sort of fancy dress, with the long black dress and the slash of lipstick on her white face. She'd been the first person they'd seen when they'd got to the Haa and Sally had been shocked. She'd heard of Celia Isbister, but never met her before. She'd expected her to look more like a real mother.

She couldn't let Robert know what she was thinking though. She could tell he'd been keen to see Celia. It was as if he was caught somewhere between his mother and his father, desperate to please them both. That was why he'd driven out here like a madman. It seemed a weird relationship to her. Not like mother and son at all. More like they were lovers or something. He seemed so pleased to see the woman when they went into the house and she appeared at the doorway as if she owned the place. He put his arm around Celia and pulled her to him. Sally never had that sort of physical contact with her parents. She wouldn't have wanted it. She didn't think it was healthy.

Before she followed him inside, she waited for a moment in the courtyard. Everything was quiet outside, though she imagined she could hear waves breaking on the beach. The tide would have turned. Looking up she saw a man's face at an upstairs window, staring down at her. He must have heard the van. She recognized him as Duncan Hunter.

Everyone was inside now. The bonfire was still alight because someone had put a huge bit of driftwood on it but even that was nearly burnt away, so there was nothing much left but embers and ash. Celia took them through to a long living room which was almost empty, to show the fire to them through French doors. Everyone else was in the kitchen. A baking tray with blackened sausages stood on the top of the stove, with some baked potatoes, cold now, their skins wrinkled, brown like a tortoise's neck. Nobody was eating. It wasn't like a party. They were still there, still drinking, but the music was turned very low and there was a quiet, subdued air.

'Duncan's daughter's missing,' Celia said. 'The police came earlier. We haven't got any details. Duncan phoned Fran, but she couldn't tell him much. It's probably nothing. She's that sort of kid. The kind to wander off. But with all that's happened lately, you can imagine what Duncan's going through. He's waiting upstairs by the phone.'

'Cassie?' Sally said. 'I babysit for her sometimes.' She thought it was quite exciting to be on the edge of the drama.

'It'll kill him if anything happens to her,' Celia said.

'Should we be here, then?' Sally didn't want to imagine what it would be like to lose a child, but she didn't think you'd want a load of strangers in your house.

'God yes, we daren't go. Duncan hates being by himself.' Celia had a way of talking which made you feel a bit stupid. Sally couldn't take to her at all, though of course she'd try for Robert's sake. It probably wasn't fair to judge. Celia had obviously been drinking very heavily. Besides the lipstick, she was wearing black eyeliner which had become smudged and close to she looked a bit of a mess. There was something sticky and disgusting on the sleeve of her cardigan. Margaret might not be a brilliant mother, but at least she maintained a bit of dignity. She knew how to behave in company. Sally would have liked to escape. Instead she started drinking again. She knew it was a mistake and she should keep a clear head, but when she saw Robert and Celia whispering to each other, standing so close that their heads were touching, she couldn't help herself.

Chapter Forty-Four

Magnus was nearly asleep when he heard voices outside his cell. It sounded like an argument. He thought,
It's Up Helly Aa. Someone with too much drink inside
him. His uncle had taken him to watch the procession
when he'd been a boy and there'd been a lot of drinking even then. One year, Agnes had been there too.
She'd have been very young. He could remember how
her eyes shone with the excitement of being allowed
out so late, and the bag of sweeties his uncle had carried in his pocket.

Then the metal flap in the thick door clicked open
and Magnus could see the face of a policeman, backlit
from the strip lights in the corridor. Magnus was lying
on the narrow bed and wriggled back on his buttocks,
so his head was higher and his back was leaning
against the wall. He wondered what they could be
wanting now. Were they going to send him away?
Surely not. The ferry had long gone and there'd be no
more planes at this time. Unless they'd chartered one.
That happened sometimes. If people got so ill that
they needed to go to the hospital in Aberdeen where
they had all the fancy machines, they flew them out in
a special plane. Despite his panic, he felt a small thrill
at the idea that they hired an aeroplane specially for

him. He swung his legs round so he was sitting on the bed.

There was the sound of keys rattling together and then he heard the key move in the lock and the door was opened. The policeman in uniform stood aside to let someone in.

'You've got a visitor,' the policeman said. He sounded bad-tempered. Magnus couldn't think what he'd done to annoy him. When the man had come in earlier to collect his tea tray he'd been all right, almost friendly. They'd chatted about the parade. 'You don't have to see him if you don't want to.' Behind the policeman in his uniform Magnus could see the detective from Fair Isle. He was still dressed for outdoors in a big padded jacket and he had his hands in his pockets.

Magnus thought then that the policeman was cross with the Fair Isle man and not with him.

'I'll see him,' he said, anxious to please. 'Oh yes. Why not?'

'You don't want your lawyer here?'

Magnus was quite certain about that. He didn't like the lawyer at all.

Jimmy Perez sat opposite him on a plastic chair. Magnus didn't hear the footsteps of the policeman moving away. He must be standing there, just outside the door. Because he was thinking about that, about why the policeman was still standing in the corridor instead of going back to his office where it would surely be more comfortable, he missed the detective's first question. There was a pause and Magnus knew he was supposed to answer. He looked around him, embarrassed and confused.

'Did you hear what I said, Magnus?' There was an impatience in the man's voice which Magnus hadn't heard before, except maybe when he'd shown the detective Catriona's ribbons at Hillhead. 'Cassie's missing. You know Cassie? Mrs Hunter's daughter?'

Magnus smiled despite himself. That smile that always got him into trouble. He remembered the girl being pulled past his house on a sledge, that snowy day when the ravens were out over the headland. 'She's a bonny little thing.'

'Do you know where she could be, Magnus? Do you have any ideas?'

Magnus shook his head.

'But you would like to help me find her?'

'Would they let me out?' he said uncertainly. 'I'd come if they would, but there'll be a lot of men to help in a search and I'm not as young as I was.' He thought of when the other girl went missing and the line of men stretched over the hill that time. He'd helped too until the two policeman had come from Lerwick to take him away.

'I don't need that kind of help. I need you to tell me about Catriona. What happened to Catriona, Magnus?'

Magnus opened his mouth, but no words came out.

'Did you kill her, Magnus? If you did and you tell me that would help us find Cassie. And if you didn't, but you know who did it, that would help too.'

Magnus slid from the bed so he was standing. He felt he couldn't breathe. 'I promised,' he said.

He could sense the detective's impatience again and backed away from him. Was the policeman still waiting outside the door?

'Who did you make the promise to?'

'My mother.'

Tell them nothing.

'She's dead, Magnus. She'll never know. Besides, she loved children, didn't she? She'd want you to help Cassie.'

'She loved Agnes,' he said and added, though he knew he shouldn't, because you shouldn't speak against your mother, 'I'm not sure she loved me.'

'Tell me what happened that day. When Catriona ran up the hill. It was the school holidays, wasn't it? One of those blustery, sunny days?'

'I was working in the field,' Magnus said. 'Cutting hay. I had nearly finished and then I was going to do some gardening. We had a garden in those days at the side of the house where there was a bit of shelter. I don't bother so much now. I only keep up with a few tatties and neeps. Then I had greens in the spring, cabbage later, carrots and onions.' He paused, sensed that the man from Fair Isle was getting impatient, though nothing about his face had changed. 'I saw the girl running up the hill. She had a bunch of flowers in her hand. I always liked it when she came to visit and I thought I'd take a break. Have a cup of coffee in the house.' He looked up defensively. 'There was nothing wrong with that, was there? To take a break and talk to the girl.'

'Of course not if that was all you did.'

He said nothing.

'Will you tell me?' Jimmy Perez said. His voice was very quiet, so quiet Magnus had to strain to hear it and his hearing was very good. Not like some old folks. Not like his mother who'd gone deaf in the end. Thoughts were racing round in his head. Pictures of Catriona and of Agnes when she was ill and his mother braced in her chair by the fire, the knitting pin trapped under one arm, clicking away in that sad, unforgiving way she had. And of sitting in Sunday school as a boy, the rough wooden chair full of splinters that rubbed in the back of your knees, looking up at the dust caught in the light coming from the long window. Listening to the things they were taught by the minister. That the only way to find happiness was through the forgiveness of God. Not really understanding the words, not all the words, but glimpsing the meaning of it occasionally like shapes in the fog. And later not believing any of it.

He decided not to tell the detective, but when he opened his mouth, it all came out.

'She danced up the bank with the flowers in her hand and I knew she was coming to see us. She would never have thought that she might not be welcome. She had her hair tied up with two ribbons . . .' He held his hands at the top of his head to show what he meant. '. . . Like horns, maybe. I was in the kitchen by then, my hands washed, ready for some coffee. She came right in. She never bothered to knock. And you could tell that she was full of mischief that day. Could it be the wind? When it's windy you see the children rushing round the playground and so noisy sometimes you can hear them from my house. My mother was knitting. I could tell she didn't want Catriona there. Some nights she didn't sleep so well. I think she just wanted to be left alone that day. She'd had a bad night and she wanted to sit and knit in peace.'

'But you wanted to see the child?'

'I liked to see her,' he said. 'I gave her a glass of

milk and a biscuit. But she said she didn't want milk; she wanted juice. We had no juice in the house. She wouldn't settle. Some days when she visited she would sit and draw a picture, or when mother was in the mood they would bake together. That day she was all over the place, opening drawers and looking into cupboards. I suppose she was bored. She said she was bored.' He spoke in a puzzled voice. Boredom was an idea he found hard to understand. Here in the police station he hated being locked in, and he worried about what was going on with his land at Hillhead, but he wasn't bored.

'So she left?' Perez said. 'Is that what you're telling me? She was bored so she left. Where did she go? Who did she see?'

There was a silence.

'Magnus?'

'She didn't leave,' he said. 'She went into my room and starting looking in there for things to play with.' He remembered the girl pushing open the door, bouncing on his bed, her head thrown back, laughing, the horns of hair flying. His confusion as he watched her, watching the small brown body, glimpsing her knickers as her skirt rode up. 'She shouldn't have done that. Not without asking first.'

'No,' the detective agreed. Magnus expected him to ask another question then, but he didn't. He sat looking at Magnus, just waiting for him to go on with the story.

'I'd kept some things which had belonged to Agnes,' Magnus said. 'You remember, I told you about Agnes. She was my sister. She died when she was still a girl. She caught the whooping cough. My mother had asked me to get rid of them. She didn't want them in the house. But I couldn't bear to. They were in a box, which I kept under my bed.' *Except when mother did the spring cleaning. Then I had to move them.* He didn't tell the detective those details. He didn't think he'd understand what it was to have just one secret, one thing only for yourself. 'Catriona found them. There wasn't much. A soft toy. A rabbit. And a doll with long hair. That was all Agnes had. It wasn't like these days when the children have so many toys.'

'You didn't want her to play with them,' Perez said. 'Because they'd belonged to Agnes.'

'No!' Magnus wasn't sure how he'd make the policeman see how it had been. 'I liked to see her playing with them. I was afraid she'd laugh at them, because they weren't like the toys she was used to. But she didn't. She took the doll in her arms and held it. She rocked it as if it was a baby. Agnes used to do that. She used to rock the baby and sing to it. Catriona didn't sing, but she was gentle with it. She asked if she could brush its hair. She wasn't a bad girl. No, not bad. She just had too much spirit. They didn't know what to do with her.'

'What happened next?' the detective asked.

Magnus shut his eyes, not to recapture the scene, but in an attempt to block it out. But he couldn't block it out. There it was playing in front of him, and when he opened his eyes again he could still see it. His mother appearing suddenly at the door, the horsehair belt holding the knitting needle still round her waist. *Give that to me.* Reaching out and grabbing for the doll. The girl, defiant, enjoying the scene she was making, the fuss all around her, doing a kind of teasing jig, with the doll held above her head. Not understanding, because how could she? Agnes was never mentioned in the house after her death. Mother must have held on to the memory in her fierce, unforgiving way, but Magnus was never allowed to speak of her. So Catriona would never even have known of her existence. *It's my dolly now. Magnus gave her to me.* The icy hatred in his mother's eyes when she turned and looked at him. Then the girl trying to dance her way out of the house, skipping and laughing.

But she never made it to the door. Because his mother had reached for the scissors. They were the scissors she used to snip the wool when she was knitting, and cut the cloth when she was sewing. Not big scissors, but narrow-bladed and very sharp. And then the girl was still and dead, looking almost like a doll herself, lying on the rag rug in front of the fire. His mother had raised the scissors above her head and using both hands thrust them down to kill Catriona. Catriona had made a little sound, hardly a cry at all, taken a small step and fallen on to the rug. Magnus had remembered his mother making that rug, cutting up the scraps of old clothing and pulling the material strips through a piece of sacking with a crochet hook. He'd knelt down on it to look at Catriona, turned to his mother, looking for guidance. What should they do? They had no telephone but he could run to the Bruce house. His mother had spoken in her quiet firm voice. *She shouldn't have played with Agnes's toys.* Then she sat back in the chair and continued her knitting.

It was Magnus who was left to deal with it. He rolled Catriona up in the rug and took her into his room. There was blood but not so much of it. He put the doll and the rabbit back in the box under his bed. When people came looking for Catriona he was out in the garden, slicing up the weeds with his long handled hoe. *No, she's not been here.* And when they came back later and asked his mother she told them the same thing. No one noticed the missing rug. Why would they? They seldom came into the house. When it was dark, he unwrapped the rug so Catriona was lying on her back in the middle of it, he untied her ribbons and spread out her hair. Then he carried her up the hill. It was a cloudy night. No moon. Raven black. The men still searching for her were on the headland and along the cliff tops. He could see the flashes of their torches but nobody saw him. They were at the coast and he went inland. Then he left the girl there on the heather, her face turned to the rain and went back to the house for a spade, a good sharp spade. He went up the hill again and he buried her in the peat bank and covered the spot with loose rocks.

It was dawn when he'd finished and was on his way home. It was summer then and the nights were still short. But still nobody saw him. In the house, he cut up the rug with his mother's scissors and threw it on the fire a piece at a time. His mother stayed in her room until it was all done, and then she came out and made the porridge for his breakfast as she always did. They never spoke of it. Only when the policemen came for him and she said, *Tell them nothing.*

'That was how it was,' he said, when at last the words had stopped and the scene had faded in front of his eyes. 'That was what happened.'

He could see that the detective was disappointed. It wasn't what he'd been hoping to hear.

'That was how it was,' he said again. 'I'm sorry.'
Then because he'd got into the habit somehow of
speaking – after having such a long time of having no
one to speak with, he was starting to get used to it – he
opened his mouth again and he started telling the
detective from Fair Isle about the last time he'd seen
Catherine Ross. Somehow he didn't care any more
about his mother's instruction to tell them nothing.

Chapter Forty-Five

All that evening Fran was aware of the time passing. With each minute it became less plausible that Cassie had wandered away and was safely caught up with a family who was looking after her. Now it was nearly midnight and in Lerwick the community halls' Up Helly Aa celebrations were in full swing. In every part of the town, people were dancing and laughing and listening to music. The men were rowdy with drink. This wasn't a time for children. All the children would be long in bed. She'd concentrated on making the minutes move slowly. She'd never wanted to reach this point. She watched the clock, the two hands coming together, couldn't bear to see them meet and turned away.

Outside it was freezing. The sort of cold which penetrates clothing and goes straight to the bones. Sitting in the house at Ravenswick, Fran was aware of the cold, even though her fire kept the room hot. She had the curtains open to watch for headlights coming down the road. Every now and then she cleared the condensation from the glass and saw the frost, thick and white on each blade of grass. She thought of Cassie, hoped that she was still wearing her scarf and her gloves, preferred to think of her outside in the open than shut up somewhere. Cassie hated the dark and always had a lamp on when she was in bed. Fran thought of the nightmares which had troubled her daughter, remembered Cassie, still half asleep, blindly reaching out to her for reassurance. Fran blinked, an involuntary response to the image, felt the tears on her cheeks but couldn't find the energy to wipe them away.

Euan Ross was sitting with her. The fat police-woman was at the table, awkward, silent. Euan had poured Fran whisky, just as she had poured some for him after his daughter had died. She sipped it to be polite. Even now, when she was going crazy, panic-frozen so she couldn't think straight, she still didn't want to offend him. He knew his daughter was dead. There was still hope that hers was alive. She wondered that she could have considered herself upset when she found the bodies of the other girls.

She'd shut the dog in the bedroom. It reminded her too fiercely of Cassie. She didn't want to see her, the smell of her at her feet made her want to retch.

The telephone rang. She sprang to her feet, reached it before the second ring, felt the adrenaline hit her brain, making her suddenly clear headed. It was Duncan.

'Any news?'

'I would have phoned you,' she said. After Perez had visited the Haa looking for Cassie, Duncan had called her, demanding an explanation. She couldn't tell how he was feeling. She'd expected him to blame her for losing their daughter. In a similar situation she would have torn his eyes out. Instead he seemed dis-tant, icy. At first she'd thought he was very drunk and trying not to show it. That intense effort to seem sober. Now she thought there was more to it. He had called every hour since. She couldn't be angry with him. It was her fault, not his. If she'd allowed Cassie to go with him to the Haa, the girl would be safe.

'I'm sorry,' she said. She said that every time he phoned too.

There was a moment of silence. 'No,' he said. 'There was nothing you could do. You can't blame yourself. Should I come over?'

'No. Stay there. There should be someone in both houses. Just in case . . .'

He was about to speak again but she interrupted him. 'Please, I'm going to hang up now. The police might be trying to get through. As soon as I hear anything I'll call you. I promise.'

As she hung up, she saw herself reflected in the window. A dark shadowy figure, unrecognizable, middle-aged. A wave of self-pity took her by surprise. She'd moved here to keep Cassie safe. It had been all she'd wanted. A better life for them both. It was as if she was the object of some twisted prank. To find the bodies had been hard enough. She couldn't be expected to deal with this too. She realized she was sobbing. Not for Cassie this time, but for herself.

Euan came up behind her and offered her a handkerchief. It was clean, white, ironed. She took it from him. The feel of the smooth cloth against her face was a small comfort.

'How can you think of ironing? At a time like this?' It was the first thought that came into her head.

It took him a moment to realize what she meant. He gave a little smile. 'Not me,' he said. 'I have help in the house. Someone to keep things going. Left to myself I'd have fallen apart. You saw that.'

Now, it seemed to her that he was entirely composed.

'Did you find anything in that writing of Catherine's?' she demanded suddenly. 'Anything which might help them find out who's doing this?'

Before he could answer there was a noise outside. Her image in the window broke up, as headlights caught it from behind. She held her breath as the car coming down the road slowed and then pulled to a stop. It was Jimmy Perez and she could tell at once that he was alone. She waited, still hoping despite herself, that he would move round the car to help a child from the back seat, but he walked straight to the house. *He's come to tell me that Cassie's dead. If it had been good news he'd have phoned. He wouldn't have wasted time driving here.* Maggie heard him approaching and started barking and jumping up at the bedroom door.

The first thing he said, as soon as the door was open, was, 'I haven't got anything to tell you. We haven't found her. Not yet.' Because she'd convinced herself that Cassie was dead in the moment of his walking from the car to the house, she felt relieved. She could have kissed him.

'I have some questions,' he said.

'Of course. Anything.'

He looked over her shoulder at Euan Ross. 'I'm sorry. We'd like to talk to Mrs Hunter alone. You understand?'

'I'll go home,' Euan said. 'Give me a ring if you'd

like me to come back. Or stay with me, Fran, if you'd prefer. Don't worry about the time. I'll be up.'

Fran wasn't aware of his leaving. She knew she should thank him, see him out, offer coffee and food to the detective, but she sat impatiently waiting for the questions. She thought Perez had an idea, ideas. There was hope. As she waited she saw the lights of another car coming from the direction of Lerwick, but it didn't stop.

He pulled out a hard dining chair and sat on that, facing her, his long legs twisted under the seat. The policewoman eased her chair back into a corner. Fran sensed an urgency. He was desperate for her to answer quickly. When she paused for a moment he didn't tell her to hurry, but she knew that was what he wanted. The questions made no sense to her. They seemed entirely random. He asked about Cassie and how she was doing at school, about Fran's social life and the friends she'd made away from Ravenswick. She didn't demand to know what the questions were about. She could do nothing more to find her daughter. She was in his hands. And if he wasted time explaining his ideas to her, it might be too late.

It didn't take long. After a quarter of an hour he stood up again. 'You shouldn't be on your own here,' he said.

'Euan said he'd come back.'

'No. Not Mr Ross. He's too close to all this. There must be someone else.'

Fran thought of Jan Ellis who'd been so kind about the dog, whose husband didn't mind making a fool of himself by dressing up as a baby. She heard Perez phone her, standing outside, using his mobile. As soon as Jan's car pulled up outside, he disappeared. He didn't say anything to her before he left and she didn't watch him go. She understood he didn't want to tell her that everything would be OK, to make promises he wouldn't be able to keep.

Chapter Forty-Six

Jimmy Perez pulled away from Fran Hunter's house and turned down the bank towards Hillhead. He stopped outside the old man's place and wiped the condensation from the windscreen. At the bottom of the hill there were still lights on in the schoolhouse and at Euan's, but no sign of the activity going on inside. Roy Taylor understood the need for discretion. The cars had been parked out of sight from the road.

It was tempting to drive down and join them. There would be something reassuring in the detail of a search. It would help him forget the panic. He could concentrate on sifting through objects and belongings, proving a theory which had already convinced him. But it wouldn't bring Cassie back. He was certain she wasn't in Ravenswick.

Perez forced himself to breathe slowly, to think rationally about what he should do next. His thoughts chased one after the other and he struggled to bring an order to them. They were strange thoughts which had little to do with the matter in hand, distractions.

The ravens. Every time he'd been here in daylight they'd been flying over these fields. Where would they go in the dark? Looking out over the frozen headland, he found it hard to imagine them sheltering on ledges of the cliff, but where else was there for them to go? Did they roost close together to keep out the cold? He didn't know how they could survive a winter like this. Magnus's raven was already dead. Perez had taken it to the woman who cared for injured birds and animals and she'd fed it as Magnus had instructed, but something about the change of home had disturbed it. It had died the first night for no apparent reason. Sometimes it happened like that, the woman said.

Then he thought about Duncan. Who had once been a friend and had become an enemy. How would Perez talk to him if his daughter was dead? And that brought him to the murderer. He knew what he should do. He started the engine and backed into the gateway opposite Magnus's house to turn round. He drove north again.

In Lerwick he made a phone call to Taylor. 'Anything?'

'You were right. We found them. Well hidden though. Easy to miss.'

But you didn't miss them, Perez thought. He could hear the triumph in Taylor's voice, subdued because he'd feel guilty for feeling that way, but there just the same. Magnus Tait hadn't killed Catherine. An Englishman had proved them all wrong. An Englishman and a Fair Islander.

'Go out to Quendale. Talk to the boy there. There was something I missed.' He shouldn't be the one to be giving orders, but he didn't care.

Perez hung up and contacted the rest of the team who were already searching the halls. By this time the dances were breaking up, people were drifting home. Those with more stamina had moved on to private parties.

'Any sign of him?'

'No one's seen him for a while.'

'You've checked the house?'

'All quiet. The door was open and we had a look round. No one's there.'

He drove slowly around the streets, stopping occasionally to talk to groups of revellers on their way home. No one had seen Robert. Not for hours. On the phone again, he said, 'Talk to taxis. And rouse the folks working on the Whalsay ferry. He could have gone to the boat.' He thought that would be an efficient way to dispose of a small child. Tip her overboard. This temperature she'd only survive for seconds, even if she could swim. For some reason the image of the raven flashed into his head for a moment. It wouldn't take any depth, he thought. Depending on the state of the tide, there was a chance her body would never be found, even if she was thrown over where the boat was moored.

Perez was thinking of friends who had boats and lived close to Vidlin. Someone he could persuade to take him across to Whalsay. Then he had another idea. Celia was at the Haa, had been at least when he'd tried there earlier. It was worth looking there first. For the second time that night, Perez drove north, across the bare wastes of heather moorland.

At the Brae junction he saw skid marks on the road and he changed gear to go down the bank to the house. There were two figures on the beach, silhouetted in the embers of the fire, but he couldn't make out who they were. He hadn't known what to expect in the house. He couldn't tell how Duncan would react to his daughter's disappearance. He wouldn't have been surprised by a riotous party in full swing, Duncan the exhibitionist pissed, trying to pretend that nothing was wrong. But it was very quiet there. Even when he switched off his engine, he couldn't hear music. The faint breeze that had come with the change of the tide had dropped again. The smoke rose in a straight line from the tall chimney. He could see it in the moonlight and he could smell the wood in it.

He opened the door without knocking. In the kitchen someone he didn't know was asleep in the Orkney chair. It was a young woman, with her legs curled under her. Two men sat at the table eating toast. They were dressed in suits and ties, could have been having a breakfast meeting in the city. They looked up when they heard him, took him for one of Duncan's friends.

'Hi,' one said, not surprised that a guest should be turning up at two in the morning. 'He's upstairs. Not really in a party mood.' He had an English accent and Perez put them down as business acquaintances.

He didn't answer and went on to the drawing room. The young couple he'd found in bed were there, on one of the sofas, arms entwined, not asleep quite, but in a glazed, self-absorbed stupor. Celia was sitting on the floor, staring at the fire, prodding it with a wrought-iron poker, making the sparks fly. He thought she'd been crying.

'Is Robert here?'

She looked up at him. 'He was,' she said. 'I don't know now. Is his van still here?' She didn't ask why he wanted to know or if there was news of Cassie. He felt the urge to scream very loudly. Anything to rouse them. What right did they all have to laze about half conscious while the girl was missing?

He said nothing and walked quickly outside. He should have thought of the van when he'd first arrived. He saw it immediately. Before approaching it, he moved his own car so the van was blocked in. He didn't want the embarrassment of Robert driving away.

He tried the driver's door. It was locked. He peered through the window, shone his torch inside. There was salt on the glass and the light was reflected so it was hard to make out anything inside. He stooped so he was closer. There was a pink glove on the passenger's seat, but it was too big to be Cassie's. He couldn't see to the back. The business end was separated from the seats by a sheet-metal casing. He tried the handle on the back doors. The handle moved, released a rod and bolt and when he pulled the door opened.

There was a soft bundle lying inside. He wouldn't let himself think what it might be. He shone his torch and caught a pair of eyes, wide and panicky. They blinked, hurt by the light. Alive. Cassie couldn't move. Her hands had been tied by twine, expertly knotted. A gag made of a strip of oily rag was in her mouth. Perez took his penknife from his pocket. He cut the ropes and pulled the gag from her mouth, then he carried her out and held her in his arms as if she was a baby. She began to shiver. He ran with her into the house, shouting for Duncan as soon as he was inside. The man loped down the stairs towards them.

Chapter Forty-Seven

Sally found herself on the beach. She couldn't remember getting there. It was cold, but now the cold seemed a long way away. Robert had taken off his jacket and put it around her shoulders. The fire was still giving off some heat. She thought suddenly that she'd had enough and it would be quite good to be at home. Her parents would be asleep and she could let herself in very quietly, make herself tea. She was tired and she could lie in the single bed she'd slept in since she'd grown out of her cot. The duvet would be warm and she'd sleep. More than anything now, she wanted to sleep. But sleep, it seemed, was impossible. Robert wanted to talk.

'Did Catherine tell you what happened the last time we were here?'

'I don't want to hear,' she said.

'What was it with her?'

'Look,' she said. 'I don't care. Not now.'

She leant back against him and felt her eyes begin to close. The knife on his belt was in the small of her back. Not uncomfortable and she was too tired to move. Was it just the drink? Was that what drink did to you, made you want to sleep and forget?

'Mam was right about her all along,' he said. The

words seemed to bounce off her skull. What was he trying to say? She saw she couldn't sleep. She had to listen.

'What do you mean?'

'She said she was a strange girl. No good.'

'She was my friend,' Sally said, though it seemed strange to be standing up for Catherine to Robert. Especially to Robert.

'She tried to make a fool of me. I couldn't let her get away with that.'

'You didn't have to. She died.'

'I liked her,' he said. 'Fancied her. That was what she intended. Mam said that was what she was up to. She was just mucking around with me, she said, trying to get a reaction.'

For God's sake, leave your mother out of this. She saw how it would be if they got together permanently. The first sign of trouble and he'd be off to Celia, looking for a shoulder to cry on, depending on her to put every-thing right. Perhaps it was healthier to hate your mother. Perhaps she should be grateful that Margaret had treated her like shit. Away from the fire there was frost on the shore now. The waves when they retreated left streamers of ice, pale reflections in the moonlight. Oh God, she thought. What a mess.

'She filmed me,' he said.

'She filmed everyone.'

'She filmed me hitting her. That night. She got me so wound up that I ended up hitting her, slapped her across the face so there was a red mark. It was what she wanted. It made good film. That's what she said. She had her camera set up on a tripod and provoked

me so I forgot it was there. Like I was some perform-
ing seal.'

Sally didn't answer.

'Did you hear me?' he demanded.

Sally tried to pull away from him, but he held on to
her shoulders.

'Are you going to hit *me*?' The words seemed to
come from someone else's mouth, not hers. She
shouldn't taunt him about Catherine. It wasn't his
fault. She knew what Catherine was like. And it
wouldn't do to make him angry.

'No,' he said. She thought he sounded like a little
boy. He could be one of the kids in her mother's
school. 'No, of course not.'

'Walk away from her.' These words though were
spoken by a grown-up. They'd been facing the fire and
beyond it the water, so they hadn't heard Jimmy Perez
coming up behind them. Sally thought he must have
moved very quietly over the shingle. He was a quiet
man. Even the words, when he repeated them, weren't
spoken loudly. They turned together to look at him.

'Your mother wants to speak to you, Robert. Come
along.'

Robert began to move and she thought, That's it
then. Celia has won. Every time Celia shouts for him,
he goes running. And she knew she'd probably never
see him again. She watched Robert scramble away
until he disappeared into the darkness. Further up the
beach there were voices, something of a scuffle. She
couldn't work out what that was about. She thought
Robert wasn't a very elegant mover. He had rather
short legs. His bum was too near to the ground. She
wondered how she could have thought him worth

bothering about. He'd left her his coat, but she shivered and turned back to the fire, feeling it hot and fierce on that side of her face. There'd be a red mark like a slap, she thought. In her hand she held the knife she'd taken from Robert's belt when he'd tried to hold on to her.

'Would you have killed him too?' the policeman asked.

She didn't answer. She angled the knife, so the blade reflected the embers. The blade looked scarlet in the strange red light, as if it was covered in blood already.

'We found Cassie,' he said. 'She's all right.'

'It was nothing to do with Robert,' she said. 'He'd left the back of the van open. Cassie had wandered away from her Mam. I said I'd help her find Mrs Hunter. There was rope in the van. I was in the Girls' Brigade. I'm good at knots.' She paused. When they'd skidded at the Brae junction, she'd heard Cassie bounce around in the back. Robert hadn't noticed.

'Why did you take her?' the detective said. 'You don't have to answer. I shouldn't be talking to you at all without a lawyer, but I wondered. A kid like that. What could she have done to hurt you?'

'She saw me that night with Catherine. She'd woken up. Some nightmare. Saw me through her bedroom window in the moonlight. I convinced her it must have been a dream. Then, when I found her this evening in Lerwick, lost, all upset, I thought I couldn't take a chance. Stupid.' *But it wasn't only that. It was the girl. You could tell she'd turn out just like Catherine. Confident, full of herself. She wouldn't be the sort of child to be bullied, to feel sick every morning before setting off*

*for school. She'd be the one making the clever comments
which would turn some other poor kid's stomach. Cocky.
Her mother had been right about that.*

'Why didn't you kill her straight away?' he asked.

She shrugged. 'I had to wait until it was quiet,
didn't I?' *Quiet, like the night I killed Catherine. A night
like this.*

'Was that what the knife was for?'

She shrugged again.

'You've no use for it now,' he said. 'Best to give it to
me.'

She didn't answer. She sat down on the sand and
held the knife on her knee. In the distance she heard
the sound of cars driving away from the Haa. The
party was over. Robert would go home with Celia.
They deserved each other.

'Sally, give the knife to me.'

She thought she might reach him with it before he
could stop her. Weighed up the possibility in her head.
The thrill of doing it. Would there be the same buzz
as when she'd killed Catherine? Perhaps it would
be more exciting. She imagined bone shattering and
blood, the power of standing and watching his life
seeping into the icy sand. There'd be no chance of getting away now, of course. She'd never thought she
would get away with killing Catherine. Not even when
they locked up the old man. This was Shetland, where
you couldn't fart without the whole place knowing.
Anyway, she'd have been disappointed if it had stayed
a secret for ever. Imagine her friends at school, their
faces when they found out. She'd give anything to be
in the house room when the news broke, when her

face was on the front of the papers and on the television. She'd be a celebrity.

'Sally. Give it to me.'

She held the bone handle of the knife in her hand,
ready to strike out at him, then was overcome by
tiredness again. She stood up, and with the last of
her energy, she threw it away from her towards the
sea. It twisted in the air, and landed in the shallow
water. She didn't see the splash because of the dark,
but she heard it.

He walked right up to her, held her hand and
pulled her to her feet. It wasn't a rough or unkind gesture. It was as if he was trying to help her. He put his
arm round her shoulder and walked with her up the
beach. From a distance, they'd look like lovers.

Chapter Forty-Eight

Perez dropped Roy Taylor off at the airport the next morning. Now he was satisfied they had the right person for the Catherine Ross murder, the Englishman didn't want to stay. The restlessness which he'd just about managed to hold in check while the investigation kept his interest was moving him on. Already he was thinking about the next case. He shook Perez's hand warmly before leaving the lounge, but didn't look back as he walked over the tarmac to the Aberdeen plane. Perez waited until the plane took off and almost wished he was on it. He still hadn't made up his mind about the move to the Isle. His mother had given up asking him about it. She'd probably resigned herself to the fact that he wouldn't be coming home.

On the way back to Lerwick he stopped at Fran Hunter's house. He told himself as he drew up that he was stopping on impulse, but really it had been at the back of his mind since leaving the airport; even before that, he'd considered it as an option when he'd set out from home. She was pulling sheets from the washing machine into a plastic basket, didn't stop when she called for him to come in.

'I wanted to know how Cassie was feeling,' he said.

'She's still asleep. By the time we got in this

morning it was almost light. The doctor looked her over. Just a few bruises he said from being banged around in the back of the van.'

He didn't know what to say. They both knew it wasn't the physical effects which would last.

She'd straightened up now. 'I don't suppose I can ask you questions about what happened. I don't suppose that's allowed.'

'Ask me whatever you like,' he said. 'You're not the sort to go to the press. And if anyone has a right to know, it's you.'

'Did you ever think I was involved?'

'No,' he said without hesitation. 'Never.'

Without asking if he wanted a drink she moved the kettle on to the hotplate, rinsed out the cafetière which stood on the draining board and spooned in coffee.

'Why did she do it? I've been trying to think. I mean, I fell out with people when I was a teenager. You do, don't you, at that age. One minute you think you're soul mates. The next you wonder how they can be so cruel. But I never pulled a scarf round their necks and strangled them.'

'It wasn't just a matter of friends falling out,' he said.

She poured his coffee, remembered that he took it black.

'She'd had a hard time at school. Since she'd been in primary. I was bullied a bit too, know what it's like. And it can't have been easy, I suppose, to have your mother as teacher.'

'God, no. Especially someone like Margaret Henry. That would be a nightmare.'

'It got worse when she moved to the high school.

A sort of routine bullying. Never physical. Not really. People knocking into her in a way which could have been accidental, tripping her up. But a sort of cold indifference. She was never included. Never wanted. Everyone made it clear she wasn't worth bothering with. Maybe it turned into a sort of paranoia. Wherever she went at school she thought people were whispering about her.'

'But Catherine bothered with her.'

'Catherine didn't care what the other kids thought. She had her own agenda. Sally was jealous of that.'

'How do you know all this?'

'Sally told us. She wants us to know everything. It's as if she's enjoying the attention.'

Fran was sitting next to the fire, with her back against the hearth. 'Did they both fancy him? Is that what they fought over? I don't really see him as Catherine's type.'

He couldn't help smiling. 'He wasn't. No, not that. Sally was besotted with him. You can see that she might be, can't you? Big, handsome, in charge of that monster of a boat. A reputation which her parents would hate. And her first boyfriend. Catherine's interest was more . . .' He paused. '. . . more academic.'

'What do you mean?'

'She had this project at school. A film.'

'Of course,' Fran said. '*Fire and Ice.*'

'As I understand it, it was a sort of anthropological study of the islands. Almost a critique. But she didn't just record what she saw. She was a director. She made things happen. A teacher at school, who invited her into his home and came on to her. She pretended to be shocked but it was what she wanted. She filmed him in secret. A young lad at Quendale who poured out his heart to her. She set him up for rejection, for humiliation and caught that on film too. He was the boy who drove the girls home on New Year's Eve. Sally claimed not to recognize him, but of course she must have done. She just wanted to create more of a mystery around Catherine.' He paused again, drank the coffee, which was very good. After all, there was no hurry now, and he could think of nowhere he'd rather be than in this small warm house with this woman. 'Catherine knew Robert's father was Guizer Jarl, knew Robert was desperate to take a leading role in Up Helly Aa. Knew he was sensitive about his father's reputation. Robert was always one for the young girls. Probably felt safer with them. He'd never really grown up. I'm not saying she set him up. Not quite. But she gave him the opportunity to behave badly, and he jumped at it.' He felt suddenly embarrassed. He didn't want to talk about Catherine provoking Robert, his reaction when she laughed at him. He didn't want to imply that Catherine had asked for the violence. How would that sound? Fran was a liberated young woman from the south. What would she think of him? But in fact Catherine had got just what she'd wanted. She'd been triumphant about it. He felt himself stumbling over the words. 'Catherine captured Robert on film. It showed him in a bad light. She was going to show it in school. You know how things get around here. By that evening everyone would be talking about it. He might even have been charged and taken to court. His father had been through enough embarrassment over Celia's affair. Imagine the publicity of a court case.'

'Robert had a motive for killing Catherine,' Fran

said. 'But Sally didn't. Did she? Am I missing something?' She frowned, but in a way which was curious, not anxious. He felt a rush of relief that it had ended well for her. He knew the response was completely selfish. He wouldn't have been able to face her if Cassie had been harmed.

'I told you that Sally was besotted with Robert. I don't think he had any plans at that stage for a permanent relationship. He'd been drunk at the market cross on New Year's Eve and they'd ended up together. That was all. But Sally was full of romantic notions. To hear her talk you'd think she'd been designing her wedding dress. Almost. That afternoon, the day she died, Catherine spent some time with Magnus Tait. He talked to her about Catriona Bruce. He didn't give away his mother's secret. Not quite. But he talked about the girl and Catherine filmed him. Later that evening she met up with Sally.'

He set down his mug and tried to picture the scene in his head. 'They were in Catherine's house. Her father was out. Catherine knew he'd be going out for a meal with colleagues after the meeting at school. Sally's mother thought *she* was in her room finishing homework. Margaret didn't like her out in the evening, even when it was only to go up the road to Catherine's and it wouldn't be the first time Sally'd slipped out without her realizing. Catherine was full of her film, of the great material she'd got. Robert Isbister behaving like an animal and Magnus Tait talking about the disappearance of a young girl and about how the whole community had shunned him for years. Not the sort of picture the Shetland tourist board would want to portray. She showed the film to Sally. They'd been drinking. Not a lot – they'd shared a bottle of wine. But it would be enough for them to talk more freely. Catherine would say what she really thought of Robert. You can imagine the taunting. *How can you bear to go out with someone like that? I couldn't stand to have him touch me.* It would be like the bullying all over again.

'Somehow they ended up outside. A notion of Catherine's probably. She liked the dramatic. Another scene for her film. It hadn't started to snow again yet. There was a full moon. Everything very icy. Cassie woke up and looked down the hill from her bedroom window. She saw the girls together, silhouetted against the white field. Catherine couldn't let the matter of Robert Isbister go. Perhaps she had Sally's best interests at heart and knew he'd only hurt her later. More likely, I think, that she hoped to provoke another outburst to catch on the camcorder. She certainly did that. Sally lost it. When we took a statement this morning, she said she just wanted to stop Catherine's taunting. She pulled her scarf tight around her neck. At last there was silence. She left her there in the snow. Cassie saw her walk alone back to the Ross house. She was half asleep, didn't realize then the importance of what she'd seen. It was only when Sally came to babysit for you, turned up wearing the same coat she'd been wearing that night, that it triggered a memory. Cassie still wouldn't have thought it significant, but it troubled her. She must have said something to Sally.'

'I left her alone with Cassie in the house,' Fran said. 'Twice.' She thought of the drawing Cassie had made on the beach at the Haa. She'd known then that Catherine was dead. 'I should have realized'.

'You couldn't have known. None of us had any idea

then.' He wanted to reach out and stroke the nape of her neck, where some hair had become unfastened from its clip, to tell her that everything was all right, but knew this time he couldn't let emotion run away with him. He twisted his fingers together to trap them and make it easier to resist the temptation. 'Magnus saw it too. Some of it. The girls going down the track together. Only one of them coming back. The next morning he went out early and found Catherine was dead. He swept the snow off her face.'

'Why didn't he say something?'

Perez paused. 'He'd had a bad experience with the police when the other girl disappeared. He didn't think anyone would believe him. He told me in time to get Cassie back safely. I asked Taylor to search the schoolhouse. He found Catherine's keys in Sally's room. She'd been in Euan's house to get the film.'

'So Sally killed Catherine to protect a man who didn't even care about her.'

'It seems she was quite calm afterwards,' Perez said. He thought Fran had a right to the whole story. 'She took the camcorder with her. She was wearing gloves, of course, had put them on before going out because of the cold. She went into Catherine's room, found the script and the disk and deleted *Fire and Ice* from the computer. Then she went home. Her parents were asleep by then and heard nothing. They never knew she'd been out. She even made herself a cup of tea before she went to bed.'

There was a moment of silence. He knew he should go. There was all the work which followed an arrest and he couldn't trust Sandy to get it right. At last, reluctantly, he got to his feet. She stood up too.

'Thank you,' she said.

He was going to say it was nothing, he was only doing his job, but before he could speak, she came up to him and kissed him on the cheek. A light dry kiss. Of gratitude.

'Thank you,' she said again as she shut the door behind him.

He drove back to Lerwick. Before going to his office he called at his house and phoned his mother.

Hidden Depths

A hot summer on the Northumberland coast, and Julie Armstrong arrives home from a night out to find her son murdered. Luke has been strangled, laid out in a bath of water and covered with wild flowers.

The stylized murder scene has Inspector Vera Stanhope and her team intrigued. But then a second body – that of beautiful young teacher, Lily Marsh – is discovered laid out in a rockpool, the water strewn with flowers. Now Vera must work quickly to find this dramatist, this killer who is making art out of death.

Clues are slow to emerge from those who knew Luke and Lily, but Vera soon finds herself drawn towards the curious group of friends who discovered Lily's body. What unites these four men and one woman? Are they really the close-knit, trustworthy unit they claim to be?

As local residents are forced to share their private lives and those of their loved ones, sinister secrets are slowly unearthed. And all the while the killer remains in their midst, waiting for an opportunity to prepare another beautiful, watery grave . . .

Look out for *Hidden Depths*, the gripping new novel from Ann Cleeves, out in Macmillan hardback in 2007.

The opening scenes follow here.

Chapter One

Julie stumbled from the taxi and watched it drive away. At the front gate she paused to compose herself. Best not to go in looking pissed after all those lectures she'd given the kids. The stars wheeled and dipped in the sky and she almost threw up. But she didn't care. It had been a good night, the first with the girls for ages. Though it wasn't the girls that had made it so special, she thought, and realized there was a great soppy beam on her face. Just as well it was dark and there was no one to see.

At the door she stopped again and scrabbled through the eyeliner pencils and lippy-stained tissues and loose change in her bag for her key. Her fingers found the scrap of paper which had been torn from a corner of a menu in the bar. A phone number and a name. *Ring me soon*. Then a little heart. The first man she'd touched since Geoff had left. She could still feel the bones of his spine against her fingers when they'd danced. It was a shame he'd had to leave early.

She snapped the bag shut and listened. Nothing. It was so quiet that she could hear the buzz of the evening's music as a pressure on her ears. Was it possible that Luke was asleep? Laura could sleep for England, but her son had never seemed to get the hang of it. Even now he'd left school and there was nothing to get up for, he was usually awake before her. She pushed open the door and listened again, slipping her feet out of the shoes that had been killing her since she'd got out of the metro hours before. God, she hadn't danced like that since she was twenty-five. There was silence. No music, no television, no beeping computer. Thank the Lord, she thought. Thank the fucking Lord. She wanted sleep and sexy dreams. Somewhere on the street outside an engine was started.

She switched on the light. The glare hurt her head and turned her stomach again. She let go of her bag and ran up the stairs to the bathroom, tripping halfway up. No way was she going to be sick on the new hall carpet. The bathroom door was shut and she saw a crack of light showing underneath it. From the airing cupboard there came the faint gurgle of water which meant the tank was refilling. And wasn't that typical? It took hours of persuasion to get Luke into the shower in the morning, then he decided to have a bath in the middle of the night. She knocked on the bathroom door but there was no urgency about it. The queasiness had passed again.

Luke didn't answer. He must be in one of his moods. Julie knew it wasn't his fault and she should be patient, but sometimes she wanted to strangle him when he went all strange on her. She crossed the landing to Laura's room. Looking down at her daughter, she came over suddenly sentimental, thought she should make the effort to spend more time with her. Fourteen was a difficult age for a girl, and Julie had been so caught up with Luke lately that Laura almost seemed like a stranger. She'd grown up without Julie noticing. She lay on her back, her spiky hair very black against the pillow, snoring slightly, her mouth open. It was a bad time for hay fever. Julie saw that the window was open and although it was so hot, she shut it to keep out the pollen. The moonlight splashed on to the field behind the house where they'd been cutting hay.

She returned to the bathroom and banged on the door with the flat of her palm. 'Hey, are you going to be in there all night?' With the third bang, the door opened. It hadn't been locked. There was a smell of bath oil, heavy and sweet, which Julie didn't recognize as hers. Luke's clothes were neatly folded on the toilet seat.

He had always been beautiful, even as a baby. Much lovelier than Laura, which had never seemed fair. It was the blond hair and the dark eyes, the long, dark eye lashes. Julie stared at him, submerged beneath the bath water, his hair rising, like fronds of seaweed, towards the surface. She couldn't see his body because of the flowers. They floated on the per-fumed water. Only the flower heads, not the stems or the leaves. There were the big ox-eye daisies which had grown in the cornfields when she was a kid. Overblown poppies, the red petals translucent now. And enormous blue blossoms, which she had seen before in gardens in the village, but which she couldn't name.

Julie must have screamed. She heard the sound as if someone else had made it. But still Laura slept and Julie had to shake her to wake her. The girl's eyes opened suddenly, very wide. She looked terrified and Julie found herself muttering, knowing that she was lying, 'It's all right, pet. Everything's all right. But you have to get up.' Laura swung her legs out of bed. She was trembling, but not really awake. Julie put her arm around her and supported her as they stumbled together down the stairs.

They stood like that, wrapped up in each other's arms on the doorstep of the neighbours' house and the silhouette on the wall thrown by the street light made Julie think of people in a crazy three-legged race. One of those pub crawls that students went in for. She leaned against the bell until the lights upstairs went on and footsteps came and she had someone to share the nightmare with.

Chapter Two

It disturbed Felicity Calvert that she'd become so pre-occupied with sex. Once, in the doctor's waiting room, she'd read a magazine which claimed that adolescent boys thought about sex every six minutes. Then she'd found it hard to believe. How could these young men lead a normal life – go to college, watch a film, play football – when they were so frequently distracted? And what of her own son? Watching James playing on the floor with his Lego, it had been impossible to imagine that in a few years he would be similarly obsessed. But now she thought that an interval of six minutes between sexual daydreams could be a conser-vative estimate. In her case at least. For a while now an awareness of her body and its responses had been with her whatever she was doing, an uneasy, occa-sionally pleasurable background to the stuff of every-day life. For someone of her age this seemed inappropriate. It was as if she'd attended a funeral wearing pink.

She was in the garden picking the first of the straw-berries. She lifted the net carefully, sliding her hand underneath between the mesh and the straw bedding. They were still small but there should be enough for James's tea. She tasted one. It was warm from the sun and very sweet. Glancing at her watch, she saw it was almost time for the school bus. Ten more minutes and she'd have to wash her hands and walk down the lane to meet him. She didn't always go. He claimed he was old enough to make his own way to the house and of course that was true. But today he'd have his violin and he'd be glad to see her because she could help him carry his stuff. She wondered briefly whether it would be the old bus driver or the young one with the muscular arms and the sleeveless T-shirt, then looked at her watch again. Only two minutes since she'd last considered sex. The thought returned that at her age it was quite ridiculous.

Felicity was forty-seven. She had a husband and four children. She had, for goodness' sake, a grand-child. In a few days Peter, her husband, would be sixty. The bubbles of lust surfaced at random, when she was least expecting them. She hadn't talked about this to Peter. Of course not. He certainly wasn't the object of her desire. These days they seldom made love.

She got up and walked across the grass to the kitchen. Fox Mill stood on the site of an old watermill. It was a big house, built in the thirties, a coastal retreat for a ship owner from the city. And it looked like a ship with its smooth, curved lines, the mill race flowing past it. A big, art deco ship, stranded, quite out of place in the flat farmland, with its prow pointed to the North Sea and its stern facing the Northumberland hills on the horizon. A long veranda stretched along one side like a deck, impractical here where it was seldom warm enough to sit outside. She loved the house. They would never have afforded it on an academic's salary, but Peter's parents had died soon after he and Felicity had married and all their money had come to him.

She put the basket of strawberries on the table and checked her face in the mirror in the hall, running her fingers through her hair and adding a splash of lipstick. She was older than the mothers of James's friends and hated the idea of embarrassing him.

In the lane the elders were in flower. Their scent made her head swim and caught at the back of her throat. On either side of the hedge the corn was ripening. The crop was too dense for flowers there, but in the field which they owned, close to the house, there were buttercups and clover and purple vetch. The pitted tarmac shimmered in the distance with heat haze. The sun had shone without a break for three days.

This weekend it was Peter's birthday and she was planning what they might do. On Friday night the boys would come. She thought of them as boys, though Samuel at least was as old as her. But if it stayed like this, on Saturday there could be a picnic on the beach, a trip to the Farnes to see puffins and guillemots. James would love that. She squinted at the sky, wondering if she could sense an approaching cold front, the faintest cloud on the horizon. There was nothing. It might even be warm enough to swim, she thought, and imagined the waves breaking on her body.

When she reached the end of the lane there was no sign of the bus. She hoisted herself onto the wooden platform where once the churns from the farm had stood to wait for the milk lorry. The wood was hot and smelled of pitch. She lay back and faced the sun.

In two years James would move on to secondary school. She dreaded it. Peter talked about his going to a private day school in the city, to the school which he'd attended. She'd seen the boys in their striped blazers on the metro. They'd seemed very confident and loud to her.

'But how would he get there?' she'd said. This wasn't her real objection. She didn't think it would be good for James to be pushed. He was a slow and dreamy boy. He'd do better working at his own pace. The comprehensive in the next village would suit him better. Even the high school in Morpeth where their other children had been students had seemed demanding to her.

'I'd take him and bring him back,' Peter had said. 'There'll be lots going on after school. He can hang on until I've finished work.'

That had made her even less favourably disposed to the plan. The time that she had with James when he arrived home from school was special. Without it, she thought, he would be lost to her.

She heard the bus growling up the bank and sat upright, squinting against the sun as it approached. The driver was Stan, the old man. She waved at him to hide her disappointment. Usually three of them got off at this stop – the twin girls from the farm and James. Today, a stranger climbed out first, a young woman wearing strappy leather sandals and a red and gold sleeveless dress with a fitted bodice and full, swirling skirt. Felicity loved the dress, the way the skirt fell and the exuberance of the colours – the young today seemed to choose black or grey even in summer – and when she saw the woman help James off the bus with his bags and violin, she was immediately drawn to her. The twins crossed the road and ran up the track to the farmhouse, the bus drove off, and the three of them were left, standing a little awkwardly by the hedge.

'This is Miss Marsh,' James said. 'She's working at our school.'

The woman had a big straw bag strung by a leather strap over her shoulder. She held out a hand which was very brown and long and bony. The bag slipped down her arm and Felicity saw that it contained files and a library book.

'Lily.' Her voice was clear. 'I'm a student. This is my last teaching practice.' She smiled as if she expected Felicity to be pleased to meet her.

'I told her she could come and stay in our cottage,' James said and set off, unencumbered, up the lane, not caring which of the adults carried his things.

Felicity was not quite sure what to say.

'He *did* mention I was looking for somewhere?' Lily asked.

Felicity shook her head.

'Oh dear, how embarrassing.' But she didn't seem very embarrassed. She seemed to be remarkably self-assured, to find the incident amusing. 'It's been such a nightmare travelling from Newcastle every day without a car. The head asked in assembly if anyone knew of accommodation. We were thinking of a B&B or someone wanting a paying guest. And yesterday James said you had a cottage to let. I tried to phone this afternoon, but there was no answer. He said you'd be in the garden and to come anyway. I presumed he'd discussed it with you. It was hard to say no . . .'

'Oh yes,' Felicity agreed. 'He can be very insistent.'

'Look, it's not a problem. It's a lovely afternoon. I'll walk into the village and there's a bus from there into town at six.'

'Let me think about it,' Felicity said. 'Come and have some tea.'

There had been tenants in the cottage before, but it had never quite worked out. In the early days they'd been glad of an extra source of income. Even with the money from Peter's parents the mortgage repayments had been a nightmare. Then with three children under five, they had thought it might house a nanny or au pair. But there had been complaints about the cold and a dripping tap and the lack of modern conveniences. And they hadn't been comfortable having a stranger living so close to the family. They'd felt the responsibility for the tenant as an extra stress. Although none of them had been particularly troublesome, it had always been a relief to see them go. 'Never again,' Peter had said, when the last resident, a homesick Swedish au pair, had left. Felicity wasn't sure how he would feel about another young woman on the doorstep, even if it was only four weeks until the end of term.

As they sat at the table in the kitchen, with the breeze from the sea blowing the muslin curtain at the open window, Felicity Calvert thought she probably would let the young woman have the place if she wanted it. Peter wouldn't mind too much if it were for a short time.

James was sitting beside them at the table, surrounded by scissors, scraps of cut paper and glue.

He was drinking orange juice and making a birthday card for his father. It was an elaborate affair with photos of Peter taken from old albums and stuck as a collage around a big 60 made out of ribbon and glitter. Lily admired it and asked about the early photographs. Felicity sensed James's pleasure in her interest and felt a stab of gratitude.

'If you live in Newcastle,' she said, 'I suppose you wouldn't want the cottage at weekends.' She thought that would be another point to make to Peter. *She'd only be here during the week. And you work such long hours you wouldn't notice she's around.*

The cottage stood beyond the meadow with the wild flowers in it. Besides the garden this was the only land they owned. Looking from the house, the building looked so small and squat it was hard to believe that anyone could live there. A path had been trampled across the field and Felicity wondered who had been here since the grass had grown up. James probably. He used it as a den when he had friends to play, though they kept the building locked and she couldn't remember his asking for a key lately.

'Cottage makes it sound more grand than it is,' she said. 'It's only one up and one down with a bathroom built on the back. The gardener lived here when our house was first built. It was a pigsty before then I think, some sort of outhouse anyway.'

The door was fastened by a padlock. She unlocked it then hesitated, feeling suddenly uneasy. She wished she'd had a chance to look around the building before inviting the stranger in. She should have left Lily in the kitchen while she checked the state of the place.

But although she was aware at once of the damp, it was tidy enough. The grate was empty, though she couldn't remember cleaning it after her eldest daughter and her husband had been here at Christmas. The pans were hanging in their place on the wall and the oilskin cloth on the table had been wiped down. It was pleasantly cool after the heat in the meadow. She pushed open the window.

'They're cutting grass at the farm,' she said. 'You can smell it from here.'

Lily had stepped inside. It was impossible to tell what she thought of the place. Felicity had expected her to fall in love with it and felt offended. It was as if an overture of friendship had been rejected. She led the woman through to the small bathroom. Pointing out that the shower was new and the tiles had recently been replaced, she felt like an estate agent desperate for a sale. Why am I behaving like this? she thought. I wasn't even sure I wanted her here.

At last Lily spoke. 'Can we look upstairs?' And she started up the tight wooden steps which led straight from the kitchen. Felicity felt the same uneasiness as when she'd paused at the door of the cottage. She would have liked to be there first.

But, again, everything was more in order than she had expected. The bed was still made up, the quilt and extra blankets folded neatly at its foot. There was dust on the painted cupboard and dressing table, on the family photographs which stood there, but none of the rubbish and clutter which usually remained after her daughter's stay. A jug of white roses stood on the wide windowsill. One of the petals had dropped and she picked it up absent-mindedly. Of course, Felicity thought. Mary has been in although I never asked her. What a sweetie she is! So unobtrusive and helpful! Mary Barnes came to clean twice a week.

Only when she was closing the padlock behind them, did Felicity think that the roses couldn't have been there for more than a few days, and Mary, an unimaginative woman, would never have thought of a touch like that without being prompted.

They stood for a moment outside the cottage. 'Well?' Felicity asked. 'What did you think?' She caught a falsely cheerful note in her voice.

Lily smiled. 'It's lovely,' she said. 'Really. But there's such a lot to think about. I'll be in touch, shall I, next week?'

Felicity had intended offering her a lift, at least as far as the bus stop in the village, but Lily turned away and walked off across the meadow. Felicity couldn't bring herself to shout or run after her, so she stood and watched until the red and gold figure was lost in the long grass.